MIND GAMES

Gary William Ramsey

Gary William Ramsey

ISBN: 1493560530
ISBN-13: 9781493560530

Dedicated to:

My new Granddaughter Ilsa.

Please remember your Grandfather.

God Laughs a Lot – A Thought

*S*ometimes, *generally at night when I am alone, I attempt to figure things out. This exercise is part of a long objective look at my soul and myself. I came to some conclusions years ago and after meticulous consideration, I think most of them still apply today.*

The conclusions concern life and God. As I consider our decisions to sacrifice our happiness and the profound self-importance we place on events in our lives, the thought struck me.

GOD MUST LAUGH A LOT.

For surely as insignificant as we are to him, we are laughable in our seriousness about life.

Humans believe that everything has a purpose. What is God's purpose? His purpose certainly is not to serve us or to be involved in every intimate thought and action of every living organism in the universe.

Humanity is significant and indispensable to each other, but God is to us as we are to ants and small insects. They are insignificant to us, and we control their universe as God controls ours in a remote way. The height of arrogance is to think that he exists only for us.

So as we sacrifice, seek purpose, and gloat in self-importance, God laughs and that makes me happy. I believe I like a God with a sense of humor.

God must be thinking, "Look at them — don't they know that in 10,000 years, no one will care or remember about them or their existence. I'll create another assemblage and the next phase of humanity may discover the real me, and then I will not laugh, but for the next ten thousand years, Humans please continue your self-indulgence. I need the humor."

And we do and GOD LAUGHS A LOT.

IMAGINATION

Imagine that you touched me,
without a trace of fear.
Imagine you said "I love you,"
for all the world to hear.

Make your mind a dreamland.
Place guilt in a forgotten place.
The world is but a fantasy.
Imagine reality is in my face.

Emotion knows the binds of time.
It dies when left alone.
Imagine our love in the magic of dreams.
Reality will turn love to stone.

Imagine things your heart desires.
Imagine the world at peace.
Imagine what could be,
and your happiness will never cease.

Imagination transports our minds,
to far and distant dreams.
Imagination is our way to cope,
with reality and heartaches it seems.

So enter your imagination and free yourself
Join your spirit with mine.
Let my soul caress your soul.
In our sweet abyss in time.

Imagine *with me as you read my book, "Mind Games."*
I promise to give your mind a ride.

PROLOGUE

Imagination is the art of forming a mental image of something not present to the senses or never before wholly perceived in reality.

Imagination is what makes our sensory experience meaningful, allowing us to comprehend and make sense of it, whether from a conventional perspective or from a different original specific one. It makes perception more that a mere physical stimulation or sense organ. It produces mental imagery, visual and more, which is what makes it possible for us to think outside the limitations of our current perceptual reality. We have the ability to consider memories of the past and the endless possibilities of the future.

Imagination makes conceivable all of our thinking about what is, what has been, and more importantly, **what might be**. I have imagined endlessly in my life about **what might be.**

I believe that imagination is one of the most extraordinary gifts bestowed on humans. Each of us possesses distinctive degrees of how we use it. As for me, imagination has always been a central and prominent force my life. It is ingrained in a special dwelling in my mind.

When I was a child growing up poor in a small town in North Carolina, I imagined and dreamed of proving to the world that I was not just another cotton mill worker walking the streets. I imagined making something significant of myself, and being respected by others for my accomplishments.

I imagined what heaven is and what hell is. I imagined what a soul is and what is its reason for existence. I imagined a true and everlasting love.

As I have grown older, I find myself imagining more about the past and the future and mortality.

Which leads me to this book. When I first heard of Higgs boson or what scientist call "The God Particle," my imagination soared.

For anyone who is not familiar with The God Particle, I'll quote to you a summary definition. You'll read much more about it in the book.

"The Higgs boson or Higgs particle was initially theorized in 1964 and tentatively confirmed to exist on 14 March 2013. The discovery has been called "monumental" because it appears to confirm the existence of the Higgs field, which is pivotal to the Standard Model and other theories within particle physics. In this discipline, it explains why some fundamental particles have mass when the symmetries controlling their interactions should require them to be massless, and—linked to this—why the weak force has a much shorter range than the electromagnetic force. Its existence and knowledge of its exact properties are expected to impact scientific knowledge across a range of fields and should allow physicists to finally validate the last untested area of the Standard Model's approach to fundamental particles and forces, guide other theories and discoveries in particle physics, and—as with other fundamental discoveries of the past—potentially over time lead to developments in "new" physics, and new technologies."

In plan English, it is the *particle*, which causes mass to form. That may lead some to believe that this *particle* was the central force in the creation of the universe, hence "The God Particle." I hope my religious friends don't get antsy. I'm just reporting scientific discoveries and theories.

It is my understanding that even though Higgs boson has been isolated and confirmed, it cannot presently be preserved or used. Also through my research I found that it only could cause mass to form in objects, not humans.

Now my friends, this subject fueled my imagination. Almost everything that we imagined 20 years ago is true today. In the 1940's we imagined going to the moon and on July 20, 1969 we did. Someone imagined a computer, now it practically controls our lives. Steve Jobs imagined a smart phone and it's now in millions of hands. Therefore anything you can imagine is possible, **anything**.

What if brilliant Physicists discovered a way to preserve the God Particle and modify it so it could be used on human body?

What if the altered and enhanced God Particle was injected into certain lobes of the human brain to increase mass, therefore increase the functionality of that particular lobe?

What if the Formula was injected into the body mass to form enhanced muscles and strength?

Could this possibility alter and cause Evolution on Steroids of Humans and allow scientist to create an individual, tailored to the specific needs of the nation who owns the Formula?

What if?

Remember, anything you can imagine is possible.

In my imagination this breakthrough would create…

Evolutionary Mind Games of epic proportions.

1

I woke, with a start, acknowledging the sensation of rain and small hail pelting my skin. I stood up, while shielding my eyes, only to find dizziness drove me back to my knees. My head was pounding and the surrounding corn stalks seemed to mock me, as I touched the open wound on the back of my head. The downpour of rain mixed with hail and pain was almost too much to endure.

Since I couldn't stand, I began crawling in the mud. The corn stalks hindered my progress, and I knocked them down as I moved forward. After about twenty yards, I attempted to stand again. This time I succeeded in remaining on my feet, stumbled forward and tripped on a large obstacle in my path. I looked down and saw the mangled body of a young woman lying in the mud. Her long blonde hair was tangled, mud-spattered and her body was twisted in a grotesque position. Large chunks of flesh had been torn from her arms and legs. I bent down and put my finger on her neck, finding no pulse. She wore only torn panties and a mud spattered bra.

I kept moving as the rain intensified, overpowering the hail. As I pushed my way through the cornfield, I saw a large brown object about ten feet in front of me. I made my way to the spot and gasped upon discovering a dead horse. The animal's legs were broken and twisted to one side. There were bite marks on the legs and a large caliber bullet hole just above its left eye.

My breath was ragged, and my head pulsated with shooting pains. I reached up to touch my scalp again, pulling back a handful of blood. The rain quickly washed it away, and I took comfort in knowing that it was cleansing my wound.

However, the comfort was short-lived. I discovered another sore spot, about six inches back from my right temple. It was a small round object, which felt like medal, and any contact only intensified the pain.

Just outside the cornfield, I fell to my knees and rolled on my back to rest, but the rain was merciless, thrashing on my body. I felt a chill and began shivering. My adrenaline had kept me from noticing the frigid air until now, and I huddled into a fetal position to compensate. It was then that I realized for the first time that I was naked.

The earth was spinning, and I threw up.

Darkness overcame me as I lost consciousness.

2

The coal-black alpha male coyote sensed helplessness as he approached the body lying motionless at the perimeter of the cornfield. His pack sat cautiously, fifty feet away. Their experiences with humans had been deadly and the leader bravely approached the prey. When he gave the signal, they would savagely feast with the alpha female first in line. Excitement was heard in their howling, and drool seeped from their open mouths.

The alpha male circled the body, his beady black eyes watching for movement. There was little food for days as the endless downpour ruined their hunting. This would be a welcome meal.

Seeing no movement, he raised his head and howled, signaling the pack that there was no danger. He glared at the body in anticipation of the choice meat, his fierce hunger encouraging him to proceed.

The alpha slowly moved forward, baring his teeth to tear at the flesh from the thighs.

Abruptly, a shot rang out. The bullet entered the right eye of the coyote and he fell dead on top of the motionless body. Seeing the alpha drop, the pack ran back into the cornfield to regroup. Leaderless, they were cowards.

The small figure in the yellow rain slicker walked forward with her Savage 110 rifle still in the shooting position. The shooter pulled back her hood, revealing long blonde hair pulled into a ponytail. She knew that coyotes were not easy to take down. Even though she used .220 Swift cartridges, she needed to confirm the kill. In this case, an additional kill shot was impossible because the animal was lying on top of the man's body. She nudged it with the barrel of the rifle and spotted the lifeless stare in the animal's eyes. She had never seen a black coyote in these parts of Texas, and she marveled at the beauty of the savage beast. She kicked it off of the body and put another shot in his head to make sure it was dead.

The girl knelt and put her fingers on the neck of the still naked body of the muscular man, observing a weak pulse. She didn't notice any bites, but there was a wound on the back of his head. He was too big and heavy to carry, and she was hesitant in leaving him for fear that the coyotes would return.

She sat down and waited for her brother to come. She was sure that he heard the shots and would come running to see if she was okay.

"Blaze, Blaze," he yelled.

"Over here Billy. Don't worry I'm fine."

Billy ran to her side.

"I need your help. Go get the big wheelbarrow and a couple of blankets. We've got an injured man here. He needs our help."

"Is he like the other one?"

"No, this one is different. He's handsome."

3

The sight of the steel cage unnerved me when I opened my eyes. I was lying on a mattress dressed in old jeans and a T-shirt about three feet away from the cage. The enclosure was approximately seven feet wide and eight feet high. An old man with a white beard and long matted white hair stood inside, holding the bars and glaring at me. He grinned when I looked at him. His face was wrinkled, and his teeth were an odd shade of tan. There was a half eaten ham bone lying on the floor at his feet and a pan of water in the corner of the cage. A large pot with a lid was in the other corner, and I assumed that it was some sort of porta potty. The door to the cage was secured with a small rope. It looked frayed as if the old man had been gnawing on it.

I attempted to get up, but then I realized that ropes bound my hands and feet, and I didn't have a clue what was going on. My head ached, and hunger pains racked my body.

"Help me!" I shouted. The old man cackled and spit at me.

Looking around the room, I noticed that other than the cage, the only additional object in the room was a worn and cracked black leather couch about three feet to my left. A bare light bulb hung over the center of the room. The paint on the walls was pealing and was formerly a light shade of grey, and the floor was a battered oak hardwood. The finish was worn off, and the boards had turned a decaying gray color. Oddly, it matched the walls.

I noticed an old poster taped on the wall. Elvis grinned, wearing his black leather suit that he sported in his comeback special on TV.

After closing my eyes, I recalled waking up naked in the cornfield and crawling to the edge, and I remembered the dead girl and the horse. Someone had brought me into this room, dressed me and tied me up. Stark fear consumed my mind as I struggled to remember anything, but my mind didn't cooperate and remained blank.

The old man howled, fell to the floor and twisted into a fetal position. I heard footsteps and looked around. I couldn't believe my eyes when I observed a girl, so beautiful that she resembled an angel. Her long blonde hair reached her waist, and her face was flawless with cream-colored skin and full sensuous lips. She appeared to be in her early twenties. Her big blue eyes gazed compassionately at me, and she stood staring, without speaking. The girl was dressed in a halter-top, cut-off jeans, was barefoot and had a stunning figure. I was speechless for a moment, but then managed to utter, "who are you?"

"Blaze," she replied.

"What am I doing her and why do you have me tied-up?"

"We were worried that you were dangerous like him," she said, gesturing toward the cage. The old man howled again.

"Pay no attention to him," she said. "Who are you and where did you come from?"

"I don't know."

"Surely you know your own name."

"Sorry, I don't remember anything before I woke up in the cornfield.

"My brother and I are not allowed to go into the cornfield," she said. "What did you see in there?"

"A dead girl and a dead horse," I replied.

Her hand flew to her mouth, and she took a deep breath. "You don't seem like the old man. He was passed out at the same place we found you. When we were trying to put him in the wheelbarrow, he came to and bit my brother. Billy subdued him, and we locked him up. We've had him for about a week."

"Why didn't you call the police?"

"We don't have a phone or a car, and I think the nearest town is seventy-five miles away."

"What are you doing here, Blaze?" I looked toward the door and a tall muscular young man entered the room. He had blonde hair like Blaze, with similar features, and looked few years older. His left hand was bandaged.

"This man seems normal, Billy. He doesn't remember anything before waking up in the cornfield. Maybe that blow to the back of his head stops him from recollecting. He said after he woke up that he saw a dead girl and a dead horse in the cornfield."

Billy walked over to me. "What are you doing in these parts?"

"As I told her, I don't remember."

"Billy, he must be very hungry," Blaze said. "We should feed him."

"Listen mister, I'm going to untie your feet and take you to the kitchen." He pulled a large hunting knife from his belt. "If you try anything, I'm afraid I'll have to stab you."

He cut the ropes binding my feet and helped me up. My legs were weak and my knee's buckled, and Billy gripped my arm and kept me from falling.

"Some food will give you strength," he said.

We walked out of the room and entered a long hallway. The old man's howl sounded like a wounded dying animal as we left the room.

"He's a dangerous loon," Billy said nonchalantly. "When the man comes to harvest the corn maybe he can take him off our hands. I'm tired of cleaning up after him."

"What about the dead girl and the dead horse? The boss has a daughter." Blaze asked.

"The Reaper man can deal with that when he comes," Billy replied. "You know he doesn't allow us in the cornfield." He looked at me. "We call him the Grim Reaper. Until the corn is ready for harvesting, only he and his daughter are allowed to go in. If we are to ever get out of here, we must do as he says."

The conversation dumfounded me.

I wish I knew what in the hell was going on.

4

Timothy Harding Olsen earned his PhD Degrees in Nuclear Science and Physics at the Massachusetts Institute of Technology at the age of twenty-two. He had overcome many obstacles in his life, including the suicide of his mentally deranged mother when he was twelve years old. His father, a university college professor of physics and mathematics, was distant and callous after the death. He held no pride in his son's mental and academic brilliance. Tim lived in solitude emotionally, and devoted all his waking hours to reading and studying. His outstanding achievements in academics were his only pleasure in life.

By the time he completed college and grad school, Tim stood 5 ft.8 inches tall with sandy blonde short hair. His baby face and boyish scowl made him appear to be a teenager. He finished at the top of his class and was serious and extremely solemn all the time. His classmates recognized that he was a genius, but they also believed that he was somewhat of a psychopath.

Tim was a loner and totally self-sufficient with no friends. His primary areas of expertise and interest were in the evolutionary development of humans as it related to the evolution of the Earth. He believed that he had the aptitude and talent to assist mankind to an advanced level in the evolutionary process. Human's Evolution on Steroids was his life's goal. He considered this enhanced progression as playing human mind games.

Tim was pursued by numerous organizations, but after pondering countless job opportunities, he decided to accept the proposal and offer of employment from the cutting-edge firm of Future Mankind Ventures. One of the corporation's missions was to develop and test ways of extending the lifespan of humans and the correction of severe behavioral and physical problems through the application of nuclear technology. Other branches of the company held other mission directions, but he was assured that this one was the prime objective. The home office was located in Houston, Texas, with branches in Paris, London, New York and Moscow.

Future Mankind Ventures had many laboratory facilities testing various theories from the brightest and preeminent scientists in the world. Most were young and classified as prodigies. Tim was designated to be the prime scientist in the Texas laboratory after his internship at Bern. There were other practical arms of the company, which were kept secret, and intended to raise money to finance the expensive projects.

The company's prize location, where Tim was to serve his internship, was a particle collider at Bern, more than 16 miles of tunnels under Switzerland and France. In that location, the scientists were searching for the "Higgs boson," known as "The God Particle." The Moscow branch was led by the world famous, Sergay Petrof, philanthropists and businessman. He also was in charge of the Bern facility.

Tim spent his first two years with the company working at Bern in the Particle Collider labs. During his first year there, after thousands of tests, the God Particle was isolated. This magnificent discovery was kept from the press because there was no apparent practical uses of the Particle. In addition, the almost insurmountable problem was the its short life span. It was estimated to decay in a less than a millionth of a second.

Tim worked on this problem for a year and to the astonishment of the older and more experienced scientists, he developed a method, using ionic disbursement, of extending the life of the Particle. By applying his method in 24-hour cycles, he could keep the Particle from decaying and develop uses to apply it to humans, and to improve and evolve mankind. His discovery would allow him to play never ending mind games.

Sergey Petrof was informed of the breakthroughs and visited the laboratory expressly to interview Tim. He was impressed with the young genius and decided to recommend to the board of directors to give Tim resources and move him immediately to the laboratory in Texas to develop his theories. He would be regularly supplied with the preserved Particle from the labs in Bern for the experimentations.

The other scientists and physicists scoffed at the young man, who was convinced that he could develop a Formula, using the God Particle, and sharply speed up the evolutionary process of humans. Most of his colleagues called him the "Loony Kid." The paramount distain shown to Tim was triggered by envy of the fact that he developed the technique of extending the life of the Particle, while they had failed, and that he was being elevated and funded above them in the organization.

The Board agreed with Petrof's recommendation, and Tim was provided a private laboratory in a remote location in Texas. Over his objections, he was also assigned an accomplished assistant, even though he preferred to work alone.

Tim was granted substantial funds and wide-ranging latitude in his research. He and his assistant had separate living quarters on the second level of the laboratory building. All the necessities of life were provided and once a week, usually on Saturday, a limo was sent to take them to the nearest town for recreation and entertainment. Tim rarely took the opportunity to leave the compound, even for a couple of days, because he was obsessed with his work and had no friends anyway. He reported his experimental results to the Board of Directors quarterly to sustain his grant.

Security guards were ever present, posted at the entrances and exits. There was another large building located behind the laboratory. Tim didn't know or care what was going on there, but he saw men entering and leaving the building regularly. Trucks loaded with whatever would depart twice a day. A large cornfield was in front of the laboratory, and he considered that strange, but could care less why it was there.

Tim worked for three years in this remote and secure location, when he discovered what he believed to be a breakthrough in the alteration of human genes with nuclear ionization, which would lead to the extension of life and the alteration of problematic emotional behavior among other things, by increasing the size of certain brain lobes. The God Particle was central to his Formula.

Presently, certain side effects revealed, when tested on chimpanzees, specific erratic and aggressive behavior, however the aging process appeared to be slowed. He adjusted the process and the Formula, and was confident that the corrections would correct the complications.

Hi assistant, Brenda Alford, held a Masters Degree in Nuclear Science and Biology from the University of Texas. She was brilliant in her own right, but had anxious feelings on where Tim's experiments were leading. Brenda developed more than professional relationship feelings for Tim. Even though she was a strikingly beautiful young woman with long black hair, green eyes and a remarkable figure, Tim didn't seem to notice her personally. He was driven and totally focused on his work.

The heat and humidity were almost unbearable in west Texas as Brenda was driven back to the laboratory that Monday morning. Her mother and father met her on Sunday and urged her to leave her employment and find something less demanding. Brenda was reluctant to leave Tim and was truly worried about his mental state.

She planned to challenge Tim about the direction of his experiments and had tossed and turned all night dreading the confrontation.

"Brenda, you look like hell. What's your problem?" Tim asked when she entered the laboratory.

"Tim I think you're going down a path in your experiments that will be highly destruction to society. These experiments could alter humans in a way that we can only speculate. We should go in another direction. The tests on chimps reflect a peculiar aging process and aggressiveness that I don't understand."

"Are you crazy?" A visibly upset Tim replied. "Listen to me Brenda, we can change the world and correct the mistakes God made when he created us."

He continued in an impatient voice to explain to Brenda, "Don't you understand that ionizing radiation is radiation composed of particles that individually can liberate an electron from an atom or molecule, producing ions, which are atoms or molecules with a net electric charge. These tend to be especially chemically reactive, and the reactivity produces the high biological damage caused per unit of energy of ionizing radiation. Although thought to be fatal if introduced into the bloodstream of a human, my experiments on Chimpanzees indicate that with my chemical alterations and with certain measured levels introduced into the brain cells of the frontal lobes located behind the forehead, lifespan, behavior and problematic emotions may be altered."

Brenda looked down at her feet as Tim lectured at her, however she remained highly skeptical and fearful of the experiments.

Cognizant of Brenda's fear and his concerned that she may complain the Board, he continued to practically shout his theories.

"Brenda, the frontal lobes are the largest lobes of the brain. They are prone to injury because they sit just inside the front of the skull and near rough bony ridges. These two lobes are involved in planning, organizing, problem solving, memory, impulse control, decision-making, selective attention and controlling our behavior and emotions. If altered with my procedures and the introduction of the Formula, I can change the course of the history of mankind! I can make humans superior to what God created and I can put evolution on steroids."

Brenda shook her head, "Okay Tim, but if asked, I will never agree to test this on humans. We are years away from safe tests."

Tim stormed out of the laboratory and went to his office to plan his subsequent actions. He was concerned about Brenda blowing his chances for huge success with her reluctance to test on humans.

His experiments on chimpanzees were decisive even, although their appearance was altered and there was an aging and aggressiveness hitch, but he had made corrections to handle those problems. Tim was extremely frustrated because the Company had postponed his request to test his breakthrough on human volunteers and now Brenda would add her objections. He felt trapped and exasperated.

Tim habitually worked sixteen hours a day and had no life outside of his job. He kept a Desert Eagle .50 Caliber handgun in the laboratory for protection, since he was alone on these late evenings after Brenda left for her living quarters. In his cynical mind, he didn't trust the security guards or the old janitor who cleaned every night. He was obsessed about someone stealing his formula. Tim was still in the laboratory at midnight when the old man came in.

"I'm sorry sir, I thought the place was empty. I'm here to clean up," the old man said in a heavily accented Hispanic voice. Tim had seen the janitor on several occasions and had insisted that the man never come into the lab until after midnight to clean.

"Get the hell out of here. I'm working," he yelled. The alarmed and frightened old man was pushing a cleaning cart, stumbled, lost his balance and fell as he attempted to rush out of the room. He hit his head on the corner of the cart as he was falling. Blood seeped from the wound on his head and he tumbled to the floor.

"You stupid asshole," Tim yelled as he walked to where the man was lying. The janitor was out cold and at that instant, an idea materialized in Tim's unstable mind. This insignificant old man might serve as his first test on a human. The janitor could be the initial recipient of Tim's genius. He dragged the unconscious body to the corner of the laboratory and prepared the injection.

It was after midnight on a rainy summer morning in West Texas, when he injected the Formula into the frontal lobe through the man's eye socket.

Tim expected a delayed reaction, however, injecting directly into the frontal lobe could have some immediate effects. He presumed that he needed to restrict the man to be safe, and he left the laboratory to locate some restraints.

He found a nylon cord in his living quarters, returned to the lab, and was shocked when he saw that the area where the body was laying was empty. Tim frantically looked around the room. Standing in the far corner was the old man, by the door, crouched and holding the pistol. His appearance had changed somewhat, but it was apparent that the evolutions and the transformations were occurring before Tim's eyes.

"Just calm down," Tim said as he approached the man. A low raucous growl escaped from the man's throat. His eyes were bloodshot, and his hands were drawn up in a claw-like position. He glared at Tim and pulled the trigger of the pistol. The boy genius crumbled to the floor in a puddle of blood. For security reasons the laboratory was sound proof and no one heard the shot.

The old man scampered from the room with speed not possible for a person of his age and ran to the outside door. He slammed the pistol against the temple of the surprised guard safeguarding the door and ran into the cornfield. He scrambled through the corn stalks like a wild animal, ripped off his clothing, and darted deeper into the cornfield.

Suddenly, he felt dizzy, grasped his throbbing head, fell to the ground and passed out. The Formula was reacting in his brain with stunning speed.

The old man had no idea of the time lapse, but woke up confused and ravenously hungry in the cornfield. He was naked except for the Desert Eagle .50 Caliber pistol clutched tightly in his left hand. Something in his mind snapped, and he wasn't aware of his complete disorientation. He steadied himself and stood, ripped off an ear of corn, with his right hand, stripped the husks with his teeth and devoured it. His hunger didn't subside at all. His body craved protein and he was driven to locate fresh meat as he ravaged his way through the cornfield.

There was movement in front of him, and he scurried to the area and sighting fresh meat, he dropped the gun and attacked with his claws and his sharp teeth.

He howled as he tore and chewed flesh from the fallen girl. He heard a noise to his right where large brown animal stood. He grabbed the gun, walked to where the animal stood and shot it in the head. He distorted mind grasped that he could feed off this protein for days. The horse crumbled to the ground, and its heart had not stopped beating as the old man threw down the gun, tore into his flesh, feeding ravenously.

After getting his fill, he walked to the edge of the cornfield. He looked around with his barbaric eyes and attempted to grasp reality. He seized his head as his brain exploded in pain, and he collapsed to the ground, cataleptic.

5

We walked to the kitchen, and Billy sat me down at the small table near the center of the room. The walls were freshly painted a sunny yellow color. There was a fridge beside the cabinet area, and the built-in stove had a microwave positioned above it. The cabinets were also freshly painted white. The door in the corner of the kitchen stood open, revealing a large pantry loaded with can goods and another essentials.

Blaze went to the fridge and grabbed three plastic containers. "Are you hungry Billy?" she asked.

"No, let's just feed him and you and I can eat later."

Blaze retrieved a plate and a tumbler from the cabinet. She opened the containers and spooned a large helping of mashed potatoes on the plate. From the other containers, she put what looked like collard greens and meat loaf on the plate and placed it in the microwave. She returned to the fridge and fetched a pitcher of lemonade, filled the tumbler and put a fork on a napkin beside the tumbler. The ding from the microwave indicated that the meal was hot. Blaze placed it in front of me.

Billy glared at me. "Okay I'm going to untie your hands. Remember I've got my hunting knife, and if you try anything funny I'll be obliged to stab you."

I nodded. Billy handed Blaze the knife and he untied the ropes. My hands were trembling as I picked up the fork, cut a large piece of the meat loaf and jammed it in my mouth. Nothing ever tasted better. It must have been days since I ate and had no way of knowing. I chewed the meat, swallowed it and drank about half of the lemonade. The potatoes and the greens tasted wonderful.

My hands were beginning to be steady when I heard a blood-curdling shriek. The old man from the cage darted into the room and sprang on Billy's back. Blood sprayed when he bit him on the right shoulder. Blaze screamed as Billy dropped the knife and tried to grab the man's head.

Without hesitation, I jumped up, moved behind the man and gave him a karate chop to the neck. He dropped from Billy's back and turned to face me. He lowered his head, crouched and glowered, preparing to attack. I intuitively moved into a martial arts position. As he leaped at me, I landed a Kung Fu Tai gurk kick to the stomach. He fell, but then immediately sprang to his feet. The kick only angered him. He swung at me with his hand, which looked more like a claw. I moved to the side and hurled a straight right hand to his nose. I immediately swung around and shot the heel of my foot to his head. He crumpled to the floor, out cold.

Blaze was screaming. Billy was on the floor, and she was holding his head. I grabbed a dishtowel from the sink. "Put pressure on the bite, Blaze. Do you have a first-aid kit?"

"In the bathroom, down the hall to the right."

I found the bathroom and threw open the cabinet under the sink and grabbed the first-aid kit. I rushed back to the kitchen, opened the kit and saturated a large piece of gauze with antiseptic and pressed it to the wound. I cleaned the bite, and it wasn't as deep as I feared. Billy lay still as I applied more antiseptic and tightly bandaged the wound.

I heard a groan behind me. Apparently, the old man was regaining consciousness. "Blaze, quickly, get me something to secure him."

Blaze ran to the kitchen cabinet, reached under the sink and tossed me a roll of duct tape. I wrapped it around his hands, tore it and secured his feet. His eyes opened wide, and he began to squirm and howl. I dragged him to the holding room, threw him into the cage, closed the door and went back to the kitchen. Billy was up sitting in a chair drinking water. Blaze hugged me when I walked through the door.

"You saved his life and maybe mine to," she was crying softly. "How did you learn to fight like that?"

"I have no idea. I guess it was instinctive." Billy nodded at me indicating his thanks too.

"Guys, what do you call the old man? Does he answer to any name? Did he have any identification when you found him?"

"No," replied Blaze. "We call him Fang because he likes to bite."

"We need something stronger than the cord you had the door tied shut with. From the looks if it, he just gnawed through it."

"I've got a chain but no lock to secure it," Billy said.

"Get me the chain and some wire, I'll secure the door."

"I'll get it. It's in the barn," Blaze said, leaving the kitchen.

I went back to the cage to see what Fang was doing and Billy followed me. The creature of a man was sitting up gnawing on the duct tape that secured his hands. His body was contorted was in position that no man could endure.

"Billy, yell to Blaze to hurry. I may not be able to contain him if he gets out again."

Fang successfully chewed through the tape binding his hands. He gawked directly at me, bared his teeth and howled. I think it was a combat challenge. As he was reaching to tear the duct tape from his feet, Blaze ran into the room with the chain. I quickly wrapped it twice around the door and the bar. I put the heavy wire through two of the loops and twisted it together and tied it. Just as I finished, Fang freed his feet, leaped forward, attempting to grab my hands. The nails on his claw of a hand could rip flesh to shreds. I jumped back out of his reach. He shrieked again and began banging on the door to the cage. When he realized that it was secure he dropped to the floor and hung his head.

"What in the hell is that thing?" I asked Blaze.

"I don't know, but you said there was a dead girl and a dead horse in the cornfield. I think maybe Fang killed them. The only other person allowed in there is the Grim Reaper's daughter. He'll be furious if Fang killed his daughter. He may murder us all."

I couldn't stand this cryptic conversation anymore. I glared at Blaze. "Who is this Grim Reaper? What does he have to do with you and Billy? What's in that damn cornfield that he doesn't want you to see?"

Billy walked to my side and put his hand on my arm. "Calm down. We don't know the man's name full name. His daughter calls him Daddy Ben. You know what we call him, the Grim Reaper.

Billy bowed his head and continued. "After our parents were killed when a tornado hit and our farm was destroyed, fifty miles outside of Waco, Texas, Blaze and I were left homeless. I was sixteen, and she was twelve. Both of us were injured and knocked unconscious by the twister. When we regained consciousness, we were in a strange place being tended to by the Grim Reaper. Blaze had a concussion, and her left arm was broken. I also had a concussion and a broken leg. We both had gashes in many areas of our bruised bodies. The Reaper's daughter helped with our care. We spent months recuperating, seeing no one but the two of them. When we could move about, we were allowed access to only the west wing of the house, and the fenced-in back yard. The man apparently has great wealth because we could see that we were in a mansion. There was lavishness everywhere. The Reaper supplied us food and clothing, and we were very thankful. After several months, Blaze and I realized that we were actually prisoners, however, we had no place to go, and we were treated kindly."

I sat astounded, listening to the story. "What does he and the girl look like?" I asked.

"He called the girl, Katy. She has long blonde hair and appears to be in her late twenties. She's very beautiful with green

eyes and fair complexion. The Reaper is probably in his late forties, over six feet tall and very muscular. He has black hair and
looks to be of Hispanic descent. His dark complexion and stark
brown eyes were so opposite of Katy's that we doubted that he
was her true father, but he said she was his daughter."

"Damn," I uttered. "That matches the description of the dead
girl I saw in the cornfield."

"We will certainly die!" Blaze cried.

Billy put his arm around her. "Don't worry little sister. I'll
protect you and now we have help," he said nodding toward me.

"How did you get here?" I asked.

Billy continued, "When our wounds were healed, the Reaper
made us a proposition. He said that he needed someone to help
his daughter guard a cornfield. If we agreed to handle this task
for seven years, he would provide Blaze and me with a home
in a location of our choice and jobs. He said he would place
fifty thousand dollars in a bank account in our names to get us
started. I asked him what if we declined his offer, would he let us
go? He replied that if we refused him it would be a great insult,
since he saved our lives. He said he would not take kindly to
our refusal. I took his meaning to be that he would do us great
harm, so we agreed. He blindfolded us and brought us to this
house. We were transported in a small jet plane. The Reaper left
us without any means of communication to the outside world,
but brings supplies monthly. Katy was put in a house a couple
of miles from here. We are not allowed to go to her home, and
we only see her when the Reaper delivered supplies. Our orders
are to guard the entrance to the cornfield. If anyone other than
Katy tries to enter, we are supposed to shoot them with the gun
he left with us. He didn't say anything about someone coming
out of the place, so we didn't shoot you or Fang. We've been here
for six years."

My head was spinning. I felt like I was in an alternate universe.
Nothing made sense. If I could only remember who I was and

how I got there, maybe my head would stop throbbing. I went to the bathroom and splashed cold water on my face and looked in the mirror. The face looking back at me had short black hair with a three-day stubble, blue eyes, and a worried scowl. I looked down and guessed that I was about 6 feet 4 inches tall, with a well-developed body. I did notice a small scar to the right of my chin. I had no idea who this man looking back in the mirror is. I walked back to the kitchen.

"Billy I've got to get some fresh air." I walked out the front door and sat on the edge of the porch, buried my head in my hands and closed my eyes.

The picture of a large group of people, on their feet, yelling and clapping flashed through my mind. I was standing behind a podium waiving to the crowd. The memory flash left my mind as quickly as it had entered.

I reached to my head again and felt the small metal object beneath my scalp. I've got to figure out what it is and get it out. It hurts.

6

Benjamin Thomas Cruise sat on his veranda overlooking the Olympic-sized pool surrounded by Fan Palms and Cocos Palms in steamy South Texas. Just to the left of the pool was a large sunning area with a flower garden and Sego Palms enhancing the landscape. He sipped his Tropical Itch drink and smiled when his bikini-clad girl friend waved at him. She was tanning her stunning body, while he watched.

Ben wore a white silk Tommy Bahama Garden of Hope shirt, dark rayon Bermuda shorts and Gucci sandals. With his black hair, dark complexion and intense brown eyes, he had always been a ladies' man. His muscular body was hard from daily work-outs defying his fifty years of life, and he considered himself to be in his prime.

The drug trade was brisk, and he was adding more distributors and customers every day.

His investment in Future Mankind Ventures was looking magnificent with breakthroughs on the immediate horizon, especially with one of the laboratories he controlled in his territory.

"Honey, come down and join me," Maria Langus shouted.

"Maybe in a while," he answered.

Ben watched while Maria removed her bikini top and turned over on her stomach. Her long blonde hair was tied in a ponytail and her firm twenty-three old body was extraordinary. Ben liked them young, fresh and blonde. The only problem was that he tired of his women easily. His former girl friend, Katy, had lasted for an impressive two years, satisfying his every need, before he shipped her off to his remote retreat where the cornfield and other facilities were located. He still cared for her and hoped to bring her back when he was weary of Maria.

Thinking of Katy reminded him that it was time to take supplies to Billy and Blaze. For six years, he had preformed this task personally even though he had many men at his disposal to handle any job he wanted. His special interest was Blaze. He watched her grow from an injured twelve-year-old girl to a stunning eighteen-year-old. Maybe when the seven-year deal was over, he would put her in his rotation of girl friends. He had other plans for Billy and those were to use him for human experimentation. Tim Olsen, the chief scientist at the facility behind the cornfield, had been clamoring for human tests.

Both Blaze and Billy knew little of the outside world, as for the last six years they were isolated.

Their parents were employees of Cruise, growing marijuana for him, when the devastating tornado hit, killing them and seriously damaging the fields. He took his men, went to the farm and discovered that the two children were alive, but seriously injured. Katy accompanied him to the devastated site. He went to access the damage and estimate what could be saved and his men would have to work hard to save what was left of the crop. Ben's inclination was to leave the children and let them die, but at the insistence of Katy, he had them taken to his home for treatment by his physician. When they healed, he hatched his scheme to assign them to guard the cornfield.

Now he had the desire for Katy again because he surprisingly missed her.

Ben was interrupted from his thoughts when his cell phone rang. He looked at the caller ID and determined that it was Carlos, his top lieutenant.

"Yes Carlos, what is it?"

"Boss, it was reported to me that there were some unusual incidents at the laboratory and in the compound behind the cornfield. One of our employees was angered by the breakdown of security and called me. Two of the subjects were reported to have escaped at different times. One of them may have killed a guard."

"Carlos, Katy usually rides her horse in that general area. Did they mention seeing Katy on her horse? I don't want any harm to come to her."

"No sir. There were two men and the incidents were three days apart. What about the people you have in the house guarding the cornfield? Maybe they saw something."

"Billy and Blaze don't know about the compound and laboratory and are not allowed to enter the field. I have to deliver supplies and I'll check on it. Get the usual provisions ready and I'll leave tomorrow. Make sure my pilot and helicopter are prepared to leave early."

"You got it, Boss."

Ben laid down his phone and lit a Cuban cigar when Maria touched him from behind. He turned and she was standing there naked.

"Daddy Ben, I'm ready for some afternoon delight," she purred.

They retreated to the pool house and Ben granted her request.

7

The coyote pack regrouped at the den area, which was near the southwest corner of the cornfield. Now leaderless, with the death of the alpha male, the alpha female looked at the beta male for signs that he was ready to take charge. She did not want to lose her status because the alpha male, and the alpha female were given preference to be the first to eat any kill and the first to mate. In this pack, she was the only female allowed to mate, and mating season was just days away.

The beta male was a large grey animal with black markings over his left eye. His left ear had been torn off the last time he challenged the alpha male for leadership and lost. Now with the death of his rival, his long-sought role of alpha was his for the taking. He gaped at the alpha female and snarled.

The beta glowered at the rest of the pack, uttered a gruff snarl deep in this throat and bared his teeth. There were no challenges. The new alpha howled and ran back toward the site where the prey was located at the edge of the cornfield. The pack was ravenous, and he was determined to lead them to food.

The pack submissively followed. When they arrived, the prey was gone and the only thing left at the edge of the cornfield was the dead body of their former leader. The alpha sensed danger, so he sent the omega, which was the lowest caste in the hierarchical society, to the area of the kill. When he determined that there was no threat present, he and the alpha female led the pack to the perimeter of the cornfield.

It was obvious that the omega wanted to feast on the dead coyote, but his fear of the alpha stopped him. The alpha lifted his nose. He smelled dead meat nearby and proceeded into the cornfield.

The carcass of the horse he came upon was filled with flies and maggots. He tore a piece of flesh from the haunches and chewed. He moved back, allowing the female to rip a piece of flesh from the dead animal. With the ritual out of the way, the rest of the pack ravenously pounced on the carcass. The Alpha sensed sweet-smelling protein and darted to the girl's body. At first, he was wary because he sniffed the scent of a wild beast on the body. The odor was so stringent that it momentarily frightened him. His hunger overcame his fear, and he snarled and tore into the flesh of the upper leg. After watching the alpha make his choice of meat, the alpha female began eating the meat from the arms. The meat was tender and sweet, much superior to the tough meat of the lifeless horse.

Suddenly, the alpha lifted his head, and his remaining ear perked up. He heard human voices in the distance. Not willing to give up the sweet meat of the girl, he began dragging the body with the assistance of the alpha female. They dragged the remains back to the den to finish their meal in safety. The rest of the pack followed. Their hunger was temporarily satisfied with the protein from the lifeless horse. The half eaten carcass of the dead girl was dropped at the entrance to the den.

The entrance was about ten inches high and thirteen inches wide and it was just to the right of a large boulder. The den was about four feet underground and the tunnel leading to the internal denning area was fifteen feet long. The girls' body was too large to fit into the entrance. So the alpha ripped huge hunks from the body and dragged them into the den. When he had completed the task, the female followed him into the den and they finished feeding. The nesting area was about three feet in diameter and was the area where the female would have her pups. It now served as a dinning space.

The rest of the pack quickly devoured the remaining parts of the body left outside the den. They dragged the bones a safe distance from the entrance.

Coyotes mark their den territories by leaving lots of scent on stumps, brush or dirt piles using their urine and scent glands. The entrance to the den is kept clean as the adult coyotes remove bones and other debris so these materials do not accumulate in or around the edges of the den.

The once vibrant life of Katy Underwood was desecrated when her body was torn apart and left in places never to be discovered by any humans. Her soul was trapped in the everlasting devastation of an unfinished destiny.

To wild coyotes, she was merely protein to be ingested to prolong their lives. They had no conception of her life, her spirit or her soul. She was merely an object to satisfy their hunger.

The new alpha had proven his worth by feeding the pack. His authority was unchallenged as his mating ritual with the alpha female began.

8

Brenda remained upset with the tone and anger Tim displayed when she gave her opinion on his testing of the Formula on humans. During the night, she decided to resign. Her feelings for him were getting out of hand, and he showed no interest in her at all. After a breakfast of grits, toast and coffee, she proceeded to the laboratory. It was very early, but she knew that Tim was up and working. He never seemed to sleep.

Brenda walked into the lab through the inside private entrance that she and Tim used. There was a cleaning cart near the door with a small slick of dried blood beside it and she immediately sensed that something was dreadfully wrong.

"Tim, Tim, are you here?" she yelled. She heard a groan and quickly turned toward the source. Lying on the floor in a large puddle of blood was Timothy Harding Olsen. He was struggling to speak, but nothing came out but groans.

Brenda sprinted to his side. Blood was oozing from a wound in his right shoulder. Brenda grabbed a lab coat and applied solid pressure to stop the bleeding.

"Help, Help!' she screamed not remembering that the lab was soundproofed. Abruptly realizing that no one could hear her, she tied the lab coat as tightly as possible around Tim's shoulder and rushed to the outside entrance of the laboratory to summon the guard. The door only opened about twelve inches and was apparently blocked. She pushed with all her might and managed to open it far enough to get out.

Lying in front of the door, partially blocking it was the life-less body of a guard. She dropped to her knees and felt for a pulse. The man was dead. There was a gunshot wound on the left temple.

There was another entrance on the other side of the build-ing. Brenda knew it was guarded as well. She scuttled around the building as fast as she could. As she approached the door the guard pointed his rifle toward her and yelled, "Stop!"

"Please, I'm Brenda Alford, Mr. Olsen's assistant. Mr. Olsen is seriously injured and the guard at the other entrance is dead. We need medical help immediately."

The guard lowered his rifle and said something into a two-way radio.

"Miss, go back and tend to your boss. Help is on the way." He unlocked the door and held it open for her. She heard the door slam hard behind her as she entered the building and ran toward the laboratory.

When she returned to Tim's side, he was unconscious. The lab coat tied tightly over the wound had apparently stopped the flow of blood. She sat down and lifted Tim's head into her lap. "Please Tim, wake up, wake up." She pleaded as tears ran down her cheeks.

The laboratory door burst open and three men rushed in with a stretcher. Without a word they lifted the unconscious body and placed it on the stretcher.

"Where are you taking him?" Brenda sobbed.

"Stay out of the way Miss. We're transporting him to the hospital."

"I need to go with him," Brenda replied.

"No," the man said and they rushed out. Brenda heard the whirling blades of a helicopter when they open the outside door. She hurried towards the entrance and observed the men loading Tim's body and the body of the guard into the copter, which immediately lifted off.

Brenda collapsed to the floor. She looked at her bloody hands and wiped them on her lab coat as she wept.

"Please, I don't know what's happening," she gasped aloud and hung her head.

9

I went back into the house. Blaze was not in the kitchen area, and Billy was sitting at the table drinking iced tea.

"Billy, I have a favor to ask of you."

"Fine, you helped me and now I'll help you, but we need to decide what to call you."

"Just call me Ethan," I said without hesitation. I startled myself with the automatic response.

"Okay Ethan, what can I do for you?"

"Billy, I've got this small metal object just beneath my scalp. I need you to cut it out."

"What is it Ethan?"

"I don't know, and I need to find out. I'll give you instructions on how remove it." I sat down at the kitchen table.

"Ready when you are, Ethan."

"Okay, the first thing is to shave the spot around the object. Cut the hair as short as possible and then shave it."

Billy went to the bathroom and returned with a pair of scissors and a razor. I guided his hand to the spot where the object was located. He cut the hair around it and shaved a one-inch area.

"Now what?" He asked.

"Get some alcohol and a bandage. Once you've cut the thing out, apply the alcohol and bandage to the area." Bill got the needed items that I described.

"Now I need you to take out your hunting knife and sterilize it by holding it over the gas burner on the stove." Billy followed my directions. When he was ready I told him to use the point of the knife to make the incision and then carefully squeeze out the object.

"Listen, Billy, there can be a lot of bleeding. Hold pressure on the cut until bleeding stops. Put direct pressure on the laceration. Do you understand?"

"I'm ready," Billy replied.

I felt a pinch as he cut into my scalp and felt him squeezing out the object. He placed the tiny bloody thing on the kitchen table on a napkin. He then held the bandage tightly on the laceration. I felt a little dizzy, but there was very little pain. When the bleeding stopped, Billy taped a bandage over the small cut. After drinking a glass of water, I picked up the device and wiped it clean with the napkin.

I can't explain how, but I immediately recognized it. My mind clicked in and somehow I knew that Applied Digital Solutions, a Florida-based company, has been in the testing and production stages of microchip products called VeriChip and Digital Angel. VeriChip, is a miniaturized, implantable identification device. It is an encapsulated microchip a little bigger than the size of a grain of rice, which contains a unique verification number. The microchip is energized and activated when passed by a specific VeriChip scanner. Previously, the chip used radio frequency to energize and transmit a signal of the verification number. More recently a chip was developed that uses satellites to transmit signals globally. The newer product, Digital Angel, integrates wireless Internet technology with global positioning to transmit information directly to the Internet. The microchip is inserted typically under the skin of the scalp. Someone had inserted the Digital Angel under my scalp to track me.

"What is it?' Billy asked.

I knew better than to tell him. "I don't know," I lied.

"I need some fresh air. Thanks for helping me, Billy." I took the chip and went outside and sat on the corner of the porch to think. Some experience in my past had dragged up the knowledge to recognize the chip. I closed my eyes and tried to remember anything. My mind was blank, and I shook my head in frustration.

Then it hit me. If there was a tracking device inserted under my scalp, someone will be here soon to get me. They must know where I am, and I don't know if that's good or bad. Maybe I'll be rescued or maybe I'll be captured or killed. I couldn't take the chance. I decided to bury the tracking device about 2 inches deep, wrapped in the napkin, at the edge of the cornfield and watch the area. Surely they would come for me soon, whoever they are.

I walked to the edge of the cornfield, dug a small hole with my fingers, and placed the device inside. I covered it, pulled an ear of corn and placed it beside the area to mark the spot. There was only one road leading to the house and I could watch from there. I now had my first hope to find out who I am and how I got here.

"Ethan, come back here," Billy yelled. "Don't get so close to the cornfield. I can't allow you to go in."

I slowly walked back to the house and Blaze opened the door for me.

"Billy told me your name is Ethan," she said. "Nice to meet you, Ethan."

Without saying anything else she hugged me. I felt the warmth of her body against mine and something stirred.

"Katrina, Katrina," I whispered and Blaze stepped back.

"Who is Katrina?" She asked.

I didn't have a clue, but my heart was beating faster at the thought of the name.

10

"Hey Ted, the signal has consistently been coming from a remote area in West Texas for a couple of days. Maybe he's staying in one spot," Herman Scott said as he peered at his computer screen.

Ted Harper was aggravated. They were at the point of getting vital information when the Operative stopped communicating. The Digital Angel was working fine, and it had tracked the Operative from Chicago to Houston, then to West Texas. They made many attempts to communicate but received no response. Ted immediately wanted to fly from Washington DC to Texas to confront the Operative and find out what was happening, but Herman convinced him that it may disrupt the investigation and the sting. The long-standing surveillance of Future Mankind Ventures was too important to be compromised, but the Piranha was the final decider.

Harper scratched his baldhead and raised his 6'3" body from the chair. At age 61, he was still muscular and could hold his own in a fight. However, he was tired of the hassle of his work and wanted to retire and live a normal life. He couldn't reveal to anyone the nature of his job or where he worked. His few acquaintances thought he was a travel agent. That cover explained why he traveled a lot.

Herman had no such problem. He was single and had no relatives or friends to lie to. He was fifty-four years old and loved the secrecy of his job. He accepted his position after graduating from West Point and serving fifteen years in Army Intelligence. Even thought the employer was strange and unpredictable, he felt it was time he earned some real money and the man paid extremely well.

Herman stood just less than six feet and was slim and well developed. He was a handsome man often told that he looked like Brad Pitt. Many women made shameless approaches to him, which he gracefully declined. Herman was gay, but not out of the closet.

"We need to fly down there now to see what's happened. It looks as though he has gone rogue. Why else would he just stop communicating with us?" Ted asked.

"I think you're right this time," Herman replied. "I'll make arrangements. If the tracking device keeps sending signals, and he stays put, we'll have to land in Odessa and drive to the spot. It appears to be a three-hour trip from the airport. I'll requisition a charter jet.

"We'll should leave first thing in the morning after I call and update the boss," Ted replied.

"If there is any evidence that he's gone rogue we'll have to eliminate him on the spot." Herman said. "You know how the Piranha is. He ruthlessly destroys anything he perceives as dangerous to his power. He's our boss, but that man scares me. I've got the feeling that he knows our every move."

"The Piranha may want him eliminated regardless, since he has been off the reservation and hasn't contacted us in several days." Ted said. "The last conversations I had with Tyler, he said he had information which would lead him to the identification of the Piranha. He wouldn't share it with me. I would love to know who that son of a bitch really is and what kind of work he does so we could have some leverage. Tyler thinks the man holds a high-ranking political position. I reported that conversation to the Piranha at the time, but before he could take any action, Tyler disappeared. I think now that Tyler's been compromised, and it's a shame. I heard that the tall sensual wife of his should never be left alone. I'd love to have one uninterrupted hour to have my way with that sexy bitch," Ted said.

"If we kill him, we'll be required to eliminate her too and maybe you'll get your chance. We don't know what Tyler told her about the operation. The Piranha can't allow us to leave anyone alive who knows anything about him." Herman replied.

Ted picked up the phone and punched in the number of the Piranha. He wanted to clarify his orders before he and Herman left to find the Operative.

"Yes," a guttural voice answered.

"Как поживаешь?" Ted replied.

"Are you a stupid man," the voice responded. "Don't you ever speak Russian when you call me. English only, fool."

"I'm so sorry sir. It won't happen again," Ted said in a shaky voice. He comprehended that the man, who he only knew as the Piranha, had people killed for mistakes smaller than this.

"We know where the Operative is, and he seems to have settled at one place. We plan to go there and determine why he hasn't been in communication with us. Do you have any specific orders?"

"Kill him. He has been compromised."

"What about his wife? She's here in Washington DC."

"See what she knows. Do whatever you have to do to make her talk, then kill her."

"Yes sir, Boss."

Ted heard the click as the phone call was ended.

"Herman, we need to talk with the Operative's wife and deal with her before we go to Texas," Ted said. "Why don't we go to Katrina's apartment this afternoon? This could be fun."

11

Shelby F. Cain founded his company fifteen years ago. The original name of the company was Cain Enterprises, but he changed it to Future Mankind Ventures when he incorporated. He limited his investors to a few handpicked multi-millionaires, and he didn't care how his investors made their money. He was interested in running his company on his terms, but with deep-pocketed resources. He only invited three of his most wealthy investors to sit on the Board of Directors. Sergay Petrof from Moscow, Benjamin Cruise from the USA who oversaw the Houston operations, and Durand Moreau from Paris.

At this juncture in time, Cain's primary focus of interest was in the Moscow branch, which had isolated Higgs boson or Higgs particle, known in scientific circles as "The God Particle" at the Bern facility. He was encouraged by reports that Timothy Olsen was near a breakthrough in using the God Particle in his experiments.

Cain sat in his office in New York City's Rockefeller Plaza in Manhattan. He was smoking a Cuban cigar looking out at his magnificent view of New York City when his secretary Ivy, stuck her head in the doorway.

"Mr. Petrof is here for his appointment Mr. Cain."

"Show him in," Cain replied.

Sergay Petrof entered the room. His imposing stature always impressed Cain. Petrof stood 6 feet 7 inches tall with short blond hair. His light-blue eyes always had a spark of defiance in them.

He looked like the Russian fighter in Rocky IV, and his rugged appearance defied the extraordinary intellect he possessed. He held a master's degree in Atomic Science and a PhD in physics. He was fearless and ruthless. He had studied the God Particle for many years, and it was his primary goal in life was to isolate it. He knew the immense wealth that would follow the discovery and isolation and the application to other scientific theories.

Cain felt physically inferior at 5 feet 8 inches tall, completely bald and slightly overweight, but he was every bit the equal of Petrof intellectually.

"Sit down, Sergay. It's nice to see you."

Sergay sat down in the high-backed soft leather chair in front of Cain's huge oak desk.

"I have many excellent things to report," he said in his heavily accented voice.

"I'm somewhat familiar with the God Particle," Cain said, "But could you educate me further so I completely understand the significance of the project that I have invested millions in." Cain was well aware of the facts, but wanted to test Sergay's knowledge.

"Some have likened the search for the Higgs boson, known as the God Particle to the search for the Holy Grail. To the outside world, it presently exists in theory, but we have proven that it's real. Professor Peter Higgs put the theory forth in 1964. The God Particle is the missing link in the standard model of particle physics, our understanding of how the universe works. It produces mass. Without mass, the earth, the planets, the stars and the galaxies could not have formed after the theorized big bang. Our scientists found it using the particle collider at Bern. They smashed the particle beams to recreate the big bang countless times. What they have seen is sub-atomic debris, including the decayed remains of what they say appeared to be the God Particle. They were successful in isolating it. We are testing the

Particle twenty-four hours a day. The God Particle joins with other particles to create mass."

"When it is isolated, what is the practical use?" Cain asked.

"Sir, we can change mankind and in theory dramatically increase and improve the evolutionary process. We may even eventually be able to create life. We can do what God did millions of years ago and do it better." Petrof said, almost breathlessly.

Cain sat back in awe. He was sitting at the threshold of becoming the most important human on the planet.

12

"Why don't we have some lunch?" Blaze asked. "I'm starving." I agreed and sat down at the kitchen table. She went to the fridge freezer and took out a frozen carton and grabbed a can of green beans from the cupboard shelf. She put the green beans in a pot on the stove and turned it on and then put the carton in the microwave and punched in four minutes. Blaze set plates and silverware on the table and poured two glasses of ice tea from the pitcher she had retrieved from the fridge. When the microwave dinged, she took out the carton and spooned a generous portion on my plate and a small helping on hers. The mixture looked like some sort of pulled pork barbecue.

"What is this, Blaze?"

"Billy shot a feral hog that came running out of the cornfield one day. We slow cooked it in a pit that Billy dug. We have been eating on it for months but it's almost gone."

She served some green beans on my plate, sat down and began eating. "Where's Billy?" I asked.

"He's in the room with Fang. Fang talked."

"What do you mean he talked?"

"He just talked and now Billy is in there talking to him."

I let the statement sink in, as I sampled the pork. It was delicious and I finished my pork and green beans and drained the tea glass.

"I think I need to see what's happening," I said as I got up and headed for the room where Fang was caged.

"Suit yourself," Blaze said nonchalantly as she continued eating.

I heard voices when I entered the room. Billy was siting in a chair in front of the cage. Fangs' appearance had somewhat changed. Maybe it was just the look on his face and in his eyes. He appeared calm and intelligent.

"What going on Billy?"

"Mr. Fang asked me what happened?"

"Who are you sir?" Fang asked in a clear, Hispanic accented voice.

I was astonished that this wild man was talking so calmly and distinctly.

"He doesn't remember anything about biting me or attacking me," Billy said.

I looked at Fang. "Call me Ethan," I said. "What's your name?"

"Juan Gomez," he replied. "I work as a janitor in the laboratory. They pay me very well. The crazy man in the laboratory attacked me, and I woke up here. I don't know why I am in your cage."

Suddenly, he grabbed his head and let out a blood-curdling scream. He fell to the floor writhing in pain while clutching his head. Then he stopped and lay motionless in a fetal position in the middle of the cage.

"Billy I need to go into the cage and check on him." As I approached the cage and began undoing the chain, Fang sprang to his feet, and with lightning speed ran to the cage door and tried to grab me with his claw like hand. His teeth were bared and he was drooling. I jumped back as he extended his arm through the bars trying to get to me.

Billy yelled, "He's a crazy loon, let's get out of here so he'll settle down. Why did he go from sane to crazy?"

"I have no idea. Just don't trust him in the future."

Fang's screams were more like the last sound from a dying animal as we went to the kitchen where Blaze was cleaning up from our meal.

"I hope the Grim Reaper comes soon because we're running low on food, but I don't like the way he looks at me. I think he wants to rape me" Blaze said.

"If he hurts you, I'll stab him," Billy replied.

I looked at both of them. They were talking about rape and stabbing someone so calmly. It was to them like talking about the weather.

I felt like I was in the twilight zone.

"Billy we can hear anyone approaching the house, can't we?"

"Sure as hell," Billy replied.

"Listen, you and Blaze call me if a car approaches. I need some sleep. My head is pounding."

"Sure thing," Billy replied.

13

Katrina Ann Tyler, alias Ann Davis, lived in the Warren Towers in apartment 707 for three years. She moved there with Ethan Tyler after their whirlwind romance and marriage. The address at 3137 Connecticut Avenue was convenient to her work, and it didn't matter to Ethan since he traveled a lot. Katrina was a law clerk for Justice Clarence Thomas on the United States Supreme Court. She was working there under her alias name, cleared by the CIA and the FBI. She operated as a sleeper agent only to be used when needed.

Katrina held that position for two years when she met Ethan at a social gathering hosted by her best friend Lisa. Apparently, Lisa's husband worked with Ethan in the armed forces.

The tall handsome muscular man swept her off her feet with his charm, good looks, and striking blue eyes. She thought he resembled Shawn Connery in the old days when he played James Bond in the movie, Goldfinger. When they met, he had just been discharged from the Navy, where he held the rank of Colonel with the Navy Seals.

Ethan accepted a position in security work with the government. The work was classified, and Katrina respected his situation. To their friends and relatives, they said that he was in the security field and avoided further discussion.

She always felt guilty about never divulging her true identity to Ethan, and prior to their marriage, she secretly broke the agreement with the CIA, revealed to him her real name and judiciously explained the circumstances. Ethan respected her autonomy as an equal and would never divulge their secret. She had signed an agreement with the CIA. Her sleeper status had never been activated, but was in force. The CIA judiciously created her new identity so all legal matters could be handled without compromise.

Currently Ethan was on assignment for several weeks. He usually kept in touch with his her, with a phone call at least once a week, but over two weeks had passed without any calls. She certainly was worried, but knew that he was extremely competent to take care of himself. She went about her daily life as usual.

Today, Katrina hadn't gone to her apartment on her lunch break as planned. She had an errand to attend to. She phoned her co-worker, agent 924, who was waiting for her at the apartment, and told her that she would bring lunch, but she would be delayed. After finishing her errand at the bank, she planned to pick up Chinese, have a quiet lunch and discuss business with the co-worker. On the way to her apartment, she received a phone call telling her to return to the office for an emergency meeting. She called her apartment to explain, but got no answer.

Several days ago, Katrina provided Agent 924 with a key. Since the apartment was debugged, it was the safest place to meet securely. She felt sure that the woman, who was an active undercover CIA agent, wanted the meeting to activate her status.

Since Ethan hadn't called, she sought to delay the anticipated activation, however she felt compelled to comply with her agreement with the CIA.

14

After receiving the call that Katrina was going to be late, the agent phoned her supervisor. She believed that Katrina might be getting cold feet. The supervisor told her to wait, keep the appointment and proceed with the activation and subsequent orders.

After a short wait, there was a knock at the door. She opened it, and observed two men standing there. They looked like professionals in dark suits. One was very tall, older, and bald, while the other man was younger, slim, muscular and carried a black briefcase.

"What can I do for you?" she asked.

"Miss, we're here about your husband. May we come it?"

"Who are you, and may I see some identification?"

"Sure," the younger man replied.

He reached for his wallet. While she watched him, the older man threw a powerful left hook to her midsection. She fell to the floor, gasping for breath. The men quickly entered, closed and locked the door.

"Great punch Ted," the younger man said, smiling.

"Well thank you Herman."

Herman set down the briefcase and opened it. He extracted a roll of duct tape and a black cloth. He pulled out two pairs of surgical gloves and he, and Ted put them on. Herman taped her hands together and stuffed the cloth in her mouth.

Ted picked her up and carried her through the living area to the kitchen. He dumped her in a straight-back chair beside the kitchen table, and taped her feet. She struggled hopelessly against the restraints and attempted to scream. The gag muffled her voice. She gaped wildly at the two men.

"Katrina, please calm down," Herman said in a soft voice. "Just answer a few questions and we'll leave. Now I'm going to take the gag out of your mouth. If you scream my partner here will hit you again. Do you understand?"

She nodded, and Herman removed the gag.

"What has your husband told you about his work and what has he been up to in the past week?" Herman asked.

Wild thoughts darted through her mind. These men believed that she was Ethan's wife, Katrina. She calmed herself and decided to go along with them. She was certain that her CIA training would get her through this situation.

"I haven't heard from him in days and as far as work goes, not much, he's in a classified job in security."

Ted slapped her hard. "Stop lying or I'll hurt you. Tell us about his work."

"Now Ted," Herman said. "Don't be so harsh. I think she'll tell us, won't you honey?"

The slap angered her. She spat at Ted. "Go to hell!"

Herman stuffed the gag back into her mouth. "She needs some incentive."

Ted went to the cupboard, grabbed a pot, filled it with water, placed it on the stove and turned the burner on high. "Maybe scalding water on your face will loosen your tongue."

"Please honey, don't make Ted scar you for life. Let's try again." He jerked the gag out.

"I promise that Ethan will kill both of you for this. I can't tell you more than I know. However, if I knew anything more, I sure as hell wouldn't tell you. If you get out now maybe you'll be allowed to live," she murmured through gritted teeth.

Herman jammed the gag back in her mouth. "We're wasting time, forget about the torture Ted. Have your fun and let's get out of here."

Ted had never seen Ethan's wife before, but certainly approved of his taste in women. She was gorgeous, sexy and feisty. He liked that and it turned him on. Ted grinned, picked her up, threw her over his shoulder, carried her to the bedroom and dumped her body on the bed. He looped more tape between her bound hands, and taped it to the headboard. He reached into his pocket, pulled out a pocketknife and cut the tape around her ankles. While she wildly kicked, he spread her legs and taped each ankle to the footboard. She was spread eagle on the bed. He cut off her shorts and rippled off the T-shirt.

"You're not so tough now are you missy?" he sneered.

Tears began to roll down her face as she grasped what he intended to do. She shook her head wildly and struggled hopelessly against the restraints as Ted removed his pants and shorts. He crawled on the bed and taunted her. He punched her several times to make her to lie still. She continued to fight and gagged repeatedly on the cloth in her mouth.

Ted laughed again and put on a condom. He wanted no DNA inside her.

Regardless of the strength of her will, and resisting with all her might, Ted savagely raped her.

When he finished, he showered, dressed and yelled to Herman, "I'm through now. Your turn."

Herman went into the room and viewed with sick pleasure, the broken bleeding woman lying on the bed. To his surprise, she glared back at him with fierce hatred. It actually frightened him.

"Time to put her out of her misery," Ted said. "Herman, you do the honors."

Herman recovered from the viciousness of her glare, giggled, walked over and unceremoniously cut her throat. Soft gurgling was the last sound that this beautiful, brave woman made in her life.

The two hired goons had no remorse or any feeling at all. Killing another human being was no more than swatting a fly to them. The Piranha said kill, and they killed.

"Now let's go get Ethan. It'll be my time to snuff him out unless you want to play with him first."

Herman laughed, "Maybe, maybe I will."

15

My Unit was trudging through the torrid heat in Eastern Afghanistan when the I.E.D. exploded. I was well back of the impact; however, I was thrown to the ground from the shockwave. My ears were ringing when I staggered to my feet, grabbed my AKM type 56-assault rifle, and ran to the burning vehicles. Screams came from the Humvees as I sprinted past burnt body parts covering the ground. Another vehicle was overturned, and I saw a body hanging out of the window. I laid down my rifle, ripped open the door, and dragged the solder to safety. My hands were blistered by the hot metal on the door. I jogged back to the Humvee and forced the door all the way open. Two additional unconscious men were inside. I managed to drag them out and checked their pulses. They were barely alive.

A gunshot rang out, and I felt a burning sensation in my upper thigh. I was hit. I looked toward the source of the shot, and six Afghans were advancing, while stepping over the body parts on the ground. I reached in my belt and in one fluid motion heaved a grenade at the advancing party. Their body parts joined my dead comrades.

I heard the whirling blades of a helicopter and gunshots while I was running to the vehicle to pick up my assault rifle. Using the Humvee as a shield, I emptied my rifle into the Afghan helicopter. I must have hit the pilot because the copter crashed to the ground and exploded into flames.

I collapsed to the ground, tore a piece of cloth from my shirt and put pressure on my wound.

Additional whirling sounds filled the air and I looked up. At first, I thought it was another Afghan copter, but I recognized it as a USA Black

Hawk. I struggled to my feet and waved. The copter landed. I watched as the men surveyed the scene.

"My God man, you saved three of our boys and killed ten of those Taliban assholes. Let's get you and the guys to the hospital at Bagram Airfield. I opened my mouth to speak...

"Ethan, Ethan, wake up. A car is coming," Blaze said, breathlessly.

The dream was as realistic as if it had just happened. My hand moved automatically to my thigh. I felt the scar, evidently from the bullet wound. For some reason, I was given this flash from my past, but I still had no clue who I am or what I'm doing here.

I sprinted to the front window. Billy was standing there looking out the open window with his rifle resting on the windowsill. A black Cadillac Escalade pulled into the driveway. Two men got out. One was a very tall bald man, and the other was younger and slender. They looked around and approached the house. Both were dressed in dark suits, and the tall one carried a small device resembling an oversized phone. I immediately recognized them and understood the danger they represented. I knew it was Ted and Herman, and the device was a GPS tracking device.

"These guys will kill me if they know I'm here," I said to Billy.

"Billy, you handle these bad men and I'll hide Ethan," Blaze whispered, gripping my arm and pulling me.

"Please Blaze, I need to hear what they say."

We stopped in the living room, and I put my back to the wall, out of sight.

I heard the knock on the door. "What do you want?" Billy yelled through the closed door.

"I recognized the surly voice of Ted answer, "We're here looking for our friend and just wanted to ask if you've seen him. We think he's been hurt."

I heard Billy open the door, "ain't no one here but my sister, and me. We ain't seen nobody."

"Son, why don't you lower the rifle? We mean you no harm." I recognized Herman's soft voice. "Do you mind if we look around the property? We're very worried that our friend is injured. It won't take us long."

"Look all you want, but just don't go in the cornfield or I'll be obliged to shoot you." Billy replied.

"To hell you say," Ted murmured.

Billy pointed the rifle at his head, "Heed my words."

Herman stepped forward in front of Ted. "Okay friend, just calm down. We won't go into your cornfield." He smiled, and Billy lowered the rifle. Herman stepped aside revealing Ted holding a pistol. Before Billy could raise the rifle, Ted shot him. Billy crumbled to the floor with blood oozing from his upper torso.

Blaze screamed and darted to the fallen body.

"What do we have here?" Ted said with a snicker.

"Why did you shoot Billy?" Blaze whispered between sobs. "I think you killed him."

"The bastard shouldn't have threatened me. I don't take kindly to that."

Blaze screamed, jumped up and tried to punch Ted. Herman stepped forward and launched a left hook to her stomach. She fell to the floor beside Billy, gasping for breath.

"Herman you take care of the girl. I'm going to follow the device to see if Ethan is on the property. It shows him a couple of hundred yards away. He'll come running if he heard the gunshot. That'll make it simple. I'll kill him, and we can be on our way."

Herman pulled his pistol from his shoulder holster and pointed it toward Blaze.

"Don't kill her just yet," Ted said chuckling. "After I take care of Ethan, I want to have some fun with that sexy little minx before she leaves this world."

Ted walked out of the door and headed toward the cornfield where I had buried the tracking device. Herman walked toward Blaze. She stood up, clutching her stomach.

"Don't give me a reason to shoot you right now," Herman said.

His back was to me, and I had one chance to attack. I carefully moved closer to him and gathered myself to chop his outstretched arm, which was holding the gun. He must have heard a noise, and he twirled around to face me. I chopped his arm as hard as I could and the gun fell to the floor. Herman was quick and well trained. He instantly threw a right cross. I moved to the side, and the blow struck my shoulder. I responded with a left to his midsection. As he doubled over, I shot a kick to his head with my left foot. I was mystified at my fighting skills, but they came instinctively.

Herman crumbled to the floor. As I moved to finish him off, he reached in his pocket and brandished a switchblade. I backed away as he sprang to his feet.

"I will gut you like I gutted your wife. She loved it when Ted raped her," he growled. "When the Piranha says kill, we kill and he wants you dead too."

My heart almost stopped. The image of a beautiful woman came into my mind. It caused my heart to skip a beat. I was stunned by what he said, then rage overcame me.

"I'm going to kill you, bastard!" I yelled.

He was one tough cookie. He swung the knife, and I leapt back. A gunshot rang out. Herman looked stunned as he grasped his chest. He looked at his blood-soaked hand quizzically, and fell forward on his face. Herman hit the floor with a sickening thud. I looked around and there stood Blaze, with tears running down her cheeks, holding the gun that I chopped from Herman's hand.

"He shot Billy, and he was trying to kill you." She fell to her knees, sobbing.

"Run to the other room now," I yelled. I knew that Ted would be there in a flash after hearing the gunshot. I grabbed the gun and gently lifted her.

"Go hide until I take care of the other guy." She bit her lip and ploddingly walked away. I jogged to the window and looked outside. Ted was nowhere to be seen. I knew he was too smart to burst into a room where he heard gunshots, without knowing what had taken place. I had to get outside to find him. Blaze was in danger if he killed me. I walked quickly to the back door and exited the house.

There was complete silence outside. I knew I was facing a trained killer. I walked quietly around the side of the house holding the pistol to my side. I looked around the entrance and toward the cornfield. Nothing. I knew I had to take a risk. I stuck the gun into my waistband and covered it with my T-shirt.

"Ted, this is Ethan. I need to talk to you. I'll surrender," I shouted.

I walked out into the open with my hands raised and stood there for about five minutes with nothing happening. I remained standing with my hands in the air.

"Lay down on the ground and spread eagle," I heard Ted's anxious voice shout.

I complied and heard him approaching.

"What happened to Herman?"

"The girl shot him. He's dead."

"Ethan, you're in deep shit. Why did you run? You knew we would find you and kill you. You're a dead man, but if you tell me what you know about the experiments in the laboratory and the names of anyone who spoke to you about it, I'll let the girl live."

"It's a deal," I said, not knowing exactly what he was taking about.

"Can I at least sit up, so I can tell you everything?"

"Okay, but keep your hands in the air."

I sat up and looked at Ted. His shaved head was covered with sweat. His gun was pointed straight at my head.

"Listen Ted, I honestly don't know what happened. I woke up at the perimeter of that cornfield. I don't remember anything. The boy and girl took me in and cared for me."

"You're a lying bastard, Ethan. I know how dangerous you are. Don't think for a minute that I trust you. You've got twenty seconds to answer my questions or you're a dead man right now, and I'll rape and kill the girl."

I knew I had to attack him, but my chances of survival were slim with the gun pointed at my head. All he had to do was pull the trigger.

Suddenly, I heard a blood-curling shriek. I looked toward the house, and Fang was looping toward us.

"What in the hell is that?" Ted yelled as he turned and shot toward the approaching ghastly creature.

That distraction was all the opening I needed.

16

Agent Hank Thompson could hardly see the road because of the torrential rain as he drove to work. It was 9am on this stormy morning in McLean, Virginia. After secretly meeting with a covert agent, he was headed for the Langley neighborhood where the CIA Headquarters were located. Thompson was deep in thought, worried about one of his most exceptional agents, who he had deployed undercover. The mission was one of the highest priorities in recent history, and if it wasn't successful, there was the potential of changing the structure of the power throughout the world.

Thompson was the lead agent in the Directorate of Science Technology. He always avoided any discussions of his job content with people outside the CIA.

The rain slackened as he neared the office. His cell phone rang. He glanced at the caller ID, and saw that it was his administrative assistant Mae, calling.

"Yes Mae."

"Agent Thompson, the Director asked me to transfer a call to you from a New York Times reporter, Sam Owens. He's doing a story on the CIA, and he's asking specific questions about the CIA and the functions of your department. He's very pushy."

Thompson groaned and said, "Okay Mae, put him through." He placed the call on his blue tooth car speaker.

"Mr. Owens, this is Henry Thompson. I'm the Agent in Charge of the Doctorate of Science and Technology with the CIA. What can I do for you?"

"Mr. Thompson, could we start with your explaining to me what your department does?"

"I'll be happy to," Hank replied.

"The Directorate of Science and Technology is one of four major components whose employees carry out the CIA's mission. The DS&T brings expertise to solve our nation's most pressing intelligence problems."

Thompson took a deep breath and continued. "We attack national intelligence problems with effective targeting of bold technology and superb trade craft. We create, adapt, develop, and operate technical collection systems and apply enabling technologies to the collection, processing and analysis of information. We also monitor scientific experiments in foreign countries to ascertain the potential effect on the United States. To spend a day with the DS&T is to spend a day inside the imagination of the CIA. All the employees are technical intelligence officers and have significant scientific training. They work in many different disciplines ranging from computer programmers and engineers to scientist and analysis. The DS&T partners with many other organizations in the Intelligence Community, the military, academia and national laboratories, and the private sect to achieve a mission's success."

Owens interrupted, "Is your department presently involved in investigating the science which is isolating what is known as 'The God Particle?'"

The question sent a shock wave through Hank's brain. He hesitated and collected his thoughts. The question clearly startled him.

"Are you there?" asked Owens, grasping that he hit a nerve.

"Sir, you know I can't speak specifically about our projects. I can neither confirm nor deny anything specific."

"Your answer tells me what I need to know. Can we speak, off the record?"

"Absolutely not!" replied Thompson. "I'm sorry, I have a meeting, and must go now. I hope I gave you some insight into our department." He hung up the phone while Owens was still speaking.

Thompson had no idea how much Owens knew about the project. His own Intel had been cut off when Ethan Tyler went off line and ceased communications. He knew that the only thing he could do was to wait for contact with Tyler. The investigation could have been compromised, but he was certain that Agent Tyler would eradicate himself as per protocol, if his cover was blown.

He drove into the parking lot, opened his umbrella and walked to the entrance. After clearing security, Thompson went to his office.

"How did it go with the reporter?" Mae asked. "He's called back twice and said you hung up on him."

"I need to see the Director," Thompson said, disregarding her question. "Please call, make an appointment and tell him it's urgent."

"Yes Sir," Mae replied and picked up the phone.

Hank walked into his office, closed the door and collapsed on his chair. He rubbed his head and tried to unscramble all the thoughts raging through his mind. He closed his eyes and abruptly a peculiar calm steadied him.

"I've got this," he said, aloud.

Mae stuck her head in the office door, "The Director wants you in his office immediately, and he sounds very angry."

Hank Thompson scowled and shook his head. *The shit is about to hit the fan*, he thought as he walked down the hall.

17

T imothy Harding Olsen was going nuts while lying in bed in the Cain wing of Memorial Hospital. The bullet, which cleanly ripped through his shoulder, had exited without damaging any arteries. His shoulder was bandaged and he felt some pain, but he wanted to get back to his laboratory. He insisted that he be discharged; however, the doctor said he needed more time to ward off any infection.

A week had passed since he injected the janitor, and he had time to figure out what went wrong. The erratic, violent behavior and the physical changes he observed were due to the increasing size of the man's brain, and the mass growth throughout his body when the Formula entered his bloodstream. That intense transformation of any human mind and body would temporarily cause confusion and put his behavior in the Id mode of animalistic actions. As soon as the brain slowed it growth in mass, if it did, the enhanced ego and superego would emerge. Of course, the janitor stood the chance of dying because the brain may keep expanding until it found outlets of mass overload through the ears, eyes and throat.

Tim already had adjustments in mind to make to his Formula to control the growth and stop the mass growth before it induced death. His only requirements were several additional humans to experiment on until he perfected the Formula.

He could hardly control himself with the excitement of what he believed that he had discovered. Meanwhile, the hospital tray, holding a plate of runny scrambled eggs and fruit, set untouched as the doctor entered the room.

"Mr. Olsen, you need to eat to build up your strength," he scolded.

"When I get something decent to eat, I will," Tim responded sarcastically.

"You have a very important visitor waiting to see you. He's the one who insisted that we keep you under surveillance until he could come here and talk to you."

"Who is it?" Tim asked.

"Mr. Olsen, you are presently in the Cain Wing of this hospital. Mr. Shelby Cain has been one of our finest supporters and donors, and we always respect his wishes. He's waiting outside to talk to you. He said that you are one of his most valued employees."

Of course, Tim knew who Shelby Cain was. He knew that Mr. Cain founded Future Mankind Ventures and was the CEO. He had no clue what the renowned man wanted to talk to him about. *Ah yes, my Formula,* he thought.

"'Take this tray away and send him in," Tim barked.

The Doctor rolled his eyes, picked up the tray and walked out. Tim ran his fingers through his hair and tried to sit up as straight as possible.

An elderly man who looked remarkably like Spencer Tracy ambled into the room. He took the chair beside Tim's bed and sat there staring at Tim, but said nothing.

"I am very pleased to meet you Mr. Cain. What can I do for you sir?"

Cain remained silent. He knew that Olsen was a young man, but the guy he observed in the hospital bed resembled a cocky teenager. He watched him, and the young man stared back without blinking.

"Son do you know what you have done?" Cain finally asked.

"I know precisely what I've done and am doing," Tim replied. "I'm in the process of changing the course of human history through enhanced evolution by using the God Particle."

"Tim, your irrational behavior and impulsiveness have caused me a great deal of trouble. I've been given a complete report about what happened at the laboratory. The man you injected almost killed you, and he did succeed in killing one of the guards. I've cleaned up that mess, but the janitor is still missing. What were you thinking?"

"The only way I can move forward with my research is to test it on humans. The opportunity presented itself, so I took advantage of the moment. This is much more important than a lowly janitor's life.

His reaction to the injection of my Formula proved that the Higgs boson particle, which is the basis of my formula, could be developed to change the evolution of man. The injection of my Formula projected itself into the man's brain and caused the lobes in his brain to increase mass. It entered his bloodstream and affected his body strength and speed. The problem is that in its present chemical composition, mass will continue to expand. I know how to alter the Formula to correct those problems. If you provide me with three of four humans to test my corrections, I know I can perfect it. We are on the threshold of changing human history and putting Evolution on Steroids."

Cain sat silently, continuing to stare at Tim. After a few moments, he got up, went to the hospital room door and closed it. He pulled his cell phone from his pocket and punched in a number.

"Cruise, I need for you to secure at least three people and deliver them to the laboratory. They must be locked up and kept healthy. I want them on the premises no later than tomorrow." After a few moments of listening, he disconnected the call. He looked over, and Tim Olsen was grinning.

"You won't regret this, sir."

"I'll provide you with everything you need. Just don't fail me. People who disappoint me have a difficult time surviving."

Cain went to the door and summoned the doctor. "Release this man immediately," he said. "I'll have a car at the entrance in thirty minutes. I expect Mr. Olsen to be there when it arrives."

Cain left the room. "Let's get you of here," the doctor said. "Mr. Cain has provided you with fresh clothing in the closet. When you're dressed I'll have your release papers ready along with some pain medication. You'll need to see a physician in a week to check on your wound. It's healing nicely and you shouldn't have any problems."

Tim Olsen was ready to change the world and become a God on earth.

"My Mind Games will be of historic proportions," he said aloud, and giggled.

18

I couldn't determine if the bullet that Ted fired hit Fang or not. He just kept loping toward us, and that captured Ted's full attention. I rose up into a crouch and launched a robust leg sweep toward Ted's ankles. When my foot connected, his feet flew out from under him, and he crashed to the ground landing directly on this right shoulder causing the gun to fly out of his hand. I leaped to my feet, ran over and kicked him in the head. The blow rendered him unconscious. I stopped for a moment when I thought I heard the whirling blades of a helicopter in the distance, but dismissed it as the looming danger of losing my life pumped adrenaline into my blood stream.

I whirled to face Fang, not knowing if I could survive his attack. He stopped directly in front of me and moved into a hunched position. I recognized it as his attack mode. His eyes were red with rage and he snarled. I maintained a martial arts stance, prepared to do battle. We began to circle each other and Fang darted toward me. I sidestepped him and delivered a pivot kick to his back. It seemed to have no effect on him as he spun around to face me again. A low guttural snarl was coming from his throat. He looked up to the sky and then to the ground and charged again. His attack was more pure animal instinct than a tactical fight maneuver. I easily sidestepped him again. This time I landed a right cross to the side of his head. He stood with his back to me for a second and turned again. He looked at me and something peculiar was happening to his eyes. They appeared to be clearing, and a look of intelligence replaced the rage. I didn't know whether to punch him out or try to talk to him.

I recalled his moments of sanity in the cage when he asked what was he doing here. The change was temporary, and he returned to his savage ways in moments.

Abruptly, Fang's hands flew to his head, and he whaled in agony. It was the most inhuman sound I have ever heard. In what seemed like an eternity, the creature straightened up from his crouch, dropped his hands and opened his clear blue eyes.

"I think that young man in the laboratory has killed me," he said in a thick Spanish accent.

I was astounded at the clarity and calmness of his voice. "What are you talking about and what happened to you?"

He opened his mouth to speak, but no words emerged. He stood there with his mouth wide open and appeared to be gagging. It was then that I noticed blood seeping from his ears. I heard a bizarre crack, and blood gushed from his left eye along with a grey matter. It looked as if his brain was escaping through openings in his skull. He collapsed to the ground. I bent over his body and felt for a pulse. There was none. I crouched over his body for a moment wondering what had happened to this strange creature. What young man and what laboratory was he talking about? Since Blaze and Billy took us both at the edge of the cornfield, it was only logical that this laboratory he was talking about was on the other side.

Another memory unexpectedly flashed through my mind.

Ted and Herman and I were sitting in a car, staking out a large building. There were armed guards at the entrance. Herman was looking through binoculars with night-vision lenses.

"This must be the research laboratory that the Piranha wanted us to penetrate," Herman said. "Ethan, with your contacts with the Future Mankind Ventures organization, you've got to get in there and find out if that young genius punk is close to isolating the God Particle. The

Piranha is getting very impatient with the progress of our work. You don't want to make him angry or you and your family are dead."

"Don't worry, Sergey will get me in. They completely trust me. Sergey appointed me his primary body guard."

I was jolted from this flashback by a noise behind me and turned to see what it was. As I was turning, I felt a blow to the back of my head and my whole world faded to black.

19

Hank Thompson held his head high as he walked into the CIA director's office. He knew he was due a chewing out for hanging up on the reporter and for losing contact with Ethan Tyler. It was the most important assignment in his career, and he blew it. He would take his dressing down and never hang his head. Hank was a proud man, and even if he were dismissed, he would not allow himself to be humiliated.

"Can I bring you water or coffee?" Mae asked as he entered the office.

"Coffee, black," he replied.

"Same for me, Mae," the Director said.

Director C.T. Henria sat in his high back leather chair reading a file. He didn't look up as Agent Thompson entered.

"Sit," he ordered and continued to read. Director Henria's had been in his position for only six months. His predecessor had tired of working for an unprofessional and timid President and had resigned in frustration.

"Sir, I can explain about hanging up on that reporter. The discussion was centering on the 'God Particle' and I couldn't divert his attention away from the subject. I felt my safest exit was to hang up and pretend we had been cut off."

"I didn't call you in about that," The Director replied and kept studying the file.

"Well, I guess it's about Ethan Tyler. He simply discontinued contact with me. Honesty I fear for his safety. He's one of the best agents we have, and he would never go to the other side."

The Director laid down the file, "One of our undercover agents has been brutally tortured, raped and murdered. A neighbor called the D.C. police. Since she worked for the government at the Supreme Court, the FBI was called in. The Director of the FBI and only two of his top aides know about her true identity as one of our operatives. He called me and sent over a copy of the file. It was a professional hit, and probably the killers wanted information about Ethan. He's been compromised. We may need to take him out."

"Oh my God," murmured Thompson.

"The real Katrina may be in danger."

The Director picked up the file and handed it to Thompson. "I'm assigning two additional agents to assist you in finding Ethan Tyler or his body. Since he is compromised, he must be extracted from the case. You'll have the full backing of the Company in this search. Anything you want, you got."

Thompson opened the file. Behind the police report were pictures of the body. The battered woman's dead eyes were still open. He remembered her elegance and her wonderful personality.

"Ethan is one of the most dangerous men alive. Knowing what he will believe, when he finds the fool who did this, it isn't going to be pretty."

"Get out of here and find him. Agents Henderson and Ratliff will be in touch. All we have is in the file."

Thompson brushed by Mae as he was leaving the office. "Here's your coffee," she said.

Thompson didn't reply as he hurried out.

"Bastard," she whispered under her breath.

20

Ben Cruise sat for a moment in silence after concluding his conversation with Cain. His substantial investment in Future Mankind Ventures paid lavish dividends, but the promise of untold riches that would be enjoyed if the Olsen kid perfected the Formula, using the God Particle, was mesmerizing to him.

Cain ordered him to secure three humans for experimentation. Of course, he would sacrifice his right-hand man Carlos, and he thought of Blaze and Billy. Billy would be no problem, but he wanted to keep Blaze for his own personal pleasure. He knew he must choose between Katy and Blaze. However, one way or the other, he would have three humans to deliver to the laboratory. His planned trip for a morning departure to deliver supplies to Blaze and Billy was arranged.

He yelled for Carlos. "Yes Sir Boss," Carlos answered.

"Carlos, there's one change to our planned trip. I want you to accompany me. Some problems have occurred nearby, and I want protection."

"Yes Sir Boss, I'll be ready."

Ben packed his Walther pistol and his slapjack. He planned to use Carlos to secure Billy and Katy and when that was accomplished, he would render Carlos unconsciousness and deliver the three of them to the laboratory.

Maria interrupted his thoughts when she appeared in the doorway wearing nothing but a towel. "Please come to bed baby," she purred.

Cruise complied, and after rough and passionate lovemaking, he drifted off into a deep sleep while Maria was massaging his back.

He woke up late the next morning and hurriedly dressed for the trip. He placed his pistol in the shoulder holster and the slapjack in his back pocket. Cruise donned a leather sports jacket, which concealed the weapons. After grabbing his suitcase, he left the house while the naked Maria was still sleeping.

Carlos was waiting in the Jeep. He tossed the bag in the back, and they drove to the Helicopter pad. Jim Cyrus, the pilot, was standing outside the copter.

"Your supplies are packed and we're ready to go," he said. Carlos took Ben's bag and placed it in the back floorboard, and they both boarded the copter.

The sound of the thunderous whirling blades shattered the tranquility of the cloudless Texas sky. The trip took a little longer than expected because they encountered a commercial airliner flying lower than normal. Jim had to veer toward the right and circle until the airliner was out of sight.

Jim landed the copter on the helipad behind the laboratory. Two guards came to the copter with weapons in hand. They recognized Cruise, greeted him and left.

"Jim, please wait in the lounge inside the building. Carlos and I should be back in a couple of hours. We'll deliver the supplies later. I want to talk to Billy and Blaze."

"What now Boss?" Carlos asked.

"I want to surprise them so let's walk through the cornfield to the house."

Carlos nodded, and they entered the cornfield. About half way through the air was filled with the strong odor of decaying flesh. As the two men moved forward toward the stink, they came across the ravaged carcass of a dead horse. Cruise covered his nose and mouth with a handkerchief and took a closer look. He recognized the animal as Katy's horse. The wild creatures that had ravaged the flesh had concentrated on the body. Ben spotted the unmistakable bullet hole in the head.

"What in the hell?" Carlos exclaimed.

Ben didn't reply and kept walking. He instinctively realized that Katy was either abducted or dead. Looking down, he observed bloody streaks in the dirt as if a body had been dragged. He followed the blood trail and noticed a shiny object in the dirt. After reaching down to pick it up, he recognized it as a bracelet that he had given to Katy. Even his cold heart felt a tinge of sorrow.

"What is it Boss?" Carlos asked.

"It appears that Katy has been injured or killed. It looks like some wild animals, probably coyotes, dragged her body off."

Carlos opened his mouth to reply when a shot rang out. Both men instantly dropped to their knees. They heard yelling, plainly coming from outside the cornfield.

"Stay down and be quiet. Let's see what's going on," Ben said. Both men crept forward to the perimeter of the cornfield.

The scene that they observed confounded them. One man lying on the ground and was either unconscious or dead. Another tall muscular man was squaring off with what appeared to be a savage. Suddenly, the strange creature dropped to his knees with blood gushing from his face and head. The other man stood over him looking bewildered.

Ben took out his slapjack, quietly walked up behind the tall man and struck a hard blow to the back of his head. The man grabbed his head and fell to the ground, unconscious.

"Who are these men and what's wrong with that weird looking one?" Carlos asked, breathlessly.

"I don't know, but you run up to the house and get some cord or duct tape from Billy or Blaze so we can tie these other two men up." He checked the unconscious bald man and found a strong pulse.

Carlos left as Ben retrieved the pistol from his shoulder holster and pointed it toward the fallen men.

I won't have to use Carlos after all, he thought. *I can turn over these two men and Billy to use for the experiments, and keep Blaze for myself.*

Carlos returned with a roll of duct tape. "There's a dead man in the house and Billy's been shot. Blaze is tending to him. He's awake and it appears to be just an arm wound where the bullet passed cleanly through. Blaze stopped the bleeding, but she's nearly hysterical."

"Let's deal with these guys and I'll handle Blaze and Billy later," Ben said.

Carlos proceeded to tightly tape the hands and feet of both unconscious men.

Ben grabbed the cell phone from his pocket and punched in the number for Cain.

"Why are you bothering me?" was Cain's abrupt answer.

"Mr. Cain, we've got a problem here. When I came to bring food and supplies to two of my people across from the laboratory complex, I came across a couple of men fighting and a dead guy who looks like some sort of a savage whose head exploded. My man told me there was another dead man inside the house on the property. I'll get to the bottom of this and report to you, but I now have your three guys for the experiments. My copter pilot is at the laboratory. If you provided him with a van, and a couple of your guards to clean up the scene here, we'll be okay.

Cain was silent for a moment; "Okay I'll make the call now to give you what you need. My men at the laboratory will check out the identities of the dead men and the 'savage' as you call him. George is in command of security at the laboratory. Have your man turn over the dead bodies to him, and the three other men we're going to use. We'll take it from there."

After hanging up, Ben called Jim Cyrus. "Jim, you're going to be provided a couple of men, cleaning supplies, and a van. I've got a crime scene here that needs a through sanitizing. We have two dead bodies, two prisoners and one wounded man. Get here ASAP."

He hung up and turned to Carlos. "You stay here and watch these guys." He handed him the slapjack. "Knock 'em out if they struggle too much."

Ben walked to the farmhouse and went inside. Blaze was holding Billy's head on her lap. She was sobbing. Billy was quietly talking to her. She turned as Ben entered the room. "Thank God you're here. Billy's been shot!"

Ben went to her side and looked at Billy. "How are you doing kid?" he asked.

"I recon the man shot me, but I ain't too bad," Billy whispered.

Ben removed the cloth and inspected the wound. "The bleeding has stopped and you'll be okay. We just need to get you to the hospital. What's going on here Blaze? I want to know everything. Who are these men?"

"I'm so worried about Billy," she cried.

Ben searched the rest of the house, and then returned with the first-aid kit, scissors, a pillow and blanket. He cut off the blood soaked shirt and applied antiseptic to the wound. Billy grimaced, but didn't cry out in pain. He applied bandages and taped them tightly over the wound. Ben put the pillow beneath Billy's head and covered him with the blanket.

"We don't want you going into shock," he said.

After covering him, he continued speaking. "Blaze, I've got men on the way to take Billy to the hospital. I'll get you a glass of water, and you tell me what's been going on." He took Blaze by the arm, led her to the kitchen table, got her a glass of water and they sat down. "Don't you worry, Billy will be fine."

Blaze drank some water and took a deep breath. "Well it all started when we found the first strange man at the edge of the cornfield. He was unconscious and when we approached him, he woke up and tried to bite Billy. Billy knocked him out cold with the butt of the rifle. We put him in the cage and named him Fang. You said we shouldn't let anyone go into the cornfield, but you didn't say anything about someone coming out. We were worried that you would be disappointed if we killed him. We kept him locked up, fed him and waited for you to come. He's a loon."

Blaze drank some water and continued. "A little later we found the second man at the same place. A black coyote was about to eat him, and I shot it. We were worried so we tied him up. He was normal and nice to us. He saved Billy when Fang got out of the cage. He said his name was Ethan. Billy took some little medal object out of his head. After a few days, the other two men came. Ethan said that they wanted to kill him. We were going to hide Ethan from them, but the slim one shot Billy. He tried to kill Ethan, and I shot him dead. Ethan went out to get the other man. That's everything I know until Carlos came in to get the duct tape. I'm sorry if Billy and I messed up. We really want to please you and get away from here." Tears were running down her cheeks when she finished.

"Well I'll be damned," Ben replied. "Did this Ethan guy tell you anything about the dead horse in the cornfield?"

Blaze began crying again. She wiped away her tears and in a shaky voice said, "He told us that he saw a dead girl and a dead horse. We figured it was Katy, and that you would be very angry at Billy and me."

Cruise exhibited absolutely no emotion. He just shook his head. "Wasn't your fault."

He heard a vehicle approaching and went to the door. Jim Cyrus and two husky men in guard uniforms got out of a long white van. Cruise walked outside to meet them.

"Jim, there are two men tied up and a dead body down by the cornfield. Another body is inside the house. Get them and put 'em in the back of the van. Also, there's an injured man inside. I'm going to tell the girl that you're taking him to the hospital, but you take him with the two men to the laboratory. Turn them over to George, who heads security. He'll handle it from there. Then I want you and your guys to come back here and clean up the area by the cornfield and in the house. I don't any trace of blood or anything that can tie back to what happened. Carlos and I will take the girl and walk through the cornfield back to the laboratory complex. We'll wait for you there in the lounge. When you're finished, we'll fly back to my ranch."

"Yes sir, boss," Jim replied and he and the two men left to follow orders.

Cruise walked back to the house. Blaze met him at the door. He put his arm around her shoulders.

"Don't you worry, honey. The men will make sure Ethan is taken care of, and they'll take Billy to the hospital for treatment. You and I and Carlos are going to walk through the cornfield to the building on the other side and wait for my copter pilot. We're flying to my place and when Billy is released from the hospital, he'll join us.

"Thank you for helping me and Billy, Reaper," Blaze said. Her hand flew to her mouth when she realized that she had called Cruise the nickname that she and Billy had conjured up for him, the Grim Reaper. "I'm sorry," she said.

"Don't you worry, honey. Please, just call me Daddy Ben."

21

The United States Supreme Court building is located on First Street NE about a block east of the US Capital. Ann Davis (Katrina) smiled as she briskly walked toward the building. It was a beautiful morning with a soft breeze blowing. She felt lucky being able to work at the center of power for the country. She was concerned about standing up the Agent at her apartment for lunch, but it couldn't be helped. She attempted to call the apartment to tell her that they had an emergency at work, and that both of them were required at the meeting to make their case presentation, but got no answer.

Ann was concerned, without any substantial reason, about her partner. She joined the team a few weeks before, and Ann was worried about her confidentiality. Ann's assumed identity may be on shaky grown if the Agent broke her silence in any way.

Her cell phone buzzed in her purse. She took it out and saw a new text message. It read code 9643. She took a deep breath. This was her activation code. Ann thought that the Agent would activate her in person at the planned luncheon, and she wondered why it was handled this way.

She deleted the message and hung up the phone. She placed it back in her purse and fished out a throwaway cell phone she purchased for this exact purpose. Ann dialed the number ingrained in her memory. There was a click on the other end of the call.

"9643," she said. A slightly distorted voice gave her the assignment. She hung up the phone, dropped it on the sidewalk, crushed it with her foot, picked up the pieces and deposited them in the nearest trash receptacle. She walked briskly to the office building.

Ann passed FBI Agent Bill Lewis as he was leaving the building. He smiled at her and stopped. She thought that maybe he had been waiting in the lobby, watching for her return.

Ann's long black hair was blowing in the soft breeze and her tall lean body stopped beside him. Bill had tried to entice this beautiful, sexy woman into a relationship for months, but she steadfastly refused to date him.

"Any chance for dinner tonight?" he smiled and asked."

Ann stared at his big blue eyes. "Why not?' she replied.

Bill stood shocked and silent for a moment. He regained his composure and said, "I'll pick you up at seven, is that okay?"

"That's fine Bill."

"Is the Oval Room Restaurant satisfactory?"

"That would be lovely."

He handed her his card. "This has my cell number on it in case you need to reach me."

Bill hurried away in fear that she would change her mind.

Ann laughed out loud, went through security and proceeded to her office. She reviewed the case presentation again for the emergency meeting and felt comfortable that she, and her partner had done a competent and professional job. She called the woman's office number, but got no answer. Her partner's office was located on the floor above her in the complex of Justice Thomas' associates. The conference room where the presentation was scheduled was on the third floor. She assumed that her partner was already there. Fifteen minutes prior to the meeting time, she gathered up her papers and proceeded to the conference room.

Each Supreme Court Justice is assigned four clerks. Ann and her partner served with Charles Williams and Berl Antze as clerks for Justice Thomas. Berl and Charles were in the room when she arrived.

"Have you seen my partner?" she asked.

"Not today," Charles replied, not raising his head from his papers.

Ann left to call the office again. The meeting was scheduled to begin in less than ten minutes. Still, there was no answer. She went back to the conference room, grabbed a cup of coffee from the refreshment area, and sat down.

The door burst open and Jim Spencer, Judge Thomas's administrative assistant, rushed into the room.

"The meeting is cancelled!" he screeched breathlessly. "The police just called, and our associate has been killed. Her body was found an hour ago in your apartment, Ann. She was raped, tortured and murdered."

Ann felt the breath leave her body. She felt faint and grabbed her face. "What are you talking about?" she managed to say.

"I'm sorry to break it like this," Jim said. "That's all I know."

Ann got up and rushed from the conference room to her office.

She looked through her files and found the number of Agent Hank Thompson. She knew he worked with Ethan and was desperate to make contact with her husband. She grabbed her cell phone and punched in the number.

"Agent Thompson speaking," answered the deep professional voice of the CIA Agent.

"Hank, this is Ann Davis. Have you heard about the murder?"

Before he could answer, the full force of the loss of her associate hit her. She burst into sobs. She knew that it was supposed to have been her.

"I'm so sorry Ann. Yes, I know and I realize how upset you are. I'll wait until you can compose yourself. We're involved in the investigation and have taken over the crime scene. As far as the public and the press are concerned, Katrina Tyler is dead.

We'll work out the details with the FBI. I've had most of your clothes and necessities moved to the Hilton Hotel. We rented you a suite there until further notice. You go directly there."

Ann bit her lip, grabbed a tissue and wiped her eyes. It was all she could do to internalize the grief and stop crying.

"Does the Company know what happened to her and who did it?" She managed to ask.

"Ann, it was a professional hit. Probably has something to do with Ethan. We don't know where he is. That's all I can say. It's classified. We're holding her body for confidentiality reasons. The FBI is handling the investigation. I'll keep you informed."

"Thanks Hank."

Ann Davis hung up the phone and sat quietly with tears running down her cheeks. She wiped her eyes and sat in a steely silence. Her inter strength regained control of her emotions. She knew that she had to carry out her assignment without feelings getting in the way. She only wished that she could talk to Ethan and let him know that she was not dead.

Agent Bill Lewis proceeded to his car and got in. He pulled a disposal cell phone from the glove compartment. The only number programmed in the phone was to the Piranha. He punched the number.

"What do you want?" the gruff, slightly distorted voice asked.

"We got a break, and I finally have a date with Ann Davis. She's Ethan Tyler's wife's friend and co-worker. I'll drug her and get all the information I can about Ethan's whereabouts. If he's not already dead, I'll find him and kill him."

"After you get the information from the girl, waste her. No loose ends. Do you understand?"

"Yes Sir," relied Agent Lewis and hung up the phone.

Within minutes his cell phone rang. "Hello."

"Hi Bill, this is Ann. We have a slight change of plans. I can't explain right now but pick me up tonight at the Hilton. When you arrive just go to the desk and have them ring me. I'll come right down and join you."

"No problem Ann," he replied. He heard the click when she hung up. Bill didn't know why the change was made, but he needed to devise an alternate plan. No way was he going to disappoint the Piranha. That would mean a certain, painful death.

22

*T*he cool breeze was tranquil and enchanted as Katrina and I lay on a blanket at the beach. Her body felt warm in my arms, and her soft breath and lips lingered on my neck. It was twilight, and the sun produced streaming lights of orange and red as it peered through the low-hanging clouds. The memories of a wonderful day in Maui lingered in my mind. We had lunch at the Japengo restaurant near the beach and enjoyed Mahi Mahi broiled and stuffed with crabmeat. We spent the late afternoon on the lanai reading and sipping Mai Tai's. We decided to end this perfect day by viewing the sunset while lying on the beach. My heart was filled with adoration for this woman, and she returned my affection. Our fifth wedding anniversary was affirming our unconditional love for each other.

She softly whispered in my ear, "I love you with all my heart, Ethan. Don't ever leave me."

"Katrina you are the love of my live. I will always protect you and I will be with you forever."

My head was spinning as I regained consciousness and departed from this wonderful dream. I opened my eyes and struggled to get up, only to find that my hands and feet were bound. I was lying on the floor in the back of what appeared to be a van. I felt the bumps as we rode over a rough road. Looking around, I saw Ted glaring at me. He was bound with duct tape on his hands and feet. Lying beside him was Billy, who was bloody and also bound with tape. He apparently had passed out. Beside Billy was Fang's body and Herman's remains.

"What in hell is going on, Ethan?" Ted sneered.

I shook my head. For the first time since waking up in the cornfield, my thoughts were clearing. The blow to the head must have brought my memory back. Thoughts flashed rapidly through my mind. I closed my eyes and remembered.

I'm a CIA undercover agent. I worked my way into an organization, which I thought incorrectly, was loosely connected to the KGB. A man, who I had never seen, only known as the Piranha, gave the orders. I worked directly with two agents in his clandestine organization, Herman Scott and Ted Harper. They did not know the true identity of the Piranha, but I overheard them speculating that he was a high-ranking government official. Ted felt certain that he knew his identity and said that he had proof, but Herman was doubtful. As information and orders came to me from the Piranha, through Ted and Herman, I think I may know who he is. Whoever he is, I had to stop him before the accomplished his goals.

The group discovered that Future Mankind Ventures had isolated "The God Particle." Herman, dealing with the Piranha, and through an outside underworld recruiting company, had arranged a meeting for me with Sergay Petrof. He was on the Board of Directors of Future Mankind Ventures and was searching for an experienced and skilled bodyguard. An agent of the Piranha provided me with a fake resume and references. After a successful interview, I was hired as Petrof's bodyguard.

My undercover assignment was to verify that the God Particle had been isolated and preserved and to locate the principal scientist responsible for the project, then abduct him. I overheard Ted saying that the Piranha already had an insider in the organization, but he didn't trust him.

My Thoughts were that The Piranha sought to acquire the God Particle research, steal the procedures to allow physicists and scientist, from what country I didn't know, to advance the findings and use it to gain immense power in the world. This was pure speculation on my part.

Cain, the CEO of the company apparently wanted to sell the procedures and the Formula to the highest bidder. I remember Ted saying that the Piranha wanted Cain out of the way and his man in charge. I knew this information was sketchy and some of it incorrect, but I was near finding out the truth when something happened.

My head was spinning as the memories flooded back. It was quite a complicated situation. I was undercover with the CIA, planted with the Piranha organization, and then planted by them with Sergay Petrof and Future Mankind Ventures.

Part of the deal included embedding a tracking device in my scalp. Ted and Herman, operatives for the Piranha, told me it was for my protection, so they could locate me in case of a life-threatening situation.

My CIA contact was Hank Thompson. I couldn't remember when the last time I talked to him.

For a reason, unknown to me, my cover was blown with Sergey. He found out that I was working for an outside organization and spying, but little else. I was subdued by three of his henchmen, after a bloody fight. I think I may have killed one of them in the struggle.

I was subsequently transported to a place unknown to me and water boarded three times. My training allowed me to resist telling them that I was a CIA agent, but I knew it was only a matter of time before they broke me or killed me.

The last time I was taken into the room for water boarding again, my clothes were ripped off. Water boarding me, while naked, was supposed to further obliterate my will and dignity.

The interrogator who was to administer the torture grew careless. He assumed I was too weak to be a threat. A chop to his Adams apple crushed his windpipe. His associate had a rifle and butt stroked me. I slid to the side and the blow was glancing, however, it almost knocked me out. The pain and dizziness nearly overcame me, but I managed to kick him in the groin. When he fell, I stomped his head, grabbed his rifle and made my way to the outside door. I burst through the door and was confronted by two guards, shot them both and ran. There was a road going east. I knew I had to throw my abductors off my track, so I ran about 50 yards down the road. I lowered my head to allow blood drops to fall to the road and threw the rifle down. There was a cornfield a short distance away to my right. I sprinted to the cornfield and stumbled in. I lingered just inside the cover of the field and watched. I heard loud voices as three men ran out of the building and looked at the two bodies. One of them yelled, "He must have run down the road. I see the rifle." They sprinted east past where I left the rifle.

I cautiously made my way through the cornfield, vigilantly avoiding leaving a trail. I came across a dead girl and a lifeless horse. At the time, I thought it might have been an illusion, as I was getting dizzier and my head was throbbing from the rifle blow.

I made my way to the other side of the cornfield, where I passed out. I must have suffered a concussion from the blow to the head and encountered temporary memory loss. Now my mind is clear and I remember everything that happened before and after Blaze discovered me. I realized that some of the memories were probably distorted, but at least I know who I am.

Suddenly, another devastating memory battered my brain. I remembered what Herman had said to me when he pulled the knife in our fight. He said he killed my wife after Ted raped her.

My mind couldn't immediately grasp the devastation I felt. Did they really kill my Wife? Did the scumbag on the floor of the van beside me rape her?

I opened my eyes and glared at Ted Harper. His eyes were open and he was looking at the roof of the van.

He turned his head and looked at me.

"You sorry piece of shit, I'm going to kill you." I said in a surprisingly calm voice. "You raped my wife and Herman killed her. You're a dead man."

23

Agent Bill Lewis picked up a dozen red roses and a bottle of Dom Perignon on his way to the Capital Hilton. The elegant hotel was located at 1001 16th street NW and was within two blocks of the White House. The valet took his car keys, and Bill gave him a twenty.

"Keep it close," he said, and walked into the lobby.

A well-dressed Asian guy stood behind the chic lobby desk. He smiled and nodded at Bill. "How may I help you sir?"

Bill looked at the gentleman and noticed what appeared to be a lunch bag sitting on the back desk. It was a strange-looking bag, and a lingering smell of lemon and vanilla was in the air. He felt a momentary dizziness; however, his head cleared quickly.

"Miss Ann Davis is a guest here and she's expecting me. Could you call her room and tell her that Bill is here?"

"Certainly sir."

The Asian guy punched her name into the computer, determined the suite number and called. "A gentleman named Bill is here to see you, Miss Davis." He apparently got a reply that surprised him and he raised his eyebrows. "Miss Davis asked me to invite you to her suite, 707. The elevator is to your right."

Bill was amazed, but proceeded to the elevator and punched seven. On the elevator with him were an elderly distinguished looking man and very pretty young lady. Her assets were well displayed in the tiny red dress that she wore. The man appeared embarrassed when Bill gazed at him. The couple got off on the fifth floor. The gentleman glanced back at Bill as they exited the elevator.

Bill recognized him as the Senior Democratic Senator from New York, Charles Erickson. He grinned knowing that the Senator had some playful activities planned for this evening. If only the general public knew what went on with the power brokers in this corrupt city. He laughed again as the elevator door opened to the seventh floor.

Bill looked to the right, and suite 707 was two doors down. He walked to the door and knocked.

A beaming Ann Davis opened the door. A beautiful single strand of pearls complimented her elegant short black cocktail dress.

"Come in Bill, it's nice to see you."

He smiled and handed her the roses and the champagne. There was a vase holding some silk greenery on the end table. Ann removed the greenery, filled the vase with water and carefully placed the roses in it. She set it back on the end table.

"Have a seat Bill, I'll put the champagne on ice to chill and maybe after dinner we can come back here and enjoy it."

Bill moved to the white leather couch and sat down. He couldn't believe what was happening. *Maybe I'll see where this leads before I drug her and get the information for the Piranha,* he thought. *What a shame to kill such an elegant sexy lady, but when the Piranha gives orders, I obey.*

In the corner of the room was a small bar with a selection of mini bottles on the glass shelf behind it. "What will it be?" Ann asked. "I could use a drink before we go."

"Whatever you're having," he replied.

She grabbed two mini bottles of Jack Daniels, retrieved two glasses from under the bar and filled them with ice. She emptied the bourbon into the glasses and added a splash of ginger ale. Ann walked over to the couch and joined Bill. She handed him the drink and raised her glass. "To an enjoyable and exciting evening."

They both sipped their drinks.

"What time are our reservations at the Oval Room?"

"We have about twenty minutes, but if you'd rather stay here and order up room service, I'm game," Bill said, grinning.

"You're a naughty boy Bill, but I'm in the mood for steak and lobster.

Afterwards we can come back here and enjoy the Champagne and each other."

"Well, we better get going, I'm anxious to get this dinner out of the way and come back here."

Ann grabbed her purse and wrap and they left the suite. Bill's black Beemer was waiting near the door and the eager valet had it there in seconds. Bill palmed him another twenty and they were off.

"Bill, are you really feeling romantic tonight?" Ann leaned over, pressing her breasts against his arm."

"Whatever you want." Bill answered, not believing his luck. "Why don't you call and delay our reservations for about an hour. I want to take you to my special place."

Bill made the call and reset the dinner reservations. "Where do you want to go?" "There's a romantic and secluded place at the East Potomac Park. We have a beautiful full moon tonight and I'd love to spend some time with you there. To be honest I'm in the mood for some relaxation." She pushed his arm against her warm breasts and kissed him on the cheek.

"Where have you been hiding this side of you?" Bill asked. "I've been saving it for you a long time," she replied. "Do you know how to get to the park?"

"I don't know exactly where you're talking about."

"Bill, East Potomac Park is located south of Independence Avenue and the Tidal Basin. The southern end of the park is known as Hains Point. That's my special place. You can access the park on foot by following the trails from the Jefferson Memorial. Just go to the Memorial. We can park and walk to my spot."

Bill proceeded to the Memorial and parked. The area was secluded. He turned to Ann. She put her hands on his cheek and pulled him to her. Her kiss was passionate and his left hand softly caressed her breasts.

"Wait until we get to my spot," she whispered.

Bill couldn't figure out this come-on, but he was going with the flow. After getting the information he needed, he planned to waste her anyway so he decided to have as much fun as possible before the messy part began.

Ann got out of the car, removed her heels and went directly to the trail that led to Hains Point. Bill followed her. After a short walk they arrived at a secluded spot. There was a small pier leading out over the water with benches at the end. The moon's reflection on the water made it shimmer with an orange glow. There was a small building holding rest rooms to the right of the pier.

"Bill go to the end of the pier and sit down. I'll be there in a minute. I need to use the ladies room."

Bill grabbed her and kissed her hard. "I'll be waiting," he panted.

Ann walked to the rest room, went inside and locked the door. She took a pistol from her purse, screwed on the silencer and placed it back in the purse. She unlocked the door and walked slowly down the pier. Her hand remained inside the purse holding the pistol.

"That didn't take long," Bill said, turning his head to look at the water.

Ann walked up to him and pulled the pistol out of her purse. Her hands were trembling as she shot him in the head. He crumpled to the pier boards. She shot him three additional times and kicked his body into the water. Tears welled in her eyes. She had never killed anyone before. Ann heaved the pistol as far into the waterway as she could and walked away. She proceeded back to the Memorial area parking lot.

The company had left a white Kia there for her. She located the key, stuck by magnet under the left back fender over the tire, and drove to the designated area about a mile from the Hotel. She parked the car and walked to the hotel. When she got back to the suite, she put the roses in a plastic trash bag along with the bottle of champagne and the drinking glasses. Ann wiped clean any other fingerprints Bill may have left. She walked down the hall to the ice machine area and stuffed the bag into the trashcan.

After returning to the room, she called the contact number. When she heard the click, she said, "8969," and hung up. The number designated that the assignment was completed successfully. She hesitated and called the number again.

"I need to know why you required that man eliminated? I'm having a hard time here."

A computer-distorted voice answered, "You're breaking protocol here."

"I don't care I need to know."

"Agent Bill Lewis does contract work on the side for a criminal known as the Piranha. We have known about this for a couple of weeks. He was ordered to kill you tonight, and then he was going after Ethan."

There was a click, and the phone went dead. Ann strained to completely grasp what he said. Now, at least, she had some justification.

She would now return to her former status, undercover. Her activation and her mission were complete. Maybe later she could find out more details on why the CIA wanted Bill Lewis eliminated.

Ann (Katrina) checked out of the hotel and traveled to the new apartment that the company had acquired for her. As usual it was properly furnished with new clothing and the appropriate essentials.

If I could only talk to Ethan, she thought. *I fear for his safety and I desperately miss him.*

24

The van stopped, and an armed stocky guy with curly black hair opened the doors. Two other men quickly appeared by his side. One had short grey hair and a grey beard. The other man was very tall with red hair. All three of them were extremely muscular and carried assault rifles. Curly handed his assault rifle to Beard, jumped into the van and cut the tape, unbinding our feet. He pulled us to our feet. Billy was conscious but could hardly stand.

"Get out," he commanded. Ted and I jumped to the ground. Billy had to be lifted down and he immediately collapsed. I knew that if he didn't get medical attention soon he would die of blood loss from the gunshot wound.

Red Hair handed Curly his weapon back. He threw Billy over his shoulder and walked away. Billy was grunting with pain. Curly punched Ted with the barrel of his rifle and grunted, "Let's go."

That left me standing there with Beard. "What in the hell is going on?" I yelled. Curly looked back toward us. Beard punched me hard in the gut, and I fell to the ground, breathless.

"Keep your mouth shut!" He bellowed and nodded to Curly that he had me under control.

When I regained by breath and stood, both Billy and Ted were out of sight. "Let's go shithead," Beard sneered and pushed me toward a large building. There was a door to the left with an armed guard standing by it.

"George wants him in a laboratory holding room. Put him in cage 3," the guard said.

"You got it," Beard replied.

He nudged me with the rifle, and we walked into the building. Beard pulled a cloth from his pocket and blindfolded me. "Walk straight forward."

I slowly walked forward for fifty steps. I decided to memorize the path I was taking in the event I might be able to escape and needed to get back to that door leading to the outside.

"Turn right here." I turned and waked 22 steps. "Left," he said. We walked 31 steps and passed a place where I heard voices.

"We need to check them physically and test their IQ," I heard a voice say." It sounded like a young man talking.

"Right." Beard ordered. I turned and walked 8 steps when he told me to stop. I heard the squeaking of a door opening. We walked a few more steps and I heard the rattling of chains. Beard shoved me forward. I tripped over something on the floor and almost fell. I regained my balance and stood still. I heard a door close, the chains again and the click of a lock.

"Come three steps forward," Beard said. I walked toward the sound of his voice. "Hold your hands straight out." I stretched my hands forward. I felt the tape being cut.

As soon as my hands were free, I removed the blindfold. The first thing I saw was Beard standing outside the door of the cage. I was locked inside. Inexplicably, he grinned at me. "Behave yourself and you won't be shot the first day," he chuckled and walked away.

I surveyed the surroundings. I was locked inside a cage about fifteen feet by about twelve feet. Nothing was in the cage but a porta potty sitting in the right corner. There was a small door just behind the toilet. It was also padlocked. I assumed that it was there to remove and empty the toilet. The floor was a white tile. The cage was situated in a large room with equipment that you would expect to see in a laboratory. There was a long table with test tubes and other containers with liquids in them. To the right of that table was what appeared to be an operating table and a small stand with surgical instruments on it. The entire room was spotless and appeared sterile.

I knew instinctively that I was back in the same building where I was water boarded and had escaped from. This time I was here for a different purpose. I have no idea what. I don't understand why they didn't just kill me on the spot.

I heard noises, and the door to the room opened. A very young man in a white lab coat walked in with Beard and another older man in a tailored suit. They came to the cage. The young guy was giving me the once over.

"What do you think, Dr. Olsen?" the older guy asked.

"He looks like a healthy specimen," was the reply.

I just stared at them, not moving. Beard squinted his eyes at me.

"Mr. Cain, we need to be sure that the three test subjects are healthy, mentally and physically, before I can proceed with the tests." Dr. Olsen said.

Cain looked at Beard. "Work with George and make sure this man is well fed and kept clean. He's your charge."

"What about the other two men?" Olsen asked.

"Each has an agent assigned specifically to them," Cain replied.

They were talking as if I was an object and not even in the room. Then Olsen looked at me again. "Would you consider yourself a reasonably intelligent man?" Olsen asked me. "What's your real name?"

I said nothing. I knew that my best bet was to remain silent.

When he saw that I wasn't going to answer him, he smiled and said, "Doesn't matter. I'll make you a man with superior intellect and skills. I can evolve you."

"Let's go check the other two," Cain said. "I understand one of them is wounded. If he dies we'll get you another."

"I need three," Olsen replied in an irritated voice.

Cain and Olsen left, but Beard stayed.

"You handled that well," he said. "Just keep your mouth shut and say nothing to anyone. I'll take care of everything else."

Before I could reply, he left the room. *What in the hell is with this guy*, I thought.

I sat on the floor thinking about how I could get out of here before the Olsen guy did whatever he planned. I knew instinctively that my life as I know it, depended on it.

My thoughts drifted back to what Henry said about raping and killing my wife. I had no way of knowing the truth, but my mind entered a dark place. *Katrina is probably dead.* The thought of that sickened me and filled me with rage.

The door opened again and an older stocky Mexican woman entered. The old woman had grey hair and walked with a limp. She was pushing a cart.

She walked up to the cage. "Who are you?" I asked.

"No hablo engles," She said.

There was another small door on the floor of the cage three feet from the main door, measuring about two feet wide and ten inches high. She unlocked the padlock, opened the small door, took a pan filled with soapy water and slid it through the opening. A second pan filled with clear water followed, and a towel. There was a washcloth in the soapy pan. I assumed I was to wash myself. She smiled and pushed a white jump suit and clean underwear through the opening. She dutifully turned her back. I remembered that Olsen said he wanted us kept clean. I undressed and washed myself as best I could. After drying with the towel, I put on the clean underwear and the jumpsuit. I pushed the dirty clothes and the pans back through the opening.

She said, "Gracias," went back to the cart and retrieved a large bowl of what looked like vegetable soup and a half loaf of French bread. She slid it through the opening with a bottle of water and a plastic spoon. She walked to the corner of the room and sat down in a chair, apparently waiting on me to eat.

I knew I needed my strength, so I ate all the soup and bread and drank the bottle of water. She watched me the entire time. When I finished she came back to the cage and motioned for me to slide the items back through. I complied with the bowl and the empty bottle of water. I slid the plastic spoon in my pocket. She didn't seem to notice and put the items on the cart. She turned to look at me before she left. I could sense a look of pity in her eyes. She shook her head and walked out. I was clean and fed and fell into a restless sleep on the tile floor.

My dreams didn't release the pain of the thought that my wife might be dead.

I sat up and stared into the still lighted room.

I've got to get the hell out of here!

25

Tim Olsen was giddy with the envisioned power that he was going to possess. Once he perfected his technique and Formula, he could build his own empire and sell his discoveries to the highest bidder. To hell with his contract with Future Mankind Ventures. He needed to pacify old man Cain, for the moment, because he required a supply of human test subjects, money and facilities. *This is my discovery, and no one can take it away from* me, he thought. *I love playing games with inferior minds.*

The first subject that he, Cain and the bearded man visited was locked inside a cage and appeared to be an ideal, healthy candidate. As they left the room, he became curious about the bearded man who accompanied them.

"Who's this guy, and why do we need him with us?"

"I've assigned a guardian for each of your three test subjects. It's their responsibility to keep the men clean and healthy as you instructed. As you know, the captives are not here of their own free will. We need to situate them to a state of mind to be compliant subjects. This will require some 'brainwashing,' Cain answered. "This man is Hedrick, he's assigned to "Case Study One." The test subjects will be designated as "Case study One, Two and Three." No need for them to have names or a past. They're yours now."

"I don't even want to know names or history. I'm going to evolve them, and build them a new future, if they survive," Tim replied.

Cain turned to Hedrick, "Get Case Study One cleaned and fed."

Cain and Olsen walked to the next holding room. Cain opened the door, and they entered the room. "This is "case study two," he said. "He's young and strong but has been wounded. We're treating his wounds, then he's yours."

"This could prove an interesting experiment," Olsen said. "Maybe my God Particle Formula can cause muscle mass to form and heal the wound faster."

"Case Study Two", Billy, was lying in a bed with an IV's in his arm. A tall man with red hair was sitting in a chair near the bed. "This is Curt," Cain said. "He's in charge of this one." Curt nodded but didn't move his gaze from Billy.

"He's been sedated and will be out for awhile," Curt said.

"I may need him very soon, so take good care of him."

Curt looked at Cain and Cain nodded. "Yes sir," Curt replied.

Cain and Olsen left the room. Tim Olsen's excitement continued to build as they walked to the third room. He couldn't help himself, but to instruct Cain on the God Particle. Cain allowed himself to be lectured. *This brash young man will see who's boss soon enough,* he thought.

Olsen looked at him and stopped. "What I've done and am going to do will answer basic questions about how the universe evolved and how man evolved. I'll improve and expand the evolutionary process. My discoveries will teach us something fundamental about the building blocks of the universe and how the major particles that build the world around us acquired mass. I will take this knowledge to the next level and use it to improve and evolve humans."

Tim's eyes were almost glazed as he continued, "In addition, my research will also lead to many important applications outside of the human elements. Particle accelerators have many applications in material science and medicine but how it is applied to man will be the most dramatic."

A stocky man with black curly hair mercifully interrupted Olsen's self-serving, narcissistic lecture.

"Mr. Cain, I'm having trouble with Case Study Three. He's extremely violent and I've had to subdue him and gag him until he settles down."

"This is Isaac," Cain said to Olsen. "Let's follow him to the next holding room."

The three men walked into the room. It was identical to the room, which held Case Study One. Inside the cage was a very tall bald man. He was bound by duct tape and gagged. When he saw them, he began to struggle. He was bleeding from a blow to the left side of his head.

"This one is going to be challenging to control," Isaac said.

"Don't worry, when he's hungry enough he'll settle down." Olsen replied.

Cain and Olsen left the room. Isaac stayed behind to monitor Ted, Case Study Three.

"I also have the body of the janitor who you injected with the Formula. It appears that his brain matter exploded through his eyes, ears and nose,"

"That was a mistake. I wasn't in a controlled situation. I'll need to examine him and see what went wrong. I've already made adjustments to the Formula. Have the body sent to my laboratory immediately."

"Okay young man, the ball's in your court. I've invested a fortune in you, and I expect a return. I'm flying back to Chicago tomorrow. Keep me informed. I want video calls and reports daily."

Tim Olsen nodded and walked back to his laboratory. He resented this old man ordering him around.

He didn't have time to concern himself about Cain at the moment. Tim knew that his immediate daunting task was to convince Brenda, his assistant, to assist him with the human experiments and keep her mouth shut. Tim was incapable of love, but he knew that Brenda had feelings for him. He planned to take full advantage of her emotions.

26

In the United States of America, people run for political office for many reasons. Their original intentions may have been patriotic, but when they get to Washington, DC and see the power granted to them by the people, logic and the good of the people appears to leave their minds. Many get wrapped up in the power and the partisan political atmosphere and simply go with the flow.

Almost immediately, special interest and lobbyist visit them with what seems to be reasonable requests. Of course in return for their support, campaign contributions are promised. After a time of conditioning, outright bribes are taken.

With the state of the partisan press, politicians are not held accountable for their actions. The result is a government that is stagnant and unresponsive. For most of them, polls guide their speeches and actions. If a poll shows that 90% of the American people favor raising the minimum wage, then they're for it. They don't realize or care that if a poll was taken asking, "Do you think everyone in the USA should make 100,000 dollars a year?" Of course over 90% would say yes.

Even though the American people give Congress extremely low approval ratings, they keep electing the same corrupt politicians, sometimes for decades. This atmosphere gives corrupt individuals and corporations fertile grounds for influence peddling.

The Piranha knew Washington, DC like the back of his hand. He took full advantage of the corruptness. For years, he selected particular politicians and essentially put them on his payroll. His stature in the thrones of political power was impeccable. His real identity was protected from the bribes and payoffs by a network of organizations. He had tentacles reaching to the highest levels of the White House and Congress. Through other organizations, he secured paid informants in the FBI and the CIA.

The Piranha carefully constructed his network so only one man knew his actual identity. He called his cohort "The Organizer." Most of his orders were given by secure phone calls to this man. He had met his Organizer just two times in person so as not to take any chance that his cover would be blown. Other than the Organizer, he only spoke to Ted Harper, Herman Scott, Agent Bill Lewis and a high-ranking CIA official. They did not know his true identity and had ever met him. Their payoffs were made in cash drops.

The Organizer was unaware of Harper, Scott and Lewis' existence. The primary purpose the Piranha had them at his disposal was to exterminate the Organizer, if it became necessary, and to eliminate any threats to his plans. This trio was highly successful in carrying out his orders. They were essentially his assassination squad.

Large sums of money were needed to fund his organizations. The money came from Drug Operations run by the Organizer along with human trafficking and child prostitution. He also made countless millions with insider trading deals on information provided to his organizations by the politicians on his payroll and no bid contracts given to companies his people made deals with.

When the information that the God Particle had been isolated and stabilized reached him, he immediately recognized that this discovery would place, whoever owned the research, in an extraordinary powerful position. He carefully laid out a master plan to be the one who controlled it. This could be the crown jewel to his "Kingdom." The potential of the God Particle, and its application elements could catapult him to the position of the most powerful man in America, and perhaps the world. That master plan was working perfectly until Tyler came on the scene.

The Piranha was informed that Ethan Tyler had escaped his confinement and knew enough to be a serious threat to the master plan. He suspected that somehow Tyler may know his real identity, however, it was only a gut feeling. He ordered Ted and Herman to eliminate him, but Tyler's whereabouts was unknown. After Ted and Herman questioned the woman in Katrina's apartment, without success, and killed her, they finally received a hit on the tracker imbedded in Tyler's scalp. When they had ultimately located him, Ted and Herman went to execute him.

Harper and Scott were recently unresponsive to his calls. He sent Agent Lewis to interrogate Ann Davis, for information about the whereabouts of Tyler and to kill her, but Lewis never reported back to him.

The woman known as Ann Davis had returned to work. The Piranha had no idea why Lewis failed to kill her. Lewis' whereabouts remained unknown to him.

Subsequently, through his informant, he learned that Agent Lewis had disappeared. He couldn't reach Ted or Herman; therefore, they must be either dead or captured. The Piranha was concerned that things appeared to be falling apart in his master plan.

There was an important task that he needed completed immediately, and he wanted it kept secret from the Organizer. Finally, the Piranha concluded that he must complete the task himself. He must kidnap the real Katrina Tyler and hold her as bait to draw in and eliminate Ethan. With this accomplished, he figured he could get his plans back on track.

The ringing of his cell phone interrupted his thoughts. He picked up the phone without saying a word. "3567" was spoken by the caller.

"Go ahead," he said to the Organizer.

Benjamin Thomas Cruise took a deep breath and replied. "I was ordered by Shelby Cain to secure three human subjects for Olsen to test the latest God Particle Formula on. I had them delivered to the compound. I think Olsen is near a breakthrough. We're need to seize power from Cain soon."

"I'll let you know when," the Piranha replied and hung up.

Cruise, not knowing about Ted and Herman or about Tyler, was completely unaware that one of the Piranha's men was killed and the other set to be a guinea pig for Olsen's experiments.

The specific threat to the Piranha's master plan was unknowingly in his custody and secured in a holding cage. Ethan Tyler was unknown to him.

27

Benjamin Thomas Cruise was anxious to partner with any-one on the board to find a way to remove Cain for his position of CEO and Chairman of the Board of Future Mankind Ventures. If this action was impossible, he could simply have Cain killed. He was certain that, working with the Piranha, he could take over the company. The best way to get total control of the God Particle research was to secure controlling interest in the company, and the Piranha certainly had the capital to do just that.

"Boss, the copter is here," Carlos said as he entered the private office where Cruise and Blaze were resting. Blaze was asleep on the sofa, exhausted from one of the most difficult days in her life. Cruise finished his bourbon and ginger and set the glass on the table.

"I'll wake up Blaze and we'll get going," he replied. He walked over to the couch and looked down at the beautiful young girl. As she had grown older, her innocent beauty had captivated him. Her body matured, and she was as sexy as any girl he had ever bedded. Cruise knew that she was a virgin, and this added to his lust for her. He realized that he had to move her to his compound and convince her that Billy was being cared for. After a while, if necessary, he would introduce her to drugs, and then he would own her. She might even last two years as his number-one girl. He smiled and gently shook her shoulder.

"Blaze, Blaze, time to leave."

Blaze opened her eyes. They were a swollen from crying.

"Is Billy going with us?"

"No honey, he'll have to stay in the hospital for a few days, then he'll join us at my ranch. I'll keep my promises to you and Billy."

Blaze sat up and clasped her arms. Cruise took off his coat and put it around her shoulders.

"Carlos, take her to be copter. I need to talk to Cain and then I'll join you in less than ten minutes."

Carlos left with Blaze, and Cruise walked toward Cain's office. There was a guard by the office door.

"I need to speak with Mr. Cain," he said.

"He's busy with the Olsen guy," he guard said.

"Tell him I left for my ranch and I'll be in touch."

The guard nodded. Cruise took the elevator to the roof helicopter pad. Carlos and Blaze were already on board.

"Let's go," he said as he boarded.

He looked over at Blaze, and she was crying again. He reached in his pocket and took a little white pill from a small container. He grabbed a bottle of water from the cooler in the copter.

"Honey, this will calm you down," he said as he handed Blaze the water and the pill. She took it without questioning him. She closed here eyes as the copter rose into the cloudless sky.

She had no idea what Daddy Ben had in store for her.

28

As I lay on the floor of the cage, trying to figure out my next move, I felt anguish and deep depression. I thought of my wife and what Herman said about Ted raping her and him killing her. I believe I may be close to giving up. I don't know what I've got to live for.

Then these words from my past came rushing into my mind.

"Get up and fight, Ethan, get up and fight." I remembered when these words were spoken to me.

It was a scorching August day in Monroe, NC. I was sweating profusely as I peddled my Schwinn bicycle as fast as I could go toward the recreation center. The Schwinn was my prized possession. It was my mode of transportation to work at Midway Café, where I was employed as a curb hop, waiting on cars when they drove into the dirt parking lot. It was also my transportation to school, to see my cousin David, and anywhere else I wanted to go.

I received that bicycle as the result of a beating. I couldn't remember what I did wrong but my stepfather was beating me with a belt. After a few licks from the short red-faced man, my mother stepped in and told him to stop. He stormed out of the door. My real father had left my mother years before. He was a hopeless drifter.

When my stepfather stormed out, my Mother with tears in her eyes turned to me and said a very cruel thing.

"He probably won't come back just like your real father, and it's all your fault."

I was too hurt to do anything but hang my head.

He did return after a couple of hours. He felt guilty and came back with a beautiful red Schwinn bicycle for me. Being very poor, I never dreamed of owning a bike like that. He had gone to the Western Auto, paid five dollars down, with a promise of five dollars a week for my prize.

That bicycle was my pride and joy.

On that day, I peddled even harder worrying that I would be late. That summer the recreation center added a new activity for young boys, a boxing tournament. This was the first addition to the existing square dancing classes every Saturday morning.

I was always a scrapping young man who could take care of himself. I continued to try to find ways to prove to the world that I wasn't just another bum, going nowhere, walking the streets of Monroe, in my case, peddling the streets.

My Mother and Stepfather had little to do with my life. They were totally unaware of my entry into the boxing tournament or my other summer activities, which included Little League Baseball. I was a good first baseman for the Cardinals and was number one in the league in walks. They also had little familiarity with my work at Midway.

I had beaten three other guys in the ring and was now in the semifinals of the boxing tournament. When I arrived, I leaned my bike against a big oak tree and went inside. There was a slim redheaded man just inside the door. His face was acne scarred and his smile looked like a grimace. I was a little afraid of him. His name was John Henry Baucom, but we called him Scarface to his back.

"Tyler, you're late," Scarface snarled at me. "Get your ass ready. Your fight starts in ten minutes."

He handed me an old pair of boxing gloves. I took them and ran for the bathroom. When I got there, I removed my jeans and shirt. I had my black bathing suit on under the jeans. They served as boxing trunks. I folded the jeans and my shirt and placed them on the floor beside the sink, to be retrieved after the fight. I put on the boxing gloves but couldn't tie the laces. When I pushed open the bathroom door, Scarface was standing there. "Mr. Baucom, sir, will you tie my gloves?"

"Come here you scrawny assed bastard," he said. "The only reason I'm doing this is you're keeping Mr. Gaddy and his son Mitchell waiting. I hope he knocks your block off."

Mr. Gaddy owned the seed and feed store in Monroe, along with a large farm. He was what we called, "A Big Shot."

"Thank you sir," I said and ran through the door to the main activities room of the recreation center. In the center of the room was a makeshift boxing ring. There were three rows of folding chairs on each side of the squared ring. Most all of the chairs were full of adults and kids. I looked closely to see if there was anyone I knew there. My spirits brightened when I saw my cousin, David, and his dad K.W. sitting on the front row outside the red corner. David saw me looking and waved. I grinned and waved back.

Scarface came lumbering through the door behind me. "Get your ass in the ring," he whispered to me as he passed. Scarface was the referee.

I looked up at the ring. Sitting on a stool in the blue corner was Mitchell Gaddy. His father was beside him, apparently giving him instructions. There was another guy with a towel and a bottle of water standing on the other side of him. I recognized him as a boxing coach that some of the better off kids trained with for the tournament. I didn't have the money to do that. I walked up the steps, crawled through the ropes and went to the red corner. I looked around but there was no stool there. I heard David yelling, "You can beat him Ethan, you can beat him."

A young boy at ringside rang a bell and Scarface beckoned Mitchell and me to the center of the ring. Mr. Gaddy came with his son, rubbing his neck.

"You boys know the rules," Scarface said. "Any dirty fighting and I'll stop the fight," he said as he glared at me.

I turned and walked back to my corner. I looked down at David and smiled.

I heard the bell ring for the first round. I walked to the center of the ring and held out my hand to touch gloves as a sign of good sportsmanship. Mitchell, instead of touching gloves, threw a left hook to my stomach. I staggered backward and he ran toward me, raining punches to my head and body. I heard his Father yelling, "Take him out now, Mitchell, he's a bum."

I lowered my hands as he landed another solid left hook to my midsection. That boxing coach had taught him well. He hit me with a straight right to the forehead. I felt dizzy and fell to the floor. I was shocked more than hurt since I had yet to even land a punch. I heard Scarface counting, "one, two."

Then I heard my cousin yell words that I remembered throughout my life when I was in difficult situations. "Get up and fight, Ethan. Come on, get up and fight!"

Those words electrified me and I jumped to my feet almost knocking Scarface backward as he was standing over me counting. He regained his balance and sneered.

Mitchell came running at me from the other side of the ring. I side stepped him and landed a left jab to the head.

"Box him, box him," I heard the coach yelling orders. Mitchell went into a crouch and circled me. He hit me with three straight left japs. I tried to rally and return his jabs but he was well coached and my blows hit his gloves. The first round ended with the sound of the bell.

I walked back to my corner. I had no stool to sit on so I leaned my back against the ropes and looked over at Mitchell's corner. The coach was talking to him while his father was wiping him off with a towel and giving him water.

"Get up and fight Ethan, get up and fight," those words rang in my head as the bell sounded for the second round. Mitchell rushed me again, but this time I was ready. I started pumping rights and lefts toward his midsection. Most of the punches were hitting his elbows and gloves, but I kept on throwing them. When he lowered both hands to protect against the punches to his belly, I threw an overhand right to his head, landing solidly. I shot another and another and another overhand rights. He raised his hands to his head and I saw a look of fear in his eyes. I knew then I had him.

With his hands covering his head, I stepped forward on my right foot, planting it, and with all my might pounded a left hook to his stomach. He crumbled to the canvass. I knew he would not be able to get up. I *walked to my corner and waited for Scarface to count him out. His father ran into the ring. He glared at me, "You little shit," he said. Then he grabbed Scarface's hand as he counted "eight, nine."*

"It was a low blow, you idiot. It was a low blow!" Scarface looked at him quizzically. He knew it was a clean shot well above the top of Mitchell's trunks. He looked over at me and then again at Mr. Gaddy.

"You better listen to me," Mr. Gaddy bellowed.

Scarface gazed at me again. I think I saw pity in his eyes as he waved his hands.

"Low blow, low blow," he yelled. "Ethan Tyler you're disqualified."

I couldn't believe my ears. I started to argue with him, but I realized that it was no use. I was a poor kid from the sticks and Mitchell was backed by the power and money of his father. I hung my head and left the ring. David was standing there with his Dad, K.W.

"Don't worry Ethan, you got up and you fought and you beat him fair and square. Way to go Ethan. Come by tonight after work and we can watch wrestling."

I smiled at him, nodded, went to the bathroom and put on my shirt and jeans. I got on my red Schwinn bike and rode to Midway lunch. It was time for work.

My thoughts were interrupted when the Mexican lady came in with a tray of food. With the bright lights shining consistently, I lost track of time. It must be morning.

She opened the little food door and slid a bowl inside, followed by a carton of milk. She smiled at me, and I saw sympathy in her eyes.

"Gracias," I said and looked straight into her eyes. She smiled again and backed away. I picked up the bowl. Another white plastic spoon was with the food.

The bowl contained either grits or cream of wheat. I ate it and couldn't tell the difference. While I was eating, she removed the porta potty at the back of the cage, and left the room, I supposed to empty it in a bathroom and clean it. She returned and placed it at the back of the cage. It emitted the smell of disinfectant.

GARY WILLIAM RAMSEY

I drank the milk from the container and slid the bowl and the empty milk carton back through the hole. I palmed the plastic spoon. She picked up the bowl and the carton and gazed at me. I knew she noticed that I didn't return the plastic spoon, but she said nothing and left the room.

At present, I had two weapons and I'm ready to get up and fight. I think revenge is an extreme motivator. Ted had to pay, and the Piranha had to pay. I grabbed my two plastic spoons and broke the spoon part off. I worked on the plastic handles until I had sharp points on both. Now all I have to do is figure out how to get the guard close enough to me to stab him in the eye.

That might prove to be challenging.

29

When Tim Olsen arrived back at his laboratory, Brenda was there working. She smiled at him when he entered.

"Where have you been Tim?"

"Mr. Cain and I had something to consider," he replied. "Brenda, there's something we must discuss."

"What?"

"A body will be delivered here in a few minutes. The man was accidentally injected with the Formula," he lied. "We need to determine what caused his death."

"What do you mean, accidentally injected? How is that possible? Tim, you know how I feel about testing the Formula on humans at this stage."

Tim walked over to Brenda. He put his hands on her shoulders and looked into her eyes. He felt her body stiffen.

"Brenda, don't you know that I love you? I'm sorry I waited so long to say the words." He pulled her close and kissed her. He felt her body go limp in his arms. He didn't have time for this nonsense, but he needed her help. If that meant lying to her and stating false emotions, so be it.

"Oh Tim, I've loved you for a long time. I'm so happy that you feel the same." "Brenda, do you love me enough to trust me in this matter? I need your trust."

"Yes, oh yes," she replied.

The door to the laboratory opened, and Tim stepped back from Brenda. Two men rolled in a gurney with a body bag on it.

"Where do you want this?" the redheaded man asked.

"Take the body out of the bag and leave it on the gurney. Roll it over there," Tim said, gesturing to the left side of the laboratory where the instruments were located. "Give us three hours and then come back to pick it up. I don't want it stinking up my laboratory."

The men complied and left.

Tim walked over to the body. The first thing he noticed was the brain mucus in the eye sockets and the mouth. The brain mucus was also matted in the man's hair just above the ears.

"Let's get started Brenda. It appears that he's been dead about four hours."

"What?" Brenda replied in an unnerved voice.

Tim thought that she was asking him a question.

"After death, all the muscles relax," he said. "About three hours after that, they start going rigid, as glycogen is converted into lactic acid. This starts at the eyelids, works through the face and down the body and is usually complete within about 12 hours. It then starts to wear off after about 36 hours. However, temperature, climate and other things affect this. Heat accelerates the process, and cold slows it down. Illnesses also causes a change. Furthermore, faced with a limp body, it could be a body that has not yet started to stiffen, or a body that has stiffened then relaxed again."

He continued, "To complicate matters, people killed in intense heat tend to stiffen immediately and stay that way. Moreover, sometimes a person stiffens at the exact time of death, such as clutching convulsively to the gun they used to kill themselves."

"Stop Tim, stop. I meant what are we doing?"

"Please Brenda, just trust me. Let's try to determine what happened to this man."

Brenda rubbed her face and walked to his side. *Tim loves me and that's all that matters. He needs me and I'm not going to let him down,* she thought.

Both of them donned surgical facemasks, smocks and latex gloves. Tim picked up a scalpel and the dismantling of Fangs distorted body began.

Cain sat in his office, watching and listening to everything. He trusted no one, and he had set up an elaborate system of cameras and microphones in the laboratory. He despised this arrogant kid, Olsen, but admired the way he convinced the pretty young assistant to help him. He needed the kid to generate all the necessary breakthroughs in the Formula before he turned the project over to a scientist who worked for him. Then he could kill, with pleasure, Timothy Olsen and his love-struck assistant.

His private cell phone rang, and the caller ID reflected Sergey Petrof was on the other line. He turned down the volume of the system in the laboratory.

"Sergey everything's going as planned. First, we want Olsen to perfect the Formula, and if he desires to use humans as test subjects, that's fine. We know there're additional uses of the Formula which will make us the wealthiest and most powerful men on earth."

"Of course," Sergey replied. "Higgs bosom as the basis of the Formula can be used to regulate the velocity of a spaceship by regulating its mass. Decreasing its mass increases its velocity, while increasing the mass decreases its velocity. Arbitrarily large distances can be traversed in arbitrarily short times by reducing the mass to a minimal level during intergalactic flights. Astronauts can take round trip to and from the edge of the universe without aging at all."

He continued his lecture to Cain. "If Higgs boson, the God Particle, conveys mass upon matter and could be removed somehow from the matter, its mass would become zero. With no mass, an object could be accelerated to and beyond the speed of light, breaking the known laws of physics, plus mass-less things could be brought into earth orbit far more easily than now."

"Wait," Cain interrupted. "Something important is happening in the laboratory. Let's talk later." Furthermore, he was tired of Sergey's endless lectures.

Cain increased the volume of the system.

"Brenda, this man's death was caused by his brain increasing its mass at an alarming rate. It literally ruptured through the only holes in the skull, eyes, ears and mouth. The other physical changes occurred when the Formula entered his blood stream. What I find most interesting is that the mass growth ceased with his death. That is remarkable. We can inject the Formula in other lifeless objects and generate magnificent discoveries. There must be an innate intelligence in the God Particle. We need to find a way to regulate the mass growth and stop it at a given point. We're at a critical stage now, and I believe that I know how to make the adjustment to the Formula to achieve our desired goals."

"Tim, we're entering an area of experimentation where human beings don't belong," Brenda pleaded. "This is God's territory and we don't need to disturb nature and evolution. It can only lead to disaster."

Tim shook his head, "If you love me, trust me."

Sitting in his office watching and listening, Cain decided at that moment that Brenda must be eliminated. He knew just the Scientist needed to replace her, and he intended to handle this matter promptly.

30

Katrina was ordered to continue using the alias, Ann Davis. She yearned for Ethan to be located soon, and she was beginning to doubt her commitment to continue to work for the CIA.

It was about 6pm when she completed her workday and drove to the new residence. The Houston heat mellowed with a cold front approaching. At first, a soft rain fell, but it quickly changed into a torrential downpour. Puddles rapidly turned into small ponds of water as she splashed her way home. Katrina parked in the underground lot of the building and entered the elevator.

She was suspicious of the well-dressed Asian guy on the elevator carrying what appeared to be an odd lunch bag. There was an eerie smell of lemon and vanilla emanating from the bag. The odor had a calm metaphoric effect, and she was a little disappointed when the Asian guy got off on the second level. He looked her directly in the eyes as he was leaving. A warm smile was on his face when he walked away.

Katrina got off on the fifth floor, unlocked the door and went in. She changed into pajamas, washed her face and sat down on the recliner to read. It was around 7pm when she stopped reading a novel by Gary William Ramsey titled "The Spirit Survives." She was enthralled by the book written by the unknown author and didn't want to put it down, however, she was hungry.

She went to the kitchen, put on a pot of water. When it came to a boil, she added grits. After about three minutes of boiling, she poured the grits into a baking dish and added grated cheddar cheese, a little milk, pepper and two crushed garlic cloves. Katrina placed it in the oven to bake. She moved to the fridge and retrieved a package of peeled shrimp. After adding butter in a frying pan, she sautéed the shrimp, pulled the baking dish out of the oven and stirred the shrimp into the cheese garlic grits. While the shrimp and grits were baking, she poured a glass of white wine and sipped it. She and Ethan had shared this dish often in the early days of their marriage. Her heart felt empty. She missed him so much.

The timer buzzed, and she took her creation out of the oven. She dished a large portion on her plate, filled the wine glass and sat down to eat dinner. She only had one bite of the delicious shrimp and grits when her cell phone rang. The caller ID read *private caller*. "Hello, this is Ann Davis."

"Hi, Ann, sorry to interrupt you at home but an urgent matter came up. I need your immediate assistance."

Ann, (Katrina) instantly recognized the deep resonate voice. She was very surprised that the man of his importance would call her informally at home. She normally dealt with people well below his rank.

"What do you need?" she asked in a cautious voice.

"I know it's highly unusual for me to call you directly, but I think there's been a security breach concerning your identity and we need to meet in person to discuss a course of action."

"When and where?" she asked.

"In an hour at Hanis Point."

"I'll be there," she replied.

She covered the shrimp and grits, placed the dish in the fridge and placed the dirty plate and wine glass in the sink. Katrina hurriedly changed clothes, grabbed her keys and hurried to the car. She was still mystified by the call, but knew that it must be critically important for him to call her directly.

Arriving at the memorial, she parked and walked the path to Hanis Point. She did not miss the fact that they were meeting in the place where she had disposed of Agent Lewis. She saw the man sitting on the bench by the water and she approached him.

"Sir, I'm here," She said, as she walked up behind him.

He turned and smiled, "Have a seat, Ann. Thanks for meeting me on such short notice."

Katrina was surprised that he was using her alias, however, she took a seat on his right side.

"It's a nice cool evening after the rain this afternoon," he said.

She looked out over the water. The moonlight reflected an orange glow.

Before she could utter another word, he wielded a slapjack in his left hand and struck her on the left temple. She fell, unconscious.

Benjamin Cruise trotted out from behind the boathouse located to the right of the bench. He looked at the comatose woman, then at the distinguished man sitting calmly on the bench.

"Are you prepared to take her to your ranch?" the man known to Cruise as the Piranha asked.

"Yes sir," he replied. "My car is in the lot. I'll load her and drive to the private airstrip. My helicopter is there. I have prepared a secure place to keep her at the ranch. We can keep her there until you draw out Ethan Tyler."

Cruise took a syringe from his briefcase. He plunged the needle into the fallen woman's arm.

"This sedative should keep her out for at least twelve hours." The two men carried her to his vehicle and loaded her in the trunk.

"I'll be in touch," the Piranha said and walked away.

When this is over I need to waste Cruise, the Piranha thought.

He knows too much.

I now have the bait I need to get Tyler. Sooner or later he'll call in.

31

I heard someone call my guard Hedrick and he left the room. While I sat on the floor of the cage, I fashioned a plan. It was simple and very risky, but I had nothing to loose. If I don't do something now, they'll experiment on me and I'll die or even worse be turned into a monster like Fang.

I knew that Hedrick would return soon. Acting immediately was a necessity. I grasped one of the plastic spoon handles. The sharp point on the end would work nicely. I dug it into my left wrist. When the skin broke, blood practically spurted out. I hope I didn't cut too deeply and hit an artery. With my right hand I cupped as much blood as possible and rubbed it on the back of my head. I dropped to my knees, squeezed the cut and produced a small puddle of blood on the floor. After checking the cut and applying enough pressure to stop the bleeding, I carefully laid my bloody head at the edge of the puddle. I concealed one plastic handle in my right hand and the other one in my left hand. Then I screamed as loudly as I could, closed my eyes and waited. Right away I heard footsteps. I didn't know if it was Hedrick or the lady. I heard a gasp. It was the Mexican woman. I lay as still as possible trying not to breathe.

"Mr. Hedrick, come quick! He looks dead," she screamed. I heard what sounded like someone running.

"What the hell happened?" Hedrick grunted.

"I don't know sir. I heard a scream and found him like this. Look at the blood."

"Go quickly and get me some hot water and towels," Hedrick said. "The boss told me to keep him healthy. He's going to be mad as hell."

I overheard the footsteps as the Mexican Lady left and closed the door. Holding my breath, I lay still. The click of the lock and the sound of the door to the cage opening was what I planned. Hedrick walked up and kicked me. I didn't move. I heard his knee hit the floor beside my head, and his hand lifted my head. He apparently was trying to find the source of the blood on my head. I knew I only had one chance. I sluggishly opened my eyes. He was staring at the top of my head.

With my left hand I thrust the plastic handle toward his eye. He turned his head, and it penetrated his cheek. He grunted and grabbed the wound. I sat up quickly and with my right hand stabbed him in the left eye with the other plastic handle. He screamed. I braced myself and threw a hard right hand to his jaw. He fell back, but wasn't unconscious. I leaped to my feet and kicked him hard in the head. That blow knocked him out cold.

As rapidly as I could, I took off his shirt, pants and boots. I put his baseball cap on my head, unbuckled his gun belt and placed it to the side. I ripped off my jump suit and put it on him. I dressed in his uniform and bucked the gun belt and holster around my waist. I turned him over with his face to the floor. The keys were still in the lock from when he had opened the door to the cage. I grabbed them and locked the door.

Just as I turned to leave, the Mexican lady entered the room carrying a pan of water, some towels and bandages. I snatched the gun from the holster and pointed it at her.

"Just be quiet, I don't want to hurt you. Put the water pan and the other items on the table."

"Please don't hurt me mister. I have four children depending on me." Her voice was shaking.

"Don't worry, just be quiet." I walked to the table, laid the gun down and wet a towel. I removed the baseball cap and cleaned the blood from my head. My wrist had stopped bleeding but was caked with blood. I wiped it off and applied a bandage. I kept an eye on the lady. She was shaking with fear. She had been nice to me and I felt overwhelming pity for her.

I reached in the back pocket of Hedrick's pants that I had put on and removed his wallet. There was a couple of hundred dollars in it. I took the money out and walked over to the lady.

"I'm sorry to have frightened you. Here take this for your children." She took the money and nodded.

"Listen I'm going to have to tie you up so they won't think you helped me. Please sit on the floor." She complied. I tied her hands and feet with two of the towels. I put a piece of a bandage in her mouth. Tears wet her cheeks as I finished restraining her.

"Just relax, I'm sure someone will be here soon to free you."

I pulled the baseball cap down over my eyes and walked out the door. I had to make my way to an exit without being discovered. I remembered the number of steps and the turns as passed a guard. He was talking on his cell phone and didn't even look at me. I turned down another hall, saw an exit door, and slowly walked toward it. I heard some commotion and was sure that they discovered Hedrick, so I sprinted to the exit door and opened it. A guard was standing there. He looked at me and pointed his rifle toward my head.

"Who are you? I don't recognize you," he hissed.

"I'm new pal, lower the rifle and I'll show you my ID," I said, reaching for my wallet.

"Hell no, drop the gun and kick it over here. Then you can show me ID," he ordered.

I took the pistol out with two fingers, dropped it on the ground and kicked it over. "Can I get my ID now?"

He nodded and I pulled out the wallet. I walked closer and held it toward his face.

When he looked at it, I kicked him in the groin. He crumpled to the ground on top of his gun, gasping. I heard voices yelling in the building. I ran as fast as I could toward the cornfield. I knew if I could make it into the field I might have a chance to loose them. My prior escape reassured me.

Just as I got to the edge of the field, I heard a volley of gunshots, and felt a burning pain in my left shoulder. I was hit. I stumbled forward into the cornfield. I didn't know how badly I was hit, but I kept running. I attempted to run between the rows to keep from leaving a trail of broken corn stalks. Men were yelling in the distance, but the voices were fading. They must be going the other way. I slowed down because I felt woozy from the loss of blood and stopped to look at my shoulder. The shirtsleeve was soaked with blood. I still had the empty gun belt around my waste. I removed it, stripped off the holster and fashioned a tourniquet. The wound was half way between my shoulder and elbow. I strapped the belt tight and continued to run.

After another twenty minutes, I came to the perimeter of the cornfield. Outside there was a road and a wooded area on the other side. I sat down to rest a moment knowing I had to make it to the wooded area.

Hearing a low guttural growl, I looked to my left. About five feet away stood a large coyote with his teeth bared. He must have smelled the blood. About twenty feet behind him was his pack. He was undoubtedly the alpha male. I had no weapon and had no chance to fend off the pack.

I stared into his eyes. Drool was leaking from his bared teeth. He took a step forward. I knew I was in deep shit.

32

*K*atrina gawked at the giant white stuffed bear sitting on the shelf behind the booth of the carnival game. All Daddy had to do was to throw a dime and have it land inside one of the small circles on the board. It didn't look hard to a six-year-old girl. Her Mommy and Daddy had taken her to the SeaWorld Water Park in San Antonio, Texas for her sixth birthday. Mommy went to the restroom and she and Daddy were waiting beside the booth with the white bears.

The carnival man was yelling at her daddy. "Come on, win one for the little girl." Daddy was ignoring him.

Katrina pulled on her Daddy's hand. "Please Daddy, please."

"Honey, that's impossible. No one can do that. The game is rigged."

"What does rigged mean?" she asked.

"It means it's impossible to win."

"Please Daddy, Please," she begged.

John Martin reached into his pocket. He had one dime. "Okay honey, but it's impossible," he said as he casually pitched the dime toward the board.

Katrina watched breathlessly as the dime hung in the air and landed on the board. It landed and stuck squarely in the middle of one of the circles.

"Daddy you did it, you did it," Katrina yelled, getting the attention of several other patrons.

Three of them came over to look. The stunned carnival barker carefully examined the dime in the circle. It was squarely in the middle, and *unmistakably a winner. He hadn't given away a bear in three months, but he couldn't get away with not giving away this one. There were witnesses.*

"Big winner," he yelled. "Come try your luck."

He picked up one of the giant white stuffed bears and put it in Katrina's outstretched arms. Her Father stood there in shock. The stuffed animal was larger than his little girl. She was giggling with glee. He smiled and shook his head. What in the world am I going to tell Susan, he thought. Just at that moment, she returned from the restroom. She looked at her husband and at the enormous bear in Katrina's hands.

"What have you done, John?"

"Honey, I had no idea this would happen. I won it even though it looked impossible."

Susan laughed, "Well you can't undo it now. We'll have to deal with it."

Katrina tried to walk with the stuffed animal, but nearly stumbled. It was simply too large. John took it from her and carried it. Katrina held on to the bear's foot as he carried it. They went to the arena and watched the water show with Dolphins and Killer Whales. The giant white bear sat proudly beside his owner, Katrina.

When the show was over they walked down the midway again. Daddy was carrying the bear and Katrina felt that this was the happiest day of her life.

She looked down the midway and a very tall Clown approached them. He had blood red lips and big yellow ears. His clown outfit was red, white and blue. His pointed teeth were stained with the lipstick from his lips making it appear to be blood. His grin was more like a snarl, as he got closer to them. Katrina suddenly became very afraid.

"Daddy don't let him get me," she cried. Suddenly her mommy and daddy were gone and she was alone with the horrible clown. He grabbed the big white stuffed bear and bit it on the neck. Blood gushed and ran down the white fur. Katrina screamed. The clown rippled the head off of the bear and threw it to the side.

"I want you now!" he hissed. Blood from the bear was dripping from his jagged razor sharp teeth. Katrina tried to run but her feet were frozen

and she couldn't feel them. The clown grabbed her and picked her up. He bared his teeth as he went for her throat.

Katrina awoke from the nightmare with her head pounding. She reached to the source of the pain and found a lump the size of a golf ball on the side of her head. She had trouble remembering what happened. She sat up, fought off the dizziness, and focused her eyes. She was lying in a king-sized bed in a room with one large window. The room was decorated expertly in shades of blue and white. There was a white dresser across from the bed with a white-framed mirror on the wall behind it. In the right corner was a matching chest. In the left corner was a large TV stand with a 48-inch flat screen TV on it. A pale blue leather love seat was in front of the TV, with a coffee table of stainless steel and glass in front of it. The light blue drapes on the window were closed. A matching blue comforter decorated the bed, neatly folded at the foot. The same shade of blue silk sheets covered her legs. White end tables were on each side of the bed. A pitcher of ice water sat beside a clock on one of the end tables. She removed the sheet, leaned over and poured a glass of water. She downed it in one gulp.

Katrina sluggishly got out of the bed. The entrance door was to her left. She stood there for a moment to get her balance and slowly walked to the door. It was locked. She went to the window and threw back the drapes. The large window had black horizontal bars about eight inches apart. She was apparently on the second level of the house. She looked down on a perfectly manicured lawn. A man and a young blond girl were sitting there on stunning horses, talking. Katrina shouted, but apparently her cries were not heard. She realized that the windows must be sound proofed. The couple laughed, and rode the majestic animals into the distance.

It was only then that Katrina realized that she was wearing silk, navy blue pajamas. She looked over toward the bed and saw a pair of slippers. She walked over and put them on. On the right wall was another door. She went over and opened it, discovering a small bathroom. She opened the cabinet under the sink and found toilet paper, towels and washcloths. The cabinet above the sink held a comb, toothbrush, tissues, toothpaste and a couple of bars of soap.

She wandered back to the bedroom and looked into the chest of drawers. It was stocked with panties and bras of her size, a couple pairs of jeans and T-shirts. Tennis shoes and socks were in the bottom drawer. Whoever her kidnappers were, they had taken care of all the details.

In front of the TV were a love seat and a matching blue recliner. She walked over and sat down on the recliner. Her head was clearing as she remembered.

She had met her Superior on what was purported to be urgent business about a breech in her cover. He rendered her unconscious. She could tell by the woozy feeling in her stomach that she had been drugged. Katrina had no idea how long she was out. Instinctively she knew that her kidnapping had something to do with Ethan. *How was the important government official mixed up in it, and why kidnap her?* she wondered.

The door suddenly opened, and a muscular black haired man with a ragged scar under his left eye rolled in a cart with a tray of food on it.

"What am I doing here?" she asked him in a measured voice.

He stared at her with cold black eyes, grunted and slammed the door. She heard the lock click.

Katrina wasn't hungry, but she knew she must eat to regain her strength. She picked up the tray and set it on the coffee table. The tray contained a piece of grilled fish, stuffed with crabmeat, twice baked potato, buttered asparagus and a yeast roll. A chocolate liquor soufflé, still warm, was the desert. White wine accompanied the gourmet meal. A master chef had apparently prepared it. She shook her head in disbelief and ate the meal. In her state of mind the fool was tasteless. Figuring out a plan to escape fully occupied her mind. She was a professional, however that did not stop tears from rolling down her cheeks. She briskly wiped them away and gritted her teeth.

Time to be tough.

33

Cain was intently watching the laboratory camera while Tim finished the autopsy. The boy was brilliant. The ringing of his phone startled him. George, head of security, was on the line.

"Boss, we've got a problem."

"What's that," Cain asked.

"One of the prisoners escaped."

"The hell you say! What happened?"

"He tricked his personal guard, stole his uniform and escaped. We think he was wounded."

"Who was his guard?"

"It was Hedrick sir, the one with the beard."

"Bring him to me," Cain hissed.

"Yes sir, right away."

Cain leaned back in his chair. *This stupid man put me in a position to have to find another test subject,* he thought.

After about five minutes, George walked in with Hedrick. The guard had a bandage on his cheek and over one eye. He was clearly shaken.

"Leave us George," Cain said. George walked out of the room.

"Sit down, Mr. Hedrick,"

Hedrick took a seat. He had yet to utter a word.

"Tell me what happened?"

"Sir, first I'm sorry that he tricked me. He was lying on the floor of the cage with blood on his head and on the floor. I thought he was badly injured and I entered the cage. My orders were to keep him healthy for the experiments. I was attempting to do just that. He attacked me, stole my uniform and left me unconscious." Hedrick hung his head.

"Describe the man," Cain ordered.

"Tall, probably 6 feet, 3 or 4 inches tall, short black hair, blue eyes and muscular."

"What was his name?"

"When he was captured, I was told that the girl at the farmhouse called him Ethan."

Cain looked stunned. "Are you sure?" he asked.

"Yes sir,"

"You fool," Cain replied. He opened the desk drawer and grabbed his Glock pistol. Without saying another word, he shot Hedrick in the face. The body crumbled to the floor. Cain walked around the desk and put another bullet in the man's skull.

The door to the office burst open and George rushed in, pistol in hand. He stopped in his tracks, stared at the dead man on the floor and looked up at Cain.

"He was a fool," Cain said, hurling the Glock to the floor. "Get the body out of here and clean up the mess."

He walked out of the room as George was calling for help on his cell phone. Cain went directly to the laboratory.

"Tim, could we talk privately?"

Brenda quickly replied, "I'll go to the break room for coffee. Call me when you want to start work again." Tim nodded.

When she was out of the room, Cain said, "One of your subjects has escaped. You still have the big guy Ted and the injured boy to start with, but it will take a little time for the boy Billy to be healthy enough to use. I'll get you another test subject as quickly as possible."

Tim's face reddened. "I don't care what happened, get me another subject now. If you want progress, you must keep your end of the bargain."

Cain controlled his anger. He needed Olsen, but the young brat was treating him disrespectfully. He clinched his teeth.

"I'll get you another test subject right away."

"I would prefer a female," Tim said. "I need to determine if a female reacts differently than a male in the experiments."

Cain nodded and left the room. He didn't even ask about the autopsy just completed, but he noticed the foul odor in the laboratory. He walked to a vacant office, sat down, grabbed his cell phone and punched in Ben's number.

Cruise pulled his phone from his pocket. He was astride his favorite stallion, Rex. "Wait here," he said to Blaze. Horseback riding, lavish meals and ostentatious accommodations were part of his carefully planned seduction of the young beautiful girl.

He rode a few feet away, "What can I do for you Shelby?"

"We lost one of the test subjects, the tall muscular one with black hair. I need another one right away, preferably a female."

"What happened?" Criuse asked.

"None of your damn business! Just get me a healthy female now."

Cain hung up the phone.

Cruise looked at Blaze. She would be a quick fix to the problem. He shook his head. It was more important to him to be Daddy Ben to her. The woman locked up in the house was another matter. Maybe the Piranha would allow her to be used.

"Is everything okay?" Blaze yelled.

"Yes sweetie, just give me one more minute. I need to make another call."

He punched in the private number. A click indicated that the call connected. "4419," he said and hung up. Within a minute his phone rang.

"What's so urgent?" The Piranha asked.

"Listen, sir. One of the test subjects escaped from the laboratory and Cain needs a replacement. May I use the girl we're holding prisoner? We can kill two birds with one stone by keeping her at the laboratory. You're going to kill Tyler when you get him anyway, and luring him to the laboratory would be easy."

There was a temporary silence on the other end of the phone.

"Tyler is a threat and I must draw him out. Don't move her to the laboratory yet. That can remain a future option."

"Sir, can you give me a description of this Tyler. If he, by chance, establishes that this woman is here, I wouldn't even recognize him if he attempted to rescue her.

"He's about 6 feet 4 inches tall, blue eyes, about 210 pounds with short black hair and a muscular build. He's easy to recognize."

"Oh shit," Cruise replied.

"What!"

"That fits the description of the man who escaped the laboratory. Oh my God, we had him and didn't even know it."

"You damn fool!" the Piranha yelled. "You damn fool!"

34

The Piranha rested on his recliner at his cabin in the Blue Ridge Mountains of North Carolina. He decided to take a two-week vacation to relax and plan his next moves. Too many things were deviating from his master plan. Even though he was in touch with his office by cell phone, no one knew exactly where he was. Matter of fact, they were unaware of the existence of the cabin. The deed to the cabin and the deed to his condo at Myrtle Beach, SC, were both in the name of Benjamin Cruise. He had exclusive access and Cruise didn't know when he was there.

He swirled the ice in the glass of Gentleman Jack bourbon and took a long drink. The mellow bourbon felt hot going down his throat. The phone call that he had just received from Cruise angered him. He took another long drink and hurled the glass against the large stone fireplace. It shattered, and the remaining liquid dripped from the hearth to the hardwood floor. Tyler had been in the grasp of the fool, Cruise, and had escaped. He was fixated on killing Tyler. He instinctively knew that Tyler was smart enough and tough enough to destroy his plans and in the process, destroy him.

The cabin was his sanctuary and his haven to unwind. When he was in his work persona, he was perceived as a calm, reasoned, highly intelligent professional. Here in the cabin, he could escape that created persona and be his real self.

The Piranha quickly suppressed his anger, and cleaned up the broken glass. He decided to have some lunch and then go on the hunt. The hunt satisfied his cravings for release and eased his psychopathic mind. Six months had passed since his last hunt. The results of that hunt, the publicity, and police activity had calmed down.

Unexpectedly, he felt a pang of hunger and went to the kitchen. He prided himself in his culinary expertise.

The kitchen décor didn't fit the furnishings in the rest of the cabin. It was outfitted with all of the state-of-the-art equipment. The stainless steel sub zero refrigerator-freezer was well stocked. A warming drawer was beneath the Viking oven. The oversized gas grill was centered in the stainless steel and oak island. To the right, over the counter, was a large stainless steel Viking microwave. Underneath was an area containing a blender, coffee center and a huge teak chopping block. The floor was done in a black-and-white custom ceramic tile.

The Piranha opened the fridge door and took out a package of fresh flounder that he has purchased the day before. He unwrapped the filets and put them aside to bring them to room temperature. He opened the cupboard doors and extracted packages of Panko and cornmeal. He mixed the Panko and cornmeal, added salt and pepper and lemon dill seasoning. Breaking two fresh eggs into a small bowl, he added milk and lemon juice and mixed it. He turned the grill on to preheat to 350 degrees, then carefully dipped the filets in the egg wash and saturated both sides. He rolled the filets in the Panko mixture until fully coated, and placed them on a plate. After checking the temperature on the grill, and finding it perfect, he poured a small amount of olive oil and a spoon of butter on the grill. The filets were placed on the grill and cooked for three minutes on each side. The beautifully browned filets were positioned in a flat pan and situated in the warming drawer.

In a small bowl, he mixed finely chopped onions, olives, lemon pepper, fresh lemon juice, parsley, and Dukes mayo. His own recipe for tartar sauce was delicious. A salad was tossed with loose-leaf lettuce, Vidalia onions, chopped banana peppers, red bell peppers and vine ripen tomatoes. He created his dressing with olive oil, tangy mustard, chopped red peppers, and lemon juice.

He uncorked a bottle of Montrachet white wine, and gave it time to breath as he placed his filets, tartar sauce and salad bowl on the stainless steel and glass dining table.

The Piranha poured the wine and leisurely devoured his creations. He was fueling up for the hunt.

After placing his dishes, utensils and glass in the Viking dishwasher, he took a hot shower and applied his disguise. The dressing room, just behind his bedroom, was well equipped with make up and various wigs and facial hairpieces. The room was concealed from view from the bedroom. Access was granted by pushing a button in the second drawer of the dresser beneath his underwear. The right wall slid back automatically when the button was engaged.

His short hair permitted a wig to be worn with no problem, and he chose a medium length black one. It was supported with a dark mustache and a two-day stubble. He darkened his skin with makeup, giving it a tanned appearance, and placed blue contact lens in his eyes. He donned a plaid flannel shirt, jeans and a scuffed pair of brown cowboy boots. Now he fit with the environment of the Blue Ridge Mountains.

The Piranha prepared his bag, placing in it chloroform, a pistol, a package of large cotton balls and plastic restraints. He was ready for the hunt.

On his last hunt, he went to the University of North Carolina at Ashville to secure his prey. After failing to catch a college girl walking around, he called a massage service, and following her assurance that she was independent, went to her in-call apartment. She was a college girl working her way through school by providing erotic massages at one hundred bucks a clip. The Piranha savagely used her to satisfy his needs.

Her body was never found and the police assumed, after uncovering that she was in the sex trade, that she had just left school. Her parents were drug addicts and didn't seem to care one-way or the other about the whereabouts of their daughter.

This time, the Piranha decided to drive to Western Carolina University in Cullowhee, NC. He desired a fresh, innocent girl. The former prey was young, but a hardened professional, and half drunk when he had his way with her.

The cabin was about two hours away from the campus. He secured the wall to his dressing room, locked the cabin, and drove off in his black Mercedes. Similar to the last hunt, he needed to get another vehicle. His red Ford pickup was stored in a rented facility along with his boat. The facility was a large building with individually locked garage-like doors located about twenty miles from the cabin. He drove to the building. There was rarely anyone there since the other renters only came during the summer to pick up their boats and go to their summer homes.

He unlocked the door, raised it and removed the pickup from the building, replacing it in the building with the Mercedes. He laid his hunting bag in the floorboard of the front seat of the truck and headed west to the campus.

When he arrived at Cullowhee, the small mountain town just outside the entrance to the college, he stopped by a service station and filled his gas tank. Paying cash covered his trail. The Piranha drove around the campus, but found no suitable young woman to subdue. His girls had to fit a precise description, blond hair, full lips, blue eyes and a nice figure. He had deviated and used a brunette on one occasion, but it left him unsatisfied.

After a couple of trips around the campus, He drove back to Cullowhee and stopped at a MacDonald's for a cup of coffee. He decided to try again tomorrow night and went to the counter to the counter to order.

There she was, wearing a smile and a nametag that read, *Jennifer.* She was about five-feet four inches tall, 110 lbs., probably

32b, with blue eyes. She resembled his former wife when he met her in college. The bitch had left him broken hearted after three years of marriage. She ran off and married a computer programmer, who she worked with. The geek was the first victim of the Piranha's string of murders. He had tied him up, skinned him alive, dismembered him, and buried the remains in four different locations.

"Welcome to McDonald's, what can I get for you?" Jennifer asked, with a smile.

"Just a cup of black coffee and one of those fried apple pies," he replied.

"Hey Jennifer," a boy at the drive-through window yelled. "What time do you get off? Maybe we can hang out."

"I get off in an hour, but I have to study. Maybe next time, I've got a customer, please."

She looked at the Piranha, "Sorry sir." She poured the coffee and grabbed the pie. "That'll be a dollar sixty-one."

The Piranha smiled and handed her the money. He took the coffee and pie and went back to the truck. He sat there thinking and sipping the coffee, never touching the pie.

After about twenty-five minutes he drove off. He returned to the convenience store where he purchased the gas and sat there for twenty minutes, finalizing his plans.

After starting the truck, he drove back to the McDonald's. The Piranha assumed that management required the workers to park in the back of the lot, so he parked in that location and waited. After a few minutes, he opened the hunting bag and took out a handful of cotton balls, the chloroform and the slapjack. He put plastic restraints on the seat beside the other items.

After about fifteen minutes, Jennifer exited the building and began walking toward the back of the lot. There were three automobiles there, a Toyota, Ford Mustang, and an old red Volkswagen. As she walked toward the Volkswagen, he got out of his truck.

"Miss, I'm here to visit my daughter. We were supposed to meet at the Student Union Center, but I don't know where it is. Can you give me directions?"

Jennifer smiled and said, "Sure, straight down the main entrance road and turn right on Wallace Street."

"Wait," replied the Piranha, "let me get a pencil and paper and write it down. I don't have a very good sense of direction." He walked to the passenger door of the truck, looked around and determined that no one was in the parking lot. Jennifer followed him. He opened the door. "Now can you start over?"

"Yes sir," she said.

When she began to repeat the directions, he grabbed the slapjack, twirled and hit her on the temple, catching her as she fell. The Piranha quickly flung her in the floorboard of the front passenger seat and secured her hands and feet with the plastic ties. He stuffed a handful of napkins in her mouth, slammed the door and ran to the driver's side and got in. He started the truck and drove off.

About five miles from the campus, he heard her groan. He pulled over to the side of the road, saturated several cotton balls with chloroform and placed them on her nostrils, and held them until he felt her body go limp. Grabbing a CD from the glove compartment, he put it in the player.

"Don't be cruel to a heart that's true," Elvis belted as the Piranha drove back to the building where his car Mercedes was stored.

"Since my baby left me, I found a new place to dwell. Down at the end of lonely street at Heartbreak hotel," Elvis crooned. The Piranha loved his Elvis oldies.

He pulled in front of the door of the building, unlocked it, and opened the door. He looked around to assure that no one was in sight. He carried Jennifer's limp body and dumped it in the back seat of the Mercedes. Even though she was out cold, he held another dose of chloroform to her nose to ensure that she remained unconscious until he reached his destination.

The Piranha wet a towel and wiped down the truck floor-board where her body had been lying. He also removed the floor mats. Didn't want any DNA evidence in the truck. He deposited the floor mats and the used towel in the trunk of the Mercedes, backed out and replaced it with the truck. He then proceeded to his cabin. Having secured his prey, it was time for the fun.

After driving the car into the garage and closing the door, he lifted the unconscious girl from the floorboard and carried her to the bedroom.

The bedroom was decorated in red and white. Mia, his first wife, loved those colors. The walls were painted white, and a soft white wool carpet enhanced the floors. Red lace drapes covered the windows. He carefully laid Jennifer's body on the white carpet at the foot of the bed. He pulled back the red comforter revealing white silk sheets and pillows. Beneath the silk sheets was a rubber cover. He didn't want the blood to penetrate the mattress.

The carved white headboard matched the dresser and chest. An eight by twelve mirror reflected his actions from the ceiling. The white end table held a clock and an arrangement of red silk roses. The flowers were another favorite of Mia's. The Piranha lifted Jenifer's body onto the bed. He slowly undressed her and deposited her McDonald's uniform in the trashcan in the corner.

With lust in his eyes and groin, he rubbed his hands tenderly over the soft skin of the young girl, lingering on her breasts, and found himself becoming aroused. He walked to the chest, opened the drawer and grabbed a short red silk nightgown, and slipped it over her naked body. He sniffed the Clive Christian No. 1 Imperial Majesty Perfume lingering on the nightgown. The scent stirred his passions for Mia.

His concentration was disturbed by a moan coming from Jennifer's lips. He quickly returned to the dresser and retrieved a roll of red ribbon and a pair of scissors. The Piranha slashed four long pieces, cut the plastics restraints, and replaced them with the ribbon. Each hand was securely tied to the headboard and each foot was tied to the footboard. Jennifer laid spread eagle on the elegant bed. He went to the bathroom and wet a towel with cold water. Removing the paper towels from her mouth, he tenderly placed the wet towel on her head.

"Oh my Mia, you look so beautiful," he whispered.

A stainless steel and glass bar stood in the corner in the living area. He retrieved two glasses and a bottle of Moët Chandon Dom Perignon White Gold champagne. When he returned to the bedroom, Jennifer opened her eyes. She blinked and looked around. Realizing that she was bound, she struggled and screamed. The Piranha grinned and watched her.

"No sense in yelling Mia," he said softly. "It's just you and me, and no one can hear you. You know I love you and would never harm you."

"Who is Mia?" the girl cried. "My name is Jennifer! What are you doing to me?"

"Oh Mia, I'm going into the other room and when you calm down, we can talk intelligently. I know you're thirsty, and I brought your favorite champagne." He held up the bottle.

"Are you insane?" she squealed as she labored against the restraints. She pulled so hard that small amounts of blood appeared on her wrists.

"Oh honey, you're hurting yourself. I'll just wait in the other room until you calm down."

The deranged psychopath walked to the living area and sat down on the white leather couch. He was in full role model mode. He placed the champagne and the glasses on the stainless steel and glass coffee table and poured himself a glass, picked up the remote control and pushed it. The lights dimmed, and the Boise CD player turned on.

"One night with you, is all I'm dreaming of." Elvis guttural voice crooned. The Piranha sipped his drink, laid his head back and closed his eyes. His beloved Mia was still screaming.

"I will spend my whole life through, loving you, loving you." Elvis was singing now. He and Mia made passion love to Elvis so many times in the past.

After about twenty minutes, there was silence in the bedroom. He picked up the two glasses and the champagne and walked back into the room. The girl was lying still.

"Mia, I'm glad that you've calmed down. Now let's have a glass of champagne together."

Jennifer looked at him, realizing that he was nuts and pretending that she was this Mia person. She figured that if she played along that maybe she could get him to untie her.

"Untie me and we can have our drink," she said.

"That's okay honey, I can help you." He set the glass on the end table, filled it and held it to her lips. She took a sip.

"Just untie me and I promise we can be together," Jennifer whispered.

The Piranha gritted his teeth. "Mia, you're just trying to trick me again. I'm tired of your hurtful games." He threw the champagne in her face. He was clearly angry.

"Please, please don't hurt me," Jennifer pleaded.

"You hurt me Mia!" he hissed, and you're going to pay over and over again. He opened the end table drawer and jerked out a scalpel.

"Please, I am not Mia," she screamed as he cut the red nightgown from her body.

"I've grown tired of your yelling and screaming, Mia," he said as he stuffed a washcloth in her mouth.

For the next hour, the Piranha tortured and slashed the young girl. His sexual pleasure was satisfied just before he cut her throat, ending her excruciating pain.

"You shouldn't have left me, Mia," he mumbled.

Serial killers keep trophies of his victims reminding them of the sick pleasure of the kill. The Piranha collected ring fingers. Mia broke his heart and rendered the wedding ring, a symbol of his love, to be defiled. The ring fingers gave him a feeling of satisfaction and revenge. After removing Jennifer's ring finger and placing it in a plastic Zip-lock bag, he wrapped up her mangled body in the rubber sheet and tied it with a nylon cord at the top and bottom. He planned to heave the body off a cliff in the Blue Ridge Mountains. Animals would feed on the flesh long before the body was found, if it ever was.

Feeling satisfied and fulfilled, he methodically cleaned the bedroom and returned to the living area to finish his Champagne. His deranged desires would be content for at least six months.

As he was sipping the sparkling wine, his secure cell phone rang. Code *4567* appeared in the text. It was Benjamin Cruise signifying an emergency. He punched in the emergency number and waited calmly for the answer. He was now ready for the next step in his quest to get control of the God Particle research and the Formula.

His only remaining hurtle was to kill Ethan Tyler and protect his identity.

35

The coyote growled and moved closer. I only had my one good arm to fend him off. As soon as he took me down, I knew the pack would tear me apart. I braced for the attack, and then heard a noise behind me.

"Just be still mister, don't move," a strong voice said. With my peripheral vision, I saw the man move beside me and then in front of me. He held an ax in his hands and had it raised over his head. His body was bent. The short grey hair was thinning, but his hands were steady. The coyote growled again.

"Listen," he said to the coyote in a cool resolved voice, "I ain't scared of you and I'll chop your head off if you attack. I'll kill your mate. I ain't got much longer to live anyway. May as well go out like this."

He stared straight into the eyes of the animal. After what seemed like an eternity, but I'm sure was a matter of minutes, the coyote lowered his head and his tail drooped. The old man became the Alpha. He stood firm holding the ax. The coyote backed away, turned and ran back to the pack. The pack disappeared into the cornfield.

"You gotta stare em down and prove that you ain't scared," the old man said and turned to me. "Mister, you're bleeding."

Those were the last words I heard as my world went black.

The smell of frying bacon filled the air when I regained consciousness. I remembered the gunshot wound and looked down.

My arm was neatly bandaged. Remarkably, I felt no pain. I tried to sit up, but was a little dizzy.

"Look who's decided to join us, Maybelle," the old man said walking toward me. "It's Mr. Hedrick." The old man grinned revealing missing teeth. The ones left were yellowed. He faced was wrinkled, but his eyes were crystal clear. "How you feeling?"

"Where am I?"

"You're here in our home, Mr. Hedrick."

"Why are you calling me that name?"

"I looked in your wallet and found your drivers license. Don't worry I didn't steal nothing."

A short woman with long grey hair put up in a bun joined him. She limped toward me and was holding an iron skillet filled with sizzling bacon. I guess that she was in her eighties. Her face was wrinkled like her husband, but I could see a face that once was very beautiful.

She smiled at me. "Glad you're okay," she said softly, "My name is Maybelle. Jacob said that the Coyote almost got you." She nodded at Jacob and walked back to the kitchen area carrying the skillet.

Jacob grinned, "She don't say much, but we been married for near on sixty years. Having a quiet woman comes in handy sometimes. Who shot you Hedrick? You had a guard uniform on. What do you guard"?

"Sir, my name's not Hedrick. That man held me prisoner and was guarding me. The people there were going to experiment on me or to kill me. I took Hedrick by surprise and got his clothes and escaped. One of those people shot me. Don't you know that place which is five or six miles from here?"

"Maybelle and me keep to ourselves," Jacob replied. "We keep to ourselves and don't bother nobody and we hope nobody bothers us. We just want to live the rest of our lives in quiet. That's why we moved out here to the backside of nowhere. Your story is quite a yarn."

"It's the truth. My name is Ethan Tyler. I very much appreciate your helping me. I can't say much else if you don't mind."

"Don't bother me none, ain't my business anyway," Jacob said. "Do you feel up to having some breakfast? You've been out for the better part of the day and night. You must be hungry."

"How did you get me to your house?"

"Well sir, I was out chopping wood and had my ax and wheelbarrow with me so I just put you in it and rolled you here."

I sat up and Jacob helped me to my feet. I looked around. The bed I was laying in was in the corner of a large room. To the right, the room contained a living area with a big couch with a log frame with blue cotton cushions and two rocking chairs. In front of the living area was a stone fireplace. A pleasant fire was smoldering. I looked to the left and there was an open kitchen with pine cabinets covering the walls. An old fridge was in the corner. Maybelle was standing beside a gas-stove top with an oven above it. A huge oak table was centered in the kitchen with four homemade oak chairs around it. Blue cotton pillows were in the seats of the chairs, matching the couch. There were two plates set and glasses filled with milk.

"Jacob, set our guest a place," Maybelle said.

Jacob set a plate for me and filled a glass with milk. "We don't drink coffee," he said matter of factly. "Milk is better for the digestion. Sit here Ethan."

I sat down and Maybelle dished scrambled eggs on the plates. She placed a bowl of grits and a plate filled with bacon on the table. She went back to the oven and took out a pan of homemade biscuits. After putting butter on them, she placed the pan on the table "Where's my gravy?" Jacob asked.

"Don't worry it's simmering on the stove," she replied. Maybelle went to the stove and stirred some flower and water into the bacon grease and added salt and pepper. She poured the rich brown gravy in a bowl and put it on the table.

"This is redeye gravy," she said. "Jacob, bless his heart, loves it."

Jacob grabbed my hand and Maybelle's hand. "Thank you Lord for this food and bless our new friend, Ethan."

"Amen," Maybelle whispered.

I watched Jacob as he spooned grits on his plate and four pieces of bacon. He opened two biscuits and put a generous supply of gravy on them. He mixed some of his eggs into the grits and began to eat. Looked good to me so I followed suit. It was undoubtedly the best breakfast I ever had. The cold fresh milk was wonderful.

"We ain't done yet," Jacob said. "Maybelle, get the blackberry jam that you made."

After two more hot buttered biscuits with homemade blackberry jam, I was full.

Jacob and I retired to the couch while Maybelle cleaned up the kitchen.

"The bathroom is through that door to the left," Jacob said, pointing toward a closed door on the far wall. I walked to the door and opened it. It opened to the delightful couple's bedroom. The bed's headboard and footboard were made of oak logs. An oak dresser was on the left wall. One end table was beside the bed with an old alarm clock on it. The closet was open with their clothes hung neatly inside. An opening to the right of the bed was apparently the bathroom. I walked into the opening and there was a toilet, a bathtub with a shower, and a table with a mirror over it. The toiletries were setting on the top. I used the toilet, washed my hands and went back to the living area.

"You're welcome to take a shower," Jacob said. "I got some new underwear that I bought from the store that I'll be happy to give you."

"Thanks Jacob I want to take a shower, but soon I need to be going. I think those people will come looking for me and I don't want to put you and Maybelle in danger."

"I ain't scared of nothing," Jacob said and nodded toward the corner where a double-barreled shotgun was leaning on the wall. Son you know that you're twenty-five miles from anything. You gonna walk?"

"I guess so," I replied.

"Well you seem like a nice young man. I guess I can let you borrow my scooter. I need my truck."

"What do you mean?"

"Come with me," he said.

We walked outside. There was an old barn in back of the house and we went there. The barn was open, and inside was an ancient battered red pickup truck. Beside it was an old scooter. "I bought this in the 60's. Kept it up and it runs good. It's full of gas and should get you where you need to go."

"Jacob, I don't have any money to pay you, but I promise I'll repay your kindness. You took me in without question and helped me. I will not forget your kindness. You can count on that."

"Well sir, me and you are human beings. I'm a darn good judge of character and I think you're a good man. Your business is your business and I don't pry. I'm glad to help you and I don't need nothing in return." Jacob patted me on the back.

We walked back inside. "Maybelle, Ethan's got to go. Fix him some food and sweet tea to take with him. Now son, go take a hot shower. You sorta stink."

I took a shower, carefully not wetting my bandages. I marveled at the professional way the wound was cared for. I put the uniform back on and checked the wallet. I had given all the money to the Mexican lady, but there was an ID and several credit cards in the wallet. I walked back to the living area. Maybelle handed me a large bag. "This'll tide you over," she said.

"Who took care of my wound and bandaged it?" I asked.

"Why Maybelle was a nurse before she retired twenty years ago," Jacob said.

"Comes in handy." Maybelle just smiled

I smiled at her and hugged her. "Thanks for everything."

"Son, I'll walk you to the barn," Jacob said.

"Jacob I don't know how to thank you but you'll be hearing from me in the future." He held out his hand and I shook it. I placed the food in the saddlebags on the scooter.

"Just go down the dirt road till you get to the hard surface road and turn left. That'll take you to civilization."

I started the scooter, took one more look at Jacob, this fine specimen of a human being, and left. I had no idea what was coming next.

36

Tim Olsen was furious. First, Case Study One had escaped, and Case Study Two, Billy, had taken a turn for the worse. The young man was in poor condition and was in no shape to be used in the experiment. Case Study Three was extremely violent and was undoubtedly going to be difficult to deal with since his Formula tended to intensify certain brain functions. That fact was discovered in his autopsy of the janitor.

Because of the results from the autopsy, he added Biophecendine and Centeneze to his Formula to better level out the mass growth in the various lobes of the brain. The Formula was ready for injection, but he had no viable subject.

Brenda walked back into the laboratory. She was perspicuously distressed.

"Tim, I love you, but I just can't continue to assist you in this project. You're tinkering with things that humans should stay out of. We were not meant to experiment with God's design of humans or their natural evolution. The God I believe in set up an evolutionary process to allow man to progress at a manageable growth pattern rate in mind development and physical development. If you alter that process, or put it in the hands of others who may not use it properly, the world could end up in chaos, ruled by the elite few who controlled the God Particle Formula. I can't allow that. If you continue, I will go to the press and the authorities and report what's going on here."

Tim gaped at her in astonishment. "Are you crazy, we're on the verge of improving mankind and making our species stronger and smarter, and giving humans the ability to change the world for the better. With the mass growth of the precise elements within the brain, we can develop scientist who can solve the most complex medical problems, such as cancer, autism, and the common cold. We may have the ability to take a psychopath, a murderer, anyone suffering from a mental illness and use my Formula to change the part of the brain that places a human in that condition. You can't comprehend what you're saying."

"This is wrong, Tim," she uttered, with tears in her eyes. "I could never live with myself if I was a part of this."

"Just listen to me Brenda, according to the left-brain, right-brain dominance theory, the right side of the brain is best at expressive and creative tasks. Some of the abilities that are commonly associated with the right side of the brain include, recognizing faces, expressing emotions, music, understanding emotions, and color. We could enhance emotions, especially love, and eliminate hate from the brain. We can make every human a Mozart or a Mother Teresa."

He continued, "the left side of the brain is considered to be adept at tasks that involve logic, language and analytical thinking, critical thinking, numbers, and reasoning. Improving the brain mass in these areas can open the universe for mankind and eliminate all sickness and pain and create a world language. You must see the immeasurable importance of the possibilities."

Tim was hoping to change her mind with these arguments although he knew that his Formula could be used to hoard power in the hands of a few rulers. He wanted to be one of the powerful men controlling society.

"No, Tim. I've made up my mind." She turned to walk out of the laboratory.

Tim grabbed the nearest thing he could find to use as a weapon. He picked up the desktop spin coater and bashed Brenda on the back of her head, knocking her unconscious. Quickly, he checked her pulse. It was strong but erratic. She probably suffered nothing more than a concussion. He dragged her body to the cage, which was set up in the laboratory to control his human experiment subjects. After locking her inside, he left the laboratory, locked the door and went to find Shelby Cain. The laboratory was sound proof, so he had no fear of anyone hearing her screaming when she regained consciousness.

Tim rushed to Cain's office. As he walked toward the door, Cain's assistant called out to him.

"Mr. Olsen, he's not there. There was a problem, and his office is being cleaned. He's in his temporary office on level two, office 212. Tim went to the elevator and punched two. He located office 212 and knocked on the door. "It's Tim Olsen," he said.

The door opened and Shelby Cain greeted him cheerfully, "Come in Tim, what can I do for you?"

"Sir, we have a problem. My assistant, Brenda doesn't agree with the experiments, and she has threatened to go to the authorities and the press."

"We can't let that happen, Tim."

"Yes sir I know that. I rendered her unconscious and locked her in the cage. I wanted to ask your permission to use her as a replacement for Case Study One, who escaped. Can you cover it so no one knows that she's missing?"

Cain admired the boy's spunk. "I can work it out without a problem. Proceed with your work and I'll also secure a replacement for her. I've got a gentleman in mind who is an exceptional scientist who I've used before."

"Mr. Cain if you can have him here first thing in the morning, I'm ready to begin. We've wasted enough time."

"I surely can," Cain replied. "Prepare everything and I'll arrange a keeper for the girl. She'll replace Case Study One and I'll have her moved to the holding cage. Her keeper will be Jesse."

Tim nodded and left the room.

Cain picked up the phone and called his assistant. "Yes Sir," the familiar deep voice of his trusted assistant, Derrick, answered.

"Derrick, I want you to send Jesse to the laboratory, Have him remove a test subject from the cage and put her in a holding room. Olsen will update him. Furthermore, call Alzar Frontier and tell him to report to this facility at 8 in the morning. Have my office cleaned by then, and I can brief him there. He's expecting a call from me. Oh, and one more thing. Put the word out that Brenda Alford has requested a transfer and will be sent immediately to our offices in Paris. She will be there permanently. Have our people there rent an apartment in her name and set up a phone in her name. Secure one of our female operatives, and I don't care how you do it, but make sure she resembles Brenda. She must pass for her while traveling to Paris. Get her the proper documentation. Purchase a one-way airline ticket in Brenda's name and have our girl make the trip and move into the apartment. When she arrives, tell her to talk to no one and make herself invisible. Use what resources you need to make this happen. If it goes off without a hitch, there'll be a bonus in it for you."

"Yes Sir," was the reply.

Tim walked back to the Laboratory. A short stocky man with a mustache was already there. He was inside the cage and had secured Brenda's hands and feet with duct tape. A gag was over her mouth. He wrapped her in a sheet and placed her on a Gurney.

"My name is Jesse. Mr. Cain assigned me to handle her. I'll take good care of her, sir."

"Get her medical attention if she needs it, Jesse. I want her back here in the laboratory first thing in the morning. I trust you to handle it."

The man nodded and left. Tim had absolutely no remorse about Brenda. She was just an object for him to use.

37

CIA Director Henria had no choice but to declare Ethan Tyler compromised.

Even though he was aware of things that he couldn't officially bring out in the open, he knew what the protocol was when an Agent was suspected of going to the other side. The Agent must be neutralized.

The intercom buzzed, "Agent Thompson is here as you requested," his assistant announced.

"Give me a minute," replied Henria. He went to the bathroom. Under the counter was a bottle of Gentleman Jack. He poured a shot, downed it, and looked in the mirror. What he saw was a very distinguished man in his early 50's. He touched his perfectly groomed grey hair to make sure that every hair was in place. He always loved it when women said that he looked like James Brolin.

Henria took a sip of mouthwash to cover the smell of the bourbon, walked back to his desk and punched the intercom button, "send Thompson in."

Hank Thompson walked in and took a seat in front of the Director's desk. "What can I do for you Sir?"

"We've had conversations previously about Ethan Tyler. Update me."

"Ratliff, Henderson and I have been contacting all of our sources. Nothing, he's disappeared into thin air."

"If he knew that his wife was, I bet he would surface," the Director said.

"No Question about that," Thompson replied.

"Listen Agent Thompson, too much time has elapsed since he's checked in. Agent Tyler has probably been compromised. I think that big money got to him. It's time that we neutralized him. You know the drill. When the time comes, I want you to personally handle it. Keep Ratliff and Henderson searching for him, but when he's located and it comes to the kill, it's yours alone. Do you understand me?"

"Yes Sir," replied Thompson. "It's still hard for me to believe that he's a traitor, but I know my duty."

"Once it's done, dispose of the body so it's never found. We must not allow the CIA to be compromised in any way. When Tyler's out of the way, we need to get another undercover Agent inside Cain's operation. We can't lose tract of the God Particle research."

"I'll keep pressure on all my sources to find Tyler, and I'll start right away locating another Agent." Thompson got to his feet and left the room.

Henria massaged his face. He had his own ways to find Tyler, but it would be cleaner if Thompson just killed him and the body disappeared.

The Director picked up his secure phone and punched in a number.

"Activate phase two," he said. "Get the information I need on Thompson, using all means at your disposal." He hung up and leaned back in the chair. The view from his sixth-floor office overlooked the well-tailored grounds. He loved the power if his position.

Henria was appointed CIA director three years ago. He meticulously built his power base and had the complete confidence of the President. He regularly briefed the President on the research on the God Particle, but not on the details of the operation. The Chief Executive didn't want any knowledge that would put his fingerprints on the CIA operation in case it went south and was uncovered. He certainly did not want to be in the loop if an Agent was ordered eliminated. Henria was *on his own* in this matter.

He shook his head and retreated to the bathroom. He needed another shot of Gentleman Jack.

38

Katrina awoke from a troubled sleep. She took a shower, dressed in Jeans and a T-shirt and chose a book from the selection that had been provided. She selected "The Long Journey Home" by an unknown author named Gary William Ramsey.

After reading two chapters, she heard the sound of the door being unlocked. Before she could get up, the man with the jagged scar entered the room with a tray of food. She noticed a pistol stuck in his belt. He set the tray on the coffee table and picked up the dishes from the night before.

"What am I doing here? What do you want from me?"

Scar glared at her. "The Boss will talk to you after you eat breakfast," he said in a gravelly voice. He sounded as if his vocal cords had been damaged.

After he left the room, Katrina thought about hiding behind the door and surprising him on one of these visits. She was well trained in the martial arts, however, she didn't know what additional security was situated outside her suite.

She laid down the book and walked to the sofa. The tray on the coffee table contained a pot of steaming coffee, with a plain white mug beside it. The plate held egg's Benedict, two strips of thick bacon and a bowl of fruit. Sourdough toast was on a separate bread plate. Her captor certainly was feeding her well and keeping her in comfort.

Katrina finished her breakfast, drank two cups of coffee and poured a third. She walked to the window. While sipping the coffee, she looked outside. Katrina saw the dark haired, middle-aged man and the young blonde girl sitting at a beautiful white wicker table, having breakfast. A waiter in a white uniform stood to the side. The dark haired man looked up toward the window where she was standing. He placed his napkin on the table, said something to the girl and walked toward the front door. She assumed that he was coming to talk to her, so she moved to the recliner, sat down and waited.

In less than five minutes she heard the door being unlocked. Scar entered with his pistol drawn. "Okay Boss, it's clear."

Ben Cruise walked in. He was wearing a black silk Mexican wedding shirt, white linen trousers, and Nike Dunk Low Pro SB Paris athletic shoes with no socks. He was a striking figure. He glanced at his gold Rolex as he entered.

"Well, Mrs. Tyler, I hope your stay at my home has been satisfactory. We strive to make you as comfortable as possible. Is there anything you need?"

Katrina was flabbergasted. He acted as if she was an honored guest in his home.

"Are you insane," she said, and she rose to her feet. "Why am I here? What do you want from me?" Her eyes flared.

Scar moved forward pointing he pistol. "Be respectful," he growled.

Cruise put his hand on the man's arm and gestured him back toward the door.

"I will answer your questions, but you must be civil. I loathe loud voices and confrontations. Do you understand me?" He smiled and sat down on the couch. "Please take a seat."

Katrina sat down on the recliner. His calmness and nonchalance unnerved her. "Why am I here?"

"Mrs. Tyler, we need to talk to your husband Ethan. We have questions of him and we don't intend to harm either of you," he lied. "Just tell us where he is or how we can make contact with him, and we can end this in a respectful manner."

"What do you want with Ethan?"

"We have questions to ask him about his experiences in the laboratory in West Texas."

"I don't know anything about that." Katrina said. "I haven't been in touch with Ethan for sometime. I don't know where he is."

"He's your husband, surely you know how to get in touch with him."

"No, I don't."

"You are lying to me Miss Tyler. Things are not going to be as nice for you if you continue to deceive me."

"I don't know where he is and I don't know how to reach him, but he'll find me for certain and he doesn't take very kindly to anyone who harms me."

Ben Cruise leaped from the couch. He scowled and gritted his teeth. His congenial manner turned dark. He looked at Scar, motioned him over and said, "Give me your gun." Scar handed it to him, and he pointed it at Katrina. He turned again and nodded to his cohort. Scar walked over and punched Katrina hard in the stomach. She bent over and crumbled to the floor, gasping for breath.

"Miss Tyler, I don't like to be lied to or stonewalled. You'll find your stay with me much less comfortable until you answer my questions. Your CIA contacts will never find you here." He and Scar turned and left the room, locking the door behind them.

Katrina struggled to get her breath. She raised herself to the recliner and sat down. Her side, where he had punched her, was very painful. *He may have cracked a rib,* she thought. *How did he know that I was a CIA Operative? I am undercover and only high-ranking officials knew my identity, yet this Cruise guy seems to know all about me.*

She stood and trudged to the bathroom and drank a glass of water. Her instincts told her that things were going to get difficult, and she must become aggressive about escaping. Even though her risks were high, she had to so something.

Katrina had no idea whether Ethan was alive or dead and the thought of his possible death devastated her. Tears filled her eyes as she stood looking out the window. She saw Cruise walking back to the wicker table to join his young blonde friend. The girl looked toward the window and clearly saw her standing there.

"How was your breakfast, Blaze?" Cruise asked.

"Great Daddy Ben, who is that woman at the window upstairs?"

"Just a businesses associate my dear. Do you want to go for a ride?"

"When will Billy join us?" Blaze asked. "You said soon and it's been over a week."

"Honey he needs medical attention. Don't worry about Billy, he's being well taken care of."

"I want to go see him."

"Well dear not now, soon okay?"

Cruise leaned over and kissed her on the forehead. He hungered to take the relationship further immediately, but knew he had to take his time with her. Sooner or later she would graduate from his friend to being his lover.

I saw that girl yesterday. I think Daddy Ben's lying to me, Blaze thought. *I want to see Billy, and maybe that woman knows something about where he is.*

Blaze made up her mind at that moment that she wanted to talk to the woman, and that she had to do it secretly. She also wondered about Ethan Tyler. He had been kind to Billy and her and Daddy Ben told her that he went home. Nothing made sense to her. Something was going on, and Blaze was going to find out what it was.

Scar had been looking at her with lust in his eyes when Ben wasn't around. He frightened her, but maybe she could use him to get to the woman at the window. Daddy Ben said that he had to go into town tomorrow. Blaze decided to take advantage of his absence and do some snooping.

39

When I reached the paved highway, I turned left, as Jacob had instructed me. The road was abandoned. Dusk was falling and all I saw was the long straight road ahead. The scooter was old, but it ran like a top. I was cruising along at about fifty miles an hour. The pinkest blaze of the sunset through the clouds was magnificent, and the cool breeze against my skin invigorated me.

Drainage ditches were on either side of the two-lane road and thick woods were behind the ditches on both sides. After traveling about two hours, I pulled to the side of the road and took a drink of the sweet tea Maybelle packed for me. It tasted wonderful. After replacing the jar back in the saddlebags, I continued my journey into the unknown.

As darkness fell, I turned on the headlight. Hours passed and I hadn't seen a single vehicle. I figured that I had traveled about one hundred and fifty miles. My stomach growled with hunger, so I stopped again and ate one of Maybelle's sandwiches. I bit down on a thick slice of fried baloney with mustard and onions.

When I got back on the scooter, I checked the fuel gauge. It was almost empty. I slowed down to about forty, hoping to save gas. Just as I thought I would be stranded in the backside of nowhere, I spotted lights in the distance. Approaching the lights, I saw a sign. It read, *Alba, Texas, population 507, home of Albert Alonzo.* I recognized the name of the major league baseball pitcher, who played about five or six years for the Texas Rangers. I don't know whatever happened to him but this is his hometown.

The lights belonged to a small convenience store with gas pumps in front. There was a red pickup truck in the parking lot along with an old Plymouth. I needed gas and access to a phone, but I had no money. I remembered that there were two credit cards in the wallet that I took from Hedrick. I pulled up to the store, put down the kickstand on the scooter and went inside.

I tall slender man in his twenties was standing behind the counter. He wore a sleeveless T-shirt and tattoos covered both arms. His matted hair was tied up in a ponytail. He grinned at me when I walked in, revealing stained brown teeth.

"What can I do you for mister?" He asked.

"I need to fill up with gas and get some supplies," I said, "but first I want to use the restroom." He nodded toward the corner. After using the restroom, I looked around the store. I hoped that Hedrick's credit card would be taken. There wasn't much I could use in the store. One section had some fishing items, including a filet knife. I grabbed one, a large bottle of water, a can of Vienna sausage and pack of cheese crackers.

"I think this will do it and I need to fill up the tank on my scooter." I handed him Hedrick's credit card.

"What you doing in these parts?" Ponytail asked.

"Just passing through."

I walked outside, filled up the tank with gas and went back in. Ponytail swiped the card and handed it to me, along with the ticket to sign. I signed it, grinned and handed it back to him. He looked quizzically at me again, 'I guess I was wondering about the guard uniform. What do you guard?"

I ignored the question. "Is there a motel nearby?"

"We ain't got no motel here in Alba, but about twenty miles down the road there's one in Burnam beside the Walmart store."

I thanked him and left. I knew that I had to get some clothes and a phone to call in. Being exhausted, I also wanted to find a motel to get some rest.

After eating the snack and finishing the bottle of water, I set out again. On this leg of my journey I did pass several vehicles, all pickup trucks. I was entering the edge of civilization. I passed several businesses, all closed for the evening except for a Burger King. The road I had been traveling on intersected with an interstate highway. Just beyond the intersection were the bright lights of a Walmart. There were few cars in the parking lot at this late hour.

I parked my scooter near the front door and went in. I picked up a pushcart and proceeded to the men's clothing area. There I picked out pair of jeans, a long sleeve blue cotton shirt, baseball cap, socks, underwear and a pair of tennis shoes. I wanted to buy a pistol, but I knew they would require a background check. In sporting goods area I chose a bicycle chain and lock. I didn't want my scooter stolen. After getting shaving supplies, I was almost finished.

I walked to the electronic section to purchase a prepaid cell phone. While the middle-aged lady behind the counter finished with another customer, I looked at the selection and chose a Straight Talk Hauwei Ascent II Prepaid Cell Phone. I wanted a low cost phone because I had no idea what Hedricks's credit limit was on his cards.

"Did you decide what you want?" the clerk asked.

"Yes," I said pointing to the phone in the glass case.

"This phone will only work with the $45/30-Day unlimited service plan or the $60/30 day unlimited international service plan," she said.

"I'll take the first one and please activate it for me."

First she swiped the credit card and then proceeded to activate the phone. I thanked her and put it in my pocket with the receipt and walked to the front checkout to pay for the clothes.

"Did you find everything you needed?" the cashier asked.

"Yes I did. What is the maximum amount of cash back I can get?"

"One hundred dollars, sir."

"Okay, do that for me."

She rung up the sale, I swiped the card and signed. She bagged the clothing and handed me five twenties.

"Thank you for shopping Walmart," she said.

I nodded and walked toward the door.

"Hey wait a minute," I heard a man yell. My first thought was that a warning had come up on the credit card. An older, fat gray haired man was waving at me. I had to decide whether to run or take my chances. I stopped and waited for him. He came up to me slightly out of breath.

"Sorry sir, the cashier didn't put your socks in the bag." He handed me the socks. I breathed a sigh of relief and left the building.

I rode back to the highway and saw the Motel 6 that Ponytail had mentioned. A diner was located beside the motel. The sign read, "*Open 24 hours.*"

After parking my scooter and chaining it to a light post, I walked into the lobby carrying my bag of clothes. A young Asian lady smiled at me from behind the counter.

"I need a room for the night," I said, handing her the credit card. She swiped it and I signed Hedrick's name to the receipt.

"Room 120," she said, giving me the room key card. "Just outside the door, second one on the right."

As I left the lobby, a well-dressed Asian man passed me. He was carrying what looked like a silky lunch bag, however I caught the strong smell of lemon and vanilla coming from it. He smiled at me as we passed. The strange look in his eyes startled me. I dismissed the incident and proceeded to the room.

After using the rest room, I deposited my new clothes in the dresser drawer. The room was equipped with a coffee pot, small fridge and a microwave. Beside the king sized bed was a recliner. On the other side was an end table holding the phone and a clock. A picture of the ocean rolling in on the sands of a tropical island hung over the bed. Nothing else decorated the white painted walls. I guess the beige bed spread was supposed to remind the guest of sand.

Beside the clock was a flier with a menu stating that the 24-hour diner delivered. I realized that I was starving. I looked at the menu and decided on a Philly cheese steak sandwich, side salad and an order of fries. I was surprised to see beer on the beverage list so I decided on two Buds.

"24 Hour Diner," the gruff male voice answered.

"Sir, I'm in room 120 at the Motel 6 next door. I want to order for delivery."

I gave him my order.

"Will this be cash or charge?" he asked.

"Charge," I provided him the card number and Hedrick's name. I wanted to save the one hundred dollars cash I had.

"Be there in thirty minutes," he said.

I grabbed the cell phone from my pocket and started to punch in the emergency number for Agent Thompson. He was my primary contact with the CIA. I wanted to let him know that I was alive and needed to be brought in for debriefing. I also wanted to know about Katrina. Herman told me that she was killed after being raped by Ted. I needed to know that she was afforded a proper burial. These thoughts tore into my heart. I laid the phone on the end table and sat silently thinking about her.

If it's the last thing I do, I'm going to return to that laboratory and make Ted pay for what he did to Katrina, I thought. My mind almost snapped. The pain in my heart was overwhelming.

"Get up and fight, Ethan, Get up and fight," I said aloud, repeatedly. Revenge is a great motivator.

My thoughts were interrupted by a knock on the door. I answered it and a young blonde haired boy was standing there with a bag of food and the beers. I took the order, signed the bill and he left.

I popped the top and sipped a Bud. After finishing it, I removed the sandwich, salad and fries out of the bag. The fries were greasy and limp, so I threw them in the trashcan. The Philly Cheesesteak was good and the salad was crisp and fresh. I felt better after eating the food and finishing off the second beer. I decided to wait until morning to call Thompson. A decent nights sleep would do me good. I took a hot shower and went to bed. Sleep did not come easily.

It was a dark rainy night when I got off at 1am from working at Midway Lunch. Mr. Lonnie, the cook, and I had cleaned the little café.

"Are you going to ride your bike home in this rain?" he asked. He was old and gray and had a slight hump on his back, but he was a kind and caring man.

"No, I'll get drenched. I'll call the old guy at Monroe Cabs to take me home. Can I leave my bike inside here and pick it up tomorrow?"

"No problem," Mr. Lonnie said.

I called the cab station, and waited under the overhang outside of the café for him to arrive. Mr. Lonnie left. After about twenty minutes, the cab pulled up. I lived seven miles away at the end of a long dirt road. I was scared to ride with the old cab driver but at that time of the night, no one else was on the road in Monroe, NC. The old cab driver would always drive on the wrong side of the road when he went around curves. I sat with my hand on the door handle thinking that if a car was coming, I could jump out before the head-on collision.

We arrived safely, and he let me off at the end of the dirt road. He wouldn't drive to my house because he feared getting stuck in the mud. I paid him and began the walk up the hill. The rain had calmed to a drizzle, but I was still drenched when I reached the door of the old farmhouse where I lived with my mother, stepdad and younger half brother. Of course, everyone was asleep when I got home.

This night something was different. There was a heavy fog in the house. My heart skipped a beat as I spotted the silhouette of a rocking chair in the corner. My revered grandfather always sat in a rocking chair like this, but he didn't live with us. I walked to rocking chair and saw his overalls, but only bones and a skull were lying there. I felt a cold wind when I lifted up the front part of the overalls. I shrieked as I uncovered Katrina's head. It was bloody with blank eyes staring back at me.

I sat straight up in the bed and was covered with a cold sweat. My subconscious produced this horrible nightmare. I got up and pulled back the drapes. The sun was rising. I glanced towards the clock, and it was 5am. I took a shower, as hot as I could stand, shaved and dressed in my new clothes. I stuffed the uniform into a bag.

Breakfast was in order before I made my call, so I walked to the 24-Hour Diner. A young lady in her late teens waited on me. She had piercings in each ear and one in her bottom lip and appeared very bored. I ordered eggs over easy, sausage, grits and whole-wheat toast, grape juice and told her to bring hot sauce. She filled my coffee cup with steaming hot black coffee.

One cup of coffee down, and I was sipping on my second when my food arrived. She placed it on the table along with the check. The grits were lumpy, but overall the food was editable. The teenager grimaced at me when she saw me putting catsup and hot sauce on my eggs. I mixed some sausage and butter in the grits and ate quickly. After paying the tab with the credit card, I proceeded back to the motel room.

At about 7am I punched in the secured number for Agent Thompson's phone. It rang five times before a groggy voice answered. "Who is this?"

"Hank, this is Ethan Tyler." I heard a sharp intake of breath on the other end of the line.

"Where in the hell are you Ethan, and what have you been doing?"

"I'm in a motel room in Burnam, Texas. It's a long story. I was injured and had amnesia for a while. While undercover, I was associated with two men who worked for a guy known as the

Piranha. I think I know his identity, and I shared the information with another trusted friend, however I can't talk about that on the phone."

I took a deep breath and continued, "the Piranha sent two men to kill me, but one of them was killed and I escaped. Before he died, the one named Herman told me that they had raped and killed Katrina. I'm still devastated. We need to meet and I can tell you everything. Don't tell anyone about this call. If it's known that you're in contact with me, your life may be in danger."

"Wait Ethan, Katrina was working undercover using the alias of Ann Davis. Another agent was at her apartment waiting for her, when the thugs arrived. They assumed that she was Katrina and killed her. As far as we know your wife is alive, but she disappeared a few days ago."

I took a deep breath. The thought that Katrina was alive overwhelmed me.

"Ethan, are you there?"

"Yes Hank. I've got to find her. Bring all the information you have. Let's set up a meeting."

"Okay Ethan, I googled it and Tyler, Texas has the nearest airport to you. I'll fly in there late today. You're about forty miles away. Do you have transportation?"

"I've got an old scooter and one hundred dollars, that's it."

"Listen, I'll wire you five thousand dollars. You can buy what you need. Wait, let me find a Western Union in Tyler."

After about five minutes, Thompson came back to the phone. "Okay Ethan, I'll send the money to the Western Union at 2020 Roseland Blvd. in Tyler."

"Just a minute Hank." I took out the wallet and looked at the license. The full name was Roark Lee Hedrick. "I don't have any ID so send it in the name of Roark Lee Hedrick. I have an ID showing that name."

"You got it," Hank replied. "Now let me google a hotel near the airport where we can meet."

After a couple of minutes Thompson said, "Ethan, book a couple of nights at the Holiday Inn Express at 3247 West Gentry Parkway. Call me with the room number when you're there and I'll come directly from the airport."

"Hank, you call me when you land and I'll give you the info." I gave him the cell phone number.

I hung up the phone, went to the bathroom and threw water on my face. *Katrina may be alive, she may be alive.* That thought kept running through my mind.

I rubbed my face and realized something else. Something was strange about the conversation with Thompson. I couldn't put my finger on it, but it bothered me. Protocol would be to send a private plane, pick me up and fly me to the Langley CIA headquarters for debriefing. *Why was Thompson deviating from accepted Protocol?* I temporarily dismissed it.

I put all my belongings in a bag and went to the office to check out. A stout older lady with white hair took my key card and checked the computer to see if I had any other charges. Her mannerisms were like those of a lifetime military person. She spoke distinctly and with authority.

"You're good to go sir," she said crisply.

"How long does it take to drive to Tyler?" I asked. "Can you give me directions to the Holiday Inn Express there?"

"Mr. Hedrick, It'll take about forty-five minutes if you follow the speed limits. I can make it in less time because driving sixty is too damn slow. I know the motel well," she said. "I formerly worked there but they fired me because they said I was too stiff and formal. To hell with them, my twenty years in the Army taught me to be precise. Motel 6 management appreciates me being accurate."

She proceeded to give me detailed directions. I thanked her, left Motel 6 and began my forty-mile trip to Tyler. Not long into the trip, the scooter began to sputter. I smelled something burning and smoke emerged from the engine. I was about a mile outside of Tyler when the scooter just quit. I pushed it to a nearby Exxon station and went inside the store. The Indian lady behind the counter smiled at me.

"Are you having trouble, Sir?"

She had evidently seen me pushing the scooter.

"Yes my vehicle has mechanical problems. May I leave it here till I can get help?"

"Yes," she replied.

"I need to get to the Western Union office on Roseland Blvd. Am I near there?"

"Only about five miles away," she said. "I can call you a taxi."

"I would very much appreciate that."

Ten minutes later my cab arrived. The driver introduced himself as Singh and delivered me to the Western Union office.

"Please wait," I told Singh. He was probably a relative of the lady at the Exxon station.

I had a little trouble getting the Western Union clerk to accept a couple of credit cards and a social security card as Id, but after a few minutes of discussions she gave me the money that Hank sent.

I went back to the cab. "Singh I need to purchase a used vehicle. Can you advise me?"

He grinned and replied, "Yes, my cousin has a automobile for sale. Do you want me to take you there?"

"Yes."

We drove back to the Exxon station and Singh walked inside with me.

"Preti is Abhay in the back? This man is interested in purchasing his automobile."

Preti went to be back of the store and returned with a short thin man with brown eyes and a balding head. He walked up to me and grinned.

"Sir, I have a very find automobile for sale. Come with me."

We walked outside and around to the back of the store. A 1995 silver Toyota Camry was parked there. It looked in pretty good shape, but had a big scratch in the rear bumper.

"What happened here, Abhay?"

"Just a minor scratch," he said.

He gave me the keys and I got in and cranked it up. The motor ran smoothly. I got out and checked the tires and they were passable.

"I'll give you twelve hundred dollars cash," I said.

"Sir, it's worth more than that."

"Take it or leave it," I said. I was willing to go as high as eighteen hundred, but I began to walk away.

"It's a deal," he said quickly. "Wait, I will get the title."

I waited and looked at the Toyota more closely. I noticed a tear in the rear seat but that didn't matter to me. I planned to ditch the car soon anyway.

Abhay returned and waved me into the back door of the store. We walked to the front counter.

"Priti is a Notary." He said as he signed the title. I counted out twelve hundred dollars, handed it to him and signed Hedrick's name to the title. Preti notarized it and gave the title to me.

"The tank is full of gas. That is my bonus to you," Abhay said, smiling.

I shook his hand, paid Singh the taxi fare, went to the back and picked up the car. I drove around to the front and put the scooter in the trunk. I tied the trunk down with a piece of nylon cord.

The drive to Tyler took about forty-five minutes. I followed the instructions of the military lady and easily found the Holiday Inn Express. When I arrived, I took the scooter out of the trunk and chained it to a light post in the parking lot.

The lobby of the hotel was located in front of the area where the continental breakfast was served. Several customers lingered there drinking coffee. I checked in and the clerk swiped Hedrick's card. She assigned me room 404. I put my bag with my meager belongings in the room and went out to find some lunch. Thompson said it would be evening before he arrived.

The first restaurant I passed was an IHOP. I tossed my phone in the glove compartment along with the filet knife. I went in and had a patty melt, fries and a Coke. When I got back in the Camry, I had the eerie feeling that I was being watched. I drove back to the hotel and sat in the car thinking. *Something's not right here.*

As I reached over to open the glove compartment to retrieve the phone and knife, the driver's side window shattered and a bullet penetrated the dash. If I hadn't leaned over, it would have hit me in the head. I ducked and slumped down as far as I could, as another bullet penetrated the dashboard no more that two inches from my head. I didn't hear the gunshots. The attacker must be using a silencer.

A red pickup truck pulled up beside me. A tall muscular guy wearing a cowboy hat yelled at me, "Are you okay? What broke your window?"

I heard screeching and looked out my back window. A black Escalade raced away. That must have been my attacker.

"Are you okay?' The cowboy asked again.

"I'm fine." I got out of the car. I didn't want him to see the bullet holes in the dash because he might call the cops.

"The window was cracked and I accidently hit it with my elbow."

He looked at me like I was nuts.

"Whatever," he said as he drove off.

Who in the hell is trying to kill me, Thompson is the only one who knows I'm here.

40

Cain's exhilaration was escalating as he sat in his office contemplating the upcoming experiments of Olsen's Formula, utilizing the God Particle, on humans. The first impulsive test on the janitor was ill conceived and immature, but it proved to be a learning experience for the young scientist. Olsen assured him that the Formula was ready and that the results would be substantially improved, however, not perfect. Perfection could only be attained through evolution of results. He presently had three test subjects, and Olsen had indicated that more might be needed.

There was a knock on the door, and his assistant entered. "Mr. Cain, Dr. Alzar Frontier is here."

"Please send him in."

A tall, lanky man in his forties with short blonde hair walked in. His eyes were an intense blue. He sported a mustache and beard and was dressed in scrubs.

"I am ready for work," he said in a heavy German accent.

"Dr. Frontier, I told you about Timothy Olsen. He's immature, ruthless and never to be trusted, but brilliant. He's taken his research with Higgs boson beyond everything I ever imagined. I need you to become familiar with his procedures and formulations. As soon as you're comfortable, we can rid ourselves of him and you can take over the project. In the near future I want to entertain bids from any country interested."

"Mr. Cain I have been working on this subject for four years. May I share some of my knowledge and findings with you?"

"Go ahead."

"Every force in nature is associated with a particle. The particle tied to electromagnetism is the photon, a tiny, massless particle. The weak force is associated with particles called the W and Z bosons, which are very massive. The Higgs mechanism is thought to be responsible for this. If you introduce the Higgs field, the W and Z bosons mix with the field, and through this mixing they acquire mass," Alzar said.

"This explains why the W and Z bosons have mass, and also unifies the electromagnetic and weak forces into the electroweak force. Although other evidence has helped buffer the union of these two forces, the Higgs discovery may seal the deal. If Olsen has perfected his Formula, the human body can be transformed both physically and mentally. No other scientist has been able to preserve the particle and adapt it to human use. It was thought impossible."

"Dr. Frontier, how would you suggest introducing the Formula into a human?"

"Intramuscular (IM) injections are given directly into the central area of selected muscles. There are a number of sites on the human body that are suitable for IM injections; however, there are three sites that are most commonly used in this type of procedure. Although none have ever used Higgs boson as the base, however, I can speculate." He took a deep breath and continued.

"The deltoid muscle located laterally on the upper arm can be used for intramuscular injections. Originating from the Acromion process of the scapula and inserting approximately one-third of the way down the humerus, the deltoid muscle can be used readily for IM injections if there is sufficient muscle mass to justify use of this site. The deltoid's close proximity to the radial nerve and radial artery means that careful consideration and palpation of the muscle is required to find a safe site for penetration of the needle. There are various methods for defining the boundaries of this muscle.

The vastus lateralis muscle forms part of the quadriceps muscle group of the upper leg and can be found on the anteriolateral aspect of the thigh. This muscle is more commonly used as the site for IM injections as it is generally thick and well formed in individuals of all ages and is not located close to any major arteries or nerves. It is also readily accessed. The middle third of the muscle is used to define the injection site. This third can be determined by visually dividing the length of the muscle that originates on the greater trochanter of the femur and inserts on the upper border of the patella and tibial tuberosity through the patella ligament into thirds. Palpation of the muscle is required to determine if sufficient body and mass is present to undertake the procedure."

Cain was bored but impressed with the detail of the research as Alzar continued.

"The gluteus medius muscle, which is also known as the ventrogluteal site, is the third commonly used site for IM injections. The correct area for injection can be determined in the following manner. Place the heel of the hand of the greater trochanter of the femur with fingers pointing towards the patient's head. The left hand is used for the right hip and vice versa. While keeping the palm of the hand over the greater trochanter and placing the index finger on the anterior superior iliac spine, stretch the middle finger dorsally palpating for the iliac crest and then press lightly below this point. The triangle formed by the iliac crest, the third finger and index finger forms the area suitable for intramuscular injection. Determining which site is most appropriate will depend upon the patient's muscle density at each site, the type and nature of medication you wish to administer."

"Okay I understand your explanation about muscle injections but what about the most important part of the experiment, the injection into the brain?" Cain asked.

Alzar looked at him and smiled, "The human brain has no lymphatic system, but produces over a half-liter each day of cerebrospinal fluid. The cerebrospinal fluid is secreted at the choroid plexus and occupies the cavities of the four ventricles, as well as the cranial and spinal sub-arachnoid space. The cerebrospinal fluid moves over the surfaces of the brain and spinal cord and is rapidly absorbed into the general circulation. The choroid plexus forms the blood-cerebrospinal fluid barrier, and this barrier is functionally distinct from the brain micro vascular endothelium, which forms the blood-brain barrier. Virtually all non-cellular substances in blood distribute into cerebrospinal fluid, and drug entry into cerebrospinal fluid is not an index of drug transport across the blood-brain barrier. Drug injected into the cerebrospinal fluid rapidly moves into the blood via bulk flow, but penetrates into brain tissue poorly owing to the limitations of diffusion. Drug transport into cerebrospinal fluid vs. brain interstitial fluid requires knowledge of the relative expression of transporters at the choroid plexus versus the brain microvascular endothelium. Cerebrospinal Fluid Transport is commonly called CSF. A drug that is injected into the CSF compartment is rapidly transported out of brain to the blood. Following the ICV injection of drug, it moves through the CSF flow tracks, and is absorbed into the peripheral bloodstream across the arachnoid villi to enter the general circulation. The drug that is injected into the CSF exits the brain, rapidly enters the peripheral blood, and then re-enters the brain across the BBB to induce anesthesia, similar to the pathway taken by drug injected intravenously to revert the control to an accessible version."

"Enough, enough," Cain felt his head spinning. He didn't understand half of what the man said, but the conversation proved his knowledge of the subject. He heard Olsen say that the best way to grow mass in the brain was to inject specific lobes, but he didn't want to enter that into his conversation with Alzar at this time.

"Let's go to the laboratory and I'll introduce you to Olsen. We've prepared a test subject for him, a female. You can primarily assist and observe his techniques on this first controlled human test, then assess the experiment and advise on the next one. We have two other humans for him to use as guinea pigs."

As they entered the laboratory, Olsen was engaged in preparing the injections for Brenda. He hardly noticed them when they walked up to him.

"Tim, this is Dr. Alzar Frontier. I have chosen him to replace Brenda as your assistant. He is well versed on the God Particle and procedures to convert it to human use."

Alzar stuck out his hand, "Nice to meet you Dr. Olsen."

Olsen looked up at him and sneered, "Just stay out of the way and hand me things when I ask." He didn't offer to shake the outstretched hand.

Anger raged through Alzar's mind. *No young punk treats me like this*, he thought.

Cain grabbed his shoulder, squeezed it, reminding Dr. Frontier that soon he would be taking over the project. Alzar relaxed.

"I'm prepared for Brenda," Olsen said. "Did you have her sedated as I requested?"

"Yes," Cain replied. He left the room to have Brenda brought in,

"I am impressed with your work, and I will assist you any way I can," Alzar said.

Olsen didn't answer and kept laboring over a vial that was heating over a blue flame.

The door opened, and Jesse rolled in a Gurney with Brenda's sedated body on it.

"Transfer her to the operating table," Tim ordered as he transferred the vile from the flame to a glass filled with ice.

Jesse complied. The operating table had restraints. Jesse buckled them on Brenda's hands and feet.

Tim filed a syringe with the Formula from the vile.

"Time to rock and roll," he snickered.

He's crazy as hell, Dr. Frontier thought as he observed the wild look in Olsen's eyes.

Jesse retreated to the corner of the room. He put his hand on the Walther pistol stuck in his belt. Something about this situation scared him.

41

After receiving the information from his informant, the Man decided to take the elimination of Tyler into his own hands. He left work and immediately booked his private charter to Tyler. He donned his disguise, black wig, mustache, and a scar on his right cheek. He retrieved his Identification for this disguise, Frank Black. His arrangements with the Charter pilot included complete confidentially for which he paid handsomely.

The pilot was a former pilot in the Mexican Air force and had done some flying for the Lopez Mexican drug cartel. His name was Enrique Santos, a thin lanky Mexican. He knew the Man only as Frank Black. Santos kept the small jet at a private airstrip. The Man arrived at the airstrip, parked his car inside an empty hanger and walked to the runway. He carried a case holding his Wilson Combat Sniper rifle with silencer.

"Mr. Black, nice to see you again. I've secured a flight plan to Tyler and we can land at Pineridge Airport."

The Man handed him a thick envelope filled with one hundred dollar bills.

"Did you secure a vehicle for me in Tyler?"

"Yes sir, a black Escalade. Completely untraceable and belongs to a business associate of mine."

After landing in Tyler, the Man drove the Escalade to the Holiday Inn Express at 3247 West Gentry Parkway. He parked in the lot, assembled the weapon and waited. In just a few minutes, he saw Tyler get into a Camry and drive off. No time for a clear shot.

After a little more than an hour, the Camry returned. Tyler turned off the engine and sat there. The Man took careful aim through the scope and slowly squeezed the trigger. An instant before he got the shot off, Tyler bent forward. The bullet went through the window and into the dash. Tyler slumped, and he shot again. The silencer reduced the noise to nearly nothing.

Unexpectedly, a red pickup truck pulled in front of the Camry. The Man cursed and hauled ass. He was furious because he knew that this failed attempt would put Tyler on guard and the possibility of another attempt was doubtful. He droved straight back to the airstrip and flew home. His fury was difficult to contain.

Just prior to the landing wheels coming down, his cell phone rang. It was his informant.

"I wanted to give you more information about Tyler," the Man said. He believes that he knows the identity of the man known as the Piranha and he shared this information with an associate. I thought you should know this."

The Man abruptly disconnected the call.

42

I glanced around the parking lot and observed only empty cars. The shot must have come from the Black Escalade. I walked to the front desk of the hotel, while constantly watching for anything suspicious.

A tall blonde young lady wearing a black pantsuit smiled at me from behind the counter. Her blue eyes and full lips reminded me of a model I once dated before I met Katrina. The pantsuit complimented her remarkable figure. The white blouse beneath the pantsuit jacket was unbuttoned far enough to show the top of her breasts, probably 34c's. Her smile was more than friendly.

"Can I help you sir?"

"I'm a guest here," I said, showing her my room key. "My name is Hedrick. I've had an accident, and I need some cardboard and duct tape."

"Mr. Hedrick, my name is Beth. I'll be pleased to help you. I know we have some duct tape in the supply room. I can supply you with a cardboard box, and you can cut it to your required size. May I ask what it's for?"

"Unfortunately a rock flew up and cracked my drivers' side window, and I need to secure it until I can get it replaced tomorrow."

For what reason I can't fully explains, she put her hand on mine.

"Come on, we'll see what we can do." She yelled to the back room, "Ramona, I'll be back in awhile. I need to assist a guest."

A short, stocky middle-aged woman emerged from the back. She also wore a black pantsuit, but she didn't fill it out nearly as well as Beth.

I followed Beth to the elevator, and she punched two. She stood very close to me, and I smelled the aroma of her Black Orchid perfume. I recognized the bouquet because it was Katrina's favorite. We got off on the second floor and took a left. The supply room was behind the area that housed the ice machine and vending machines. She opened the door and turned on the light. To the right, there was a shelf holding cleaning supplies, and I spotted a roll of duct tape. When I reached for it, Beth pressed her breasts against my back.

"Here let me help you," she murmured.

When I turned, she whispered, "Mr. Hedrick I find you very attractive, and I noticed that you're alone in your room. Would you like some company tonight? I get off in forty-five minutes. My rates are very reasonable."

I inhaled deeply and realized that Beth must be conducting a side business as a call girl from the front desk. There may be a way that I could use this to my advantage when Hank arrived. I was still skeptical of him.

"What will it cost me?" I inquired.

"Are you a member of law enforcement?"

"Of course not."

"Two hundred for the hour."

"Call my room in one hour and we may be able to set it up," I replied.

I planned to use the call as a distraction if I discovered that Hank had an agenda. If he did, I would say, "Come on," and her subsequent presence would maybe unnerve him.

She pressed her breasts against my chest and kissed me on the cheek. Beth backed up a little, took my hand and pushed it against her 34c's.

"I'll blow your mind," she whispered.

"Just call in one-hour," I said, drawing back my hand. I slipped her two twenties, took the duct tape and the box and proceeded to cover my broken window.

After taping the cardboard over the window, I went back to the hotel room. I put the duct tape on the dresser and took a hot shower. I wanted to clear my mind.

Since Thompson was the only one who knew where I was staying, either he took the shot at me or had informed someone else about my whereabouts. I turned on the TV and waited. Hank said that he would call when he landed.

I dozed off.

I was playing on the front porch of our rented house on the Mill Hill when he came up the steps. He was wearing a white T-shirt and khaki pants. He patted me on the head as he passed. I had not seen him for weeks, and mother said she didn't know where he was. I guess my father didn't care about my sister and me because he was rarely at home. My cousin Betty stayed with us when mother was working the third shift at the cotton mill. Betty would leave when mother got home. Mother slept most of the day consequently my sister and I were basically on our own. I heard yelling in the house, so I went towards the screen door, so I could listen.

"You said you were going to the store to get bread and I haven't seen you in three weeks. I can't live like this," my mother was crying.

"Listen if you don't stop yelling at me I'm leaving again," he said.

"Then go," mother yelled.

He almost knocked me down when he threw open the front door and stormed off. He didn't even say goodbye and I never saw him again after that day. I was almost three years old when my father left us for good. An empty feeling in my stomach caused tears to flow. I ran outside and hid under the house. I didn't want my mother to see me cry. I had to be a big man now.

The ringing of the cell phone awoke me from that reoccurring nightmare. The dream was exceptionally realistic and reflected exactly the last time I saw my father. These days I was having a hard time keeping the nightmares at bay.

"Hello, is this Hank?"

"Ethan, I just landed, I'll be there within the hour."

"What airport did you fly out of?"

"Out of Ronald Regan in Washington Why do you ask?"

"No problem, I'm in room 404."

"I'll be there in about an hour."

As soon as we hung up, I called the airlines and ask when the plane from Washington landed. I was informed that it arrived twenty minutes ago. That would have made it impossible for Thompson to be the one who took a shot at me.

I knew that I must remain vigilant because someone wants me dead. After about forty minutes, there was a knock on the door. I walked over and looked through the peephole. It was Beth. I opened the door.

"Beth I told you to call in an hour." She grinned. I looked down and she had a Beretta 92f pointed at me. I knew that only professionals handled that type of handgun.

"Back up," she said.

I held my hands up and obeyed.

"Mr. Benjamin Cruise sends his regards," she purred. "He wanted me to give you a message. Too bad you didn't immediately take advantage of my offer, and maybe I could have delivered the message in a very sexy way."

"Who is Cruise?"

"He's a friend of the Piranha, and he has your wife. If you ever want to see her alive, tell me all the information you have on the Piranha, and who you've told."

"I need to talk to Katrina to assure that she's alive."

Beth or whoever she was, pulled a cell phone from her shoulder bag and dialed a number.

"I've got him," she said and handed the phone to me.

"Listen, you better not harm Katrina or you're a dead man," I bellowed.

"You're not in a position to negotiate Mr. Tyler. Here's your wife."

"Ethan is that really you?"

I recognized her voice, and my gut knotted up.

"Katrina, are you okay?"

"Yes Ethan, but don't you dare tell them anything," she gasped.

I heard the sound of a blow or hard slap on the other end.

"You tell my agent all you know, and I'll release her."

I knew that as soon as I gave them the information, Katrina and I were both dead.

"Okay, I'll cooperate. Just don't harm her."

"Give the phone back to Beth," he said, and I obeyed.

He gave her instructions, which I couldn't hear. She answered, "Okay," and hung up.

Beth placed her phone in the record mode.

"Who did you give the information about the Piranha to and what did you tell them?"

There was a loud knock on the door. It startled Beth, and she glanced toward the door. That was all the distraction that I required. I landed a Kung Fu front kick to the stomach. She grunted, dropped the pistol and phone, and tumbled to the floor. I grabbed the gun and walked to the door as she lay gasping for breath.

I looked through the peephole. It was Hank and I opened the door.

"Come in," I said, pointing the pistol at him. "Join the party."

"What in the hell is going on?" he asked, gaping at the girl on the floor.

"Get the duct tape from the dresser and tape her hands, feet and tape her mouth." I ordered.

He looked confused, but followed my orders, probably because there was a gun pointing toward him. Beth was catching her breath and tried to resist, but Hank was an experienced law enforcement officer. After securing her, he turned to me.

"Who is this?"

"She works for a man named Cruise. He abducted Katrina. She wanted information and if I had provided it, I'm sure that she would have shot me. No doubt Katrina would have been killed too. What model car are you driving Hank?"

"What does that matter?"

"Just tell me." I said motioning with the gun.

"A gray Ford Explorer," he replied.

"Someone took a shot at me from a black Escalade, and then this girl came at me. I think more than one person wants me dead and maybe you're one of them."

I picked up Beth's cell phone and erased the commotion that she recorded. I looked at the last number dialed. Now have the number of the kidnapper.

43

Tim struggled to steady his hand as he completed the first injection just below the Femur bone on the left side of Brenda's naked body. Not noticing the trembling hand, Alzar nodded his approval at the location of the injection. *Maybe this kid knows what he's doing,* he thought. Tim repeated with an injection to the other side.

"We're just testing the arms and legs today. We'll inject the brain tomorrow. Doctor, why don't you do the honors and inject the arms and shoulders?" Tim merely wanted to test the ability and knowledge of his new assistant.

Alzar picked up a new syringe and injected Brenda's limp body just to the right of the Deltoid muscles on both sides. He discarded the empty syringe and picked up a fresh one and filled it with Tim's Formula. He carefully chose the area on the left and right sides of the Infraspinatus muscles and made injections.

Timothy Olson knew that his new assistant knew his stuff. "We should see a reaction in less than ten minutes," he said.

Tim poured himself a glass of water, and just as he was about to take a drink, Alzar yelled, "Get over here something's happening!"

Tim rushed to the table. Brenda's eyes were open wide. She glared at him with unabashed fear. She attempted to scream, but nothing came out but a hiss. Then she gritted her teeth and bit her lip. Blood gushed from the split lip.

"Alzar, get something between her teeth," Tim shouted.

Alzar grabbed a towel and tried to pry open her mouth. It was clenched inhumanly tight.

"I can't do it."

"Get back," Tim hissed.

They both backed away from the table.

"Look at her arms and legs," Tim said. Both were growing in size and were already twice as large as normal.

"If the inhibiting substance doesn't kick in quickly, she'll bust open," Alzar was not aware that he was shouting.

"Don't worry it will," Tim replied. His voice was now calm and steely.

The swelling of Brenda's arms and legs subsided. The new muscle definition was astonishing.

"This is how we're going to evolve super beings," Tim said, laughing. "And with brain mass expansion, we will develop the perfect human."

Brenda's head turned sluggishly toward them. Her eyes were bloodshot. She opened her mouth and tried to speak, but no words emerged, only grunts. Tears filled her eyes.

Tim scrutinized his test subject as if she was nothing more than an object. Her humanity was irrelevant to him. He had no compassion for whatever was going through her tortured mind.

She's an odd-looking creature, he thought. Her face was chalky white, and blood seeped from her mouth where she had chewed her lips. Her head was the normal size, but her body resembled a pumped-up weight lifter.

Tears flowed from her eyes freely as she stared at Tim. He giggled. Anger replaced the tears, and Brenda hissed. She strained against the straps around her hands and feet.

"She can't break them can she?" Jesse yelled from the corner of the room.

"Don't be silly," Tim sneered.

Alzar backed away from the table. The incredible rage in the girls face alarmed him. Brenda let out what only could be described as a blood-curdling howl. As the shriek escalated in volume, the straps snapped. Adrenalin had increased her new power.

Brenda leaped off the table, looked down at her deformed body, and went straight for Tim. Alzar grabbed a chair and attempted to hit her. One slap from her hand shattered the chair. She lifted the screaming doctor and effortlessly flung him across the room.

Brenda's eyes flashed at Tim because she knew that he had turned her into a monster. Her strength was astounding and she destroyed everything in her path. She bashed a table when Tim attempted to run. He glanced wildly around the room and saw Jessie cowering in the corner with his pistol drawn.

"Shoot her, shoot her!" he screamed.

With his quivering hand, Jesse shot and hit her in the left leg. She looked down at the bloody wound and turned to face her attacker. Jesse pulled the trigger again and the bullet ripped into her shoulder. She sprinted toward him. He emptied his revolver into her upper body and face as she seized him. After clubbing him with her fist, she put her hands on his neck and squeezed. He wailed as she crushed his Adams apple and flung him aside.

Blood oozed from her wounds, and she staggered. Tim was against the wall not ten feet from her. She looked at him, wavered, and strained to form words.

"I loved you," she croaked, and fell on her face dead. The once promising scientist and loving daughter lay mutilated and lifeless in a puddle of blood.

Tim rested on the floor, struggling to catch his breath. Alzar stumbled toward him. His left arm was twisted and appeared to be broken.

"You screwed up you little bastard," he murmured.

No one outside the laboratory had heard anything because the laboratory was soundproofed.

"Get your ass up and get me some medical help. I don't know what all is broken." Alzar said, and promptly passed out.

Tim grinned. *So far, so good, I need stronger restraints and stronger sedatives,* he thought in his genius, deranged mind.

"Live and learn," he said aloud as he got to his feet and walked toward the door.

44

Ben Cruise departed for town at about 10am. He had been good to Blaze, but she was worried and suspicious concerning his statements about Billy and Ethan. All Ben would tell her was that Billy was recovering at the hospital. Regardless of how much she begged to go to visit him, Ben refused, saying that Billy would be okay. He said he knew nothing about Ethan. She yearned to get away from the ranch and see Billy. Sometimes she felt like a prisoner. She also wondered about the lady in the upstairs room. When she asked Ben about her, he said she was a member of the household help, and that she was sick. That's why she stayed in the room. That didn't make sense to Blaze, but she didn't want to anger Daddy Ben.

Blaze was also disturbed about the way Ben was acting lately. He made comments and insulations about sex to her. One night she woke up in the middle of the night and found Ben standing over her. He told her that he was just checking to see that she was okay. He was old enough to be her father, but she believed that he had other ideas and uses for her. She was not going to let that happen.

On several occasions, he even copped a feel, acting as if it was an accident. Yesterday he kissed her. She pushed him away and he got angry. For a moment she thought he would hit her. Blaze just wanted to get away from the ranch and attempt to find Billy. Things were getting too bizarre for her here.

Another problem was the man with the jagged scar. He constantly gaped at her, and she was frightened of him.

Maybe the lady in the upstairs room could give me some information and help me, she thought. Blaze didn't understand why the lady never left the room, even if she was sick, unless she was a prisoner.

As time passed, she became convinced that Ben kept the woman locked up. She was determined to talk to the lady alone, and today was the perfect time to do it with Ben away.

Blaze persuaded herself that if she was able to restrain Scar, she could get away to see Billy, but she needed the lady's help. She never learned to drive, and it was stupid to leave the ranch on foot.

To begin with, she needed Scar's keys. She knew he had a master key to the house and rooms. She had seen him use it on several occasions. She also observed him driving Ben around in a Black SUV. To escape, she needed the vehicle and a driver. If the woman was a prisoner, as she suspected, the room would be locked. She needed the SUV keys and the master key.

Scar stayed at the ranch to guard them while Ben was away. Blaze recognized that it was now or never. She went to her room and picked out a skimpy white bikini and put it on. She grabbed her purse, went to the kitchen and put a butcher knife inside. Scar was sitting in a lounge chair in the area where she and Ben ate breakfast. He was drinking coffee.

Blaze walked to the area and stood in front of him. "Who is that woman I see looking out the window?"

"None of your business," Scar replied, admiring the sexy young body standing in front of him.

"Can't I talk to her?" Blaze asked, putting on a pouty face.

"Not a chance in hell," Scar responded.

Blaze had little experience acting sensual and seductively, but instinctively she dropped her purse and let her straps fall, revealing most of her firm breasts.

"You know I've always liked you and Daddy Ben is too old for me," she purred.

Scar looked up into her eyes. "Cruise would kill me if I touched you."

"He doesn't have to know," Blaze replied. "I promise I won't tell."

She was in way over her head, but she hoped she could handle it. Her objective was to get his keys before the sexual aggression advanced too far. She could always threaten him with telling Ben, if he became uncontrollable.

Scar grinned, showing his two gold front teeth. "Don't tempt me Blaze."

Blaze unhooked the bikini top and let it fall to the ground.

"Opps," she said. "Why don't we go inside?"

Scar couldn't believe what was happening. He was simply too aroused to care about the consequences. He knew he had to get her inside before the gardener saw them. Cruise had given the other help the day off.

Blaze picked up her purse and began walking. He followed Blaze into the house.

"Where can we go?" Blaze asked.

"Follow me to the study," Scar replied.

They walked into the study, Scar immediately seized her, knocking her purse to the floor. He grunted and grabbed her breasts. After squeezing them for a moment, he moved his hands to her face, held it tight, and kissed her hard on the lips.

"Don't you think you should lock the door?" Blaze whispered, trying to keep her voice from trembling.

Scar turned, took his keys from his pocket, and walked toward the door. Blaze unplugged the brass lamp that was setting on Cruise's desk. She didn't have time to get the knife from her purse. While he was fumbling to get the key into the lock, she quietly walked up behind him and bashed him on the head with the base of the lamp. He fell to his knees and grabbed his head.

With all her might, she hit him again. He fell, unconscious. Blaze grabbed the keys from this hand. The key ring contained car keys and the master. She pulled his wallet from his back pocket, grabbed the cell phone and stuffed both of them in her purse.

Blaze left the study, locked the door and walked up the stairs. She tried several doors that proved to be unlocked and empty.

"Can you hear me?" she yelled. No response. "I know you're up here somewhere. I want to help you."

There were eight rooms in the upstairs of the mansion. She heard what sounded like a woman's voice.

"I'm in here."

"Keep yelling," Blaze shouted.

She walked down the hall and around the corner. The sound was coming from the corner room. She tried the door and it was locked. Unlocking it, she walked in and looked around. A woman lurched from behind the door and grabbed her from behind. Katrina put a headlock on Blaze.

"Who are you?" Katrina asked, breathlessly.

"My name is Blaze and I need your help. Daddy Ben brought me here and won't let me leave to see my injured brother. I locked up the man he left to guard me. He's in the study, and no one else is here but the gardener outside, please, please. I want to leave here. Help me and I'll help you."

Katrina released the girl. "If you're telling the truth, we have to leave right now before Cruise gets back. You can tell me your story when we're away from here. My name is Katrina."

Blaze held up the keys. "I have the keys to his SUV. It's parked out front in the driveway. I don't know how to drive, do you?"

"Of course I do. Let's get going, but young lady you need to put on a shirt. Blaze had forgotten that her breasts were exposed.

Katrina went to the closet, pulled out a T-Shirt and gave it to Blaze. The young girl put it on. They rushed down the stairs and heard banging on the door to the study. The door was solid oak and not likely to be busted down. A gunshot rang out and the bullet came through the door near the lock.

"Lets get out of here fast," Katrina said. "He'll be out soon."

As they sprinted out of the front door, the gardener came running toward them. He was carrying a shovel.

"I heard a gunshot. What's going on Miss Blaze?" he said in severely accented English. "Why is this woman with you?"

Another gunshot rang out from the house. He turned to look.

"I don't think Mr. Ben would want me to let you go anywhere," he said, holding up the shovel as a weapon.

Katrina moved closer to him, "Get out of the way now!" she yelled.

He swung the shovel at her. She side stepped it and crashed a pivot kick to his groin. He collapsed, groaning and holding his crotch.

"There's the truck," Blaze yelled, pointing to the right.

They sprinted toward the vehicle. Katrina grabbed the keys from Blaze's hand and they jumped in. She heard yelling and looked back at the front door. Scar was running toward the truck, pointing the gun. He ran directly in their path. Katrina started the truck and lurched forward.

A bullet from Scar's gun shattered the mirror on the driver's side door. She floor boarded the gas pedal and crashed into him. Specks of blood splattered against the windshield. Katrina backed up and drove around Scar's crushed body.

She was driving eighty as she barreled down the private road to the ranch. When she arrived at the main road, she turned left. She had no idea where she was going, but knew that they needed to get as many miles as possible from the ranch. She made several turns in the next thirty minutes, seeing very little but land and trees. Finally she slowed down and turned to a frightened Blaze.

"Do you have any idea where we are?"

"No, I don't."

"Okay tell me how you got there, and what's this about an injured brother?"

Blaze recounted the story about her parents dying and Ben Cruise putting them in the house outside the cornfield.

Katrina glanced at her, not believing the farfetched story, but the girl appeared sincere.

Blaze told her about Fang and the other man who she found at the edge of the cornfield. She detailed how dangerous Fang was and that the other man saved Billy from him. She recounted the entire story that the man didn't remember anything. Blaze had tears in her eyes as he told Katrina about the two men who came to kill the nice man who helped Billy.

After Blaze finished talking, Katrina sat silently for a moment.

"What happened to the two men who came to kill the stranger?"

"I shot one of them dead, and the other one was taken off by Daddy Ben's men to I don't know where."

"Where is your brother?" asked Katrina.

"Ben said that they took him to the hospital. He was shot."

"They also took Ethan away too, but I don't know where." Blaze said.

"What did you say?" Katrina asked in a startled voice.

"I said they took Ethan away. He was the nice man who I found and who helped us. He said his name was Ethan."

"What about a last name?" Katrina asked in a wavering voice.

"He didn't say."

"Describe him to me."

"He had short black hair, blue eyes and very tall. He was a handsome and rugged looking man, very muscular. Oh yes, he has a small scar near his chin. He was an excellent fighter and was very nice to Billy and me. I really like him and I'm worried about him too."

Katrina pulled over to the side of the road. She had to calm her trembling hands.

"What's wrong?" Blaze asked.

Katrina wiped a tear from her eye. "That was my husband Ethan Tyler. I talked to him a couple of days ago. I was afraid they killed him."

Katrina gathered her emotions.

"We need to get some food and fill the tank with gas. The man I worked for, and trusted most, is the one who kidnapped me and passed me to Cruise. I've got to figure out who to call to help us. We must find your brother and Ethan."

"Bye the way, I got Scarface's cell phone and wallet and I have this," she said, pulling out the butcher knife with the other items.

"How much cash is in the wallet?" Katrina asked.

Blaze counted it. "A couple of hundred and two credit cards"

Katrina smiled. "Good girl. We can work with that."

45

Benjamin Cruise went by the bank and picked up some cash. He also purchased two bottles of Gentleman Jack bourbon and some sexy lingerie to give to Blaze. He was ready to be Daddy Ben to her and deflower the beautiful young girl. He waited long enough, and his lust was at its peak.

Ben checked his cell and was surprised that Beth had not called him with the information that the Piranha wanted. He used her several times on difficult jobs, and she never failed. He also wanted to get in her pants when this was over. As soon as Beth got the information from Tyler, her orders were to kill him. Then after having some fun with Tyler's luscious wife, he would have Carlos kill her and rid himself of the nuisance of having her at his ranch. He wanted to concentrate on Blaze and have her all to himself.

On the way back to the ranch, Ben tuned his radio to the oldies' station.

"I did it my way," Sinatra's golden voice crooned.

Ben loved it and sang along. The sky was Carolina blue with scattered odd-shaped clouds. Another hot beautiful day as he cruised at ninety miles an hour back to Blaze. He invested a lot of patient time and effort, and it was time to collect.

Something is horribly wrong, he thought as he drove to the end of his private road and in sight of the house. Carlos or Scar, as Blaze called him, was lying on the driveway with the gardener bending over him. He screeched to a halt and rushed over.

"Alpio, what happened?" he asked the gardener.

"Miss Blaze and a woman from the house ran him over with the truck," he said in a quivering voice. "I tried to stop them, but the woman kicked me."

Ben pushed him aside and put his finger on Carlo's neck. He felt a faint pulse. It appeared that he had a broken leg and a broken arm. His body was so mangled that Ben had no idea of the extent of the internal injuries.

"Go inside and get some blankets to cover him. He's in shock," he ordered Alpio.

He knew not to move him. Ben jerked out his cell and punched in the number of the Mexican doctor he used. He couldn't take Carlos to the hospital because the police would ask questions, and he didn't want any law enforcement involved. He paid handsomely for Dr. Jay Delgado to handle any medical emergencies, and keep it to himself. Delgado primarily worked for the drug cartels.

"Dr. Delgado's office," a cheery female voice answered.

"This is Benjamin Cruise. I need to speak with him immediately."

"Yes sir, Mr. Cruise."

After a five-minute wait, the unruffled, resonate voice answered, "What can I do for you, Mr. Cruise?"

"I need you here immediately. A car hit one of my men. He's unconscious and in shock. I think he has a broken leg and broken arm. He's breathing but his pulse is weak."

"I will be there in thirty minutes and will bring my nurse and the necessary medical supplies. I have a fully equipped van. Where is he located?"

"He lying on the driveway, and we've covered him with blankets."

"Here's what I want you to do. If he's on his back lift his feet about a foot higher than the head. If raising the legs will cause pain or further injury, keep him flat and still. Check for signs of circulation problems, breathing, coughing or movement, and if absent, begin CPR. Keep him warm and comfortable by loosening any belts or tight clothing and keep him covered with a blanket. Even if the person complains of thirst, give nothing by mouth. Turn him on his side to prevent choking if he vomits or bleeds. I'm leaving now to take care of this."

Ben threw the phone to the side, and with Alpio assistance, followed the instructions. In a few minutes, Carlos opened his eyes. He tried to speak but couldn't.

"Just lie still, the doctor's on his way."

The black van stopped ten feet away. The Doctor, and his male nurse rushed to the place where Carlos lay. The Doctor knelt his short stocky body and looked at Carlos. Beads of sweat dotted his bald forehead. The nurse was tall, lanky, muscular and wore a white uniform. He carried a large bag.

"Just get out of the way and let us work," Delgado ordered.

Ben and the gardener moved. The nurse ran back to the vehicle and brought a gurney. After preparing splints on the arm and leg and wrapping his ribs tightly in gauze, they lifted him onto the gurney and wheeled him to the van. They took out a stand pole and hooked up two IV's. A rolling oxygen tank was removed from the van, and a mask was placed over Carlos' nose.

"Let's get him in the house and situated in a bed," the Doctor said.

"Go back to work Alpio," Cruise ordered. "I'll talk to you later."

Carlos was placed in a guest room, and Delgado continued working on him. Cruise went to his study and directly to the bar. He poured a large shot of Gentleman Jack and downed it. He knew that the Piranha would be furious.

After about thirty minutes, Dr. Delgado joined him. "I'll have one of those," he said pointing to Cruise's drink.

"Your man has a broken arm, a fractured leg and two cracked ribs. He's also suffering from a concussion. His injuries are severe and he is lucky to be alive. He needs caring for and watching. I'll leave the nurse here for a couple of days until he's out of danger."

"Thanks Doc," replied Cruise as he walked to his safe. He filled an envelope with cash and handed it to Delgado. "I included a bonus for your quick response and for the nurse. I sincerely appreciate your availability and discretion."

Delgado took the envelope, finished his drink and left without saying another word.

Cruise knew it was impossible to know where the two women went. They were probably a hundred miles from his ranch now, and who knows in what direction.

He rubbed his eyes and picked up the cell phone. He knew he must inform the Piranha immediately or suffer severe consequences. The only thing in the world that he feared was that psychopath. On the third ring, the deep voice answered.

"This better be an emergency, Cruise."

Cruise got straight to the point. "Tyler's wife escaped, and I haven't heard anything from Beth. I don't know if she obtained the information you wanted or not."

"You incompetent asshole!" the Piranha roared. "How did you let this happen?"

"A young female guest, who was staying here, somehow subdued the guard and got her out. That's all I know."

There was silence on the other end of the line. The Piranha composed himself and said in a calm resolute voice. "I doubt that she knows how to reach her husband. Because of her kidnapping, she will be hesitant to call her superiors. We must assume that Tyler thinks she's still there. If he somehow got away from your assassin, he'll still try to contact you. When that occurs, you just say that his wife is still there, and he must come to meet you, if she is to remain alive."

"Yes sir, I keep you informed."

"You better clean this up Cruise. I need to know what Tyler knows about me and who he's discussed it with. If I fall, you fall."

Cruise hung up the phone and poured another Gentleman Jack. There was nothing he could do now but wait.

46

I had to make a determination about Hank. I've known him for a long time, and he has never given me any reason to distrust him. I lowered the gun.

"Sit down Hank and tell me what's going on at Langley."

"Wait," Hank said as he walked to the bathroom and grabbed two washcloths. He stuffed them in Beth's ears and secured them with a piece of duct tape around her head and ears.

"Director Henria is convinced that you've been compromised and gone over to the other side. You know the directive when that happens, elimination."

"Did he send you here to kill me?" I asked, tightening my grip on the pistol.

"Listen Ethan, I've known you long enough that I tried to convince him that you would never turn, but he's a stickler for undercover CIA procedures. That's why I didn't tell him that you contacted me, or that I'm here with you. We need to work together to get this mess straightened out and find Katrina."

"How did Cruise get her? She's too smart to be led into a trap, unless it was someone she knew and trusted."

"I don't know. She just disappeared," he replied.

I knew that I required his help in obtaining the necessary information about this Benjamin Cruise and his location. Sources inside the CIA would have to be contacted to secure the information.

"I'm going to trust you Hank. There's no other choice. I have information that will gravely affect the United States government and the CIA. While I was undercover working with Herman and Ted, I heard information that astounded me. With all that's happened, I haven't had any opportunity to act on it and I didn't know who I can trust. I'm sure you've heard of the criminal kingpin they call 'The Piranha."

Hank nodded, stood up and lowered his eyes.

"Herman and Ted worked directly for him. Herman figured out that he's inside the CIA. They received information from the Piranha that could only have come from the highest levels of the CIA. They speculated as to who he is. Ted was certain that the speculation was correct. Herman joked about it to me stating that no matter what happened, the Piranha would protect us. I'm sure if this was investigated that we could find additional proof of his identity. A source of mine already has some questionable proof. All we would have to do is to put our suspect under secret surveillance, using the Espionage Act."

Beads of sweat gathered on Hank Thompson's brow. He took a deep breath. "I'm sure that if we shared this information with the Director, he would clear you and agree to the surveillance."

"No," I said. "That won't work."

"Ethan, we need his help."

I rubbed my eyes and was silent for a moment. I looked up, and Hank was staring at the gun in my hand. I thought that was curious, but I decided to disclose the information to him. I was powerless without some help from inside the CIA.

"I believe the Piranha is Director C.T. Henria."

Hank expelled a deep breath, "Who else have you told?"

"One other person knows and has some critical information, which may prove or disapprove my suspicion, but I can't reveal the name now. He's certain, if given the chance, that he could name the Piranha."

I was stating half-truths because of my instinctive distrust of Thompson.

"This is going to be tricky," Hank said. "We'll need to go directly to the Attorney General, but we must have proof rather than speculation."

"My friend has the proof and again, he can validate if my belief is correct or not about Henria."

Hanks body language was disturbing to me, but I continued, "Let's discuss the prevailing disaster. Katrina's life is in danger and we can't report it. I've got to rescue her, and I hope that you'll help me." I heard a racket and looked to the source. Beth was struggling.

"She must know Cruise's whereabouts, maybe we can get the information from her."

I walked over to her, knelt and ripped the cloths and tape from her ears.

"Beth, I'm going to remove the tape from your mouth. If you scream, I'll put it back on and just leave you in the trunk of your car. Perhaps someone will find you or maybe you'll just die there. That would be horrible. If you lie to me, it's the trunk of your car. This gentleman," I pointed to Hank, "can verify what you disclose to me, so don't lie. Do you understand?"

She stared at Hank and nodded. I tore the tape from her mouth. She gasped and coughed. I turned on the record function on her phone.

"Beth, what's your real name?"

"Adla Bagrov," she replied with a Russian accent. The girl certainly mastered English, as I didn't detect any accent before.

"Okay, so far so good. You said that Benjamin Cruise sent his regards. Did he hire you to extract information from me and kill me?" she nodded.

"Answer me."

"Yes," she murmured.

"Do you know the girl Katrina?"

"No," she replied.

"Where does Cruise live?"

"I don't know. We communicate by phone or meet personally in Abilene."

''Do you work exclusively for him?"

"No, I do contract work for many people."

Hank and I both were trained in reading body language and eye movement. I looked at him, and he nodded, indicating that he agreed that she appeared to be telling the truth.

"Where is your car and what model?"

"White Lexus, parked in front."

I turned off the record function, picked up her shoulder bag from the floor, and emptied the contents on the bed. In the wallet, I found a drivers license that read, *Bethany Hopkins.* Obviously fake. In the compartment behind the driver's license was an American Express card bearing the name, Alda Bagrov. There was about two hundred dollars in the wallet. The remainder of the bag contained car keys, a switchblade knife, makeup items, condoms and a bottle of pills.

"I'll be right back Hank. I'm going to check the car." Hank was unusually quiet during the whole process.

The white Lexus was parked just outside the entrance. I unlocked it and searched the glove department. The rental-car papers were there in the name of Bethany Hopkins. A thick envelope was under the papers. I opened it, and discovered about twenty thousand dollars and a picture of me. I pocketed the money since it was becoming increasingly dangerous to continue to use Hedrick's credit cards. The money must have been the partial payment for the contract to kill me. There was noting else of interest in the car, so I returned to the room. As I walked in, Hank was talking to her. They stopped talking as soon as I closed the door.

"I was attempting to get more information," he said.

I stuck the tape over her mouth and replaced the cloths in her ears.

"Hank, I'm going to call this Cruise guy and attempt to set up a meeting. Can you call a trusted contact in the CIA and get some information on him, primarily where he lives?"

"I can probably acquire that information by tomorrow afternoon," Hank replied. "I'll return to Langley and also attempt to secure additional information on Henria's activities, but I need the proof that your friend has."

"I swore to keep his name out of this," I said, "but I'll call and ask permission to tell you and convey the information to you."

I grabbed a pen and note pad from the desk and sat down.

"I'm calling Cruise now," I said as I punched the phone to redial the last number called.

On the second ring a man answered, "Yes."

"Is this Benjamin Cruise?"

"Who wants to know?" he replied.

"Ethan Tyler here. Beth failed in both her attempt to get information from me or to kill me. We must deal one on one. First, if you lay one finger on Katrina, I will hunt you down and kill you deliberately and painfully. I'm good at what I do, and I promise it will be excruciating."

"We need to meet," Cruise replied. "If you give me the information I want, I'll release your wife to you. No tricks, even trade."

I knew he sought a face-to-face meeting to arrange an ambush. There was no way he would intentionally let Katrina and I live. However, if I had any chance to rescuing her, I had to play along.

"Okay, where and when?"

"Where are you now?" he asked.

"Tyler, Texas."

"Athens, Texas is about seventy miles away. Meet me there tomorrow. You call me at precisely 8pm and I'll give you directions to a secure meeting place. I'll have Katrina with me. Be alone or she's dead and by the way, your threats are meaningless to me."

I wrote down the details and hung up.

"The meeting set for 8pn tomorrow night near Athens," I told Hank.

"You know he'll not be alone and probably have a sniper waiting on you," he said.

"I don't have any choice Hank. I'm leaving now. Call me tomorrow as soon as you have any information on Cruise or Hernia. I'll call you if anything changes here. I really appreciate your help."

"What about the girl?" Hank asked, motioning to Adla.

"Hank, she was honest with us and she won't dare try anything considering the information I have on that recording. Let's just put her in her rental car and secure her to the steering wheel. I'm sure she's very resourceful."

I walked to where she was lying and removed the ear cloths and the tape from her mouth.

"Listen, Alda, we're not going to kill you. I've got your confession recorded, and I know your actual identity. If you try to find either of us or have any additional involvement, I'll release the tape to the police, and tell this Cruise guy that you crossed him and took off with the money. You know if I do that your life won't be worth two cents. Your best bet is to get as far away from here as possible."

She nodded.

I looked outside, and there was no one in the parking lot. I taped her mouth, grabbed the roll of duct tape and carried her to the Lexus. I sat her behind the steering wheel and securely taped her hands to it. I stretched a piece of tape around her neck and around the lower part of the wheel to keep her head out of sight, closed the door and locked it.

Hank was on the phone when I returned to the room.

"Beth is secure, and I'm leaving now. Will you dispose of her purse?" I threw the keys to the car on the bed with the other items. I stuck her gun in my belt.

"Will do Ethan, I'll be in touch."

I wanted to get to Athens, get a room and check out the area in the morning. That nagging feeling about Hank Thompson remained as I drove out of the parking lot.

When Ethan Tyler left, Thompson wiped the room clean of fingerprints. He placed the remaining items in the purse, except for the switchblade and keys and left the room. Thompson stuck the car keys and the knife in his pocket.

After depositing the purse in his SUV, he walked to the white Lexus and opened the door. Without speaking, he snatched the switchblade from his pocket, opened it and thrust it deep into Alda's neck at the base of her skull. Grunts came from beneath the taped mouth. He plunged it deeper until the grunts ceased. For no reason other than viciousness, he slit her throat from ear to ear.

Thompson wiped the door handle, and the knife clean with his handkerchief and threw the switchblade inside the car with the dead body. He bumped the door shut with his hip and returned to his SUV. The flight to Langley was leaving in forty-five minutes.

He popped in a CD. "Love me tender, love me sweet. Never let me go," Elvis sang as he drove toward the airport.

Hank Thompson chuckled and sang along.

47

The restraints on the operating table were replaced with steel cuffs for the hands, neck and feet. The table was stainless steel. Tim Olsen was taking no chances on this experiment going array, as did the one with Brenda. Case Study Three's heavily sedated body was brought in by his keeper Isaac, and placed on the operating table. The cuffs were securely locked and tested. Drugs deadened Ted's violent mind.

Dr. Alzar Frontier walked into the room with his left arm in a cast and sling.

"Are you sure he's secure?"

Tim glared at the Doctor. "If you don't like it, get out."

"Cain wants me here and he's the boss," Alzar replied.

"Then keep your mouth shut and do as you're told," Tim hissed.

Alzar gritted his teeth and remained silent. As soon as it was feasible, Cain had assured him that he could take over the project, and he was looking forward to personally muzzling this young punk.

Tim prepared the Formula and the syringes.

"I'll handle the injections and you observe," he said to Alzar. "You're not much help with that busted arm."

Tim turned on the recorder. He planned to record all his actions, and the Case Study's responses. Hence if successful, he could duplicate the procedures. He adjusted the headset and the microphone and began.

"I am going to conduct this experiment differently from the initial test. The first experiment, on the female, produced pronounced mass in the muscles of the arms and legs without the improved mental capacity to handle the changes within the body. I will start on Case Study Three with injections to induce mass growth in the lobes of the brain. I'm going to generate brain mass growth in all the lobes. The Frontal Lobe, which is associated with reasoning, planning, parts of speech, movement, emotions, and problem solving will receive the maximum mass growth. The Parietal Lobe, which is associated with movement, orientation, recognition, and perception of stimuli, will be increased by twenty-seven percent. The Occipital Lobe, which is associated with visual processing, will need less improvement. The Temporal Lobe, associated with perception and recognition of auditory stimuli, memory, and speech will be selectively enhanced."

He walked to the table, which contained the Formula and turned to Alzar.

"I decided that you can participate, Prepare the patient by hooking up an IV drip and attach the oxygen mask. Isaac, you assist him. The stress on the brain could cause breathing problems."

Tim moved to the cabinet and grabbed a low-speed drill.

"Contrary to your theory of allowing my Higgs boson Formula to enter the brain through the blood stream, Dr. Frontier, I prefer to inject it directly to the lobe areas, so I can differentiate the amount of mass growth in each lobe. I will do this by drilling small holes in Case Study Three's skull in the specific areas where the lobes are located. These holes will remain open to release the pressure as the brain gains mass."

"How will the skull, which has definite space, hold the increased mass?" Alzar asked.

Tim looked at him and laughed while dismissively lecturing him.

"Humans use virtually every part of the brain, and most of the brain is active almost all the time. Let's put it this way: the brain represents three percent of the body's weight and uses twenty percent of the body's energy. The average human brain weighs about three pounds and comprises the hefty cerebrum, which is the largest portion and performs all higher cognitive functions; the cerebellum, responsible for motor functions, such as the coordination of movement and balance; and the brain stem, dedicated to involuntary functions like breathing. The majority of the energy consumed by the brain powers the rapid firing of millions of neurons communicating with each other. With the brain weighting just three pounds, an increase in mass even at a fifty percent would only add one and a half pounds. The skull can handle this increase, I believe. With appropriate mass growth in the muscles, enough additional energy can be produced to handle the increased brain activity. Does your brain have the necessary mass to understand this?"

Alzar gritted his teeth, but said nothing. Tim walked over with a marker and placed four X's on different locations of the sedated man's skull.

"Isaac, get a sterilized straight razor from the cabinet and shave the areas I marked, under the supervision of Alzar. I know he's bald but there may be a stubble of hair in the areas. I will perform the craniotomy."

While Isaac complied with Alzar standing over him, Tim prepared the Trepanation instruments which had diamond-coated rims. Again, he lectured Alzar.

"These are less traumatic than the classical trephines with sharp teeth. They are smooth to soft tissue and only cut the bone."

Tim placed the instruments and vials containing the Higgs boson Formula on the stand beside operating table. He added four syringes, all remained in the sterilized packages.

"Gentlemen shall we begin?" he said, donning his headset.

Tim flipped down his magnifying scope and proceeded to cut small incisions in the scalp, pulled back the skin flap and precisely drilled the minuscule holes in the designated areas. Dr. Frontier assisted by keeping the area clean of the bone and matter with a surgical vac. When the holes were completed and the areas cleaned and sterilized, he took the first syringe, ripped open the package, and filled it with a measured portion of the Formula. He was specific in his placement of the injection. He proceeded to perform the next three injections with different amounts of the Formula. Since Alzar only had one usable hand, Tim stitched the flaps and bandaged the areas.

"If you administered the correct amount of sedative, our patient will be awake in about thirty minutes. The mass growth should be completed by then. Watch the patient and call me if there is any movement or physical reaction. I'll be back in twenty-five," he said to Alzar, and walked out of the laboratory.

Cain was observing the entire procedure in his office through the cameras and microphones installed in the laboratory. He had Tim's recording of the procedure and the film of the operation. If this brain procedure and the muscle mass enhancement are successful, he would posses the necessary information to perform future procedures using a qualified surgeon, with or without Olsen. He had the exact formulation of the Higgs boson Formula, but it might be changed depending on this experiment.

In precisely twenty-five minutes, Timothy Olsen walked back into the room. He was sipping a cup of coffee.

"Any reactions from Case Study Three?" he said casually as he removed the oxygen mask from Ted's face.

"None," replied Alzar.

All of a sudden, an excruciating howl filled the room. Ted's bloodshot eyes flew open and frantically looked around the room. Perspiration popped out, drenching his face. The neck clamp securing his head limited his movement.

"Don't worry he just disoriented and trying to control the massive increase of neurons firing off in his brain. The brain must adjust to its present capacity," Tim said, principally to himself.

Alzar wet a cloth with cold water and wiped away the perspiration. Ted seemed to be calmed by this action. His lips moved as he tried to form words. "Paaҏnnnnn, paineeee," came out in breathless gasps.

"I know it hurts man," Tim snickered. "Your body is not producing enough energy to make up for the increased brain activity."

Ted struggled, but the steel clamps held him down. As suddenly as the howl occurred, he calmed down. His eyes cleared and he appeared to be thinking.

"I can control the pain with my mind," he said clearly, but with a detached voice. "I need additional energy."

"He's reasoning now," Tim said. "His control and brain lobe adjustments are realigning. We need to perform the muscle mass procedures to produce the additional energy to allow the brain to operate at full capacity."

Tim introduced a sedative into the IV drip. Ted watched him with his peculiar intense eyes. Within minutes his eyes closed, and he was unconscious.

"Okay Alzar, observe a master at work."

Tim proceeded to inject the Formula in the same areas where the successful mass growth in Brenda has occurred. The three men observed as the skin stretched in the arms and legs as muscle mass ensued. The transformation took less than ten minutes.

"Now we must to wait to observe the alignment of the augmented brain and the enhanced body. We're watching the evolution of a human that before now could only be accomplished with God and time. If successful, we have skipped a hundred years of evolution. Gentlemen, you're observing a human God at work. This is Evolution on Steroids. My mind games are epic. The scientist should change the name from the God Particle to the Olsen Particle."

He's truly a psychopath and as people have said there is only a thin line between genius and madness. He's crossed the line, Alzar thought.

48

After setting up the meeting with Tyler, Ben Cruise punched in the secure number of the Piranha.

The familiar voice answered, "What now Organizer? Conversely, do you prefer Daddy Ben?" maniacal laughter filled the phone signal.

"I've set up a meeting with Ethan Tyler for tomorrow. He believes that I still have his wife."

"Through my sources, I know there is another person who has evidence of my identity. I need that name and presently only Tyler can provide it. Get the information any way you can and have him killed. Send someone better than the Russian girl. She's dead."

"Alda is dead?" Cruise said in a stunned voice. "Did Tyler kill her?"

"He raped her and killed her," the Piranha lied. Cruise had enjoyed a sexual relationship for three years with Alda. He had grown fond of her, and the news angered him. He wanted to kill Tyler and make him suffer before he died.

"And another thing Cruise, I must have control of Future Mankind Ventures. That young scientist had a breakthrough in his Higgs boson Formula. I'll need Cain out of the picture. Sergey Petrof is the Vice Chairman of the Board. He'll take over when elected by the board. Meanwhile, you can manage the firm. I demand that Cain disappear without a trace straightaway. Are you capable of handling this?"

"Hell yes," Cruise replied.

"Also, we can begin the process of purchasing stock through our phantom companies to gain controlling interest of the company."

Immediately after ending the call with the Piranha, Cruise made another call to The Man.

"It's time to initiate the plan we discussed."

"I'm pleased that you called. This place is transforming into a house of lunatics. That kid Olsen is certifiable and I'm afraid he'll screw up the long-term uses of his Formula."

"Right now, Cain controls him, and Cain is a conniving bastard. Cain needs to disappear without a trace. I don't want the body ever found," Cruise said.

"I'll have this accomplished within twenty-four hours," The Man replied.

"Dump the body in the cornfield. There's a pack of coyotes that have established territorial rights and will drag the body to their den and devour it. I'll have a crew there tomorrow to harvest the marijuana fields on the other side of the laboratory. The crew boss is Roy Lopez, in case you need help."

"I can handle it. Cain trusts me." The Man replied. Alzar hung up the phone. He was the Man and soon he would be very rich.

Cruise had everything in order. After these present situations were handled, he would initiate the search for Blaze. He had too much time invested to give her up. When he got her back to the ranch, he planned to get her hooked on drugs, and she could service him probably for a year before her body and mind would begin to break down. Then, as usual, he would target another young lady. Daddy Ben likes diversity.

Cruise had no intention of personally attending the meeting with Tyler. He planned to send a crew of his henchmen and a Katrina look alike. He wanted to be finished with Tyler, so he could proceed with more important matters, which would elevate him to one of the wealthiest and most powerful men throughout the world.

Cruise's drug cartel regularly contracted a man they called the Midnight Slicer. The Slicer was of Asian descent and was a master of martial arts, especially in the art of Gōjū-ryū. In the few lessons that Cruise had taken, he learned that the style incorporates both circular and linear movements into its curriculum, combining hard striking attacks such as kicks and close hand punches with softer open hand circular techniques for attacking, blocking, and controlling the opponent, including locks, grappling, takedowns and throws. He quit after five lessons. It required too much meditation to suit his style.

The Slicer acquired the name because he never used firearms. He preferred to use a knife or Japanese akaiittou- red blade sword, and preferred his killings as near to midnight as possible. He worshiped Amaterasu, the goddess of the sun. She did not allow blood to be spilled while she dominated the skies. Only in the cloak of darkness when the God Emma-hoo ruled did death take it rightful place. Even though the Slicer did not use firearms, his henchmen did. He wasn't a fool.

Cruise punched in the number. After eight rings, he was prepared to hang up when he heard a click.

"Moshi Moshi." The tranquil voice answered.

"This is Benjamin Cruise. I have a job for you and I'm willing to pay 100,000 American dollars if you're capable of fully accomplishing what I require. The job is in Athens, Texas tomorrow night. Are you available?"

"Hai," the Slicer replied.

"You will be meeting a man at a designated place of my choosing near Athens, Texas tomorrow night at approximately 9pm. You'll need to bring a woman with you." Cruise described Katrina.

"She must fit that general description of height and weight and hair color. You can cover her face with a bag to make it more convincing. Stay at least forty feet away from the man you're meeting. The women should be bounded and gagged, and you need to be prepared to slit her throat. Stand in front of your vehicle with the lights on. I'll be engaging the man in conversation over the phone to get information. He'll be told that if he doesn't give me the information you will kill the woman. He believes it's his wife. Once he gives me the information I'll ask him to give the phone to you. After I verify, kill him."

"I understand," was the placid response.

"You can use as many men as you need, and I'll increase the payment accordingly."

"I only need myself, Gensai and a sniper," the Slicer replied. "But the meeting must be at midnight, otherwise I decline."

"I'll arranged it at midnight and I'll call you tomorrow with the location."

"Oyasuminasai," the Slicer replied and hung up.

Cruise rubbed his eyes. He was so tired of dealing with eccentric people, nonetheless the deal was set up to his satisfaction.

He poured a shot of Gentleman Jack and sipped it. The next two days would be eventful and if The Man and the Midnight Slicer accomplished their tasks, he and the Piranha were set for their reign of power.

Ben figured he could handle the situation from the ranch. No need to fly to Athens. He poured another shot of bourbon and walked to the door of his office. The household help had returned, and he required some relaxation. He yelled for Miranda, his chief housekeeper. She hurried to the door.

"Yes Sir, Mr. Cruise."

"Send Simone to my bedroom."

He proceeded to the bedroom suite and undressed. He pulled back the comforter on the bed and lay down on the black silk sheets. There was a soft knock at the door.

"Come in Simone," he said.

The door opened, and the ravishing young lady strolled in. Her long black hair flowed past her shoulders, and her brown eyes were sparkling. Ben especially loved her sexy full lips.

"Daddy Ben, I'm delighted to serve you," she said as she undressed. She climbed into the bed and pressed her soft breasts against him.

"I want to make you happy."

Cruise didn't utter a word and after thirty minutes of intense lovemaking, he rolled over on his back.

"You can go now," he said.

The gorgeous young girl picked up the four one hundred dollar bills laying on the end table.

"Thank you Daddy Ben."

After a hot shower, Cruise fell into a deep sleep. He never dreamed because he never denied himself anything.

Tomorrow would be an important day and he required his rest.

49

Katrina and Blaze drove for another thirty minutes until the local road intersected with State Highway 71. Once turning on the highway and driving a few miles, Katrina glanced at the fuel gage and saw that it was flat on empty. She was sure that they were going to be stranded on the highway, when she noticed a sign that read, *Entering the city limits of Brady, Texas.* There was a convenience store just beyond the sign. She pulled in, and using Carlos' credit card, filled the tank with gas.

"I need some cash," she said. Blaze handed her all the cash in the wallet that she had taken from Carlos.

After using the facilities, Katrina told Blaze to wait in the car while she went into the store. She grabbed a couple of Cokes, cheese crackers and two cellophane wrapped ham sandwiches.

The counter guy's head was buried in a book. Katrina looked at the title, actually expecting a porn novel. Instead the title was "The Spirit Survives."

"Good book?" she asked as she placed the items on the counter.

The young guy looked up. He was probably in his late teens with a shaved head and acne scarred face. Rings penetrated his nose and lips.

"This guy Ramsey is the best I've ever read. His apprehension of several genres at once is different from most writers." He said in a clearly educated voice.

Looks can often fool you, Katrina thought.

"Did you find all you needed Miss?" he asked.

"I want these items and a map of Texas."

Shaved Head reached under the counter and pulled out a worn map and handed it to her.

"On the House."

"Thanks, can you tell me where the nearest Walmart is located?"

"Get on US highway 87 about a mile from here and go north. Exit on South Bridge Street. You'll see it on the right."

She paid for the items, thanked him and returned to the SUV. Katina pulled the truck away from the gas tanks and parked near the entrance of the store. She and Blaze ate the sandwiches and crackers.

"Blaze, we need to pick up a few things. We'll require a change of clothes, underwear, and some toiletries. We can pick them up at Walmart. After that, we should have a decent dinner while we figure out a place to stay, and what we're going to do next."

"We gotta find Billy. I think Daddy Ben may have hurt him and lied to me about where he is." Blaze had tears in her eyes. "Maybe Billy went back to the house."

"I understand," Katrina replied. "When we find him, maybe Ethan is with him or Billy knows where to find him. We need Ethan to help us figure out what to do."

They proceeded to the Walmart and picked up jeans, T-Shirts, underwear and the necessary toiletries. She went through the self-checkout area and the stolen card was accepted without a problem.

"We ought to find a motel and plan what we're going to do tomorrow," she told Blaze.

They got back on Highway 87, and shortly saw signs for The Gold Key Inn. Katina exited, drove to the motel and they checked in. It was a comfortable room with two double beds, a desk and chairs and a coffee pot. After showering, Katrina sat on the bed and opened the map. The nearest city of any decent size was Abilene. It was a couple of hours away.

Blaze fell on the other bed after finishing her shower. "What do we do now Katrina?" she asked. She was clearly frustrated.

"The nearest city is Abilene. Wichita Falls is close by. Ethan and I go there every year for relaxation and fishing at Lake Arrowhead. There is a beautiful quaint bed and breakfast there with magnificent views of the lake. We both love to fish and Lake Arrowhead has some of the best large mouth bass fishing in Texas. It's our place to unwind."

"Wait," Blaze said in an excited voice. "When Daddy Ben came to bring us supplies, sometimes we needed other things. I heard him tell Carlos to go to Abilene to pick them up. Carlos would be gone for a couple of hours, maybe a little more. The house where we stayed, and the cornfield we were guarding, has to be near there. Maybe Billy went home. I don't know, I don't know." She began crying. "I don't know what to think."

"Please Blaze, what you said is important. That's the only lead we have. We'll go to Abilene and see what we can find out. Tell me more about the area where your house is located."

"It was secluded and at the end of a dirt road. There was a large cornfield behind the house. Billy was walking at the end of the dirt road one time when Carlos left to pick up additional supplies, and he said that Carlos went north. One other time Billy and me walked to the end of the dirt road to the paved road. There was a sign that read *State Highway 84*. We trusted Daddy Ben and never thought of running away."

Katrina breathed sigh of relief. Now she had something to work on. If they could find the house that Blaze was talking about, maybe they could discover leads about the whereabouts of Ethan and Billy.

"Blaze, we're off to Abilene first thing in the morning. Get some sleep."

There was a lite mist coming off Lake Arrowhead on that cool September morning. They had gotten up at 5am to take their rented Bass boat to the fishing sweet spot. The stress of their jobs melted away when they were here. Ethan kissed her and started the motor.

"I love you, Katrina," he said softly.

"Oh Ethan, I love you too," she said, hugging him. She was the happiest when she and Ethan were alone together.

"Woman, get off me if you want me to drive this boat," he said, laughing. "We've got to catch dinner and with an albatross like you hanging around my neck, we'll probably catch nothing." Ethan was an expert fisherman and Katrina usually only caught three-inch perch.

Katrina punched him on the arm. "We'll see about that," she said.

When they reached the sweet spot, Ethan tied on a top water plug and began casting. Katrina reached into the box of night crawlers, strung one on the hook and cast it toward the grass along the shore. She sat back and waited.

"You lazy girl, you won't catch anything like that," Ethan said, and laughed again.

The water exploded on his plug and he set the hook. "Got a big one here," he said. "Get the net."

Katrina laid her rod down and grabbed the net. Just before Ethan got the fish to the boat, it jumped and shook the hook out of its mouth."

"Ethan, you've got to set the hook better," Katrina giggled.

"Oh, shut up," he said, casting again.

Katrina picked up her rod and immediately saw the line slowly peeling out. She waited patiently and put a little pressure on the line. The fish began taking out line fast. Katrina lifted the rod in the air and jerked back hard to set the hook. The fish kept taking out line and drag. Ethan dropped his rod and came to her side.

"Just take it easy," he said. "Keep pressure on him and tire him out."

Katrina would reel in a couple of yards and the fish would take off again, pulling drag. Her arm was getting sore, but she wasn't about to ask Ethan for help. She fought the fish for twenty minutes when it began to tire. Finally she brought him to the boat and Ethan netted him.

"Now, that's a whopper," he said.

Ethan removed the hook and weighted the Bass.

"Twelve pounds," he said. "Oh my God, a twelve pound large mouth Bass."

"Well Ethan, maybe I can instruct you on successful techniques to catch fish," Katrina said, and punched him in the side.

He dropped the fish in the cooler. Except for a few Bluegills that Katrina caught with worms and threw back, no other fish were landed.

"You'll probably never let me live this down, will you Katrina?"

"Not for the rest of your life," she replied, and kissed him.

Miss Barth, the manager of the Bed and Breakfast, prepared the Bass for diner. They watched her as she expertly prepared to bake the fish.

"Okay guys this is my special recipe. First I take 3 cloves garlic, minced, jalapeno, minced, kosher salt and freshly ground black pepper, 5 tablespoons butter, plus more for greasing the foil. Then add 1/4-pound okra, chopped red bell pepper, diced, 2 tablespoons chopped fresh parsley leaves and 2 tablespoons white wine."

She preheated the oven to 450, scored the sides of the filets, three times on each side. She combined the minced garlic and jalapeno and stuffed the mixture into each of the slits. Then she rubbed the fish with salt and pepper and marinated it for 30 minutes.

Miss Barth served it to them with grilled mixed veggies.

That evening, accompanied by a French Sauvignon Blanc fine white wine, they enjoyed the expertly baked delicious fish. They sat alone on the deck of the bed and breakfast with candles flickering. Katrina thought her heart would melt on that wonderful evening. Ethan was with the love or her life and he felt the same endless love for her.

"Katrina, wake up, wake up," Blaze said as she shook her shoulders. "We need to get started."

She opened her eyes with the soft glow of the magnificent dream still tenderly lingering in her mind.

Blaze had already showered and dressed. She looked like an innocent teenager, and was eager to find her brother. Katrina showered and donned her new jeans and T-Shirt.

They checked out and stopped at the first drive though fast food restaurant. Katrina ordered a large black coffee and a sausage biscuit. It was orange juice and a bacon breakfast taco for Blaze.

Katrina stopped in the parking lot and studied the map. Since there were populated areas and small towns to the north of Abilene, she figured that the location they were looking for was probably south in the less populated areas. The main highway coming into the city from the south was Highway 84. That was probably the road that Carlos took when he went for supplies. She realized that these were assumptions, but all she had to go on was her gut.

"Blaze, we're going to take this road for about an hour, and then catch Highway 84 and go south of Abilene. We'll pass Dyess Airforce Base and keep driving from there."

"If we pass any hospitals can we stop in and see if Billy's a patient?" Blaze asked.

"Of course."

After passing the Airforce Base, Katrina stopped at a gas station and topped off the tank. She knew that there were stretches in West Texas with miles and miles of nothing but mesquite trees and dried up land. They used the restroom, picked up a couple of Cokes and snacks and continued what she thought was probably a wild goose chase.

After they passed by Buffalo Gap, population 463, they hit a stretch of road that could be best described as nothingness.

Blaze was staring out the window when suddenly she yelled, "Stop Katrina, stop!" Katrina braked, and pulled over to the side of the road. They had not seen another car in over forty-five minutes.

"Back up. See that dirt road. It looks familiar to me. When Billy and I walked to the end that day to the paved highway, it resembled this place."

Katrina backed up, knowing that a lot of dirt roads connected to this Highway and the chance that this was the one to the house was miniscule. She turned and drove down the road anyway.

"Do you remember anything on this road?" She asked Blaze.

"No, it isn't the one," she replied and hung her head.

There was no place to turn around on the narrow road. There were deep ditches on either side for rain runoff. Katrina had to continue until she found a place wide enough to turn around.

They proceeded about a mile and came upon a clearing with a log cabin situated in front of several large oak trees. There was a shed visible in the back and a truck parked at the side of the cabin. Texas Blue Bonnets bloomed all around the yard. Several rose bushes were in full bloom in front of the house. The blooms were dark blue. Katrina had never seen roses that color. The house was clearly inhabited.

"Maybe we can ask these people about the cornfield and the surrounding areas," Katrina said.

While opening the vehicle door, she heard a loud voice, "Stay put."

She looked around and an old grey haired man holding a double-barreled shotgun stepped out from behind right side of the house. He was bent over with age, but his voice held authority. He walked directly in front of the vehicle and stared inside.

"What do you two girls want, and what are you doing on my property?"

"We're looking for this girls brother and we're lost."

"Get out of the car with your hands up," he ordered.

Blaze and Katrina obeyed.

"Sir, we don't want to bother you, but I need to find my brother. We don't mean you no harm," Blaze said in a wavering voice.

An old woman with long gray hair opened the screen door and walked on the porch.

"Jacob, you lower that gun. Don't point it at those girls. What's wrong with you."

"Maybelle, since that man came here, I been worried that people would come looking for him, and he said they were dangerous."

"Well these girls ain't dangerous. Why one is a teenager and the other one looks nice."

Jacob lowered the shotgun.

"Sorry, I'm just being cautious. All Maybelle and me want is to live in peace by ourselves. We're tired of civilization and all that's going on with this stupid world. We just want to live out our lives here in peace."

"You girls come in and make yourself to home. I'll get you some lemonade and cookies and we can help you if we can," Maybelle said, and smiled.

Katrina and Blaze lowered their hands.

"I'm Katrina and this is Blaze."

"Nice to make your acquaintance," Maybelle said. "I'm Maybelle and this old fool is Jacob, who's the love of my life."

Jacob grinned. His smile was warm and comforting.

"Howdy," he said.

They walked into the house. There was a big table sitting in front of the stone fireplace.

"Just have a seat and I'll get you some cold lemonade."

Jacob put his shotgun in the corner and sat down with them. Maybelle returned with a pitcher of lemonade and four glasses. She filled the glasses and placed them in front of her guest and Jacob. She revisited the kitchen and came back with a plate of cookies.

"I baked these this morning," she said. "Let's have our snack and settle down and maybe then Jacob and I can help you."

Katrina and Blaze ate a cookie and drank some lemonade.

"I've never tasted cookies this good," Blaze said.

"Maybelle cooks everything good," Jacob said. "You otta taste her garlic cheese grits bake."

"Now how can we help you girls?" Maybelle asked.

"I use to live in these parts," Blaze said. "But I'm lost. I need to find my way back to my house to find my brother."

Katrina knew that she must keep Blaze from repeating the bazaar story or these people would think they were crazy.

"She doesn't drive and rarely left the area of her house," Katrina said. "There was a large cornfield behind the house. Probably covered several acres."

Jacob and Maybelle looked at each other. Maybelle nodded indicating that it was okay for Jacob to tell the story.

"I know the place," Jacob said. "I found it when I was hunting. It's several miles from here. I travel a lot of miles when I am hunting. Them deer are sometimes hard to track and kill, but I don't give up. I noticed that house in front of the cornfield, but I left it alone. I didn't want anyone to know that we live here. On the other side of the cornfield is a large building that has guards outside. People are coming and going all the time. On the other side are many acres of Marijuana plants. I never went back there until a couple of days ago. Don't want no trouble. I took my axe and wheelbarrow to chop some wood. Maybelle warned me against going near there, but there's good wood there."

He stopped for a moment and looked at Maybelle. She nodded so he continued.

"I found a wounded man at the edge of the cornfield. A coyote was about to git him."

Blaze gasped, "Billy was wounded. Maybe it was him."

"What does your brother look like?"

Blaze described Billy.

"Nope," Jacob said. "This man was very tall with short black hair, probably in his forties. He said his name was Ethan Tyler."

Karina's heart pounded. "What?" she gasped. "My husband's name is Ethan Tyler."

"Missy, when I was fixing his arm, I noticed a little scar on his chin," Maybelle said.

Tears came into Katrina's eyes. "That's my husband. Was he hurt bad?"

"No," replied Maybelle. "Honey I use to be a nurse and I fixed him up. He's fine.

"Where is he now?" Katrina was breathless.

"I loaned him my scooter and he took off," Jacob said. "I liked him. He went north. I expect he made it to Alba, Texas. He'd need gas by then. You'll see a sign and I expect you can find him somewhere in that area."

Katrina rubbed her face and stood up. "You are so kind and we appreciate it. How far away are the house and the cornfield?"

"You pass two more dirt roads and it's the third one. A sign is there that says *no trespassing*. It ain't safe for you girls to go there alone. I'll go with you."

"No sir,' Katrina said. "You stay here and take care of Maybelle. I can handle my self."

"Well I can't let you have my shotgun. I need that, but I got an old colt 45 I can lend you."

He walked to an old black trunk setting in the corner and opened it. The old man pulled out a towel. Wrapped inside it were the old pistol and a box of shells.

"Here this'll help you," he said, handing it to Katrina. "I've kept it oiled and it works fine."

Katrina took the gun and shells. "I don't know how to thank you both for helping us and taking care of Ethan. I will not forget this and one day I'll find a way to repay you."

"You don't owe us nothing," Jacob said. "Years ago before the world and the USA went crazy, neighbors helped each other without expecting anything in return." He put his arm around Maybelle.

Blaze went over and hugged them. "I won't forget you."

Katrina walked over. "People like you come few and far between," she said. "Thank you both." She hugged them. "We need to get going."

The old couple stood on the front porch waiving goodbye as they drove away.

"Okay Blaze, we're going to your house to see if Billy's there and then we're going to find Ethan. We'll need him before we investigate what's in the big building on the other side of the cornfield. Billy may be there, if he's not in the house."

Katrina now had a ray of hope. Ethan is alive and well, and she would find him. She would.

50

The one and a half-hour drive to Athens presented me time to access my situation. About half-way there a lite rain began to fall. The wipers made their steady swish, swish in a rhythmical timing. I knew I had only one chance to save Katrina. The odds were against either of us getting out alive, so I had to do something to even the odds. My best bet is to set up a unique distraction after I confirmed that Katrina is alive. I had no problem giving up the information that Cruise wanted because my other source was a man I despised. However, his name and the information were my only bargaining tools.

The rain stopped as I passed the sign reading, *Athens City Limits, Population 12,875.* I have always found it strange that on every city limits sign, it stated the population of the city as if that mattered to people passing through.

I spotted a billboard advertising *The Super 8 Motel of Athens at 205 Highway 175 West.* I followed the directions and was there in less than ten minutes. I checked in, paid for one night in cash and proceeded to the room. I really wasn't very hungry, but I ordered in a pizza from Ken's Pizza. I picked up a couple of Diet Cokes from the vending machine, went back to the room and took a shower. Shortly after that, I answered the knock at the door and paid the teenager for the pizza. Actually, it tasted pretty good, and I ate about half of it.

After eating, I lay on the bed attempting to come up with a distraction, so I could gain an advantage during the trade. I genuinely didn't think Cruise would be there in person. My CIA training pushed me to believe that he would probably send a couple of henchmen with Katrina, and position a sniper somewhere out of sight to kill me after he received the information he wanted. An outrageous plan began to form in my mind. Maybe it had a chance to work. I dozed off into a restless sleep and awoke at about 6 am.

I showered, dressed in my Walmart jeans and shirt and went to the motel desk. The freckled faced young lady with burgundy hair smiled at me as I approached the desk. Her nametag read *Rose*.

"Rose, I just want to check out. I prepaid the room charges."

She checked the computer. "You're set to go."

"Is there a Walmart near here?"

"Yes sir, open 24 hours a day at 1405 East Tyler Street."

She gave me directions, and I thanked her and left.

I drove to the Walmart, went directly to the MacDonald's located near the grocery entrance, and ordered a large coffee and a sausage and egg biscuit. After consuming my breakfast, I ordered another cup of black coffee, grabbed a shopping cart and headed to the toy department. I went straight to the area where the remote control toys were stocked.

The first thing I saw was a remote control RC Fire Truck with lights, music and sirens. I threw two of them into the cart. After looking at the other remote control items, I chose an Air Hogs RC Sharp Shooter Helicopter and an AZ Parachute Sky Paraglider. I grabbed a 20 pack of D batteries and checked out. I sat in the car in the parking lot and prepared my remote control toys, unpackaging them and sticking the batteries in the vehicles and the remote controls.

After leaving the Walmart parking lot, I drove to a vacant lot on the west side of town. There I tested the equipment. I found that I could control the two fire trucks with one remote, but the other items required separate controls. Those remote controls were small enough that I could put them in my pocket. The one for the fire trucks was larger and I would be forced to hold it. The lights on the trucks were exceptionally bright and the sirens were loud enough to wake up a dead pig. I reloaded the items in the trunk and decided to scout the area. Having no idea where Cruise would set up a meeting, I drove around the outskirts of the town for hours. I knew they would need some type of structure to protect their backs and a place to station a sniper behind me. I found three locations that would meet those criteria.

At about 6pm I drove back to town and had dinner at a place called Cripple Creek Smokehouse. I enjoyed a half rack of ribs with Brunswick stew and cold slaw. I chased the food with a Bud light.

After dinner, the time was 7:30 pm. I sat in the car in the parking lot waiting to make the 8pm call. I felt strangely calm as I always do before an extremely challenging situation. Much of this particular deal, I had to play by ear.

At exactly 8pm I punched in the number for Cruise on Alda's cell phone.

"Tyler?"

"Yea," I responded,

"There's been a slight change of plans."

A cold chill ran up my spine, "What's the problem?"

"Get a pen. You may want to write this down," he said.

I grabbed a pen and paper from my pocket and waited.

"The meeting must be at midnight. Drive due west on Highway 175 for fifteen miles. Turn right on 1960 south and go twelve miles. After passing an Exon station on the right, drive precisely one mile, look for a dirt road with a mailbox on the side. The red flag on the box will be up. Turn left on that road and go to the end. My people with be there with Katrina. They will be positioned in front of the barn. If you're not alone, I'll have her throat cut."

"I got it," I said. I hoped that Cruise would be at the meeting, but apparently not.

"One more thing," he said, "call this number at midnight when you get to the dirt road. I'll be on the phone with you during the exchange." He hung up before I could ask any questions.

I didn't understand why he required the meeting to be at midnight. I'm sure that he thought that I would be extremely careful to follow his instructions precisely because of fear of my wife's death. I knew that if either of us had any chance of survival that I must be bold in my actions.

I decided to drive straight to the meeting place. On the way I stopped by a convenience store and picked up a large flashlight. I had four hours to set up my diversions. The most probable circumstance was that they would position a sniper somewhere out of sight to take me out once I provided Cruise with the information he wanted.

I spotted the mailbox with the red flag raised and turned on the dirt road. It was in very bad repair with potholes everywhere. Mesquite trees lined the sides of the road. It was a cloudy night with the moon covered.

When I reached the end of the road, I saw the old barn on the right. The wood was grey and rotten, but none of it had collapsed as far as I could tell. I left my headlights on and got out of the car. There were no other structures near the barn. I walked to the barn, turned on my flashlight and looked around. Trash littered the ground as if some homeless person had once made this his residence. Beside what looked like a bed made of straw, there were cigarette buts and candy wrappers. I heard a noise and pointed the flashlight to the area. A giant rat's eyes shined in the light. It squealed and ran for cover. There was no second level in the barn, therefore a sniper couldn't be positioned here. I returned to the car and grabbed one of the toy fire engines, placed it inside the door to the right and covered it with straw.

I walked off forty feet from the barn. This is the spot where I'll be standing during the exchange. Ten feet to the left of the spot, I placed the other fire engine. Ten feet to the right, I positioned the helicopter. Just behind the spot where I would be standing, I positioned the Paraglider.

I went back into the barn several times and retrieved straw to cover my distractions. I didn't want to disturb the functions so I covered them lightly and threw a little dirt on top. They appeared to be part of the dilapidated landscape.

It was about 10pm and I had to hurry to detect where the sniper may be located. Fifty feet behind the area where I would be standing was a hill with several rotten wooden flats stacked on top. That was the only place I could figure that a sniper could be positioned without me seeing him when I drove up. I moved my car behind the barn, went inside and waited. I had a hunch that the sniper would arrive an hour or so ahead of time to position himself.

Sure enough in about twenty minutes, I heard a noise and saw the headlight of a vehicle coming down the road. I recognized it as a Harley motorcycle.

The rider switched off the lights and apparently lay the cycle down so it couldn't be seen from the road. I had the element of surprise because he had no way of knowing that I was there. I screwed on the silencer to the gun and quietly went out the back door of the barn. In a crouch I circled the hill, successfully got behind it and saw the silhouette of the man. He turned on a flashlight to apparently check his rifle. I dropped to my belly and crawled closer. In the light, I could see that he was Asian.

He evidently finished checking his weapon and placed it on the top flat. He switched off the flashlight and dropped to a prone position. I knew I had one shot at him or the whole plan would be in shambles. I lifted the pistol and carefully aimed at his head, and gently squeezed the trigger. There was a splat sound as the bullet left the barrel. My target slumped. I jumped to my feet and ran to the body. I had no way of knowing if he was dead. I put another slug in his head at close range.

I noticed that on his head was a cordless telephone head set. Apparently he expected to have communications during the ambush. I put on the headset and fished the phone out of his pocket. Carefully I positioned his body in a prone position with the rifle in his dead hands. From a distance he appeared to be ready to shoot.

Looking at my watch, I saw that it was 11:15. I went back to the car and drove it to the area in front of the barn as if I had just arrived for the swap. I checked the remote controls and shoved them in my pocket. I placed the gun under my shirt in my belt at the back. The Asian guy's phone rang at 11:30.

"Are you in position?" the heavily accented Asian voice on the other end asked.

"Yea," I grunted and hung up.

Suddenly I remembered that my instructions were to call Cruise when I arrived at the entrance of the dirt road. I jumped in the car and drove to the entrance and parked beside the mailbox. At precisely midnight, I called Cruise's number.

"This Tyler?"

"Yes."

"Drive to the end of the dirt road and park about forty feet in front of the barn. Get out of your car and wait. My men will arrive soon with your wife. You remain on the phone with me. When you see that your wife is safe, give me the information and she'll be safely returned to you. Do you understand?"

"Yes."

I set the phone on the seat and drove to the end of the road. Everything was in place and I hoped that the exchange could take place without Katrina being hurt. I understood that the possibility of that happening was remote.

I grabbed the phone, got out of the car and stood there in the darkness. The two remotes were in my pocket and the piston in my belt. The cell phone of the sniper was in my back pocket set on vibrate, and the headset was on.

"I'm here," I said to Cruise.

"Just hold on," He grunted.

Within moments, the headlights of a vehicle appeared. A white van passed on my right. I could merely make out the shapes of the people inside. The van stopped to the left of the barn and the headlights were turned off. Two men got out of the van and pulled another person from the back seat. They walked to the front of the barn, dragging her between them. The man on the right turned on a large flashlight. As far as I could tell it was a woman at about the same height and body features as Katrina. There was a bag on her head.

The men were Asian, and one of them held what appeared to be a machete. He put it against the women's throat. The second man had a phone to his ear and was talking. I didn't see any weapons on him.

"Okay, Tyler, are you ready?" Criuse asked.

"Take the bag off her face. I want to see her."

"You're going to get her killed," Cruse said tersely. "Give me the information and the men will turn her over. Refuse and she's dead. I'm through with your shit."

I didn't have choice. I had to play along a little longer. The man holding the machete yelled to me, "It would be my pleasure to slice her throat." The voice was heavy Asian accented.

"Okay," I said to Cruise, "Tell your man to remove the machete from her throat."

The guy with the phone motioned and the machete was lowered.

"The man who has the information and proof on the Piranha is Ted Harper. He told me, while we were working together, that for his own safety and to keep open the possibility of black mail, he recorded two minutes of a phone conversation with the Piranha. He has this information on a computer chip. Only sixteen seconds of conversation is necessary for the current voice recognition equipment to verify beyond a doubt who the voice belongs to. With two minutes the results will be ninety-nine percent accurate. He speculated to me who he thought the voice belonged to, but the chip will prove it. The Piranha holds a high position in the CIA, that's certain."

"Who do you believe it is?" Cruise asked.

"CIA Director C.T. Henria," I replied.

"I'll be dammed," he said, laughing. "Wait while I instruct my men to release the girl."

I gritted my teeth and got ready for anything. The phone in my back pocket vibrated. I reached around and turned it on.

"Take him out now," I heard Cruise say.

Game on, he was ordering the sniper to kill me.

I immediately dropped the phone that Cruise was on. I carefully reached in my pocket and retrieved the two remotes. It was apparent that the men holding Katrina were waiting for the sniper to take me out.

I turned on the remote for the fire engines and pushed the button. Garish sirens filled the air. I switched the remote to automatic. The fire trucks came screaming from the barn and the side. Both men holding Katrina gaped wildly around. The man with the machete took a martial arts position. The other man pulled a pistol from his belt and shot toward the sirens. The girl dropped to her knees.

I activated the other remote and the paraglider soared and the helicopter rose and the swish, swish was audible. The men were clearly confused. I dropped to the ground, grabbed my gun, took aim, and shot the guy with the pistol. The spit from the silencer was barely heard, but the machete man saw his partner drop to the ground with blood gushing from his neck. I moved the gun sights to him, but he moved quickly, grabbing the girl and using her as a shield. He dragged her into the barn.

I turned off the remotes. I needed silence to track him. In a crouch, I ran to the barn door, gun in the firing position.

"Just let her go and I'll spare your life!" I yelled.

I heard a laugh. "Show yourself or she dies," was the reply.

I knew he had a machete, but didn't know if he had a firearm. Remaining quiet, I slipped around the corner to the door and went inside. It was pitch dark. Abruptly, he turned on a flashlight and shined it on the bag on her face. I could see his face too. He had short black hair and was about the same height of the girl. He was Asian and had a smirk on his mouth. The machete was at her neck.

"This is your last chance or she dies," he hissed.

He pressed the blade against her neck, producing a trickle of blood.

"Wait!" I shouted.

"Throw down your gun and step back," he said. The girl was whimpering.

"Okay, just move the blade away from her neck. I gave your boss what he wanted. Give the girl to me and we can both walk away."

"I said throw down the gun," he bellowed.

I assumed that his only weapon was the machete. I pitched the gun to the ground at my feet. He moved the flashlight to the gun.

"Kick the gun to the side and move away," he demanded.

I complied. Then something happened that devastated me. He shined the light on the girl again and sliced her neck, almost decapitating her. He dropped the body and jumped to the side between the gun and me. I felt dizzy, but forced myself into a martial arts position. The main remote was still in my hand. He swung the machete side to side and charged me. I jumped to the side as he bellowed; "Now you die!"

When he lunged at me again, I punched the remote to the fire engine. The blaring lights and sirens exploded the silence. He looked away then back to me.

"That won't work again," he smirked.

I edged closer to him and threw the remote, luckily slamming him directly between the eyes. He momentarily stumbled.

I dropped to the ground and launched a leg sweep. He fell to the ground, dropping the machete. I grabbed it and swung it hard at his body. He rolled to the side and sprang to his feet. Blood oozed from the cut on his side. He circled me and I swung the weapon again. He ducked and launched a side kick to my arm. The machete flew away. My arm was momentarily paralyzed. He grabbed the machete and lunged at me again.

I backed up and felt something under my right heel. It felt like the gun. He swung again toward my leg. I fell to the ground groping for the object under my foot. He stood over me with the machete raised.

"I will split your skull," he shrieked.

I grabbed the gun, raised it, and shot him in the stomach. He looked down stunned, and grabbed his midsection. I pumped another bullet at his head. The right side of his skull exploded when the bullet tore through the flesh and bone. I shot again as he was falling.

"Die you bastard, die," I shrieked with fury and hatred. He killed my wife and my rage was uncontrollable. I jumped to my feet and emptied the gun in his head.

With tears brimming in my eyes, I turned and walked to the fallen body of my lovely wife. The bag over her head was saturated with blood. I sat down, cradling her head in my lap, and removed the bag. The dead eyes of a strange woman blankly stared back at me. It was not Katrina.

I took deep breath and attempted to calm myself. Apparently Katrina had escaped from Cruise otherwise it would be her body lying in the dirt in the barn.

I walked outside to where I had thrown the phone and picked it up. "Are you still there Cruise?'

After a moment of silence he said, "Who is this?"

"All of your men are dead and the woman with them is dead. You better send a clean up crew here to get rid of the bodies." I took a deep breath. "I'm coming after you Cruise. I'll search the ends of the earth until I find you. Be fearful Cruise, I'll catch you and make you suffer like I have. You're a dead man walking." I hung up.

Katrina is out there somewhere and I will find her.

51

The Piranha decided to take some time off from work. The weekend at the cabin had not taken the edge off his tension. His master plan was still on track, but that damn Tyler was still on the loose. He knew Tyler well enough to fear that he was the only man on earth who could stop him.

He hadn't been on vacation in awhile, and he missed Caroline. His superiors chided him to take a well-deserved holiday. He drove to his vacation retreat at South Padre Island. The stunning beach house was situated near the water with expansive views of the ocean from every room. This house, along with his other retreats, was listed in Ben Cruise's name. As far as his associates knew, he was staying in a hotel.

The Piranha unlocked the front door and walked into a large living area, decorated in white wicker and pale colors. He dropped his suitcase and went to the deck. It was a beautiful day, cloudless blue sky with a lite breeze blowing. After unpacking in the master suite, also decorated in white wicker, he proceeded to the bar in the living area. He opened the bar fridge, pulled out a bottle of chilled Magnum Grey Goose Vodka by Chopar and poured a generous portion in his Harcort Abysse Vodka glass. He picked up a cigar from the velvet-lined box. He was accustomed to the very best of everything when his Piranha persona was in charge. His mundane work personality bored him. Here he was the Piranha and when he acquired control of Future Mankind

Ventures and the Higgs bosom Formula that the kid Olsen had mastered, he could live this way in every waking moment.

Sitting on the lounge chair on the deck, he sipped the vodka. The silky smooth liquid felt warm sliding down his throat. The Piranha smiled as he clipped the end of the Gurka cigar. He lit it, and took a deep drag. *When I get Caroline here for some loving, this day will be complete,* he thought.

He loved diversity in his women. When he felt the anxiety of loosing his wife, he desired violent sex with younger blonde women. Presently he wanted consensual sex with a sexy, intelligent woman that he owned.

Caroline Foster Torres was the daughter of a high level Mexican drug cartel boss. She had several disagreements and fights with her father when she became pregnant and got an abortion. After being thrown out of his home, she moved to South Padre Island. Before leaving, she stole forty thousand dollars from her fathers safe.

Caroline was a tall slender woman, twenty- six years old with shoulder length black hair. Her deep brown eyes were striking and her full lips positioned her in the magnificently beautiful category. Her 34c-24-36 figure, tan flawless skin, and sexy walk caused any man to turn his head when she passed by.

The Piranha met her at Louie's Backyard Bar, an upscale hangout for wealthy tourists. When he first saw her she took his breath away, even though she was the direct opposite of his ex wife. He sent over a bottle of 1978 Dom Perignom Champagne. She was intrigued with his generosity. With her stolen money almost depleted, she was searching for a Sugar Daddy. Her ostentatious life style required lots of cash. Caroline walked to his table and introduced herself. They ended up at his beach home having passionate and sometimes violent sex.

After a week's fling with the Piranha, they struck a deal. He would provid her with an upscale condo and ten thousand dollars a month, and she would be at his beck and call. This was just another reason he needed the endless stream of cash that the God Particle Formula would provide him.

He punched in her number.

"Hola," her soft sexy voice answered.

"It's me. I'll expect you in two hours," he said, and hung up.

Immediately upon hanging up, his cell phone rang. The Id informed him that it was Ben Cruise.

"Yeah," he answered.

"I've got good news and bad. I've have the information you wanted, but Tyler escaped."

"How is that possible?"

"He's a tough and crafty son of a bitch," Cruise said. "He killed my sniper and two other professionals. The girl we had, posing as his wife, is also dead."

"You better clean this up Cruise. I want Tyler in hell and I want it done quickly!" the Piranha hissed.

"I'll take care of that, but in the meanwhile he thinks that Director Hernia is the Piranha. I think that it's only a matter of time till he finds out that you are the Piranha. If he's able to find his wife, it's a done deal."

"I'm safe for the present, and if you do what I pay you handsomely for, he'll be dead before he finds her. What about the other man who he said has proof?"

Cruise took a deep breath. "The man is Ted Harper. He suspects that Hernia is the Piranha as well, but he has a computer chip with a conversion with your voice on it. Using voice recognition techniques and newly developed electronic equipment, it could prove that it's you, not Hernia."

"We need that chip," the Piranha yelled.

"Here's the complication," Cruise replied. "Ted Harper is at the laboratory in West Texas. He was apprehended and is to be used as a human test for Olsen's Formula. He's been injected and is presently in some sort of coma. They're waiting for him to regain consciousness."

"You go there, and as soon as he is able to communicate, do what's necessary to find the location of the chip. I don't give a damn about the experiments for now, just get the chip. Olsen can use his voodoo Formula on another human."

"Yes sir," Cruise replied, and the phone was disconnected.

The Piranha took another long sip of Vodka. There was a soft knock on the door. He opened it and Caroline stood there wearing a short black cocktail dress.

"Mi querido," she purred and hugged him, pressing her soft breasts against his body. "Hagamos el amor." She knew speaking Spanish turned on her Sugar Daddy.

The Piranha picked her up and threw her over his shoulder. He walked to the bedroom and heaved her on the bed.

"I need you baby," he said as he ripped off his clothes.

52

Ted Harper thought that his brain was exploding. The piercing agony was excruciating. He attempted to sit up, but there was no connection between his brain waves, nervous system, and the rest of his body. He realized that he was completely paralyzed and was seized with terror. The pain eventually overwhelmed the fear. After what seemed like hours, although only minutes passed, the pain moderated and shifted to his arms and legs. He closed his fists and squeezed as sensations of pain and power spread through his muscles and veins. He strained to raise his arms, but something kept them pinned down.

Ted's brain was reconnecting with his body and was integrating the massive changes that had taken place after the injections of Olsen's God Particle Formula. Another horrifying wave of pain engulfed his mind and body, and he passed out.

Alzar stood with Isaac and watched as the body of Ted Harper writhed and twisted in apparent agony. The stands on either side of Harper held bags for intravenous feeding and dripped liquid into the tubes attached to the needles in his arms.

Alzar stood outside of the cage where Olsen had ordered Harper's body placed on a table and secured with metal clasps. The grotesque muscles on his arms and legs budged, revealing enlarged arteries, and they strained against the clasps. Abruptly, the body went limp.

Cain observed from the screen in his office. He sensed a scientific breakthrough of breathtaking proportions.

"How's my superman doing?" Timothy Olsen asked as he sauntered into the room. "The synchronization between his mind and his body should be aggregated soon."

"He either passed out or dead," Alzar said.

"Open the cage Isaac. I need to check on his vitals," Tim said, ignoring the comment.

Isaac opened the door but kept his hand on his pistol, which was holstered behind his back. He was fearful of the monster these deranged doctors created. Tim walked up to the table and checked the pulse on the wrists and neck.

"Strong as a horse in heat," he laughed. As he removed his hand, Harper's eyes flew open. Tim was startled by the silver tint on the pupils. Harper's eyes were brown but now contained that weird silver circle. Harper looked straight into Tim's eyes without blinking, and Tim detected a strange sensation as if his mind was being penetrated. He felt dizzy after he turned and walked out of the cage, a little shaken.

"What's your problem?" Alzar asked.

"Nothing asshole," Tim replied. "I'm going back to the laboratory to work on adjustments. I want this man constantly fed intravenously until it's safe to feed by mouth." He hurried out of the room.

When Ted Harper peered into Olsen's eyes, he actually felt the phobia in the young man's mind. His first thought was that he wanted to slaughter the little bastard. He sensed a powerful force inside his brain that was unfamiliar to him. He looked down his body as far as he could see, and was astonished at the muscular configuration of his arms. He could not see, but he felt the power in his legs. Through rapid deduction, he ascertained that he now possessed power that could overcome any human obstacle. This deductive power was new to his mind and it felt bizarre.

Ted turned his head and gazed at the two men observing him outside the cage. The man dressed in white, with his arm in a sling, apparently was in command. He discerned intelligence and cunning. The other man was far less enlightened and was staring at him with bewilderment in his eyes. Ted focused his brain and engaged the stare. He sensed fear and anxiety. He gathered himself, and the silver ring in his eyes illuminated, emitting a red glow. He sensed a surge of energy leave his brain. The bewildered man grabbed his head and fell to the floor. It was at that moment that Ted Harper realized that he possessed mental dominance that these humans had not comprehended. He quickly closed his eyes knowing that he must control and temporarily conceal his supremacy, if he was to concoct a plan to escape.

The evil that always existed in Ted Harper's mind was exacerbated ten fold with the evolution of his brain, triggered by the injection of the God Particle Formula. His eyes remained closed as his newly magnificent, enhanced brain envisioned a plan.

Alzar was looking down at the floor, considering his orders to kill Cain, and his imminent plans to rid himself of Olsen. He had never been treated so disrespectfully by anyone. Maybe he would use Olsen as a human guinea pig when he enriched the Formula for massive use on a selective populace.

Alzar heard a noise and turned toward the source. Isaac was writhing on the floor, grasping his head. A trickle of blood dripped from his ear.

Alzar knelt beside him, "What in the hell is going on?" he yelled. Isaac gaped at him with bloodshot eyes. Raw horror filled the glare. He raised his arm and attempted to point toward the cage. Alzar looked at Harper, and the man was lying placidly with his eyes closed. Isaac's body went limp as consciousness departed. Alzar touched his neck and felt a weak pulse. He knew he had to get this man immediate medical help. Isaac was obviously in shock and probably had suffered a stroke.

"Alzar, Alzar," Cain's voice bellowed from the intercom. "I saw the whole thing. Harper did it to him. Get Isaac out of there.

I'll call one of our in house medics to treat him. Don't look at Harper!"

Alzar dragged the body to the hallway. Within minutes, two men arrived with a gurney. They loaded Isaac's body and left.

Alzar rushed to Cain's office.

What did Cain see? I think we've opened the door to hell, he thought.

53

After leaving Maybelle and Jacob's cabin, Katrina and Blaze drove back to the paved road. Katrina turned right. They drove in silence since both of them were in deep thought.

A loud crack of thunder and jagged lighting filled the sky. West Texas storms come suddenly, and usually leave as quickly as they appear. Heavy rain beat against the windshield. Katrina could barely see the road. After a few minutes of virtual blindness, she decided to pull over and wait for the downpour to subside.

"Katrina do you really think we can find Billy? I fear that The Grim Reaper, that's what we called Daddy Ben, lied to us all these years. I miss Billy and I wonder if he's alright."

"I promise you Blaze, we won't quit until we find him. You saved my life by helping me escape and I won't forget it, ever. Sooner or later we'll find Ethan and I guarantee you he'll help us. Ethan is tough and persistent, and I miss him like you miss Billy."

The blinding rain continued, water accumulated and flowed in streams in the ditches on each side of the road. Katina noticed what appeared to be an approaching car in her rearview mirror. She nearly panicked knowing that the vehicle couldn't stop in time and would probably rear-end them, since the rain would implead their vision. She quickly started the car and screeched forward. The car was rapidly approaching them. She floored the gas pedal, but the car kept gaining. When the vehicle was about ten feet behind them, it veered to the left and zoomed passed. The rain subsided as they continued the journey.

"There it is!" Blaze shouted.

Katrina looked to the right and saw a dirt road with a no trespassing sign posted beside it. The sign read, *trespassers will be shot*. Texans don't usually mince words. She turned right on the rain soaked road. It was extremely muddy.

"I hope we don't get stuck in the mud."

She drove slowly to the end of the road, saw the small wood framed house, and spotted the cornfield behind the structure.

"That was me and Billy's home," Blaze said in an almost inaudible voice.

The house was dark and appeared empty. Katrina grabbed the old colt 45.

"Okay let's check it out."

She left the headlights on and they walked to the front door. Katrina tried the doorknob. It was locked.

"Wait," Blaze said as she went to the corner of the front porch and reached underneath the overhang. She came back with a key with tape on it.

"Billy taped this under the overhang in case we lost our key. She inserted it into the lock and opened the door.

"Let's take this slowly. We don't know that the house is empty," Katrina whispered.

She entered the house holding the pistol in a firing position. It was dark with the car headlights providing meager light. The front door opened to the living area. Blaze stayed close behind her. As they walked toward the kitchen, a loud clunk broke the silence.

"Stay here," she said to Blaze as she walked forward toward the kitchen. Katrina nearly stumbled and looked down. The floor was cluttered with empty food cans and other debris. Dirty dishes were piled on the kitchen table. It was apparent that someone was staying here. She heard the shuffling sound of a person moving.

Blaze screamed. "He's in here, help me."

Katrina rushed back to the living area.

"He went into the bathroom," Blaze whispered.

Katrina walked to the door.

"I'm armed and if you don't come out, I'll shoot through the door. Silence was her answer. Katrina pointed the gun at the center of the door and shot. The door splintered as the bullet penetrated it.

"Stop, stop!" a high pitch voice cried.

The door opened and a dirty-faced young boy came out with his trembling hands held up high. He appeared to be in his early teens with long shaggy blond hair. He had a barren look in his blue eyes and he was shivering. The young boy wore a pair of cut-off jeans and a filthy T-Shirt. An old ragged pair of Nike running shoes were on his feet.

"What are you doing here and who are you?" Katrina asked, lowering the pistol.

"My name is Josh," he mumbled. "My daddy beat me all the time and I ran away. I found this empty house with food in the pantry so I've been living here."

"Have you seen anyone else?" Katrina asked.

"You're the only guys who came here," he replied. "Please don't make me leave. I don't have nowhere to go. There's a man staying in the house down the way, but he don't come over here."

"Josh, my name is Katrina and this is Blaze. We won't hurt you. We're looking for Blaze's brother Billy. What does the man in the other house look like?"

"He looks mean and he's got a rifle. I think he's guarding the cornfield. He's got a baldhead and is very tall. I saw him when he went on the back porch with his rifle. I was careful and he didn't see me. I'm scared of him."

"That ain't Billy," Blaze said. "Katy lived there, but I think she was shot and killed with her horse in the cornfield. She was Daddy Ben's niece, I think."

"We have to question him. Maybe he knows where Billy is or something about Ethan," Katrina said to Blaze. "We need to be careful and sneak up until I can get the drop on him with the pistol. Otherwise he may just shoot us."

"I know how to get to Katy's house. It's not far from here," Blaze replied.

"Josh, you stay here. When we've finished we'll come back for you. I think I know a couple of people who will be glad to help you and take you in."

Katrina and Blaze walked out. Josh sat down in the corner frowning. He didn't know whether to trust these women or not.

Just beyond the house was a wooded area. Katrina followed Blaze. The undergrowth was thick and as they proceeded she felt the briars scratching her legs. After walking for a few minutes, Katrina spotted a clearing and a small house. The cornfield was to the left of the house. To the left of the cornfield, green leafed plants were growing as far as the eye could see. She recognized them as Marijuana plants.

She pointed and turned to Blaze. "That's what the man is guarding, not the cornfield."

"What is that?" Blaze asked.

"That's a drug called Marijuana, and that field holds millions of dollars worth of it."

In Blaze's sheltered life, she knew little of such things.

"Blaze you stay here. I want to surprise the man. When I get him covered with my gun, I'll call you and we can question him."

"No way," Blaze said. "I'm going with you."

The two women crouched and crept slowly toward the front of the house. There was no sign of any movement. They walked to the side of the dwelling. Katrina raised her head and looked in the window. A large bald man was lying on the couch asleep.

He wore overalls over a dingy white T-Shirt. His mouth was hanging open and spittle was leaking out of the corner. There was an empty vodka bottle on the end table.

"I think he's drunk and passed out," she whispered. "Follow me quietly Blaze."

They returned to the front door and tried the knob. It wasn't locked and Katrina slowly opened it. The hinges squeaked and she froze. Hearing no sounds, she opened the door wide enough and entered with Blaze close behind. The man on the couch was snoring loudly as she approached him. Katrina put the pistol to his head and punched him with her other hand. He groaned, sniffled, but did not open his eyes. She punched him harder in the ribs. His bloodshot eyes opened and turned toward her. He stared into her eyes without flinching and she pushed the barrel of the pistol against his temple.

"Blaze get him a glass of water," she said and turned again to Baldy. "Sit up and don't try anything. I won't hesitate to shoot you."

Katrina backed away, keeping the gun pointing toward his head. Blaze returned with a glass of water and placed it on the end table beside the couch.

"Drink the water and clear you head," Katrina said. "I just want to ask you a couple of questions and if you cooperate, we'll leave you unharmed."

Baldy grunted and drank the water. He looked at Blaze and again at Katrina, focusing on the gun in her hand. He raised his eyes, glared at her and laughed.

"You think you too bitches scare me." He chuckled and stood up.

"Sit down right now," Katrina said in a calm voice.

Baldy rubbed his face, wiping the spittle from his chin. "Go to hell bitch," he hissed and lunged forward reaching for the gun. Katrina shot him in the leg and he tumbled to the floor. Blaze screamed and covered her face.

"Shit, you shot me," he screamed. "I don't believe you shot me."

"Don't test me again or the next bullet will be between your eyes," she said. Katrina looked at Blaze, "It's okay Blaze, just calm down."

She turned her attention to Baldy. "Are you going to sit there and bleed out or are you ready to answer my questions?"

He ripped off of a piece of his T-Shirt and pressed it against the wound. "What in the hell do you want to know?" He bellowed.

"Who's your boss and what are you doing here?'

"Go to hell," he said.

"Blaze, get that chair from the kitchen table and bring it here." Blaze retrieved the chair and set it down beside Katrina. "Take this gun and if he moves shot him," Katrina said, handing Blaze the gun. The young girl nodded.

Katrina picked up the chair and walked to where Baldy was sitting. Without saying a word she crashed the chair down on his wounded leg. He screamed in pain.

"Don't tell me to go to hell again or I'll shot you in the other leg." She walked back and took the gun from Blaze's trembling hand.

Baldy gasped and caught his breath. "Mr. Benjamin Cruise is my boss and I'm guarding the Marijuana fields."

"Now that wasn't so bad," Katrina said. "Tell me about the buildings on the other side of the cornfield."

Baldy gaped at her again, holding his bleeding leg. "One of the buildings is the drug processing plant. The other building is a laboratory. Some young genius kid is conducting experiments. Before Mr. Cruise send me here I was a guard at the laboratory."

"What kind of experiments?" Katrina asked.

"It's weird and I don't know the details but he's using humans to experiment on. They brought in three men but one if them escaped."

"Did you see the men?"

"Yes I did," he said.

"Describe them to me," Katrina said.

"The one that escaped was tall with short dark hair. I heard them call him Ethan."

Katrina took a deep breath. "Where did he go?"

"How in the hell can I know that? He got away," Baldy said.

"Describe the other two men."

"One was a young fellow who was wounded. I think he had been shot. He's okay and they plan to use him for the experiments."

"That's Billy," Blaze said and tears welled in her eyes.

"What about the third man?"

"Probably shouldn't concern yourself about him. He was a tall, mean son of a bitch, but they already injected him. He's probably dead by now like the other two. Why in the hell do you bitches care anyway?"

"The one that escaped is my husband and the wounded boy is her brother." Katrina said. 'There's going to be hell to pay when I find my husband and we go back to that place."

Baldy giggled, "Missy, you'll never get by the guards."

"Okay, we're going to tie you up and you better hope one of your cohorts finds you. You won't die from that wound if you keep pressure on it, and stop the bleeding. I'll tape your hand against the wound so the pressure is applied. Blaze, look around for some duct tape."

"You can't leave me like this," Baldy pleaded.

"We sure as hell can," Katrina replied as Blaze returned with a roll of black duct tape. "Blaze I'll keep him covered while you tape his hand tightly against the wound on his leg. Then tape his other hand to his neck and bind his feet together."

Blaze walked over to Baldy. "Lift your leg so I can get the tape under it," she said. Baldy lifted his leg and as she bent over, he grabbed her by the throat and pulled her body in front of him. His hand was tightly against her Adams apple.

"Drop the gun or I'll break her neck," he hissed. "I was an Army Ranger before Uncle Sam threw me out. With one snap, she'll be dead."

Katrina lowered the gun. She noticed movement behind Baldy. Josh had creped up behind him. He was holding a shovel. Before she could say anything, Josh crashed the shovel against Baldy's scull. The big man grunted and fell backwards, releasing his hand from Blaze's neck. Josh hit him again and again, squarely in the face. Blaze coughed and stood up holding her neck.

"Are you okay?" Karina asked.

"Yes, I'm sorry I got careless."

She turned to the young boy. There was a look of terror on his face as he dropped the shovel. "Just take a deep breath and calm down." Josh sat on the floor, breathing heavily.

"Josh, why did you follow us?"

"I thought you might need my help," He said as he stared at Baldy's crushed and bloody face. "I knew he was an evil man."

Katrina knelt and put her fingers on Baldy's neck. There was no pulse. "We need to get out of here," she said. "Josh you're coming with us. You probably saved both of our lives."

They made their way back to the house, got into the car and drove away. Katrina went straight to the log cabin where Jacob and Maybelle lived. Jacob was standing on the porch when they arrived. She got out of the car.

"Girl did you have trouble?" he asked. Maybelle joined him on the porch.

"I have one more favor to ask of you," she said. She turned toward the car. "Josh, come here."

The boy got out of the car and walked to her side. Josh this is Mr. Jacob and Ms. Maybelle. This is Josh," she said to the old couple.

"Why he needs a bath and looks hungry," Maybelle said. "Son come with me and I'll fix you up."

"This boy saved our lives. He ran away from home because his father beat him almost to death."

"Bless his heart," Maybelle said.

"Will you and Jacob take care of him for awhile? I need to find Ethan and I promise we'll come back for him. He has nowhere to go."

"Surely we will," Maybelle said.

"He reminds me of our son who died," Jacob said. "We'll keep him for you."

Katrina turned to Josh. "You stay with these fine people, be good and help them with chores. I'll be back for you."

"Yes Ma'am," Josh replied. "They seem nice."

Katrina wiped a tear from her eye. "Blaze and I have to go find Ethan and try to rescue her brother. Thank you for everything."

"Wait," Jacob said. "When Ethan left here I told him to turn left. The nearest little town is Alba. He would have to get gas there. That may be a start for you to find him."

Katrina and Blaze departed and turned left at the end of the dirt road.

"Alba here we come," she said. She had no idea what was in store for them.

54

After the incident at the barn, I decided to retrace my steps. I knew that Cruise's ranch was somewhere in West Texas and that at one time Katrina was there. I was depending on Thompson to get me the address, but he hadn't called.

Since the Asians didn't have her at the exchange, she must have escaped. My wife is a trained operative and would immediately begin looking for me. My only choice is to retrace my steps and hope we cross paths. It's a long shot.

My best option is to drive back to Alba and determine if anyone was asking questions about a man fitting my description.

The morning sun was rising, splashing red spears through the clouds. The beauty of the spectacle amazed me. I didn't realize that I had drifted into the left lane while beholding the beauty of the sunrise. A blast from the horn of a trailer truck brought me back to earth. I swerved to the right and barely avoided a head on collision. In my rear view mirror I saw the driver stick out his hand and give me the finger. I didn't blame him.

It was precisely then that I realized I was utterly exhausted, not having slept in at least 36 hours. On the outskirts of Alba, I saw the Walmart where I purchased my clothes and supplies. I pulled into the parking lot, switched off the car and lowered my head. I was out like a light. When I awoke my head was pounding and I was starving. Four hours passed since I nodded off. Time for some breakfast at the MacDonald's inside Walmart.

When I entered the store, the greeter looked at me and shook his head. *I must look like shit,* I thought. I went to the bathroom, used it, walked to the sink and looked into the mirror. My face was dirt streaked. I looked like a homeless down and out bum. I grabbed a bunch of paper towels and washed up as best I could, combed my hair with my fingers, and wiped the dirt from my clothes. Now at least I looked like a decent homeless bum. I could shower later at a motel. Now I needed to eat.

At the counter I ordered two large black coffee's, two sausage and egg biscuits and a fruit cup. I sat down and devoured my breakfast. Carrying my second cup of coffee with me to the pharmacy, I purchased a bottle of Advil and downed three tablets, chasing them with a swig of coffee. At least my headache was subsiding. When I was walked back to my car I passed an old familiar pickup truck. I immediately recognized it as the one Jacob kept at his cabin. Looking inside, I spotted a shotgun in the back seat.

"Hey you, get away from my truck." I heard a voice shouting.

I looked around and there was Jacob with a young boy. The boy was pushing a cart filled with bags. He was wearing what appeared to be a brand new pair of jeans, a flannel shirt and a new pair of running shoes.

"Well I'll be gol-dern," Jacob said, holding out his hand to me.

I shook his hand. "I can't believe you're here," he said.

"Well Jacob, I'm glad to see you too. I hope Maybelle is well."

"She's fine. Man do I have a story to tell you. This is Josh by the way. Josh meet Ethan." The boy shook my hand and smiled.

"Let me put these bags in the truck and let's go back in to the MacDonald's and sit down. You ain't going to believe what I got to tell you."

Jacob loaded the bags on top of the shotgun behind the front seat and we went back into the store. After paying for Cokes for the three of us, we filled out cups at the drink fountain and sat down.

Jacob was grinning like a boy who just got a chocolate milk shake. "What do you have to tell me," I asked. *I really liked this old man and one day I will repay him properly for his kindness,* I thought.

"See this boy Josh here, your wife Katrina and the girl brought him to Maybelle and me. She said he saved her life. He's a very nice boy and we're having a great time with him. I brought him here to buy some new clothes and get some supplies."

The news took my breath away. Finally I managed to say, "When did this happen and how do you know it was my wife?"

"We done some talking and we told her about you, and after we described you, she said it was her husband Ethan. She said she was looking for you and the other girls brother."

Who was the other girl?" I asked.

"She was a young blonde girl whose name is Blaze," he replied.

Things began to fall into place in my mind. Cruise had apparently taken Blaze to his ranch and Katrina was a prisoner there. Blaze must have helped her escape.

I turned to Josh, "Tell me how you saved their life, son?"

"My daddy beat me all the time and I ran away," he said. "I came across this empty house in front of the big cornfield with food in the pantry. I decided to hole up there until I could figure out what to do. There was a mean man living in the little house down the way, but I was able to hide and he didn't know I was there." He took a sip of his coke and continued, "Katrina and Blaze found me and were nice to me. They were looking for you, I guess, and a boy named Billy, who is Blaze's brother. They went to talk to the mean man and I followed them. Katrina shot the man in the leg, but he got Blaze by the neck. That's when I hit him in the head with the shovel. I didn't mean to kill him, but I did. They brought me to Mr. Jacob's house." He looked down and bit his lip. "I ain't never kilt nobody before."

I sat there for a moment allowing the information sink in. Billy was at the laboratory and if Katrina knew that, she would devise a plan to rescue him. Her professionalism would lead her to recognize that she needed help to get Billy. She now knows that I'm alive, and in the general vicinity. Surely she's searching for me.

"Jacob, where did you tell her I went?"

"I told her that you probably went to Alba, and that you would need gas for the scooter by the time you got there."

I realized at that point that I needed to start at the beginning, talk to the pony-tailed clerk at the convenience store and retrace my steps.

"Okay, please give Maybelle my regards. Josh is lucky to have you taking care of him."

"He's a fine young man like our son was," Jacob replied, and patted Josh on the back.

I left them and drove back to the convenience store in Alba. Thick black clouds gathered in the sky, and I could smell the rain. Soon crackles of thunder filled the air, and lightning crashed across the sky. A Texas gully washer was rapidly approaching and soon the rain was so dense that I could barely see the road. Finally I arrived at the store. I was soaked when I walked in.

A young black lady was behind the counter. Her hair was up in cornrows and when she opened her mouth I noticed two gold front teeth.

"Hey man you're soaked," she said, handing me a towel. "Dry yourself off before you get a puddle of water on my floor."

"Thanks," I replied. "I need some information. Did two women recently come in here looking for a man fitting my description?"

"Not while I was here. I just came to work an hour ago. Lenny was here the rest of the time. Lots of women looking for good-looking dudes like you," She said, laughing and baring her gold teeth.

"Is Lenny the slim guy with a ponytail?" I asked.

"Shore is, he's sleeping out back in his trailer."

"I really need to talk to him. It's a matter of life and death."

"Well you can bang on the trailer, but he's a sound sleeper and I can't guarantee he'll answer."

"Thanks," I said, and walked outside in the pouring rain. I went around to the back, and saw a small camper trailer. I banged on the door. Not a sound except for the rain pelting on the medal walls of the trailer. I banged again harder. Finally the door opened a couple of inches.

"What the hell do you want?" A high-pitched man's voice asked.

I reached into my pocket, pulled three twenties from my money clip and stuffed them through the crack of the door. "More of this If I can ask you a couple of questions," I yelled over the pounding rain.

He opened the door and backed up. I walked in, dripping and soaked to the bone.

"Do you remember me Lenny?"

"Yea, you're the dude who came on that scooter. Earlier today a couple of hot women came here looking for you. They described you and said your name was Tyler, but I looked up the credit card receipt and told them that your name was Hedrick. Hey man can you fix me up with the young blonde chick? She's a looker."

I knew he was talking about Blaze. "What did you tell them?"

"I told them that you asked about the nearest motel and I sent you to Motel 6 in Burnham, just down the road."

I gave him another twenty, thanked him and left. Just as I began walking around to the front to get to my car, he opened the door and yelled, "Hey dude what about fixing me up with that hot blonde?" I ignored him and kept walking.

The rain slacked up, and I raced to Burnham knowing that I wasn't far behind Katrina and Blaze. I drove straight to the Motel 6. The same stout, grey haired military lady was behind the desk.

"Well Mr. Hedrick, you just missed two woman looking for you," she said as I approached the counter.

"You remember my name?"

"I told you I am precise. I don't forget names and faces. There was a woman about your age and a young blonde asking about you, approximately an hour ago."

I knew that Katrina was using her training to track me. "What did you tell them?"

"I told them I gave you directions to Tyler and the Holiday Inn Express, and they rushed out."

"If they come back would you be so kind and give them this number to call." I wrote down the cell phone number and handed it to her.

"Sure thing, Mr. Hedrick."

I thanked her again and hit the road for Tyler. This time, I topped ninety miles an hour on the deserted road. I was getting so close. I raced to the Holiday Inn and parked in the lot. I knew that by now the authorities or some locals would have found Adla Bagrov, and I didn't know what, if anything, she told them. I couldn't risk going to the office and asking questions. They might get the police involved.

I looked at the entrance and couldn't believe my eyes. Katrina and Blaze walked out the door and got into an SUV. I didn't want to talk to them in the parking lot in fear of being recognized by the clerk. I decided to follow them a little way before revealing myself.

Katrina turned right and headed for the freeway. I pulled in close behind her. All of a sudden she floored it and sped away. Apparently she thought I was a bad guy. I had to get close enough to pull up along side her so she could see me. My old car could barely keep up with the new SUV.

She made several evasive turns, but I was able to stay behind her. Her driving skills had been carefully honed at the CIA, and so were mine. She turned down a side street, which was unusual, and went around a corner, out of site. I slowed down and made the turn. The SUV was setting sideways, blocking the road. I slammed on the brakes and stopped within inches in the driver's door. The vehicle was empty. I got out, looked around and saw no one.

"Face down on the ground," a female voice yelled from behind me. "Face down or in the next five seconds I'll shoot you in the head."

I went to the ground and put my hands on the back of my neck.

"Who are you, and why are you following us?" I heard my wife's voice demand.

"Katrina, it's me."

"Ethan," she whispered breathlessly.

I turned and sat up. My heart was beating wildly. After thinking she was dead and then discovering that she was a prisoner, there she was in front of me as beautiful as ever. Blaze was standing behind her. Tears rolled down her cheeks as she dropped the gun and came to me. I stood up and held her tightly in my arms.

"I love you Katrina."

"I love you too Ethan."

I felt the wetness of her tears on my neck as I lifted her head and kissed her. I knew we had mountains to climb and impossible odds to overcome, but for the moment, I just stood there hugging and kissing her.

"Katrina, we need to call Hank Thompson. He's helping me and is the only one I can currently trust in the CIA."

"Ethan," she whispered. "It was Hank Thompson who drugged me and turned me over to Cruise."

55

The Piranha was furious with Cruise. Not only was he responsible for Katina's escape, he failed to have Tyler killed during the phony swap. Cruise was always efficient in carrying out his orders. This failure was compounded by the fact that Cruise was the only human being who knew his true identity. His trust in the man was decimated. The time may be approaching to have him eliminated, but he needed to accomplish a few vital things first. Cain must be killed, and he wanted to use Cruise to gain control of Future Mankind Ventures.

Untold riches were on the verge of being harvested via Olsen's God Particle Formula. He would, of course, offer the Formula to the highest bidder. He figured it would be Russia, China or maybe even Iran, and didn't give a damn which. With the proper use of the Formula, the balance of power could be tilted in the direction of anyone owning the power of the Formula's transformation and evolution of humans. Legions of intellectual genius with super strength could develop weapons that had not even been dreamed of. The Piranha's mind was yearning for power and immense riches, but there were things to be done.

He grabbed his cell phone and called Ben Cruise.

"Cruise here."

"Cruise it's time to move on Cain. Is your man in place and ready?"

"Yes sir," Cruise answered.

"Implement the plan now. Regardless of this mission, I'm still holding you responsible for having Tyler's killed."

"I've placed a half-million dollar contract on him with cartel hit men. It's just a matter of time. These guys are vicious and blood thirsty, and willing to do anything for money. I have several teams competing for the half-million. Probably a dozen of these killers are out looking for Ethan and Katrina as we speak."

"Don't fail me on this," the Piranha hissed, and hung up the phone.

Cruise punched in the number for Alzar. He got a response on the third ring.

"What now Cruise?"

"Alzar, implement the plan. I want Cain out of there and dead by tonight."

"With pleasure, and when can I kill Olsen? That little son of a bitch is treating me like shit. I can carry on his experiments without missing a beat."

"We need him to complete the experiments on Ted Harper, and determine if the Formula needs to be revised. We haven't tested Harper, and Olsen is the best man prepared to do that. Once the adjustments are complete, and another human is injected to measure the success of the alterations, we can move on him. For now, leave him in place and do what he says."

"Okay, Cain will be dead my nightfall," Alzar said, and hung up the phone. He didn't know how much longer he could tolerate following Olsen's orders. Right now however, he had to handle Cain.

Alzar checked on Harper's condition. The big man was lying quietly on the bed in the cage with his eyes closed. He then proceeded to Cain's office.

"I need to see Mr. Cain," he said to the assistant.

"Just a moment, "she said, and she walked into the office. Momentarily she returned, "Go right in."

Alzar walked into the office and took a seat in front of Cain's huge desk.

"What do you want?" Cain asked. "Any problem with the experiments?"

"Nothing other than Olsen's arrogance," Alzar replied. He hesitated and looked down.

"What is it?" Cain asked.

Alzar leaned over and lowered his voice barley above a whisper. "Sir, there's a conspiracy against you. Your life is in danger and I have the evidence, but I don't know who all is involved. I'm fearful talking about it in your office. I have the evidence of the conspiracy hidden outside the building. Can we meet at the edge of the cornfield in two hours? I'll show you everything I have. You can probably figure out who the conspirators are when you study the papers. Just don't tell anyone where you're going. We don't know who all is involved in the plot."

Cain stared into the man's eyes. He had known Alzar for a long time and trusted him. He handpicked him to take over for Olsen. There was no reason not to believe him. "I'll be there and thanks for your allegiance," he said.

Alzar returned to the laboratory, wrapped a scalpel in a cloth, and put it in his pocket. He also grabbed a large plastic bag and a small roll of white medical tape. Just as he was leaving, Olsen walked in.

"If Harper doesn't respond by morning, I want him shackled and brought back in here," Olsen ordered. "We need to conduct some physical and mental test to see exactly how much he's altered and evolved."

"Will do," Alzar said, and left. After an hour and forty-five minutes, he walked outside the building and to the edge of the cornfield. He went in about five feet and cleared a spot on the ground. He pulled an ear of corn and buried it. Then he walked back to the perimeter and waited.

Ten minutes later he saw Cain walking out of the building. Cain approached him and said, "show me what you have, Alzar."

"Mr. Cain I've got it buried just about 5 feet from here," he said, walking into the cornfield. Cain followed. He stopped at the spot he cleared, "It's here."

Cain stepped in front of him and looked down. "Well, dig it up."

Alzar unwrapped the scalpel. He came up behind Cain and with surgical precision, slit his throat, severing his jugular vein. Blood spurted from the slice. Cain fell to his knees and grabbed his neck. A gurgling sound came from deep in his throat, and blood leaked through his fingers. He fell forward on his face, dead.

Alzar didn't want to leave a trail of blood when he dragged Cain deeper into the field. He moved the body a few feet and threw dirt on top of the blood that had soaked into the ground. He covered the dirt with dead cornstalks. He took the plastic bag and shoved Cain's head and neck inside it, and sealed the bag with the tape.

Grabbing Cain's feet, he dragged the body deep into the cornfield. Alzar removed the plastic bag, allowing blood to again soak the ground. He knew the smell of fresh blood would draw coyotes to the body.

Alzar strolled back to the building and went to his bedroom. He picked up his copy of Crime and Punishment by Fyodor Destoyevsky and read until he fell asleep.

The alpha coyote lifted his head. The smell of fresh blood triggered drool to leak down the sides of his mouth. He followed the smell with the alpha female. The rest of the pack followed about twenty feet behind them. When he located the body, he howled and the alpha female came to his side. They fed on the upper leg of Cain's body, ripping off flesh and devouring it. The pack watched with ravenous eagerness, but was waiting to be summoned by the alpha. When the alpha and his mate got their fill, he howled again and the pack came running. There was growling and gnashing of teeth as the coyotes fought over the prime meat.

After a time of savage feeding, they dragged the remains of the body to the den area. They would finish it off later and chew on the bones.

The once powerful, wealthy man, who founded Future Mankind Ventures, was reduced to bloody meat and bones lying on the ground outside the coyote den.

Flesh to dust sayeth the Lord.

56

Timothy Olsen stood outside the cage glowering at his Guinea pig, Ted Harper. He was at a loss on why the man had not regained consciousness. Ted just lay there, motionless as a dead mam. "Hey man, wake up. I know you can hear me," he yelled. Continued silence was the response.

He left the holding room and went back to his office. "Call Alzar and tell him to get his ass over here now," he ordered his assistant.

Five minutes later his assistant came into the office. "Mr. Alzar doesn't answer. I left him a message."

"Okay, call Cain. Tell him that I want to proceed to inject the boy, who was wounded, so I can have duel experiments working. The kid, I think his name is Billy, is mentality dissimilar to Harper, and I've customized the Formula to account for his temperament. Harper's mind has a malicious physiological configuration, whereas Billy's is simpler and innocent. I intend to produce different Formulas for different personality types for optimum results. Inform him and have him call me in the laboratory. Cain requires personal authorization for each human experiment."

His assistant took notes, nodded and left. Tim walked to the laboratory, stopping by the holding room on his way. Harper was still lying motionless on the bed in the cage. As he entered the lab, his cell phone rang.

"This is Alzar, what do you want?"

"I've asked Cain for permission to inject the boy, Billy, so I can understand the effects of the Formula on different personality types with different brain configurations. These duel experiments will help me determine how my Formula acts inversely in dissimilar humans. Meet me in the laboratory right now. I also want to inject a stimulant into Harper's blood stream to get him conscious. I need to test his mental and physical reactions."

"What about Isaac? Harper somehow injured his mind?"

"Don't be ridiculous you fool," Olsen sneered. "Mental telepathy is not a possible reaction of my Formula."

"You don't know all the side effects," Alzar replied angrily. His hatred for Olsen dripped from his voice.

Tim was too self involved to even notice. "Have we been assigned another guard and keeper for Harper? Isaac is no longer effective."

"Yes, a man named Hillard."

"Get him in here," Olsen ordered.

Alzar hung up and went to get the man. Olsen punched in his assistant's number. "Did Cain agree?"

"Sir, I can't reach him. He's out of his office and his assistant doesn't know where he went, or how long he's going to be absent."

"Keep trying," Olsen said and hung up.

Alzar walked in with a hulking man wearing a baseball cap. Tim could see his short blonde hair below the cap line. His muscles stretched the arms of his T-Shirt. He wore Khaki pants and combat boots. A holstered pistol was strapped around his waist. His stark blue eyes were intense.

"This is Hillard," Alsar said.

"I'm here to serve you sir," Hillard said, with a strong German accent.

"Are you aware of the man in the cage in the holding room?" Tim asked.

"Yes sir," Hillard replied.

"I want you to go get him and bring him here. Be careful. Even though he's shackled, he still may be dangerous."

"I have no fear," Hillard grunted and left.

Tim looked at Alzar. "I've been thinking about inherent brain cells and genes.

Some humans are born with an evil streak or better said an absence of conscience. It may be inherent or developed with life experiences, but it exists."

Tim continued to lecture Alzar. "Conscience is an aptitude, faculty, intuition or judgment of the intellect that distinguishes right from wrong. Moral judgment may derive from values or norms (principles and rules). In psychological terms conscience is often described as leading to feelings of remorse when a human commits actions that go against their moral values and to feelings of rectitude or integrity when actions conform to such norms. The extent to which conscience informs moral judgment before an action and whether such moral judgments are or should be based in reason has occasioned debate through much of the history of Western philosophy. Therefore, in the absence of a conscience, humans can commit any acts and feel no guilt. I don't think Harper has a conscience, and with his evolved brain the evil in his mind and his ability to connive is substantially enhanced. He may now kill and commit violent acts and crimes just for the pleasure of it."

Much to Alsar's chagrin he continued. "The kid, Billy, appears to have a conscience and is basically a decent person. With the introduction of the Formula, this goodness would be enhanced causing him to live to help others and be vulnerable to the harshness of life. So, Alzar, you see I must prove this theory by injecting Billy and then testing him and Alzar. If I'm correct, and I probably am, I can isolate the various adjusted Formulas to be used as needed. As an example, for soldiers we would need to delete the conscience and enhance the evil tendencies of the mind. For medical personnel, teachers, and ministers, we would enhance the conscience. We can mold society and humans any way we want. I will certainly become God on earth."

Alzar glared at the young man who he knew was a psychopath. However, he couldn't resist having admiration for his genius.

When you're dead and I'm in control of the Formula, I can take it to even greater levels and applications, he thought.

"Where is that damn Cain?" Tim said in frustration. "We need to get this show on the road."

57

Ted Harper lay perfectly still although he was completely conscious. The alignment of his augmented brain and his superior body strength had transpired and he was wholly aware if his abilities. He knew that he also possessed the ability to project thoughts, pain and confusion onto the minds of others. His anger of being shackled projected pain and disorientation into Isaac's brain.

In his contemplated state of mind, he figured out how to control his telepathic powers. Nothing was challenging to figure out now. Solutions to problems came lightning fast to his thought processes.

Ted also knew that Olsen had underestimated his strength. He could produce adrenalin in massive amounts to increase his power. He realized that he still couldn't break the steel shackles, however the chains that connected the shackles to the bed could be snapped. He was biding his time.

Ted was not yet aware of how bullets would react in his body. He assumed that he was still mortal so his escape from this facility must be planned and executed to avoid getting shot.

Ted Harper's eyes widened when he heard the door of the cage being opened. The silver tent sparkled. He looked around and saw a very large blonde man enter. The man appeared surprised to see his eyes open, but the fellow's mind didn't reflect fear. Ted noted that the nametag that he wore read *Hillard*.

"Where are you taking me Hillard?" he asked softly.

"Shut the hell up," Hillard said.

Venomous fury burst into Ted's mind. He released adrenalin and snapped the chains to the restraints on his hands. In one fluid motion he swung the steel shackles on his right wrist and hit Hillard on the back of the head. He heard the skull crack with the force of the blow. Ted experienced immense gratification in knowing that he killed the man. He sat for a moment and gloated in the intensity of the pleasure. He instantaneously knew that this pleasure of killing would be addictive and he would need it often.

Ted ripped off the chains to the shackles on his feet and walked to the corner of the holding room. A set of keys hung on a hook. He unlocked the restraints and threw them aside. He went to the door and locked it.

He removed the surgical smock that he wore, undressed Hillard, and put on his T-shirt, khaki pants and combat boots. He checked the man's wallet and found a couple of hundred dollars in twenties. Depositing the wallet in his back pocket, Ted pulled the baseball cap down over his eyes, buckled the gun holster around his waste and chambered a round in the pistol. Ted scrutinized Hillard's corpse, then put the smock on the body. After placing him on the gurney, he covered his body with a sheet, and pulled it over his head.

He pushed the gurney to the door, unlocked it and walked out into the hall. A guard was stationed about twenty feet to his left.

"Where are you going with that," the guard asked.

"That young doctor wants him in another room," Ted replied, using a strong German accent. He went in the opposite direction from the guard. He passed another guard, but no words were exchanged. As he turned the corner at the end of the hall, he heard a door open. A maintenance guy, pushing a mop bucket, was going outside. He turned and proceeded to the door, left the gurney in the hall and walked outside. The maintenance guy was smoking and talking to an armed guard. The guard glared at him, "My orders are that no one leaves the building without being cleared. I know all the big wheels and you're not one of them."

"I can show you my ID and clearance papers," Ted said, again utilizing a German accent.

The guard walked toward him. "Just get back in the building, asshole," he said.

In a move faster than any normal man could achieve, Ted grabbed the man by the throat and crushed his windpipe, busting his Adam's apple into small pieces. He tossed the guard aside. The maintenance man held up both hands. "I got no issues with you," he said picking up the mop to use as a defensive weapon. Ted was in front of him in an instant. The man swung the mop and Ted parried it and landed a crushing blow to the man's head. When the guy fell, Ted stomped his head.

He was in a frenzy of pleasure and only wished there were other humans to kill right here and now. He took solace in the fact the he was free and there were 313.9 million people in the USA. He could take his time and kill as many as possible.

Ted Harper ran from the building in a pace the defied the possibilities of human speed.

A superhuman evil man was now loose in society.

58

I was shocked hearing the news that Thompson was a part of the conspiracy. God know who else in the CIA was on the payroll of Future Mankind Ventures, Cain and the rest of his lavishly rich hoodlums.

"Ethan, I'm so glad you're okay," the meek voice of Blaze spoke from behind Katrina. She walked over and hugged me. "Do you know where Billy is?"

I felt a tremble in her body as she asked the question. "Blaze he's at the laboratory on the other side of the cornfield that you guys were guarding. Ben Cruise delivered him there with Ted Harper and me. He was wounded, but he's okay."

"Ethan," Katrina said, "If it weren't for Blaze I would probably be dead at the hands of Cruise or his henchman. She risked her life to save me. We must do whatever we can to get Billy out of there."

I nodded, but inside I knew that we would need help getting into that heavily guarded facility and extracting Billy. I just hoped Olsen hadn't injected him and turned him into another Fang.

"I promise you Blaze, we'll get him out, but we're going to need help."

"Katrina, Harper leaked to me that he thought that CIA Director Hernia was the criminal known as the Piranha."

"Based on what Thompson did to me, I think maybe it's him," Katrina replied.

I knew at that moment that we couldn't call anyone at the CIA for help. The risks were too high.

"I have an old friend with the FBI. He's the Regional Agent in Charge based in Houston. We were in service together, went through hell in the Mideast. We had each other's back for over a year, and I trust him completely. "I'll give him a call. I have this throwaway cell phone, but Thompson has the number. I need to ditch it and buy another one. We don't want to take any chances of it being traced."

"We also need to ditch the SUV. Cruise may have reported it stolen or at least he has men looking for it," Katrina said.

"I know just the place. You and Blaze take my car and follow me." A master plan was materializing in my mind.

I drove the SUV to the location where Cruise had sent the Asians to kill me. The place was undisturbed. I parked the SUV in front of the barn and wiped my prints from the steering wheel. I also wiped clean the back seat and the passengers side in case Katrina and Blaze had left prints. After closing the door with my elbow, I joined the girls.

"What happened here?" Katrina asked.

"I'll fill you in on details later, but Cruise sent men to kill me and they pretended to have you as a hostage. I managed to eliminate them."

I took the wheel and drove back to the main highway, and drove about ten miles back toward town.

"What's your plan?" Katrina asked.

"I'm going to place an anonymous call to the police and tell them where the crime scene is. When they find the SUV and trace it to Cruise, at least that'll keep him occupied for awhile."

I stopped the car on the side of the road and dialed 911 with my throw away phone. "Where's your emergency?"

As briefly as possible I reported that gunshots were heard, gave directions to the site and hung up. I wiped the phone with a tissue, dropped it to the pavement and crushed it with my foot, picked up the twisted remains with the tissue and threw them as far as I could into the woods adjacent to the highway. I got back into the car. "Let's go to Walmart since I need to purchase another throw away phone to call Gerry Stewart, my FBI friend."

We drove to the store and had something to eat in the MacDonald's. I devoured my quarter pounder, went to the phone department and purchased a new cell phone while Katrina and Blaze finished their food. We picked up a 12 pack of water and returned to the car. I called long distance information, got the number of the Houston FBI Headquarters, and punched in the number.

"FBI regional offices," a deep male voice answered.

"I'm trying to reach Agent Gerry Stewart. It's urgent that I talk to him."

"Wait, I'll connect you to his office."

On the second ring a professional female voice answered. "Agent Stewart's office, this is Brenda. How can I help you?"

I remembered talking to Brenda on a prior occasion when I was in town and had called Gerry to have lunch with me. "Brenda this is Ethan Tyler. It's urgent that I speak to Gerry right away."

"Oh yes Mr. Tyler, I remember you. Gerry told me about your friendship in service. I set up a lunch for you and Gerry a while back."

"May I speak with him please?"

"I'm so sorry he's on a hunting trip with another friend, Nat Armstrong. It's the first vacation he's had in two years and he's staying near Beaumont, Texas. His wife Susan and the kids are visiting her family in South Carolina. He plans to join them in a couple of days."

"Please Brenda, this is exceedingly important."

"I'll tell you what Mr. Tyler, I can't give out his private cell number, but I'm sure he would want to know that you called. I'll call him and give him your number and he can call you back. Is that okay?"

"That's fine, thanks for your help." I gave her my cell number and looked over to Katrina.

"Nothing we can do until he calls. Why don't we check into a motel, get some rest and plan our next moves? Beaumont is about three hours from Tyler."

We drove until we spotted a Comfort Inn, got a room for Katrina and me and one for Blaze. Blaze was quiet and seemed nearly in shock from what all she'd been through. Katrina comforted her and assured her again that we would rescue to Billy as soon as we got some help.

Katrina was shaking her head when she returned from Blaze's room. "She cried herself to sleep worrying about her brother," she said.

I started to answer her when my cell phone rang. I answered, "Yes."

"Ethan is that you? This is Gerry."

I breathed a sigh of relief. "Thanks for calling me my friend. Katrina and I are in deep trouble and we need you help."

"You know you can count on me, "What's going on?""

I spoke to him in detail about my undercover work at Future Mankind Ventures and the period of amnesia. I covered Katrina's kidnapping, her escape and articulated to him in detail about the experiments with the God Particle at the laboratory in West Texas. I continued for about twenty minutes outlining my situation and finished by telling him about the involvement of the CIA at the highest levels with the principals of Future Mankind Ventures.

"My God Ethan, you guys are lucky to be alive," he said. "First what in the hell is the CIA doing working on USA soil? They're confined to work in foreign nations only. The FBI handles domestic issues."

"Gerry, Future Mankind Ventures has offices in Paris and London as well as in this country. The investigation began in London. Director Hernia refused to give up jurisdiction when it moved to USA soil. Since the situation started on foreign soil, he was allowed by the White House to continue because of the high stakes and his close ties with the Attorney General. This operation is top secret and was not even shared with Director Stancil of the FBI."

"That means I can't officially be involved," Gerry said.

"But Gerry, I was counting on your help."

"Wait Ethan, I said officially, you know I got your back personally."

"Another thing Gerry, are you familiar with the man known as the Piranha?"

"Yes we've been tracking him for over a year. He's a suspect in several murders and in international fraud. He's on our ten most wanted list, but we don't have a clue who he is. His identity is veiled under an impenetrable cloak of secrecy. What's he got to do with this?"

"I don't want to discuss that on the phone. I'll tell you my suspicions face to face, but he is involved."

"Ethan, do you know Nat Armstrong?"

"Yes, before he became a private investigator and was with the FBI, we worked some cases together. He was a hell of an agent before the thing with his kid. I hear he married Layla, rescued his son from Mexico, and is doing very well as a PI. Does he still have that little dog, Nick? Smartest dog I ever saw."

"He's one of the most respected Investigators in the country now and Nick still goes with him everywhere. He and Layla added a little girl to the family to join David, his son. We 're great friends and he and Nick are here with me on a hunting trip near Beaumont. Where are you?"

"I'm near Tyler about three hours from you."

"Ethan, what do you need from me?"

"Gerry, I'm shut off from the CIA right now and there's evidence that they want to eliminate me. First, I want to rescue a young man held captive at a laboratory not far from here.

They're planning some ghoulish experiment on him. His sister helped Katrina escape captivity, probably saving her life, and I owe her. Furthermore, there's another man there who worked directly for the Piranha. I want to capture him and question him about the identity of the Piranha. I believe he has physical proof to nail the guy. Finally, we need to stop the illegal activity at the laboratory and clear my name."

"Ethan, wait a minute while I speak with Nat."

I waited and heard voices in the background. Apparently, Gerry was briefing Nat on the situation. He came back on the line.

"Ethan, Nat and I are going to help you unofficially for now, as private citizens. Just tell me where to meet and we'll be there as quickly as we can. I'll call Susan and Nat will phone Layla, informing them we may be here a few days longer. We'll let everyone else think that we are extending our hunting trip."

I gave him my location at the motel and thanked him. I knew I could count on Gerry.

"Katrina, help is on the way. Gerry Stewart and Nathanial Armstrong are the best there is. There's a light at the end of this tunnel."

She smiled, however there was a look of pronounced distress on her face.

59

Ted was ravenous. The dynamism of the energy to perform his activities would necessitate much more food than he would have typically required. He was burning calories at twice the normal rate of a human. He knew that he had to find a food source.

Ted didn't know where he was or where the nearest populace would be. He realized that hitching a ride was his best option, however he looked menacing in the uniform, combat boots, and holster strapped to his waist. No one would pick up an armed hitchhiker. He unbuckled the holster, removed the pistol, and threw the belt into the woods by the side of the road. He stripped off his shirt leaving only the white undershirt and pulled the shirttail out of his pants. Ted placed the gun in his belt in the small of his back. The T-shirt concealed it. Now he looked rather harmless as he began walking down the highway.

Several cars passed him, disregarding his outstretched thumb. He cursed, since they didn't even show down, and his energy was waning. He needed food desperately. Finally after about thirty minutes of walking, an old red pickup truck stopped.

"You look like you need some help," a voice from inside the truck hollered.

"I need a lift, my car broke down a few miles back," Ted replied.

Ted could see two men in the truck. One of them got out. He was wearing overalls over a red plaid flannel shirt. The man was chewing tobacco and spit as he approached Ted. He was over six feet tall and probably weighed more than three hundred pounds. His beard was mixed red with gray. His nose apparently had been broken in several places and it grew back harshly twisted.

"Name's Eudy. You willing to pay for a lift to Brady. It's miles down the road."

"How much?" Ted asked.

"Forty would do it," Eudy said, spiting another wad of tobacco juice to the side.

Ted pulled the wallet out of his back pocket, fished our two twenties and handed it to him. He noticed Eudy eying the other bills in the wallet. "Fine with me," Ted said.

They walked to the pickup. "This here's Butch," Eudy said, pointing to the driver. Butch was thin, arms covered in tattoos, in his twenties, black hair in a ponytail and acne covering his face. He smiled, showing his brown stained teeth.

"Obliged to see you," he said. "You got to ride in the back."

Ted climbed in the back of the pickup. He wanted to kill the bastards right now, but he needed to get his bearings. The road was bumpy and Ted was bounced all over the bed of the truck. The sky was clouding up and the smell of rain was in the air. Ted's enhanced senses made the smell of the storm enthralling.

After driving about twenty minutes, the pickup turned on a dirt road. Ted realized something was up. As soon as they were out of sight of the highway, the truck stopped abruptly. Eudy came out of the passenger door holding a double-barreled shotgun.

"Get the hell out of the truck," he snarled.

Butch was behind him, hooting. His laugh sounded like an anxious duck. "Eudy said you had money in that wallet of yours," he said. "We want it, shithead."

Ted grinned at them. "You're a pair of dumb ass sons of bitches," he said.

"I'm going to rip off your arm and jam it up your ass."

"Shoot him Eudy," Butch bellowed. "He's a crazy bastard."

With lighting speed, Ted jerked the pistol from his back and shot Eudy between the eyes. He fell forward on his face, dead. Butch's mouth dropped open.

"You kilt him," he blubbered.

"Take off your pants," Ted ordered, pointing the pistol at Butch's head.

"What the hell?" Butch was drooling.

"Take off your pants or I'll shot you in the balls."

"Okay, Okay," Butch stripped off his jeans.

'Underwear too," Ted ordered.

Butch stripped off his underwear and stood there naked from the waste down. Ted laid down the pistol and walked toward him.

"What in the shit are you doing?" There was a wild look in Butch's eyes. "Are you a pervert?"

"I told you I would rip off your arm and shove it up your ass," Ted replied, chuckling.

"To hell you say," Butch said, turned and ran.

Ted caught him easily and threw him to the ground. "Take it like a man."

Butch kicked at him and Ted caught his leg. He twisted it and the bone snapped. Butch screamed in pain, grabbing his broken leg. Ted grabbed his arm and with his superior strength twisted it hard. He heard the bones cracking. Butch passed out from the pain. Ted took both hands and twisted, grunting as the bones cracked and the flesh tore. He gave it one last twist and the arm separated from the shoulder. Blood spurted from the hole. He turned Butch over, and jammed the arm into his ass.

Ted felt such a strong feeling of ecstasy that he almost swooned. The Formula had dramatically enhanced the evil in his spirit and his thirst for killing was even becoming stronger. For now he need food. This exertion had further weakened him.

He searched the bodies of Eudy and Butch and found another couple of hundred dollars cash. He fished the keys to the truck from Butch's front pocket, picked up the shotgun and his pistol, and went to the truck.

The rednecks had mentioned Brady, Texas. The town couldn't be far.

Ted sped away and soon saw the lights of a convenience store. A soft rain was falling when he pulled up to the gas pumps. He parked the truck and walked inside. There was a slouchy young man behind the counter. His nametag read *Lenny*.

Ted pulled two twenty's from his wallet and laid them on the counter. "I need a fill up."

"What are you doing with Butch's truck?" Lenny asked.

"I bought it from him," Ted said. "Eudy said they needed the money."

Lenny looked at him suspiciously, "okay."

Ted walked to the cooler and pulled out three ham and cheese sandwiches. "The forty should cover these too," he said as he walked out the door and back to the truck.

He gobbled down the sandwiches while filling the tank with gas. He still felt insatiably hungry.

The gas bill came to $29.00. He walked back into the store. "I'm going to need some more food."

Lenny looked at him. "I don't think that Butch would ever part with his truck. When did you say you bought it?"

"Listen asshole, it's my truck now. I'm going to get some groceries."

Ted picked up a hand basket and went back to the cooler. As he was filling it up with sandwiches, he heard a noise behind him. He turned and saw Lenny standing there with a baseball bat.

"I need to see the bill of sale. Butch would never sell his truck mister."

Ted grabbed the bat and with speed that astonished Lenny. "You stuck your nose in the wrong place," he said as he swung the bat at Lenny's head. "Home run," he roared as he followed through with the swing. Lenny fell dead with a busted skull.

Ted fed on sandwiches, donuts, hot dogs, and potted meat until his hunger was satisfied. He loaded up several boxes of food and drinks and put them in the truck. He walked back into the store, emptied the cash register and went to get Lenny's wallet, when a woman entered the store.

Ted went to the front. "Where's Lenny?" the woman asked. "What's Eudy's truck doing out there?"

"Lenny and Eudy are the same place you're going," Ted replied, as he grabbed her neck. "Whew," he grunted, "thanks lady for pleasure of a twofer." He heard a noise and dropped her. Rushing to the front of the store, he didn't see anyone, so he left the store and drove away. Places to go and people to kill.

He ignored the minor headache and the pressure he felt inside his skull.

The woman opened her eyes and heard the door slam as Ted left, then passed out again. There was still a breath of life in her.

Thirty minutes later when Ashton Pressley came in to get his daily six-pack of Bud, he found her and called 911. She was rushed to the hospital.

Ted was a little careless and had unintentionally left behind a witness.

60

Timothy Olsen was highly pissed when he learned that his prime test subject had escaped. He needed to perform tests to resolve necessary control adjustments to the Formula. Evidently the results of the injections were considerably more pronounced than even he had anticipated. The test subject Harper, according to witnesses, could exert some type of mind control and generate mental pain. His speed and strength defied human limits. Tim demanded that the man captured so he could proceed with intense testing. Figuring out how to control his superman would be challenging.

Azar walked into the room. "What are your plans for the boy, Billy?" Are you going to proceed with injections on him?"

"Hell no you fool. I want Harper captured and returned to me for analysis. I must make additional alterations to the Formula prior to injecting anyone else. Does Cain have people hunting for Harper?"

"Cain vanished and no one knows where he is or how to get in touch with him. Ben Cruise is temporarily in charge until either Cain can be located or replaced. The board authorized his immediate assignment of temporary CEO because you're in the critical stages of your experiments. They're getting antsy for useable results."

"I need to see Cruise now," Olsen snapped.

"He's traveling from his ranch in Texas and should arrive in about thirty minutes.

Mr. Cruise demanded an emergency board meeting for to-morrow, and requires that you deliver a detailed presentation on the status of your project. I think he also wants you to perform a live experiment on the boy, so they can observe first hand the extremity of the transformations."

Olsen ignored the last comment. "I'll must have Harper at the meeting. He is the stalwart example of my ability to success-fully evolve humans. Now I ask you again Alzar, are there men searching for him? He couldn't have gone far."

"You can talk to Cruise about it," Alzar replied.

Tim stormed out of the laboratory and went to the holding room where his only remaining subject was being held. He was still furious that his first two experiments with the janitor and his assistant, Brenda, culminated in their deaths, and now his only successful living subject had escaped. He felt as if he was working for an army of fools.

A large black man was sitting in a chair by the door reading a book when he entered.

"Who are you?" Tim barked.

"I'm Baako," the man replied with a British accent. "I was ordered by Alzar to be the keeper of this boy."

"Get out!" Tim ordered.

"You are not the boss of me," the man replied. "I will stay until Alzar tells me to go."

"Okay, asshole, but when I talk to Cruise, he'll fire your ugly ass."

Baako nodded, smirked and returned to reading his book. Tim noticed the name of the book was "The Long Journey Home," by some guy named Gary William Ramsey. *Probably a piece of trash,* he thought.

Tim went to the cage where Billy was sleeping on a gurney. A porta potty was in the corner of the cage and an untouched plate of what resembled meat loaf and mashed potatoes were on the small table to the right of the gurney. A half empty glass of milk set alongside the plate. One straight chair was by the table.

"Wake up boy!" Tim shouted and Billy's eyes flew open. He got off the gurney and gazed despondently at Tim. A bandage was visible under his white shirt.

"Who are you sir?"

"I'm the guy who is going to evolve you into a superman. Are you recovered from your injuries?"

"Yes, I'm okay, but why am I locked up and where is my sister Blaze?"

"I don't know any Blaze, however soon you will be thanking me for your grand evolution. I will play games with your mind and make you superhuman."

Billy shook his head. He had no idea what this guy was talking about.

The door to the room opened and Alzar strolled in.

"Mr. Cruise is here and wants to see you immediately. He's in Cain's office."

Tim hurried to the office and straight past the protesting assistant.

"Hello Mr. Olsen. Have a...."

Tim interrupted him in mid sentence, "How many men do you have looking for Harper? I want him here immediately. The fools running this place are irresponsible and incompetent."

Cruise stared at the arrogant young man. He bit his lip to control his anger. "Sit down, Mr. Olsen."

"I don't want to sit down."

"Get you scrawny ass in the chair right now before I force you down," Cruise ordered. His face was red with contempt for the arrogant young genius.

Tim was startled by the firmness and anger in the man's voice. No one had talked to him that way before. He was the company's prize scientist and Cain and the others usually revered him and gave him anything he wanted. Nevertheless, fear gripped him and he sat down.

"I desire to have a civil conversation with you so show me some respect," Cruise said. "I realize that incompetence allowed your test patient to escape. I've called in two of the best bounty hunters in the country and put a 100,000-dollar price on Harper's capture and return to you. These guys are connected, tough as hell, and they won't fail. I expect to have Harper back in the facility soon."

"Since I evolved him, he's a dangerous son of a bitch too," Tim replied.

"Believe me these guys have brought in men rougher than your man could possibly be."

He just doesn't understand, Tim thought, *but no sense arguing with him.*

Cruise stared straight into Tim's eyes and the young man flinched. "You just present to the men at the meeting what you've accomplished and how you plan to use your Formula to make it worth their investment. I also want you to tell them when the Formula will be beneficial and totally ready for mass practical use." Cruise watched as Tim's face reddened with anger. "The agents will also demand a live experiment on the boy. I demand tangible results since the Formula is on the market."

"What are you talking about?" Tim replied, astonished. "I'm not going to sell the most important scientific breakthrough ever in the history of man. Don't you understand, this will change the path of human evolution?"

"You don't own the project, we do," replied Cruise. "Your contract specifically grants the ownership to Future Mankind Ventures of anything you discover while on our payroll."

Tim was livid, but strained to control his anger. "There're still some glitches in the Formula that I need to advance and alter. For example, there is a space between the brain and the skull, which is filled with a three-layered membrane known as the Meninges.

It helps to cushion and protect the brain from vibration and knocks to the head. It envelops the brain in a protective cushion the keep the delicate brain tissue safe. With the mass growth in selected lobes of the brain in my experiment with Harper, this cushion was eliminated to allow enough space to expand the selected lobes. If he's hit severely enough on the skull to cause brain swelling, the pressure on the skull will be insurmountable and the brain tissue will seek outlets such as the eyeball sockets and the ears. I believe I have the Formula modified, but I can't be sure until I can get Harper back, examine him, and apply the altered Formula to the young boy, Billy."

"I don't care about this scientific mumbo jumbo. The meeting is set and we're going forward with the sale of the Formula. If you value your life, you'll be convincing to the foreign agents," Cruise sneered.

"What foreign agents? I was told that this was a board meeting."

"Who attends the meeting is none of your damn business," Cruise replied.

Tim's psychopathic mind was spinning. He had not anticipated this turn of events.

Cain had lied to him, but this Cruise guy was apparently laying the truth on the line. He needed years of experiments to conduct before sharing his discoveries with the world.

Cain promised him full credit and enormous sums of money. If the Formula was sold now, in the infancy of the possibilities, other scientists would surely massacre his intention of definitively evolving the entirety of mankind. In his mind, Timothy Harding Olsen deserved the worldwide adulation of all humans for his discoveries. He was being cheated out of his destiny.

"You'll sell it over my dead body," he whispered to himself as he stomped out of the office.

61

The Piranha was frustrated with the incompetence's of the laboratory's security force in allowing his "show pony" Harper to escape. He was ready to sell the Formula forthwith and start living his life of luxury. He was tired of his profession and the constant demands placed on him by his boss.

The Piranha masterminded the activities that placed him in the position of controlling Future Mankind Ventures. Through his agent and partner Cruise, and dummy corporations set up by Cruise's lawyers and accountants, he had accumulated eighty percent of the stock of the company. Cruise owned another ten percent. However, the Piranha promised Cruise another thirty percent when the sale transaction was complete.

The enormity of the investment left him extremely sort on funds. Presently through sources who did not know his true identity, the bidding war began and China and Russia were offering billions, if he could prove that the God Particle Formula could be successfully applied to humans. Recently Iran entered the race. The Piranha was ready to consummate the bidding war and sell. There were an enormous set of circumstances and activities that made his ability to continue to hide his identity remote. He desired to cash in, get his fortune and leave the country. He had his sites on a remote island near Belize, to purchase and to control his empire in anonymity from there.

The agents from China, Russia and the dark horse in the bidding, Iran, had been invited to the laboratory. He instructed Cruise to tell Olsen that it was a board meeting, although Cruise reserved the right to be truthful with Olsen if necessary. The Piranha depended on the displaying of Harper to prove that the Formula was adapted for use on humans, but the bastard had escaped.

Also the participants demanded a live demonstration of the use, and subsequent effects of the Formula on humans. The only subject available, the young man Billy, was the designated guinea pig.

The Piranha picked up the phone and dialed Cruise.

"Yes Sir, what now?'

"I want you to call our prospective buyers and postpone the meeting to give us enough time to capture Harper. In the event he's not apprehended by the end of the week, we'll go forward, allowing them to view the injections and the mental and physical impacts on our other test case."

"Sir we have a problem delaying the meeting. The perspective buyers are getting impatient and will interrupt a delay as problems with the Formula, which will diminish the bidding price."

Frustration filled the Piranha's voice. "Do what you must to protect the value."

"I may have some trouble with Tim Olsen. He's not very corporative," Cruise said.

"If he doesn't follow orders, that's the reason we have Alzar there. He can conduct the experiment in the event Olsen balks. Who are the men you hired to capture Harper? Are they the same ones searching for Tyler?"

I have the men I told you about looking for Tyler. No success yet, and I think it's wise to let them concentrate on him. I hired a separate team to find Harper."Alek Glinka and Faddel Vasin, they were former assassins for the KGB. These guys are malicious and rough. I told them that Harper must be brought in alive for them to get paid. They'll find him. I promise you that."

"How can I contact them? I may want personal updates."

Cruise gave him Alek's cell number. "I'll telling you. These guys are the best," he said.

"By the way Cruise, I plan on attending the meeting. I'll be in disguise, but I can't trust these negotiations to anyone else."

The Piranha abruptly hung up his private cell phone when his assistant entered the office.

"The boss wants to see you immediately," she said. "I'm sorry that I had to barge in, but he appears extremely irate."

The Piranha took a deep breath. He didn't know how much longer he would put up with this shit. The end game is near, and his dreams of living the rest of his life on a private island in audacious luxury, calmed his nerves.

"Tell him I'll be there directly," he said. His assistant left the room. He took a bottle of Absolut Crystal vodka out of the bottom drawer and took a swig. He corked the bottle and picked up his briefcase to respond to his present Master.

When he walked into the office, the man behind the desk was reading some papers. He looked up and glared at the Piranha. "Why in the hell haven't you located Ethan Tyler and his wife? This is a top priority and you have nothing. If you don't produce soon, you're off the case and I'll put Mick Henderson on it. I'm sure that he can produce positive results. Now get out and when I see you again, I want a full report on whether the Tyler's turned to the other side or confirmation of his death? You know the protocol. If in doubt, he and his wife must be eliminated." He gave his hand a flip, looked down and continued to read the papers on his desk.

The Piranha wheeled on his heels and left the office. He was seething with anger. Sweat filled the pores on his forehead. *When I complete my deal, I'll discredit him and then leisurely kill him,* he thought.

He stomped out of the CIA building and went his car. He desperately needed a distraction and relaxation before the pressure of the End Game commenced.

After a short drive, he arrived at his apartment at the Ritz Carlton in Tysons Corner. He would have rather have been at his condo in the Blue Ridge Mountains or at Myrtle Beach because in both places he had autonomy. He never satisfied his cravings this close to his place of employment. However, he needed an immediate distraction. His nerves were raw. The Piranha went to his closet and removed the panel in the ceiling and pulled out a suitcase containing his disguises and makeup.

He left the building and made the nineteen-minute drive to Bethesda, Md. He found an Econo Lodge, checked in, paid cash for one night and went to the cheap room. The desk clerk was a young man, too busy talking to one of the Hispanic maids to really notice him. The Piranha undressed, wrapped body padding around his waist. He donned a brown wig, a matching mustache and darkened his skin. A pair of wrap around sunglasses finished off the disguise. He grabbed a wallet with fake identification matching the disguise. Resembling an overweight salesman, he went back to the reception area.

"Son I need to rent a car. Can you help me?" He slipped the guy a twenty.

"Yes sir, there's an Enterprise office just around the corner. Do you want me to call them?"

"I'll just walk."

"Turn right outside the door and go to the corner of Washington and Second Street."

He proceeded to the office and rented a grey Toyota SUV. American University was a short drive away, and he would search for his prey on campus. The Piranha reached into his suitcase, removed the chloroform, a soft cloth, and a roll of duct tape and placed the articles on the front passenger seat. He threw the suitcase in the back seat.

The drive to American University was pleasant, and his anticipation peaked when he entered the campus and drove to the Hughes Dorm. This building was in a quiet and more secluded part of the campus. He parked and waited. Several groups of students passed him, talking and laughing. *Arrogant Assholes,* he thought.

After waiting about forty-five minutes, a young girl with long red hair tied in a ponytail came strolling out of the dorm, alone. She was wearing tight jeans and a sweatshirt with *No Shit Please* written on it. The girl was exceptionally tall and her ass swayed when she walked. Red had earphones on her ears and was softly singing to whatever music was playing on her phone. The Piranha could tell from the two large bulges in her sweatshirt that she had a very substantial rack. She was not the blonde he desired, but she would have to do. He looked around and no one was in sight.

He got out of his car, "Excuse me miss. Can you direct me to the student union? I'm supposed to meet my niece there."

Red stopped and removed her earphones, "What?" she asked.

He repeated the request.

"Sure just go to Hightower Street and turn right, the next left and it's on the right."

"Wait," he said, "Let me get a pad and write it down."

"Gezze," she said.

The Piranha grabbed the chloroform from the seat, and soaked the cloth. Red had her back turned to him.

"What is that God awful smell?" she said, turning toward him.

He grabbed her head and jammed the chloroform soaked cloth to her nose. He locked his other arm around her torso. She struggled, but his grip was strong and unyielding. Quickly, her body went limp.

He opened the trunk, tossed her inside, grabbed the duct tape and taped her hands and feet. After wrapping a piece around her head and mouth, he slammed the trunk, and leisurely drove away from the campus.

The Piranha's anticipation intensified during the drive back to the motel. He chuckled at the thought of his impending sexual pleasure. *My gratification is much more important than this college bitch,* he thought. Her body and life was an insignificant price to pay to calm him for the negotiations.

When he arrived at the motel, he parked directly in front of the door to his room, and went inside. He ripped the comforter from the bed, returned to the vehicle and popped the trunk. After looking around the parking lot and seeing no one, he wrapped the comforter around Red. He threw her over his shoulder, closed the trunk, carried her unconscious body into the room and dumped her on the bed.

The Piranha locked the door, went to the bathroom and soaked a towel with cold water. He unwrapped her body from the comforter, dropped it to the floor, and placed the cold towel on her head. She opened her bloodshot eyes, and shook her head. She was undoubtedly confused and terrified. When she focused on his ghoulishly grinning face, she panicked and struggled violently against the restraints. The Piranha punched her in the stomach. She gasped and struggled to get her breath.

"Stay still or I'll hurt you badly," he hissed. "Listen Red, I'm going to remove the tape from your mouth. If you scream, I'll slash your throat. Do you understand?"

She nodded and lay still. He ripped the tape from her lips. She wheezed again.

"I'm going to have sex with you," he whispered in her ear. "If you help me and don't struggle, you'll survive this night. If not, I'll rape you and kill you slowly and sadistically." He lied, having no intention of allowing her to live.

"Okay," she managed to mumble. "Just don't hurt me."

The Piranha slowly removed her sweatshirt, and took off her bra. He chuckled bizarrely while he fondled her pale breasts. She had nipples the size of half dollars. She gritted her teeth, but said nothing. He reached down, unzipped her jeans and pulled them down to her ankles. She was wearing a white lace thong. As he moved to tear it off, his cell phone rang. He ignored it, and it went to voice mail. Ethan Tyler's voice came on the line.

"I need to meet with you right away," he said. "I know who the Piranha is and I need your help to move on him. Meet me at the Holiday Inn, where we met before. I'll be in room 207. You know the place. If you're not here within four hours, I'll go to the FBI for help."

The line went dead. The Piranha, Agent Hank Thompson, leaped from the bed. He grabbed the cell phone, went to the bathroom, and punched return call. Ethan Tyler answered, "is that you Hank?"

"Yes Ethan, don't call the FBI. We don't need their interference. I'll arrange a flight on the Company's private jet. I can be there in less than four hours. Don't talk to anyone and wait for me."

"Will do Hank, thanks."

The Piranha immediately dialed the cell number of Alek Clinka.

"Yes," the Russian answered.

"I'm sure Cruise told you about me. I'm his boss and I know that you're looking for Ted Harper. If you need verification, confirm this call with Cruise. Just tell him the Piranha called and give him the code IUE378. I want you to delay your search for Harper. I have a more urgent job for you. There's a man named Ethan Tyler, who'll be waiting for me at the Holiday Inn in room 207. I want you to go to his room, find out all he knows about the experiments of the God Particle Formula, and about me. He thinks he knows my identity and may have some proof. I don't care how you extract the information. When you have satisfied yourself that you have everything, kill him. Call me with the information, and then continue your search for Harper. Your fee will be doubled. You have my cell number now in your phone's history. Cruise has other men looking for Tyler, but they're getting nowhere. He told me that you are the best there is in what you do. I want you to handle this."

Thompson gave them the address of the hotel. "Any questions?"

"What does the man look like?" Faddell asked.

The Piranha provided him with the description and hung up. He needed to deal with the girl, and then get to the laboratory to prepare for the meeting with the foreign representatives.

He gazed at the wide-eyed sexy redhead lying on the bed. She was crying. "You are a lucky bitch," he said as he slapped the tape back over her mouth. After retrieving the chloroform from the SUV, he administered a heavy dose to the struggling Redhead. He wrapped the comforter around her body, went back to the rented vehicle and dumped her in the trunk. He wiped his prints from the SUV and cleaned all prints from the room.

The car he had arrived in was in the lot. He jumped in and drove away. On the way to the private airport, he called the pilot, who was on call 24/7, and arranged a flight to Texas to depart as soon as possible.

Two days later, the dehydrated redhead was discovered in the trunk of the rented SUV. The police were called when the rental car company was informed by the desk clerk that the vehicle had been abandoned.

Shela Hemsley, the pre-med redheaded honor student was rushed to the hospital. After three days of care, she was released.

Her description of the disguised Piranha was not helpful to the police.

62

Katrina and I rested and had some dinner as we waited for Gerry and Nat to arrive. The Chinese food we ordered delivered from Wong's Chef was wonderful. She checked on Blaze to offer her some food, but the young girl was still sleeping.

"Ethan, we need to do something about Hank Thompson," she said. "He's the key to finding out how far the corruption goes in the CIA. I'm sure that either he or Director Hernia is the Piranha, but we need to be able to prove it."

I thought for a moment. "Katrina I have Thompson's cell number. I can call him and set up a meeting in the motel where we met before, record the session and attempt to acquire damning evidence. He's dangerous and may try to kill me, but with you in the closet holding a gun on him, I'll be okay."

I dialed Thompson and set up the meeting. I could hear the eagerness in his voice as we talked. He agreed on the location and we hung up.

Just as I finished the call, there was a knock on the door. I looked through the peephole and it was Gerry and Nat. I opened the door.

"You guys are a sight for sore eyes," I said, shaking their hands.

Nat was holding his little brown mutt, Nick. I patted his head. "You and that mutt are always together aren't you?" I asked, laughing.

"Never go anywhere without him," Nat replied. Nick barked and licked my hand.

Nat put him on the floor and he immediately ran to greet Katrina. She was sitting on the couch and he jumped up and curled up on her lap.

"I have a new friend," she said, patting his head.

"Nice to see you again, Katrina," Gerry said. "Do you know Nathaniel Armstrong?"

"No, but I've heard a lot about him. Nice to finally meet you Nat, and thanks for helping us."

"Okay Ethan, what are we facing here?"

There was a couch, a lounge chair and a small desk with a chair in the room. Nat sat on the couch beside Katrina and Nick, and Gerry and I took the other seats around the desk.

"Since we talked, I set up a meeting with Hank Thompson at a Holiday Inn not far from here. He's flying in. We suspect that he's the Piranha, but have no proof. Also Director Hernia may the Piranha or at least is involved. I plan to be provocative at the meeting, record it, and hope I entice him to admit something. If he is, in fact, the Piranha, he's deeply involved with Future Mankind Ventures and their illegal activities." I took a breath and regarded the amazed faces.

"After the meeting, we have to go to the complex where Blaze's brother is being held prisoner and rescue him. I hope he hasn't already been used for extermination.

Additionally, we must stop Timothy Olsen's project before it can be militarized and sold to foreign governments. To have a chance against the guards in the secure complex, we're need to be heavily armed. What are you equipped with?"

"Don't worry about that," Gerry said. "Nat and I come fully prepared when we go big game hunting. We both brought our handguns of course, and in addition Nat has a Westly Richards .375 Magnum with scope. That baby would drop an elephant with one shot. I have my Weatherby Mar 5, and I also brought my UZI 20 round semi automatic. It's new and I wanted to try it out. In addition I have a plain, old fashion Remington double barrel shotgun."

I smiled. "That should do the trick." Nick barked and licked Katrina's hand, as if to add his approval of the arsenal.

"Exactly what's your plan of deployment?" Nat asked. He had served in the Special Forces, which required specific planning.

"Well Nat, Gerry, you and I will go to the meeting with Thompson and attempt to gather information to nail him. We need to begin by cutting off the head of the snake, and if I'm correct in my assessments, he is the head. Hopefully we can take him into custody and find out how far up the corruption goes in the CIA. We have to know who we can trust. I'll waterboard his ass if I have to, after we determine that he's the Piranha. I'll do what has to be done and worry about the consequences later."

"What about Blaze and me?" Katrina asked.

"I want you and Blaze to go to house where Blaze and Billy lived, just outside the cornfield. After we deal with Thompson, we'll meet you there. We'll use the cornfield as cover when we approach the complex to get Billy."

Nick barked as if asking, *what about me?*

"Take Nick to the house with you," Nat said. "He'll be safer there."

Nick barked again, jumped from Katrina's lap and ran to Nat. "You're staying with Katrina Nick, and that's my final decision." The little dog looked up at his owner, whined, and slowly walked back to the couch and jumped back into Katrina's lap.

"We need to get going," I said. "I want to get there in plenty of time to get set up before Thompson arrives."

"I'll get Blaze and we'll leave directly after you," Katrina said.

I grabbed my pistol and Gerry, Nat and I walked out to Gerry's vehicle. Gerry lifted the trunk lid of the black Humvee and showed me the stash of weapons and ammunition.

"We could conquer Cuba in a flat bed wagon with these arms," I said, laughing.

However, hidden deep in the shadows of my mind, I was worried about the safety of my friends who came to my aid. Both were married with children, and we were going to be facing savages. Handling Thompson was one thing, but storming the laboratory complex to rescue Billy would be another matter.

One thing at a time, I thought, *one thing at a time.*

63

Timothy Olsen walked back to the laboratory. His head was pounding from the extreme anger he felt. He required considerably more time to perfect his formula, and he couldn't do it without the money and facilities provided by Future Mankind Ventures.

These greedy bastards want to sell it now, even in its non-perfected form. Of course it will work on humans, but refinements are required, he thought. Abruptly another thought blasted into his head. *They brought in Alzar to replace me in the event I objected to their plans. The reason Cruise was so blunt, and told me the truth is they believe Alzar can take over the project.* This thought triggered blind fury.

As he calmed his psychopathic mind, two things became very clear. First, he had to kill Alzar to protect the secrets of his Formula, and secondly, he had to gather his papers and all remaining samples of the Formula. The laboratory must be destroyed to eliminate any traces of his Formula and experiments. When these two actions are accomplished, he would search for another company to finance his project.

Before he signed on with Future Mankind Ventures, a Swiss company called Debkiar Enterprises had contacted him, showing extreme interest in his theories. He was sure that after reviewing his successes with the God Particle Formula, that they would provide him with everything he needed to continue his work.

While studying at The Massachusetts Institute of Technology, Tim discovered that the most effective and simplest bomb to make involved the introduction of aluminum to sulfuric acid. He learned that initially a container is filled with sulfuric acid, and then a piece of aluminum is inserted. The lid is tightened securely. The glass container will swell. Subsequently, the resulting cloud that bursts from the container is a mixture of Hydrogen gas and Sulfuric Acid vapor. The vapor will kill anyone in close proximately, and the explosion would ignite a fire when coming in contact with flammable liquids or objects.

Tim had a large supply of sulfuric acid in the chemical inventory in the supply room. That would work nicely with plain, store bought Aluminum foil. He also had, at his disposal, a supply of quart size L-Mark vials with caps.

He went to the break room and filled a cup with steaming hot coffee. In the cupboard he found a roll of heavy-duty aluminum foil. He casually sipped his coffee and left the room with the foil. Tim placed it in the laboratory, got his pushcart and went to the supply room. He set a gallon jug of sulfuric acid on the cart, four of the L-Mark vials and took the items to the laboratory. On the back table, he filled four vials with the acid. He tore four pieces of foil from the roll, crumpled them up and put them on the table. He transferred the items to the cabinet, locked it, and shoved the key into his pocket.

Just as he finished, Alzar walked in. "What are you doing?" he asked.

"What in the hell do you think?" Tim scoffed. "Getting ready for the meeting. Did you know those bastards are going to auction off my Formula?"

"You'll be taken care of," Alzar said. *I will personally kill your arrogant ass,* he thought. "What can I do to help?"

"The best way you can help me is to get the hell out of my laboratory," Tim screeched.

Alzar looked at him, sneered and left.

Tim's plan was simple. On the day of the meeting, he would gather everything relating to his Formula, hide the items in the cornfield outside the complex, and return to the laboratory. He planned to place three of the sulfuric acid filled vials and the foil on a pushcart and station the cart at the door. After summoning Alzar to the laboratory, and sending him to the cabinet in the back to fetch some supplies, he would drop foil in the fourth vial and heave it toward Alzar. Then, he would leave the laboratory, locking the door, trapping Alzar inside. With all the flammable chemicals in the laboratory, an intense fire would erupt. Of course the bomb would kill Alzar and any remaining information concerning his Formula would be destroyed.

Following that, he planed to detonate one bomb in the Boardroom, one in Cain's office, which was now occupied by Cruise, and the last one in the electrical room to render the complex powerless. The explosions should create blazes in each area.

Timothy Olsen planned to then leave the burning building and escape through the cornfield. He figured that surely there was some sort of civilization not to far away.

His plans set and the bombs prepared, he felt a deep feeling of satisfaction.

"None of these stupid bastards should have screwed with me,"he said aloud.

64

During the drive to the Holiday Inn, we talked about how to best handle the situation. We decided that Nat would check in at the desk of the motel, since no one would recognize him, and he would specifically ask for room 207. Nat volunteered to be the lookout outside the door when Thompson arrived. He would alert us if anyone was with Thompson. Gerry's job was to hide in the closet with the door-cracked open with the recording device, his smart phone, with his pistol drawn and ready. In the even that Thompson pulled a gun on me, Gerry could intervene.

My job was to entice Thompson to talk voluntarily about the Piranha. I hoped through my training in interrogation techniques, I could trick him. To accomplish this, I had to take some risks, and to lead him to believe that I was a rogue CIA agent just looking for a big payday. If he took the bait, we'd have something to nab him on. If not, I was ready to use some techniques, which in today's liberal world would be considered torture. In any event, regardless of the information we acquired, my plan was to incapacitate him while we went to the laboratory complex to free Billy. He may even supply us with information to make that task easier.

We arrived at the Holiday Inn and Gerry and I stood outside room 207 while Nat checked in. The West Texas sky was clear with thousands of glimmering stars. The Texas nights like this were meant to enjoy without violence, but you have to play the cards dealt to you.

Nat arrived with the key card, "I'm going to hang around out here, out of sight. I'll be by the vending machines, and I'll ring your cell if I see a problem."

Gerry and I went inside and set up, according to the plan.

I looked at my watch and realized that it would be at least thirty minutes before Thompson arrived. We made ourselves comfortable with Gerry at the closet door and me sitting in the lounge chair. We were talking about Thompson when Gerry's cell rang.

"What's the problem Nat?" he asked. "I'll put you on speaker phone so Ethan can hear."

"I think we have a problem. A white van just drove up and these two really huge rough looking men got out. No question they're professionals. Both have guns in their belts, and are looking around, checking out the place. They haven't spotted me. Wait, they appear to be walking toward your door. I'm going to move closer." He hung up.

Just as he hung up, the door was kicked open and an enormous man, holding a pistol, rushed into the room. He appeared startled when he saw Gerry with a gun pointed at him. As he turned to shoot Gerry, I kicked him in the groin and followed with an uppercut to his chin. To my surprise he didn't fall. When he turned toward me, Gerry slammed him in the head with the butt of his gun. Blood seeped from his scalp, and he fell to the floor. He attempted to get to his knees so I kicked him in the ribs. I heard a crack as the toe of my shoe connected. This time he lay still, out cold.

Nat rushed into the room. "What the hell?"

"We got this one, what about the other one?" I asked.

"He evidently was the lookout. I rushed him and he pointed the damn colt 45 at me. I chopped him in the neck and I'm afraid I collapsed his larynx. He'll live, but it'll be awhile before he can talk. I hog tied him with his belt, big man, long belt."

"Drag his body in here,' Gerry said. "There were no shots fired so maybe no one heard the commotion. We need to find out who these guys are."

Nat dragged the man in, stuffed a washcloth in his mouth and placed him in the corner of the room.

"I'm going to grab some duct tape from the Humvee," Gerry said.

The big guy with the broken ribs groaned. He was regaining consciousness. Gerry returned with the duct tape and taped his hands, feet and mouth.

"Nat, would you take a look in the van and see what you can find?" I said. I emptied the pockets of the thug with cracked rips and found his keys and wallet. I pitched the keys to Nat and he left to search the van.

Gerry grabbed the wallet from the other guy and searched his pockets. "Look what I found?" he said, holding up a plastic packet of what appeared to be coke. He opened the packet, smelled it and touched the white powder to his lips. "High grade cocaine."

We emptied the wallets on the bed. The guy who Nat subdued was named Faddel Vasin, obviously Russian, and he had a Texas driver's license. It was possibly fake, but we had no way of knowing. The wallet was flush with cash. Gerry pulled out a folded note. The name Ben Cruise was on the note with a telephone number and directions to the Holiday Inn. Scribbled at the bottom of the note was the name, Piranha. Faddel's cell phone was also in his pocket and we put it with the other items.

The other guy's license read *Alex Clinka*. No other identification was found. "No sense in trying to question Faddel," I said, noting that the big Russian was wheezing. The cloth in his mouth exacerbated his crushed larynx.

We'll have to get the information from ole Alek here," Gerry said.

Nat returned to the room. "I searched the van and there's a stash of weapons in the back along with chloroform, handcuffs and cocaine. There was also a police scanner, which could intercept police radio chatter. It appears that they were going to abduct or kill you Ethan."

He held up a phone. "Better yet I found this phone. Apparently these guys didn't trust anyone and recorded all their conversations. Let's get out of earshot of these goons and let me play the recordings for you." We stepped outside the door.

The first recording he played was Ben Cruise hiring the Russians to find Ted Harper and return him to the laboratory. The next conversation was the Piranha telling them to postpone the search for Harper, and to find Tyler at the Holiday Inn, question him and execute him. Following was a call to Ben Cruise to verify that the instructions from the Piranha were okay to execute.

"I recognize that voice on the call from the Piranha. That's Hank Thompson of the CIA. This proves what I already suspected. Thompson is our man. He was the only one who knew I was here waiting."

Gerry looked at me and said, "The voice recognition devices at the FBI can prove in a court of law that this Thompson guy ordered your murder. We'll have unimpeachable proof when this action is complete.

The FBI also has an open file on the Piranha. We suspect mail fraud, murder, robbery and a myriad of other crimes linked to this felon. Several criminals, who we have in custody, mentioned him as the mastermind of felonious activities, but none had ever met him in person or knew his true identity."

Nat grinned, "Glad I could help with this phone, but we need a confession recorded by one of these guys to lock the case linking the phone to them and to Cruise and Thompson. If we don't get that, they can claim that the phone isn't theirs and deny everything."

"I can handle that. Nat, grab Faddel's cell phone from the bed and record my conversation with Alek. Don't record any threats. Start recording when he agrees to talk." I said.

We went back into the room. I dragged Alek to the bed and propped him against it. His eyes were darting back and forth between Gerry and me. I placed my hand against his cracked ribs and pushed hard. The gag muffled his grunts of pain.

"Here's what's going to happen," I said. "You're going to tell me who you take orders from, who sent you here and for what reason." I ripped the tape from his mouth.

"Eat shit," he hissed.

I put the tape back over his mouth and punched him in the ribs. He grunted again in pain. "Listen carefully asshole, this is what I'm going to do." I took off his shoes and socks. "First, I'm going to take a knife and cut off your toenails, one by one. Then I'll tell my friend here to pour lighter fluid on them and set your toes on fire. If you remain silent or say anything like *eat shit* again, I'm going to get a screwdriver, jam it against your teeth, and punch all of your front teeth out. If you still don't talk, Gerry here is going to gouge out your eyeballs. It's up to you. I really don't give a damn."

Nat reached in his pocket, grabbed his pocketknife and pitched it to me. "Ethan take one off just for fun. Remember, this man was going to torture and kill you."

I opened the knife and stuck it about an eight of an inch under the toenail of his big toe. Blood seeped around the tip of the knife. The big man shuttered and shook his head violently. I ripped off the tape again. "Anything you want to say?"

"You crazy son of a bitch, I'll tell you anything you want to know, just stop."

So the big brave killer believed me and is not so brave at all when faced with intense pain. I smiled at Gerry and nodded to Nat. He was ready to record.

"Start from the beginning with who hired you and why." He hesitated. Cold fury was conspicuous in his eyes. I smiled at him and pushed the knife a little deeper under the toenail. "I'll just take this thing off. I'm tired of you shit anyway."

"Wait, wait," he screeched. "Faddel and I have done work from time to time for Daniel Cruise. He called me a few days ago and hired us to find this guy named Ted Harper. He gave us a description and where the man was last seen. It was a $25,000 dollar job with bonuses to capture him, take him to a complex, and turn him over to Cruise. This guy was supposed to be some kind of superman, but we are tough bastards too."

"Unless someone fools with your toenail," I mocked him.

"We had a lead on where this guy was after we intercepted a police call where a man fitting Harper's description had killed a convenience store clerk and seriously injured a female worker. We also acquired a description of the truck he was driving. On our way to where he was last seen, we got a call from this guy, who called himself the Piranha. He ordered us to postpone the search for Harper and come here to extract specific information from you, using any means necessary. He substantially raised the payoff. After we confirmed the call with Cruise, we came here. That's it asshole."

I twisted the knife, "Come on now Alek, be respectful and don't call me an asshole." He gritted his teeth.

"Can I just gouge out one eyeball, Ethan?" Gerry said and walked to where we were. He put his finger in the edge of Alek's eye socket and applied a little pressure. He was playing the mind game perfectly.

Alek whimpered and Gerry removed his finger. "Were your orders to kill Ethan after you questioned him? If you lie to me you will be called a one-eyed bastard for the rest of your life."

Alek lowered his head and nodded. He was a broken man. Gerry put his mouth within three inches of his ear. "Were you ordered to kill him?" he shouted.

"Yea, yea, the Piranha wanted him dead and told us to make him suffer and kill him."

"That's all we need," I said, placing the tape back over his mouth and then removing the knife from under his toenail. "Get me a couple of wash cloths from the bathroom please Nat."

Nat handed me the washcloths and using the pocketknife, I cut both of the cloths in half. I stuffed a piece in both of Alek's ears, pushed them in deep, and wrapped duct tape around his head securing them. I did the same to Faddel. "I don't want these thugs to hear anything else we say," I explained.

"What's your plan?" Nat asked.

I looked at him and Gerry. "Lets wipe this place clean of our prints. Then, let's load these goons in the back of their van. Just before we leave, I'll call 911 and report where these guys are. I'll bet that those weapons in the van are illegal, and with the cocaine in their possession, they're going to jail. We'll put the phones with the confessions and the recorded calls from Cruise and Thompson (The Piranha) in the front seat and label them. The local cops will certainly call in the FBI."

"Great," Gerry said. "Conspiracy to comment murder, conspiracy to kidnap Harper, illegal possession of fire arms and illegal possession of cocaine. That should keep them locked away and in addition give evidence of criminal activity of both Cruise and Thompson. I like the way you think Ethan."

"The fun is just beginning," I said. "We need to meet Katrina, Blaze and Nick at the house by that damn cornfield and get to the laboratory complex. I'll bet Cruise is there, and probably Thompson is headed there. After we rescue Billy, we'll deal with them."

Nat backed the van to the motel door and we loaded the Russians. After wiping everything clean of our prints, we placed all our stuff in the Humvee and drove away. When we were about a mile away, I called 911 and reported the situation as I had planned. I wiped the phone clean and threw it into a ditch by the road.

This was going to be a long night.

65

Ted Harper recognized that he had to ditch the truck. It was just a matter of time before it was reported to the cops. He continued down the road and spotted a sign reading, *Burnham, Texas.* Soon he saw the lights and the sign of a Walmart, and he pulled into the parking lot. Ted waited in the lot for about ten minutes when he saw a young woman walking toward a green Lexus parked about two cars over from him. She opened the trunk and began loading her groceries. Harper got out of the truck and went to where she was standing. She closed the trunk and looked at him apprehensively.

"Excuse me Miss," Harper said. "Can you tell me where Stewart Street is?'

The girl had long blonde hair in a ponytail, and she wore no makeup. Her athletic body was displayed in white shorts and a tank top. She was probably in her late twenties.

"I never heard of Stewart Street," she said.

Harper shook his head and threw a straight right hand to her nose. He heard her nose bone fracture. She fell to the pavement unconscious and barely alive. Ted's enhanced strength was overpowering. He grabbed the keys, opened the back door and tossed her in the back seat.

"What's going on there?" An old man with gray hair yelled as he hurried toward him. He was carrying a tire iron, which he must have grabbed from his trunk when he saw Harper hit the woman.

"You don't want to mess with me," Harper murmured.

The old man kept coming. "What did you do to that girl?" He raised the tire iron over his head, ready to strike. With lightning speed, Harper seized the old man's left wrist and broke it. The weapon fell to the pavement. He grabbed the man's neck, twisted it and tossed the lifeless body aside.

Harper jumped into the Lexus and started the engine. He drove to the old truck, threw his stuff in the back floorboard of the Lexus, and sped out of the parking lot. He turned toward Alba, Texas. His energy was waning, and he needed to eat. He knew the trunk was filled with groceries, so as soon as he was a few miles away he pulled into the parking lot of a closed Western Auto Store. He checked on the girl. She was still out cold, and barely breathing.

Ted opened the trunk and searched the bags of groceries. He pulled out a quart of fat-free milk, a loaf of bread and a package of smoked ham. He slapped half of the ham between two slices of bread, devoured the thick sandwich and drank half the milk. He stuffed the remainder of the ham in his mouth and chewed. Looking further in the trunk, he found a six-pack of energy bars and consumed them. After finishing off the rest of the milk, he felt his vigor returning.

The girl was too much trouble even though he craved to rape her. He dragged her body from the back seat and threw it in a dumpster located at the back of the store. Ted looked around. His mind was racing.

I need a place to hole up for a while to make plans and get my act together, he thought. *Surely, the police are looking for me, and it's only a matter of time before the girl, and the Lexus will be the subject of an all points bulletin from the cops. The house where I found Ethan Tyler would be a perfect place to hide out. That cornfield provides cover, and maybe I can get revenge on the men who took me to the laboratory and locked me up like an animal.* With plenty of groceries in the trunk, he could maintain his strength. He also needed rest. The house in front of the cornfield was his best option.

Ted Harper cranked the Lexus and headed back to Alba. His destination was not far from there. After driving ninety miles an hour, he spotted the dirt road and the no-trespassing sign and turned right. While he was rounding the corner and driving toward the house, he noticed a vehicle parked in front. Lights illuminated the house. He killed his headlights and pulled to the side of the dirt road. After switching off the engine, he grabbed his pistol and got out of the car, quietly closing the door.

In a semi-crouch, he trotted toward the house. When he reached the front porch, he went to the right and ducked below a window. He slowly raised his head and peaked inside. Harper recognized the young blond girl from he and Herman's encounter when they came to kill Ethan. The other sexy, gorgeous woman, he didn't recall ever seeing. The two women appeared to be alone. The older woman was preparing some food in a frying pan, and the young blonde was sitting at the kitchen table. He didn't observe any weapons.

Well, since I didn't have time to have sex with the woman from Walmart, maybe now I can satisfy my cravings. Enhanced strength and enhanced mental acuity probably is accompanied by enhanced sexual prowess. Harper thought. He was anxious to test his sexual powers.

Harper crept back to the front porch and proceeded to the front door. With one daunting kick, he devastated the door and rushed in. Katrina dropped the frying pan, and Blaze screamed.

66

Tim Olsen felt smug knowing that he was prepared and willing to take the lives of the men he despised most. In his twisted mind, he was a genius and the rest of them were fools. They had delayed his progress in the research, and now he would take his miraculous innovations and perfect them at a place where he was more treasured.

He strolled to Cruise's office. "I need to see him immediately," he uttered to the assistant.

"He's with our special guest," she replied.

"Interrupt him," Tim scoffed.

The woman scowled at him, but got up and entered Cruise's office.

Immediately, Cruise came out, red-faced.

"Who is the hell do you think you are interrupting me? I'm in a critical meeting," he hissed.

"Are you proceeding with the sale of my Formula?"

"It's not yours, you little arrogant bastard. It belongs to the company. You'll be paid according to the terms of the contract," Cruise wheeled and went back into his office. Before he slammed the door, Tim caught a glimpse of a weird looking man standing by the desk. *He must be a part of this fiasco,* Tim thought. *Maybe I'll eliminate him too.*

At that exact moment, Tim absolutely concluded that he must immediately implement his plan and destroy Cruise, Alzar, the foreign visitors who were there to buy his beloved formula, and the strange man he saw with Cruise. The laboratory must also be totally destroyed to exterminate all traces of his discoveries. He knew that the authorities would never be called because of all the illegal activities, and the acres of marijuana plants adjacent to the complex.

Earlier Tim was ordered to be prepared to make a presentation tomorrow at ten to the board and visitors, however he knew this was a ruse to get him to demonstrate his accomplishments to the foreign bidders. Tim was also aware that Cruise figured that if he balked, that Alzar could take over. Therefore, Alzar, as in his carefully concocted scheme, must be the first to be eliminated.

When he returned to the laboratory, Alzar was waiting for him. "Are you ready to demonstrate you formula to the board and use the young man as the live exhibit?"

"I'm ready," Tim smirked. "You have the boy prepared at ten. It's essential that you to have a guard bring him to the meeting precisely on time. Furthermore, I require that you meet me here in the laboratory in the morning for a final briefing before the meeting."

He could see the profound loathing in Alzar's eyes, but the man said nothing and left. Tim noticed the Russian's hands were shaking as he walked out. He didn't know if it was the result of anger or fear. Regardless, he didn't give a shit.

Tim's last task of the evening was to gather all of the important papers defining his discoveries, and all of the remaining vials of his Formula. He placed everything in a waterproof backpack, proceeded to the cornfield and hid it about thirty feet inside. His original plans were to do this the morning of the meeting, but he knew tomorrow would be fun filled. He giggled when thinking of the havoc he was going to invoke.

After eliminating his enemies who wanted to steal his Formula, he could escape through the cornfield with the satisfaction and pride that he did not allow himself to be bullied.

That night Tim slept like a baby. He dreamed of the time when he could use the Formula on himself and be evolved to a super human status.

67

When Katrina, Blaze and the little dog Nick arrived at the house, the night was pitch black. The twinkling stars were cloaked behind thick clouds. Katrina kept the headlights on as Blaze went into the house and turned on the lights. Her first thoughts were, *was Baldy's body found and did the thugs in the complex replace him?*

She switched off the car and the headlights and she and Nick joined Blaze inside. Nick ran to Blaze and licked her ankles. She reached down and stroked his head. He barked and whined.

"I think he's hungry, "Blaze said. She filled a saucer with water and put it in the corner for him. Nick lapped up about half of it and lay down.

"Blaze, I've got to check the other house in the event someone is there. We don't want to be surprised by any goons. Is there a flashlight here?"

Blaze walked to the kitchen counter, retrieved a flashlight from the drawer and handed it to Katrina.

"While I do this, you can begin preparing some food, if there's any here. I could use some nourishment and so could you and Nick."

"There's plenty of can goods in the pantry," Blaze replied.

Katrina grabbed her pistol from the car and walked toward the other house. As she got closer, she turned off the flashlight and went to the front door. There were no lights in the house. She tried the door and it was unlocked. When she opened the door, she was overwhelmed with the stench. She covered her nose and went in. Baldy's body was on the floor just where they left him. The foul stink was coming from his decaying corpse. Katrina backed out of the room and left the house. Apparently no one had checked on the guy, so they were safe for the moment.

When she returned, Blaze was at the stove cooking a pot of grits. The young girl looked exhausted.

"Honey you just get a couple of plates and silverware, a bowl for Nick, sit down at the table and I'll finish. We'll feel better when we get some food in our stomachs." She looked over at Nick and the little brown dog was sleeping.

Katrina searched the pantry for anything with protein and spotted a can of Spam. Well, fried Spam and grits wasn't a gourmet meal but it would have to do for now. She sliced the Spam and put it in an Iron skillet frying pan and turned on the stove. Soon the Spam was sizzling. She picked up the pan from the stove and walked toward the table.

The sounds of a resounding crash erupted and the air was filled with pieces of the splintered door flying past her. She dropped the pan and covered her eyes to shield them. She heard Blaze scream and looked toward the demolished door. A huge man with tremendously defined muscles was standing there grinning with a gun pointed toward her.

"Get over to the table and join you blonde friend," he bellowed. His voice had a strange hollow ring to it making it sound surreal. Katrina obeyed. She felt a force against her skull as he glared at her. For a moment she thought that his mind was piercing hers. Blaze grabbed her head, also experiencing the same bizarre force.

Ted Harper walked toward the table, reached down and ripped the front of Blaze's shirt, revealing her bra. "Take that damn thing off and show me what you got. The three of us are going to have some fun tonight." His grin was more like a snarl and his eyes were glowing with lust. The force of his intense mental sexual arousal made Katrina's head feel impaled with pain, like a screwdriver being stabbed into the brain.

All of a sudden the pressure lifted when she heard a growl and barking. She looked down and Nick was barking, growling and nipping at the big mans ankles. She saw blood as the little brave dog sunk his teeth into the lower leg of the monster. The big man turned and tried to kick him. The little dog was quick and scampered out of the way, only to turn and attack again. The man pointed the pistol at Nick, who was trying to bite the other ankle. It was apparent that he hesitated because he didn't want accidently shoot his foot.

With his attention on Nick, Katrina leaped to her feet and grabbed the iron skillet from the floor. She swung the cast iron frying pan at the back of his head and connected powerfully. He rocked on his heels, but didn't go down. When he turned toward her, she crashed the heavy frying pan squarely on his temple. He grabbed his head and she clobbered him for the third time. He went to his knees dropped the pistol and screamed with pain. His body began shaking and his shrieks were getting louder and louder.

With all her might, Katrina crashed the heavy iron pan squarely against the top of his head again, and backed off. Nick ran to the corner and sat down, watching intently. He was apparently ready to attack again if needed.

Blaze jumped up, grabbed her chair and smashed it against his blood soaked head. He grunted, let out an earthshattering shriek and fell to the floor, face down. He immediately turned over and screamed again. Katrina could see what appeared to be brain substance bursting through both ears. His left eyeball popped out and the slimy grey substance leaked from his eye socket. It appeared that his brain was exploding from his head. One final gush of the grey substance spurted from his mouth like vomit. He wheezed and his breathing ceased.

Katrina had no idea what had just happened. She had no way of knowing that Timothy Olsen had removed the protective membrane that was cushioning the brain in Ted Harper's head in order to produce mass growth in several lobes. The repeated blows from the iron skillet bruised the brain, causing it to swell. There was simply no room in his skull for the brain swelling, consequently it took the only outlets available, the ears, eyes and the mouth.

The flaw in Olsen's Formula rendered his application to humans and their Evolution on Steroids with a fatal error. Continued robust blows to the head would destroy them.

Katrina and Blaze sat, trying to calm down from the trauma of the events. Nick ran to Katrina's feet and barked. She picked him up and rubbed his head.

"Thank you for saving our lives, Nick," She kissed him on the head.

Nick whined and laid his head on her lap. He knew that Nat had sent him to protect these two women. He was just doing his job, but he really wanted some Spam. He was even hungrier after fighting the big evil man.

68

It was after 1am when Gerry, Nat and I arrived at the cornfield house. I immediately knew something was wrong when I spotted a late model Lexus parked on the side of the dirt road. When I drove closer, I saw lights blazing in the house and the front door was shattered. The girls had visitors and that can't be good.

"Gerry will you cover the back door? Nat and I will cover the front." I said, as we exited the Humvee. With pistols drawn, we cautiously approached the house. Gerry sprinted to the back.

"Nat move to the side and cover me." Nat moved to the side of the shattered door.

"Whoever's in there, you're surrounded. Come out with your hands up, we're armed."

Katrina came running out of the house. "Ethan, thank God you're here. The man's dead."

I yelled to Gerry and we went into the house. "Who is this guy and what happened to him," Gerry asked, while looking at the mess on the floor. "It appears that his brain leaked out of his head. Excuse me, I mean exploded from his head."

I knelt and examined the corpse. "His name is Ted Harper. He was a goon hired by the Piranha to kill me. His body is very different from the last time I saw him. He couldn't have naturally enhanced his muscles to this degree. Cruise and his men captured him, Billy and me after Blaze shot Harper's partner. All three of us were captured to be used as guinea pigs in the evolution experiments of Timothy Olsen. It appears that Olsen experimented on Harper. Exactly what happened Katrina?"

Katrina described the confrontation in detail including the force emitting from Harper's brain causing pain in her head.

"If it wasn't for Nick I'm sure we'd be dead. He bravely attacked the man and it distracted him long enough for me to bash him in the head several times with the cast iron frying pan. Blaze also busted a chair on his head."

Nat picked up his little brown dog. "Way to go boy." Nick licked his hand and barked.

"It's obvious that the blows to the head caused the brain to swell. Olsen's formula has a major flaw, however everything else seems to have evolved Harper. His grotesque, highly defined muscle structure must have given him superhuman strength and speed. He also probably possessed telekinetic powers to have the ability to apply pressure to your brain. Depending on which lobes in the brain Olsen enhanced, his mental powers would have been super human." I said, took a breath and continued.

"That's Evolution on Steroids and Mind Games of the highest order. We must stop Olsen before he corrects this defect and sells his discoveries to the highest bidder. China, Russia, Iran, Syria or Al Qaeda would do or pay anything to acquire this Formula. There's no telling what they would be able to do with it. It could cause a significant power shift in the world."

I heard sobs and looked toward Blaze. She was crying. "Do you think he did that to Billy?"

"I honestly don't know Blaze, but come morning we're going to attempt to rescue him. It's late. Why don't you go to the bedroom and try to get some sleep. We have to devise a plan of attack on the complex." Blaze nodded and left.

After we dragged the dead body outside and buried it, Nat, Gerry and I returned. Katrina had cleaned up the mess on the floor.

We all sat down at the kitchen table. I located a sheet of paper and a pencil and drew a rendition of the complex, location of entrances, distance to the adjacent cornfield and the marijuana field on the other side. I outlined as much of the interior as I could remember, including the holding cells. One of which should be the cage where Billy is being kept.

"To start, We're going to need the UZI assault rifle, a couple of hunting rifles, pistols, binoculars, and bolt cutters to get Billy out of the cage." I said. "Katrina you can stay here with Blaze and Nick."

"To hell you say, Ethan. I'm going, and you know that I'm a better shot than you are."

"We to use her as a sniper," Nat said. "Can you handle a semi-automatic deer rifle with a scope?"

"No problem," Katrina answered. "I also owe Ben Cruise a payback, and I would love to get my hands on Hank Thompson."

"Ethan, we've got a couple of pairs of Bushnell 10x42 Ultra HD binoculars in the Humvee. Nat and I used them for hunting."

"Perfect," I replied.

It was against my better judgment, but I knew when Katrina's mind was made up there was no changing it. I saw the starkness in her eyes when she mentioned Cruise and Thompson.

"Okay Katrina, we'll station you in a strategic position and you can pick off anyone who causes a problem with our entrance or exit to the compound."

"How many guards would you estimate?" Gerry asked.

"I'd say at least a dozen."

"We're need a distraction to keep some of them diverted," Gerry continued.

Nat was looking at my sketches of the complex. "What better distraction than to set fire to the marijuana fields? With the possible loss of that gigantic valuable crop, surely it would be all hands on deck to extinguish the fire."

"Great Idea," I said. "There are several propane tanks out back that Blaze and Billy used for the grill."

"Okay we'll need to get there, fully armed, early in the morning, and scope out the place for a couple of hours to understand what we're facing. The cornfield will give us cover." Gerry said.

"Let's gather our equipment and then try to get a couple hours of sleep," I said. We all agreed, knowing that the possibility of sleep was far fetched. At least we could get some rest.

We gathered the binoculars, bolt cutters, and one full propane tank. We loaded with ammunition the pistols, the UZI, The Weatherby Mar V and the model 750 Woodmaster. Katrina grabbed the Semi-automatic deer rifle with scope, and got the feel of it. She was dead serious as she adjusted the scope to her liking. I pocketed a box of stick matches, which were on the hearth of the fireplace.

Katrina and I went to the other bedroom, Gerry and Nat sacked out on the couch and recliner in the family room. All of us remained clothed as we tried to get some rest. Before we went to the bed, Katrina looked in on Blaze. The young girl had cried herself to sleep.

I actually dozed off for a little while, and when I opened my eyes the sun was rising. The sunlight streamed through the bedroom window. I smelled coffee and jumped out of bed. Katrina was already up.

I went to the kitchen. Gerry had made coffee and he and Nat were sitting at the table with cups of coffee. The little dog Nick was in the corner eating what looked like an open can of tuna fish. Blaze was sitting on the couch.

Katrina poured us a cup of the steaming java. "Are you guys ready to do this?" I asked.

"Hell yes," Gerry said, and Nat nodded.

We finished out coffee. "Blaze you stay here with Nick. We'll leave you a pistol for protection. We'll be back with Billy as soon as we can," Katrina said.

We walked outside. The four of us resembled a Navy Seal 6 team. We were ready to kick ass.

69

Hank Thompson slept in the living quarters where Olsen's first assistant and victim, Brenda, had lived. Her clothes remained in the closet, and he loved the fragrance of her underwear. Looking out the window, as far as he could see were marijuana plants glistening from the morning dew in the rising sunlight. He wondered if the dead girl had recognized the plants.

Today was the day he had waited for years to experience. The bidders from China, Russia and Iran arrived the night before and were opulently entertained by Cruise. He knew that Alzar was with them at the specially prepared dinners. Cruise had brought in Chinese, Russian and Iranian master chefs to accommodate the guest.

Alzar briefed them on the present accomplishments and the future possibilities of the Formula. This briefing outlined the expectations for the presentation by Olsen, and the live demonstration to be executed on Billy.

Each bidder was instructed to bring 500,000 in American dollars to be paid as a deposit for the winning bidder. The losers would have their cash returned. The money was kept in the safe in the CEO's office.

The rules were simple. There would be two rounds of bidding. After the first round, the highest bid would be shared. The second round would be final and the premier bid would win the prize. Billy would be a prisoner, accompanying the winner for evaluating and further testing.

Thompson showered, shaved and dressed. There was no need for his disguise today because Cruise had set up a closed circuit camera in the conference room to be transmitted to the TV in the CEO office, with picture and voice feed. Thompson would be able to participate in the discussions without being seen.

There was a knock on the door. "What do you want?" The Piranha asked.

"Breakfast, compliments of Mr. Cruise," was the reply.

"Leave the cart by the door and leave."

Thompson heard footsteps departing. He opened the door and wheeled in the cart. On top of the cart was a menu which read, *fresh squeezed orange juice, Kona dark roast coffee, eggs-a-la-golden rod (chopped poached eggs in a white wine sauce to be spooned over fresh baked ciabatta bread), blackberry muffins and homemade peach jam.* He smiled. *That Cruise knows the high life,* he thought. *Soon everything in my life will be ostentatious.*

He sat down and enjoyed the breakfast. Afterward, Thompson made his way to the CEO's office. He opened the safe and removed one of the briefcases. He gaped at the stacks of one hundred dollar bills. Thompson placed it on the desk alongside all the papers detailing Olsen's experiments, and the final composition of the God Particle Formula. He chuckled with the knowledge that the arrogant kid Olsen had no idea that Cruise had copied all of this information.

After switching on the TV and tuning up the sound, he observed Cruise and Alzar making final preparations for the meeting. Olsen was not in the room. In less than ten minutes a portly Chinese man arrived with a young lady accompanying him, probably his interrupter.

"Thanks you for coming Mr. Chewng," Cruise said, nodding to the man. Please be seated. He pointed to a specific seat.

A tall blonde muscular Russian man walked in, accompanied by a very thin Iranian male. They were glaring at each other.

"Mr. Zharkov and Mr. Adeli, may I respectfully welcome you?"

Cruise invited both of them to their designated seats. There were thick bound reference books at each seat containing a summary description of the Formula, and its potential uses. One book was in their native language and the other in English. A third book described the results of the experiment on Harper and information on the intended live demonstration using a young white male subject.

"By the facts presented, we will persuade you gentlemen that this Formula advances the evolution of mankind by probably one hundred years. The social, scientific and military uses are not only astonishing, but will change the course of history." Cruise made eye contact with each bidder. "Now I'll give you a few minutes to browse the contents of the books. Our brilliant scientist, Dr. Timothy Olsen, will explain everything to you in detail and perform the live demonstration. Look over the books and my colleague will get Mr. Olsen and the test subject." He nodded toward Alzar, and the man left the room.

Alzar walked to the holding room and told the attendant to place Billy's sedated body on a gurney, and to wait in the hallway while he fetched Olsen. Olsen was supposed to already be at the meeting with the test subject. He was being difficult to the finish.

Then Alzar remembered, Olsen had ordered him to meet in the laboratory to finalize his presentation. He had been tied up with Cruise and had forgotten. "The little bastard is going to be angry," he said aloud.

He made his way to the laboratory. Olsen was standing beside a pushcart, which was covered with a sheet. He looked frazzled as if he hadn't slept at all.

"Where in the hell have you been?" Tim barked.

"Cruise had me tied up with the visitors," Alzar replied. "Let's get going. The participants are ready in the conference room."

Olsen didn't answer and pushed the cart by Alzar into the hall. Olsen returned, closed the door and stood starting at Alzar. He was holding a vial.

"What is that?' Alzar asked. "Is it a sample of the Formula?"

Olsen removed the lid and dropped in what appeared to be a small silver article. Replacing the lid, he went to Alzar and handed it to him. Time was running out and he changed his plans of sending Alzar to the back of the laboratory.

Tim immediately turned and left the room, slamming the door. The lock clicked. Alzar looked at the vial in his hand and felt the intense heat. The glass was swelling rapidly. He threw it to the floor. The vial exploded instantly, expelling the deadly gas. Alzar felt his lungs burning and tried to scream. He was dead before he hit the floor. The explosion ignited the flammable liquids that Olsen had placed nearby. A succession of small explosions resulted, and the laboratory exploded into flames.

The Conference room was located at the other end of the building. The laboratory was soundproof. No one heard the explosion, however smoke seeped beneath the locked door.

Tim spotted two guards running toward the laboratory with guns drawn. He ripped the sheet off of the cart. The remaining vials of sulfuric acid had small wads of aluminum foil next to them. These bombs were sufficient to destroy the building, and kill his targeted enemies.

As he was rushing to the conference room, he heard an explosion that appeared to come from outside the building.

He ignored it and remained focused on his plan.

70

The four of us trudged through the cornfield lugging our equipment. When we reached the clearing, everything looked calm at the complex. Two guards were smoking by the east entrance. I assumed, based on my prior observations, that there would be only one guard at each entrance.

We watched the building for about thirty minutes and decided that now was the time to move. One of the guards went inside after his smoke break. The other guard was leaning against the structure, apparently dozing.

"Okay, I'm going to skirt the building and go about fifteen feet inside the marijuana fields," Nat said. "I'll wait exactly ten minutes and then turn on the flow of propane gas. I'll put some distance between the tank, and me. Then I'll light a corn stalk, toss it toward the tank, and run like hell. The explosion should trigger the guards to check it out and you guys can go inside. If the west entrance guard comes to check it out, I'll enter the building through that entrance, after I put him out of commission."

"Katrina, you stay in this location and pick off anyone who threatens us," I said. "Especially when we come out with Billy, I expect them to follow us and you'll be needed for protection."

Katrina nodded.

Gerry and I stood ready to storm the building as soon as we heard the explosion. We checked our watches and noted that eight minutes had passed since Nat left. At about thirty seconds to go, we heard frantic shouting coming from inside the building.

A severely loud explosion from the marijuana fields followed. Flames immediately were visible. The guard at the east entrance stood up and ran toward the field.

Gerry and I darted to the door. I tried to open the door, but it was locked. "Stand back," Gerry shouted, aiming his assault rifle at the lock. One shot busted the lock, and I kicked door open. When we entered, shots rang out from the marijuana fields.

"The holding rooms are this way," I said and Gerry and I turned left. At that moment, we heard at additional, successive explosions coming from the other end of the building.

"I don't know what the hell is going on," I said. "Lets find Billy and get out of here."

As we ran down the hallway, I heard a man yelling behind us. I turned just in time to see him draw his pistol. I put him down with a shot to the chest. "Turn right here," I yelled to Gerry. We ran head on into another guard. Gerry butt stroked him in the neck.

I looked down the hall toward where I knew the laboratory was located. The door was closed and smoke was pouring from the crack at the bottom. The holding rooms were located just past the laboratory. I heard yelling and screaming coming from the hallways behind us. Someone was on a killing rampage, but I had no idea who.

I kicked the door open to the first holding room. It was empty. Gerry was already at the second door and kicked it in. I ran to his side. I saw Billy in a cage looking at us, holding the bars. A very large man was standing by a gurney. He reached for his pistol. Gerry eliminated him with a burst of bullets from his rifle. I ran to the fallen body and searched his pockets for keys. I located a key ring and ran to the cage, with Gerry guarding the door. The second key unlocked it.

"Thank God you're here Ethan. I thought they either killed you or experimented on you," Billy said, breathlessly.

"Come on son, let's get you out of here. Blaze is waiting for you. She's safe."

I grabbed his arm, "Stay between Gerry and me."

We walked into the hallway and were confronted by three guards. "Stop or you're dead," the rough one with the beard roared. "Drop your weapons."

Three shots rang out and the men fell to the floor. Nat emerged from behind them. "Guys we got trouble," he said. "I was almost shot in the marijuana fields, but Katrina heard the shots and came to my rescue. She's fine, but the other end of the building is on fire. Someone detonated bombs, I think. The fire is spreading rapidly."

Just then another explosion came from the laboratory. The fire must have reached more explosive chemicals. "Follow us Nat, we've got Billy and let's get out of here fast. The fumes from the chemicals could be deadly."

As we turned the corner toward the door, I saw Timothy Olsen. When he saw us he stopped. The psychopathic genius looked like a young boy caught in the headlights. I could see that he was unarmed. He stared at us, and then turned and ran out the door.

Just as we approached the door, I glanced behind us and I was shocked to see Hank Thompson running down the hall.

"Gerry, you and Nat get Billy out of here. I can't let Thompson, the Piranha, get away."

"Wait, I'll go with you," Gerry said.

"No, stay with Nat and Billy and make sure Katrina is okay. I got this."

After watching them run out the door, I turned and jogged in the direction that Thompson was going. I caught another glimpse of him turning the corner. He was apparently heading for the west entrance. The halls were filled with smoke and I ripped off my shirt and held it over my nose. I felt a burning sensation on my skin. The halls were now empty as anyone left alive had the sense to leave the building.

When I turned the corner and saw the open door to the exit, I heard a pop and felt a bullet whiz by my head. Thompson was standing at the entrance holding a gun pointed in my direction. In the other hand he held a briefcase. I fell to the floor and returned fire. I thought I shot him in the shoulder, but couldn't be sure. He stumbled out the door.

I jumped to my feet, followed and noticed blood on the floor at the entrance. I must have hit him in the arm or shoulder because he had dropped the gun, kept the briefcase and ran. The blood trail turned right toward the road and away from the burning marijuana fields. The cornfields were on the other side of the complex.

I was apprehensive that he had a vehicle there and would escape, so I scampered forward. I spotted him running toward a silver SUV. To my dismay he reached it and got inside. I ran as fast as I could, firing at the vehicle.

The motor roared and the wheels spun in the dirt as he turned the SUV toward me. I realized that he intended to run me down. I stood my ground, rapidly firing at the windshield as he sped toward me. I jumped to the side and the bumper brushed my leg as the SUV propelled forward and crashed into the building. I must have hit him again. I ran to the vehicle and yanked open the door. Hank Thompson was slumped over the steering wheel. Blood was oozing from his right shoulder, and I noticed most of his left ear was missing. I dragged him about twenty feet away from SUV when it began to burn. I fell to the ground exhausted as the gas tank exploded. The briefcase was still clutched tightly in his left hand.

I reached over and felt Thompson's neck for a pulse. He was alive. He opened his eyes and gazed at me with blank eyes.

"Ethan, you son of a bitch, you got me," he whispered. "I would have made it but that bastard Olsen blew up the conference room and killed Cruise and the guys who were going to make me one of the richest men in the world. I watched it all on the cam." He coughed and passed out.

I heard yelling and Katrina, Nat, Gerry and Billy came running to my side. Katrina gasped when she saw me covered with blood. "Oh Ethan are you hurt bad?"

"Honey it's his blood. I'm fine." She grabbed me and hugged.

"Hank Thompson is alive. Let's get him some medical help and it's time for you to arrest him, Gerry. All the other bad guys are dead and the drugs are destroyed." I looked at the burning building. "Olsen's formula and all the papers are going up in flames. He had no right to mess with God's evolution of man. His Mind Games are over."

"I saw a young guy running into the cornfield," Katrina said. "It must have been Olsen. He was unarmed so I let him go."

I shook my head. He'll never find anyone to fund his experiments when news of this story gets to the press. He tried to master speed up Evolution, but he failed. That must be left to God and nature.

I tore the briefcase handle from Hank's hand and opened it. Inside were papers outlining Olsen's experiments and the composition of the God Particle Formula. Underneath were bundles of one hundred dollar bills. I took the papers from the briefcase, walked over to the burning building and threw them into the fire.

I handed the briefcase to Billy. "You and Blaze can use this to buy a home and start a new life," I said.

Gerry and Nat looked at me, but said nothing. "If Thompson says anything about a briefcase, it burned in the fire," I said.

"Let's take this bum, go back to the house and get Blaze and Nick. It's going to be a busy night at the FBI and the CIA, after they see what we brought them. When this place is investigated, or what's left of it, a national news buzz saw will follow.

I took Katrina's hand. Gerry patted me on the back. "The world is a better place because of what we did tonight," he said.

I smiled, nodded and hugged my lovely wife.

71

Timothy Harding Olsen, PhD Massachusetts Institute of Technology, Valedictorian, boy genius, psychopath, murderer, and scientist, who masterminded one of the greatest breakthroughs in the science of human evolution, trudged through the dirt in the cornfield. His mind was racing. He felt a peculiar sense of amusement and pride that he eliminated all the individuals who were trying to steal his cherished Formula.

They say that there's a fine line between a genius and insanity. On this remarkable night, Timothy Harding Olsen crossed that line.

He trudged to the area where he had concealed his backpack and retrieved it. Just when he grabbed the flashlight from his backpack, he heard chattering and noises. He moved away and crouched to the ground. The sounds were coming from several people walking through the cornfield, holding flashlights. Two of the men were carrying a makeshift stretcher with a wounded man on it. The bandages on the body were blood-soaked. There was a woman holding tightly to the hand of another man. Tim recognized him as the first case study who escaped from the laboratory.

Tim remained silent, scarcely breathing, for ten minutes after they passed.

He decided that turning on a flashlight was too dangerous, so he proceeded deliberately in the dark. The dense clouds covering the moon intensified the darkness. He stumbled on something on the ground and fell face first to the dirt. His arm and cheek were cut by what felt like jagged rocks. Tim cursed, jumped to his feet and wiped away the blood that was trickling down his cheek. He ignored the blood that was soaking his shirt-sleeves because he was more concerned about whether or not he broke the vials of Formula in the backpack.

Tim reached inside and breathed a sigh of relief when discovering that the vials were intact. He placed them in his shirt pocket for safekeeping.

He moved forward about a hundred feet, and heard another sound brushing against the cornstalks. He had an eerie feeling that whatever it might be was not human. Tim stood still for a moment, and then walked faster. The noise got closer, and he turned to face it. The first things he saw were two beady eyes glowing in the dark. A low guttural growl scared the hell of him. He stood there trembling, and switched on his flashlight. A large grey coyote was standing there, with spittle dripping from his bared teeth.

The alpha male smelled blood and was stalking his prey. The pack was not far behind, led by the female alpha. As soon as the alpha gave the signal, his mate would approach first, followed by the pack. The alpha male and alpha female would have the initial choice of the meat, and the pack would feast on what remained.

Tim was terrified. He turned to run, but stumbled and fell to the ground. He felt the vials burst and the Formula saturating his skin. The liquid felt hot, and it appeared to penetrate his chest. He turned over to get to his feet when the alpha attacked.

Tim shrieked as sharp teeth pierced his outstretched arm. The stench emitting from the savage's mouth was overwhelming. The alpha howled and his mate quickly joined the attack. As Tim was trying to fight off the alpha, the female went for his throat.

On the second attempt, the ravaging animal chomped down on his Adams apple. She shook her head and ripped out part of his throat. Blood spurted from the severed arteries. The alpha tore at what was left of the throat and ravenously chewed on the bloody meat.

The alpha male and female fed on the chest meat and squealed at the pleasure of the feeding. Tim's Formula soaked chest meat gave the coyote's a shock as it burned in their throats and entered their blood stream. Both felt a burst of power and stepped back from the body, and shattered the night with blood-curdling howls.

The alpha roared again with amazing power, and the rest of the pack raced to the lifeless prey. They tore and ripped flesh from the body.

After they had their fill, the pack, led by the alpha male and female, dragged the remains to the den.

When stripped of all the meat, Tim's bones would be bleached by the sun and eventually return to the dust of the earth. Ashes to ashes, dust to dust.

Nature has won the battle against the human who desired to take God's power and put the Evolution of Humans on Steroids. His Mind Games destroyed him.

The Silence of the night penetrated the now empty cornfield. Clouds dissipated and the moon appeared to take on an exceptional brilliance as millions of stars twinkled in the sky. A falling star streaked across the horizon.

God laughed.

God must laugh a lot at the egotism of humans and their menial cognitive processes. Humans are but a speck of dust in the immense and eternal universe. To think that humans could alter the evolutionary processes and the ultimate plans of God is the pinnacle of infernal ignorance and insanity.

God laughed again.

EPILOG

I n an extremely unusual joint effort, the FBI and the CIA's forensic teams scoured the ashes at the complex. The intense heat from the chemical explosions destroyed virtually all the evidence. The remains of the dead bodies in the building were never identified, except the remains of Benjamin Cruise. Their final conclusions for public consumption was that scene proved that it was a drug operation run by Cruise and the Board of Directors of Future Mankind Ventures.

The FBI searched for the Chairman, Shelby Cain, but never found him. Unknown to them, he was long gone from the digestive tracks of the coyotes. His bones lay beside those of Tim Olsen and many other wild animals.

Sergay Petrof fled to Moscow and the Russian government refused extradition. Durand Moreau of Paris disappeared and was never found.

Hank (Piranha) Thompson was charged with the kidnapping of Katrina Tyler. Upon further investigation the FBI determined that he was the primary stockholder of Future Mankind Ventures. Possession and distribution of drugs and fraud were added to the charges. Even though he was suspected of multiple murders, there was no direct evidence. Thompson was convicted and Federal Judge Edgar Eury gave him the maximum sentence because he was a government employee who betrayed the public trust. He is presently serving fifty years in the high security federal penitentiary in Beaumont, Texas. He will be eligible for parole in thirty years.

Neither the CIA nor the FBI ever disclosed to the public the information about the God Particle Formula or the human experiments that had been conducted in the complex.

Timothy Olsen had also vanished and the search for him was closed three years later. The dossier was placed in the cold case files.

After testifying in confidence, and the information obtained from them classified top secret, Ethan Tyler and Katrina were allowed to resign from the CIA. They signed a non-disclosure agreement, never to talk about any of the information concerning the case.

Ethan Tyler now is a full tenured Professor at the University of Houston, teaching Criminal Justice. He is the proud father of a baby boy born to Katrina two years after the incident.

Katrina writes novels based on her experiences while working undercover for the CIA. The mystery-thrillers are fiction and have never mentioned the God Particle. Her latest novel, "Hidden in the Shadows of the Mind," has been on the New York best selling list for 8 consecutive months. She is thrilled to stay home, write and raise her son, Gary Maurice Tyler.

Blaze and Billy were kept out of the spotlight. Ethan helped them buy a house in Kingwood, Texas. With the five hundred thousand in the briefcase, they had countless options.

Blaze remembered, with great fondness, the kindness that Jacob and Maybelle had shown Katrina and her. She also recalled how the young boy Josh had saved her life. Blaze wanted to reward Josh, Maybelle and Jacob. She and Billy went to see them and gave them one hundred thousand dollars. Jacob declined, but Blaze insisted that he needed money to raise Josh. Some of the cash could be used as a college fund for the boy. Jacob and Maybelle reluctantly agreed.

Blaze got her GED and enrolled at the University of Houston. She had two courses with Professor Tyler on the way to earning a law degree. She is presently married to a successful investment banker and has three children.

Billy also continued his education and became a Computer programmer. He developed a video game called, "Emperor of the Cornfield." He sold the rights to Samsung and started his own development company. He is presently engaged to a beautiful lady from Galveston.

Recently several hunters were in the area where the cornfield and the building complex had been located. They swore that they saw two gigantic Coyotes that resembled the werewolves in the movie Twilight. They said that the Coyotes actually spoke four words to them, "Get out or die."

They were dismissed and the authorities suspected that they had been drunk when the incident occurred. The incident was not investigated.

The evolved Coyotes that had ingested the Formula from Olsen's meat, mated and had pups.

The pups could speak.

24991178R00210

Made in the USA
Charleston, SC
12 December 2013